BURNING BRIGHTLY

for
Linda Dégh, Master Scholar
and
Alice Kane, Master Teller

BURNING BRIGHTLY

NEW LIGHT ON OLD TALES TOLD TODAY

Kay F. Stone

broadview press

Canadian Cataloguing in Publication Data

Stone, Kay F., 1939-   .
  Burning brightly : new light on old tales told today
Includes bibliographical references and index.
ISBN 1-55111-167-5
1. Storytelling.   2. Tales.   3. Title.

GR72.3.S766 1998   808.5'43   C98-930922-3

Broadview Press Ltd., is an independent, international publishing house, incorporated in 1985.

North America:
P.O. Box 1243, Peterborough, Ontario, Canada K9J 7H5
3576 California Road, Orchard Park, NY 14127
TEL: (705) 743-8990; FAX: (705) 743-8353; E-MAIL: 75322.44@compuserve.com

United Kingdom:
Turpin Distribution Services Ltd., Blackhorse Rd., Letchworth, Hertfordshire SG6 1HN
TEL: (1462) 672555; FAX (1462) 480947; E-MAIL: turpin@rsc.org

Australia:
St. Clair Press, P.O. Box 287, Rozelle, NSW 2039
TEL: (02) 818-1942; FAX: (02) 418-1923

www.broadviewpress.com

Broadview Press gratefully acknowledges the support of the Ontario Arts Council, and the Ministry of Canadian Heritage. We acknowledge the financial support of the Government of Canada through the Book Publishing Industry Development Program for our publishing activities.

Text design and composition by George Kirkpatrick

PRINTED IN CANADA

CONTENTS

IN GRATITUDE

A STORYTELLING revival has been growing in North America for most of the twentieth century, inspired by a new appreciation for the spoken word, and also in part by a yearning for a legendary age of folk creativity. In the last quarter of the century storytelling groups and activities have appeared throughout the United States and Canada, and the number of individual tellers has skyrocketed. I spent several years visiting a number of these communities and interviewing individual performers, focusing on those who favored fairy tales in their repertoires. The people I queried were so articulate and introspective that I found myself answering questions as often as asking them. There would be no book at all without them.

It is an understatement to say that no author composes a book alone, so I want to give some idea of just how many people can be involved in the writing of a single work. I am grateful to those who agreed to participate in interviews and to converse and correspond informally, and to storytellers and story enthusiasts, folklorists, editors, teachers and students, and everyone else who has been part of this very long adventure. Since I do not want to miss anyone I will name them in alphabetical order in the acknowledgements at the end of the book. For now I will keep these tributes brief.

To begin with, I am deeply grateful to Bob Barton, Stewart (and Dianne) Cameron, Susan Gordon, Marvyne Jenoff, Joe Neil MacNeil and John Shaw, Carol McGirr, Marylyn Peringer, all of whom generously shared their stories and their comments.

The thoughtful editorial suggestions and corrections of careful readers Marvyne Jenoff, Janet Langlois, and Celia Lottridge contributed greatly to making this book more readable and more accurate (though the many mistakes that remain are obviously my responsibility).

My research with specific storytelling communities has been supported by an internal SSHRC grant (Social Sciences and Humanities Research Council) enabling me to visit a number of groups and festivals in the United States and Canada. Earlier research was funded by two small grants from the University of Winnipeg. A writing grant gave me two fine weeks at the Hambidge Center in Rabun Gap, Georgia.

I am grateful to Don LePan of Broadview Press, who has given me encouragement and advice in response to my anxious messages which always had the subtext, "I don't think I can do this!" And without the careful editing and advice provided by Barbara Conolly my errors would be rampant. I also appreciate the eagle eyes of indexer Renée Fossett.

Patty Hawkins, secretary of the University of Winnipeg English Department, gave me expert technical advice and assuaged my frequent bouts of frustration. And speaking of frustration there will no doubt be errors despite endless checking and rechecking, but they will surely not be as bad as my misspelling of "resources" throughout my geography master's thesis, nor my placing of Charles Perrault in the wrong century in my doctoral dissertation on fairy tales.

One person above all is responsible for my continued studies of *Märchen*. Linda Dégh, whose dedicated work on tales and tellers is known internationally, has been an encouraging teacher, colleague, and friend who never quite gave up hope in this long-awaited book.

USEFUL TERMS

Emergent Quality: the characteristic of orally told stories, jokes, anecdotes, or any other narrative that changes when it is told; imagine a joke told or heard several times, each time a bit differently.

Fairytale: see *Wondertale* below.

Folktale: a traditional story that has passed through many generations of spoken life. In the Tale Type Index (see below) these are categorized as: animal tales; ordinary folktales (here called wondertales—see below); jokes and anecdotes; and formula tales.

Narrator: used here in the folkloric sense rather than the literary; that is, as the actual storyteller in a living tradition, not the fictional narrator in a work of literature.

Oral Tradition: an elusive term, here used to mean a community (often rural) where stories and other traditions were learned and passed on orally, and were absorbed naturally as part of the culture as a whole.

Organized Storytelling: consciously scheduled and presented performances of stories in formal settings, to children or adults, whether in schools or libraries, on concert stages, or at storytelling festivals or other events.

Platform Performer: a storyteller who takes part in organized storytelling events, whether as part of another profession (for example, library work, teaching, therapeutic counselling) or as a full-time professional storyteller.

Professional Storyteller: see Platform Performer above.

Storytelling Event: a formally arranged event during which stories are told; see Organized Storytelling, above.

Tale Type Numbers: identification numbers from the Tale Type Index (Aarne/Thompson 1973) that classify and describe the basic Indo-European folktales; for example, "Beauty and the Beast" is AT 425, while "Cinderella" is AT 510. The Tale Type Index allows readers to find different texts of any known folktale.

Traditional Storytelling: in strict terms, the kind of narration that takes place in full oral tradition (see above); it usually takes place in more casual contexts than do organized storytelling events, though it can be just as formal and performance-centered. That is, oral narration (see above) can be much more than casual "kitchen table storytelling."

Wondertale: also called fairytale, magic tale, *Märchen*, or Ordinary Folktale. As used here, it is the kind of story that presents extraordinary events, characters, and objects within an everyday world. That is, the worlds of ordinary and extraordinary reality are not separate: common beans can grow up into the clouds and an ordinary girl can turn a single strand of hair into a bridge over a deep river.

FOREWORD:

THE PATH INTO THE WOODS

S OMEONE is lost in the woods. They have gone there to find firewood, perhaps, or water from the well at the world's end, or strawberries in winter. They are looking for a path to safety but what they find will be unexpected, probably frightening or challenging or transformative. And they will survive to have their tale told, again and again. These seekers people the folktales of the world, ancient stories that still resonate when told today. You might find postmodern variants written by authors who challenge and deconstruct the old forms and create new transmutations for contemporary audiences, but these authors are not my focus here. Contemporary storytellers have found new words for the old stories, and this is where my interest lies. I want to know why, on the edge of the turning century and in the midst of increasing social, technological, and human challenges, people are still retelling and rehearing the old stories, still wondering if that path could be found and the challenge met—and if it matters.

For me it is poetic justice that the heart of this book is these old tales, stories that I did *not* enjoy as a child. I was the eldest of three sisters and an adventurer; such girls did not fare well in the collection of Grimm tales I was given at age eight, a Christmas tradition in my family (and many others in both North America and Europe). The well-worn book is inscribed in my mother's neat handwriting:

Kay Frances Mitchell
Christmas
1947

As I read the stories over the next few years, every one of them, I was disturbed and also intrigued by the shadowy nature of the tales. When I open the book at random I still feel a twinge of anxiety just glancing at the illustrations (a prince on a white horse followed by three men carrying a dead dragon), or reading through the titles ("The Goose Girl," "The Six Swans"), or simply smelling the aging paper.

Somehow these were not "my" stories, and yet I kept being drawn back to the book until I put it away in adolescence, forgot about it for many years. I only have it now because my mother was cleaning out her attic one year and insisted I take it back or throw it away.

I took the book back because by this time my early love-hate relationship had developed into academic curiosity. In the early 1970s, after reading many traditional tales as a student of folklore, I realized that the Grimm collection was not at all typical of orally gathered folktales. I was surprised to discover that they had not actually collected their stories "from the lips of the peasants," as they claimed, but gathered bits and pieces from many sources and stitched tales together to fit their own ideas of what a folktale should be. I was surprised, too, to find that in more recent collections (the Grimms were working in the early part of the nineteenth century) female characters, old and young, were generally more interesting, less docile. There were even a few stepmothers who were helpful rather than cruel.

Eventually I decided to write my dissertation on women in folktales (Stone 1975). At that time there was almost no scholarly work on folktale heroines so it was an exciting prospect. While reading countless stories in dozens of popular collections I found heroines who did not always sit and wait for the prince to appear with their missing shoe or a reviving kiss. A few years later, when I began telling stories, these atypical adventurous heroines had a chance to speak out. Subsequently I met and heard other tellers and realized that their responses were often quite different from mine. I began to see that some of the stories I had rejected as demeaning and destructive to women revealed another, more positive side. My growing curiosity not only led me further into performing stories but also into writing about them, and about the people who told such stories professionally. Why did many tellers still prefer these old tales and who were their listeners?

I began research and interviews in the mid-1980s with the intention of writing a general survey of organized storytelling in the past three decades. After several frustrating years of trying to bring order to an overwhelming mass of material from Canada and the United States I felt like the folktale protagonist with the proverbial impossible task, and no magical helpers to offer aid or advice or enchanted objects. I gave up, did nothing for an entire summer. It felt like sitting at the murky bottom of a very deep well waiting for a golden ball to fall at my feet. In retrospect what seemed like wasted time down there in the dark was a necessary resting time, like a needed 100-year sleep. When I finally woke up I understood that a general survey was not at all what I wanted to do. Besides, Joseph Sobol was already working on a very thorough study of American storytelling (Sobol 1994).[1] So I began again.

This time, instead of a general survey of tellers, I set out to investigate tellers who favored traditional folktales, and particularly fairy tales, in their repertoires. I do not mean to suggest here that folktales still dominate performance repertoires as they did for several decades. In fact, many performers now favor original creations and personal experience narratives, partly because of conflicts over performance rights.[2] Still, traditional tales figure prominently in professional story-telling, especially for the tellers included here. In this book I will explore these kinds of stories as they are told in North America today by professional storytellers. In collaboration with a number of contemporary performers, I have investigated how traditional stories continue to be evocative and relevant for both tellers and listeners. My training and experience as folklorist and as storyteller provide a dual perspective that brings together scholarly and popular interests. I introduce many of the tellers I have met in more than two decades of work in Canada and the United States, I discuss their own interpretations of their art as well as mine, and I offer eight story texts that illustrate the kind of work these tellers are doing and how they themselves respond.

Folklorists explore individuals and their expressive forms within their communities, not just as isolated artists, and that is what I am attempting here. This community might be a town or village, a family or a group, or a consciously formed gathering of people who come together to hear and tell stories. Here my focus is on these consciously formed groups, often but not always in an urban environment. I begin by looking at storytelling from the viewpoint of group dynamics in Section I, then look at several individual tellers and their tales in Section II.

Almost any intentional storytelling community could be used as an example for such relationships. I used the Toronto area community as an example here because I was familiar with the people, their stories, and the social setting in which they functioned; this allowed me to see correlations that evolved over two decades of development. I propose that my portrait of this particular community of tellers provides an overall model for comparison with other storytelling groups in both Canada and the United States. I do not mean to suggest that it is a special community, but simply the one that I knew well enough to explore the relations between individuals within their significant group. I am certainly aware that each community has its own unique history, its own personal and artistic dynamics; but each one also shares recognizable features with other groups of comparable size and complexity.

In the last three decades of the twentieth century organized storytelling has increasingly attracted large adult audiences, despite the continuing popular assumption that storytelling is only for children. It is a challenge to determine whether the so-called storytelling revival is a momentary phenomenon, a nostalgic yearning for an idealized past, or a deep and abiding hunger for an archetypal literature that crosses the boundaries of language, geography, history, and life spans. Like the folksong "revival" that preceded it, storytelling is carried on by both amateur and professional performers. I have great respect for the thousands of beginning tellers across the continent who make an important contribution as active listeners and as disseminators of stories. They are, in many ways, the ones who keep oral telling alive. However, it is established professional performers with many years of experience who are the central subject of this study; we can learn from them how repertoires developed over the years in response to esthetic considerations, personal experience, and audience influences.

Many people assume that the revival of storytelling as a profession began in the 1970s, but in fact its origins are found in the development of training programs for teachers and librarians at the very beginning of the twentieth century. In these early decades tellers focused their attention on children in libraries, schools, churches, and other areas where children were gathered. This focus began to shift in the 1970s with the rise of popular storytelling festivals. The storytellers we will meet here have performed for adults as well as children, and some tellers even prefer exclusively adult audiences. National storytelling directories listing hundreds of tellers in Canada and the United States, as well as countless local directories for centers and communities across the continent, indicate the wide-spread nature of this artistic resurgence in the last decades of the twentieth century. Storytelling of this sort is not limited to North America, of course, but it would have taken a multi-volume work to do justice to the full range of activities in Europe, Asia, and other parts of the world.

I said earlier that I chose to focus on tellers who favor the kind of story we misnamed "fairytale." Narrative scholars have attempted to change this somewhat demeaning term by replacing it with the Germanic word "*Märchen*," but for my purposes here I have used "wondertale" as a description. These kinds of stories interweave the world of everyday reality with extraordinary events—throwing a handful of ordinary beans out a window and finding they have grown overnight into a beanstalk that reaches into the clouds. One folklorist describes such stories as a "magic sandwich" because "the miraculous events of the hero's [and heroine's] travels are framed by mundane beginnings and endings" (Lindahl 1994, xvii). A boy sets out to sell a cow but trades her for a few beans, visits a giant in the sky, and eventually brings the giant's miraculous treasures home to his mother. He is an ordinary boy yet he does not question how ordinary beans can grow up into the clouds nor how the clouds can support a giant and his castle. He accepts his astounding adventures and returns home to—presumably—live a mundane life (with a very good story to tell his grandchildren). Obviously this is not a story about the everyday reality of tellers and listeners, as it is for the characters who live in the tales. Why, then, are these stories still so well received by so many adults (not just children) in the twentieth century?

Popular writers from Bruno Bettelheim in 1976 to Marina Warner two decades later have explored how and why such old and seemingly irrational stories continue to excite our imagination (Bettelheim, 1976; Warner, 1994). There are as many explanations as there are writers who have attempted to address the issue. Some suggest that their appeal comes from the escapist potential of the "happily ever after" conclusions that momentarily take us away from the disappointments and drudgery of daily existence in a world that seems to be falling apart around our feet. Others propose deeper explanations, crediting a profound potential for expressing the all-too-real pains and joys of inner realities, a response to the eternal quest for meaningful identity. That is, the wondertales touch a profound psychic reality, tapping into archetypal depths.

One thing certain about wondertales is that they speak on many different levels, some touching only the surface and some reaching into an abyss of darkness and despair and rising to heights of joy and completeness, as we will hear from many of the tellers presented here. These are not simply "happily ever after" stories—quite the opposite: one moves into the light by facing inner darkness, and it is a steady struggle and not a "once upon a time" occasion. But I am getting ahead of my story here.

In preparing the book I corresponded and conversed with a multitude of storytellers and formally interviewed dozens. I listened to 1001 stories from the Yukon south to Florida, and from California east to New Brunswick—and many places in between. The tellers represented many professional backgrounds: library and educational work, performing arts, therapeutic and spiritual training, among others. I met only a handful who were raised in non-urban communities where oral telling had been an important and viable part of everyday life; for example, Ray and Stanley Hicks in North Carolina, Cree tellers Nathaniel Queskekapow (Manitoba) and Louis Bird (Ontario), and Joe Neil MacNeil from Nova Scotia.

As I said earlier, Section I is a general survey of the evolution of professional storytelling in North America; I look at the variety of backgrounds of tellers, the stories they prefer, how they have developed their identities as performers, and how they function within a community of tellers. This first section sets the stage for Section II, which introduces individual performers and the significance of storytelling as expressed in their work. Each chapter in this section is followed by a story text from each teller. Throughout this section, and in my concluding comments, I elaborate on the idea that folktales, and most particularly wondertales, retain their age-old relevance for tellers and listeners today because of profound reflections on the human condition.

Many of the chapters, especially those in Section II, were tested in other publications; each was written with this book in mind, and the responses I gratefully received from readers and editors helped me rework them as they appear here.

In writing this book I had to discard my own biases about authenticity and authority in order to appreciate the verbal artistry of tellers who were not, in purist folkloric thinking, "traditional" performers, even when they described themselves as such. When I first began writing about contemporary storytelling in the 1980s I challenged such self-descriptions, but then I began to wonder why tellers were so insistent.[3] I wanted to discover why they felt compelled to identify themselves with an oral tradition, however vague, even when it seemed "wrong" from a folkloric viewpoint. I also began to question why it had been so important for folklorists to use their scholarly authority to deny authenticity to nontraditional performers, even when folklorists themselves continued to be influenced by nineteenth-century romanticized notions of oral tradition.[4] These issues are not central here but they lie just below the surface. It was both a frustration and an advantage to look at different sides of the issue and to find that storytellers often misunderstood and distrusted academic folklorists as much as folklorists frequently misunderstood and distrusted revivalist tellers. I hope that this book provides an even-handed presentation that will be valuable to performers and scholars alike. I see that both have been, in their own ways, concerned with tradition, authenticity, authority, and most importantly, with finding ways of expressing uncommon insights about our common existence.[5]

The fluid moments I describe here are frozen in time on these printed pages; this is always a frustration for folklorists and others who explore living human expression, especially in the case of stories into which tellers literally breathe life. Cheryl Oxford put this more poetically in commenting on a traditional narrator's printed text of a Jack tale, the essence of which, as she said,

> lies preserved as in literary amber in this transcription of [Marshall] Ward's encore performance. The genetic code for its reproduction lies dormant on these pages. In a favorable climate this story's seed could again take root, sprout, and blossom into performance. The breath of a living voice could again resuscitate the story's perennial folk hero (Oxford 1994:68).

All but two of the tellers I interviewed were still very much alive at this writing;[6] I have captured their comments and their story texts at a single point in their careers. The tellers, of course, have continued to develop their art; communities and groups have continued to evolve and dissolve, despite their momentary preservation in amber here, using Oxford's imagery. Still, their tales can speak on the breath of another teller who finds that these words ignite their imagination. The story continues.

Notes

1 Sobol completed his doctoral dissertation, *Jonesborough Days: The National Storytelling Festival and the Contemporary Storytelling Revival Movement in America*, in 1994. At this writing (1997) he was in the process of preparing a published version (Sobol 1998).

2 Sobol discusses these controversies in some detail in his dissertation,

describing storytellers' responses to attempts at creating a code of ethics that would ideally protect tellers' repertoires. At the same time there was a movement to discourage performers from using material from Aboriginal and other racial and ethnic sources not their own. Many tellers reacted by dropping all traditional narratives from their repertoires.

3 For example, in the first article I wrote on this topic in 1979 in *The National Storytelling Journal* (Stone 1984), I was still politely criticizing performers who called themselves "traditional tellers" when they had no direct connection with an oral tradition. This purist folkloric approach was too limiting.

4 Charles Briggs suggests that folklorists still have a touch of romantic nationalism (Briggs 1993), and proposes that we become more aware of our biases and acknowledge them more explicitly in our work. I note, for example, that Lindahl, whose description of folktales I cite in this chapter, creates a nostalgic image of "performers who have their feet planted firmly in traditional soil" (Lindahl 1994:xiii); he ignores non-traditional tellers who are not so firmly rooted in an oral milieu.

5 A more recent book deals with precisely this issue, and includes articles by both folklorists and storytellers (Birch/Heckler 1996).

6 Stewart Cameron died in 1989, Joe Neil MacNeil in 1996.

SECTION I:
ORGANIZED COMMUNITIES
AND THEIR MEMBERS

E ACH of the five chapters in this section gives background information on the broad spectrum of organized storytelling. Chapters 1 and 2 discuss the close connections between folktale collections and storytelling, and describe the historical development of organized storytelling. I use the analogy of four streams flowing into a wide and vibrant river. Chapter 3 reviews the development of groups, guilds, centres, and communities that experienced spectacular growth in the relatively short span of two decades, in both the United States and Canada. Since many individual tellers had their first experiences in such organized gatherings, I want to show how an actual living community and its individual members interact; I focus on one particular location with the idea that my description will allow readers to compare and contrast this community with their own.

In Chapters 4 and 5 I turn my attention to an overview of tellers themselves, first considering how and why they select and develop the stories that make up their on-going repertoires, then exploring how their self-identity as tellers arose and evolved as they gained experience in performance.

Section I, with its exploration of the evolution of the movement as a whole and the groups and individuals who have carried it forward, prepares the way for the individual tellers featured in Section II.

ONE

FOLKTALES AND ORGANIZED STORYTELLING

FRIENDS often send me modern cartoons based on popular folktales such as "The Frog Prince" and "Little Red Riding Hood." In one cartoon a sad frog and an aloof princess sit in the waiting room of a marriage counselor, and in another the princess herself turns into a frog after disenchanting the prince. In a weekend comic page Little Red Riding Hood is told by her mother not to worry about the wolf, but to run away from any man she sees; in another cartoon she is reprimanded for abusing an endangered species. Pop culture often features bits and pieces of folktales as a fine foil for humor and critiques of modern life in the form of jokes, cartoons, and commercial advertisements. Modern literature also draws on folktales for parody and satire in books such as *Politically Correct Bedtime Stories*, whose tongue-in-cheek introduction suggests that "we cannot blame the Brothers Grimm for their insensitivity to womyn's issues, minority cultures, and the environment" (Gardner 1994:ix).

These jokes and parodies reveal one way that folktales manage to stay alive today. They are effectively amusing when we remember the stories they are based on, however vaguely. They also reveal very clearly that most adults no longer take the stories seriously. They are "kid stuff." This is not new, of course. For at least three hundred years since Charles Perrault's small collection of stories based on French folktales was published in 1697, traditional tales have been regarded as light amusement, more appropriate for children than for adults. The publication and translation of the Grimm tales in the early part of the nineteenth century firmly established children as the primary audience for these "bedtime" stories.

Library story hours that began in North America and elsewhere in the early part of the twentieth century relied substantially on collections of folktales, with children as the primary audience. From the very earliest storytelling in the 1880s, teachers and librarians used traditional folktales to encourage children to read books. Stories that were told, recited, or read were identified by the books in which they appeared, in hopes that children would read them and move on to more sophisticated literature. This regular use of folktales in library and school contexts provided the initial pattern for the evolution of storytelling as an organized activity; folktales and traditional story-telling were (and still are) held up as models for competent storytelling. In this context the term "traditional storytelling" was loosely used to describe non-theatrical presentations; "authentic" oral narrators were extolled as the "real" storytellers, though in an idealized past, not the living present.[1] As the movement continued to evolve in the first half of the twentieth century, those with backgrounds in the-ater were also drawn to this performance art, particularly as children's entertainers in recreational settings.

From a well-established place in Sunday schools and summer Bible camps, storytelling found an ever-growing realm in spiritual and, more recently, therapeutic settings for adults. The connection between chil-dren and folktales was already very firmly set when Walt Disney studios produced the first feature length cartoon based on the Grimm tale of "Snow White." I want to note that when this film was released in 1937 cartoons were not yet regarded as strictly for children; the sur-prising success of the film brought the folktale additional popularity with both children and adults.

In fact these seemingly anachronistic stories still attract our atten-tion, however much they may strike some as absurdly fantastic, sentimentally romantic, and utterly irrelevant in a world firmly com-mitted to rationality, materialism, objectivity, and "virtual reality." It would be a task worthy of a folktale protagonist to consider the full range of psychological, social, historical, and artistic aspects that con-tribute to our continuing fascination with these kinds of stories; even one of these topics would require a book-length survey.

Rather than offering yet another interpretation of the meaning of folk and fairytales I want to follow a different path into the woods by looking at some of those who tell these stories now, not as parodies or as deconstructed postmodern tales in poetry or prose forms,[2] but as oral re-creations. Since the early 1970s there has been a dramatic rise in performances for mixed age audiences, and tellers have a wider variety of professional training, beyond educational and library work in which storytelling arose earlier in the twentieth century. Many tellers still begin as children's librarians or teachers, but may move out of their institutions and onto the concert stage, performing for adults as well as children. Performers also come from dramatic, literary, therapeutic, spiritual, and other kinds of professional training. Storytelling draws on a growing wealth of tellers from such a variety of interests and experiences that I can do little more than mention them here, and try to find patterns that connect them, that reveal the oral contexts in which they work.

I am interested in the kind of storytelling that takes place in organized events: for children in library story hours or in school classrooms, for adults on concert stages and at festivals. Most of the tellers who perform at these events have at least some training and experience, either in formal professional programs or through workshops and short term classes offered by other experienced performers. A few tellers are able to make a full-time career of storytelling, but most perform part-time, sometimes as part of another career in writing, teaching, library work, or the ministry, for example. On any concert or festival stage you can hear personal experience stories, exaggerated anecdotes, original compositions, myths, epics, folktales, and the ever popular tall tale or "lie." Published collections are still a major source of stories from around the world, but stories are also learned from other tellers who hear them at storytelling events and pass them on.

In order to avoid getting lost in the overwhelming multiplicity of both tellers and tales I keep my focus on the kinds of stories still of deep and abiding interest to many tellers and listeners; these are variously called folktales, fairy tales, wondertales, magic tales, or *Märchen*. Folklorists have struggled in vain to define the genre precisely; no single term suffices to capture the essential nature of these tales that bring together the worlds of common experience and uncommon happenings. I prefer *wondertale* as a description, since it seems to me a more open term not as bound up in stereotypes as the popular term "fairy tale." Wondertales are filled with commonplace things that behave in most uncommon ways: ordinary animals give extraordinary advice; trees and rivers speak; prosaic objects contain mystical powers so that simple rings may give fabulous wishes, crude sacks or bowls or boxes prove to be sources of unending wealth, and ordinary cloaks confer invisibility. Most wondrous of all, creatures transform into human beings and people become enchanted animals, flowers, trees. These stories have an intense bond with the natural world, negatively and positively.

Many of the fantastic characters in wondertales are archetypal figures who appear in dreams as well, and indeed wondertale and dream seem often to come from common sources of inspiration. These kinds of stories appeal to something profound and numinous that drifts on the edge between the consciousness and the unconscious. The wide acceptance of best-selling books offering specialized psychological interpretations of folktales underlines the continuing fascination that these stories inspire.[3]

Folklorists have explored oral tales, and particularly wondertales, for much of the nineteenth and twentieth centuries. They were curious about the literary artistry of tales and tellers as well as the social and cultural aspects that were reflected in and expressed through the stories. They wondered, for example, if the beastly husband who was a white bear in Scandinavia, a snake in Hungary, a frog, lion, or brown bear in other tales was culturally determined or was the preference of particular tellers (see, for example, Dégh 1990). Why were there so many stories like these "beauty/beast" tales that were both similar and different at the same time?

Some scholars have answered these question by centering their attention on the stories themselves (for example, Lüthi 1976, 1985, 1986; Holbek 1987; Bausinger 1990; Röhrich 1986, 1991).[4] Their descriptions and commentary make it clear that wondertales have functioned as a significant form of literature for adults. Max Lüthi, in particular, details the formal, abstract essence of wondertales that allow them to "give an answer to the burning questions of human existence" (Lüthi 1982:84) and also to offer "a reply to the demons" (93). We will see how contemporary tellers respond to this aspect of stories and storytelling.

Some scholars have explored telling and tellers as a vital part of living communities (Dégh 1979[5]; Glassie 1982[6]), and some have put particular stress on the importance of the most skilled tellers and how their lives influenced their stories (most particularly, Azadovskii 1974; Adams 1972; Dégh 1995; MacNeil 1987).[7] The study of storytelling in actual performance situations, highlighting storytelling as a dramatic rather than as a strictly literary art, has inspired context-oriented scholars (for example, Georges 1969; Bauman 1977, 1986).[8]

Women are strongly associated with storytelling, as tellers of tales and as tale characters. It is no accident, then, that wondertales have caught the attention of feminist scholars who have discussed the importance of gender in traditional stories (Bottigheimer 1987; Dégh

1995a:62-69; Rowe 1991; Stone 1975, 1985, 1993; Tatar 1987, 1992; Warner 1994; Zipes 1979, 1983).

Most of the studies mentioned above center on traditional folktales, stories reworked by the Grimms, or oral tales learned and told by people who spent their lives in communities where tales were told and heard rather than written and read. However, a handful of scholarly anthologies have moved beyond the traditional oral milieu to examine folk revivals of the twentieth century (for example, Rosenberg 1993; McCarthy 1994; Birch/Heckler 1996).[9] Rosenberg's anthology focuses on the folk music revival and offers some observations relevant to storytelling as well. Contributors to McCarthy's book describe performers from both traditional and revival milieus and provide sample texts for each teller. Birch and Heckler offer a varied collection of articles by folklorists, anthropologists, and storytellers, each chapter highlighting a different aspect of the complex dynamics among tellers, tales and listeners. Birch and Heckler attempt to address what they call a "pivotal issue," the development of "a critical language for approaching and assessing contemporary story occasions with widely diverse audiences, tellers, and types of material" (Birch/Heckler:9). In their introduction they delightfully suggest that in terms of human cultural evolution we might consider stories as "a mental opposable thumb, allowing humans to grasp something in their minds—to turn it around, to view it from many angles, to reshape it, and to hurl it even into the farthest reaches of the unconscious" (Birch/Heckler:11). This evocative metaphor reverberates throughout their anthology, and has been an inspiration in this book as well.

Of course there is an abundance of books written by storytellers themselves, far too many to include here. Extensive bibliographies can be found in the now-classic work of Augusta Baker and Ellin Greene, *Storytelling: Art and Technique* (1987) and in Anne Pellowski's survey, *The World of Storytelling* (1990). These works and others provide historical and comparative information valuable to understanding the developing role of storytelling, particularly in the library-educational milieu.

In addition to published works, there have been a small number of doctoral dissertations, of which two in particular provide detailed and invaluable information on the development of professional storytelling in the twentieth century (Alvey 1974; Sobol 1994). Richard Alvey uses the term "organized storytelling" to describe the context in which these storytellers functioned.[10] His study centers on the early years of the twentieth century when organized storytelling was a child-centered activity. He traces its origins and its steady development in schools and libraries, Sunday schools, summer camps, recreational programs, and other formal contexts. Alvey identifies three main stages: "The Foundation Years" from 1875 to 1915 when storytelling slowly came to be recognized as a pedagogical tool; "The Burgeoning Years" from 1915 to 1940 when it spread to libraries and schools across North America; "The Mature Years" from 1940 to the early 1970s when oral telling encountered growing competition from other media—radio, phonograph records, films, and television. After this, organized storytelling appeared to have gone into a steady decline as libraries and schools ceased to be as active in the promotion of stories and storytelling on a widespread and regular basis. By coincidence, Alvey completed his dissertation in 1974, at exactly the moment (unbeknownst to him) of a vigorous rebirth of organized storytelling that would carry it beyond schools and libraries and into the festival setting, with adults rather than children as listeners. Still, his historical study is an invaluable aid in understanding the background of this new burst of creativity, all the more so since many modern participants seem to be unaware of the historical roots of the movement.

Joseph Sobol begins his study where Alvey stops, carrying the dramatic story of the recent storytelling revival movement into the 1990s. His observations are based on his own fifteen years of experience as a performer and on extensive interviews with American performers caught up in the sudden revitalization of storytelling, spurred by the establishment of a "national" festival and organization in Jonesborough, a small Tennessee town, in 1973-74. Sobol notes that for many of the people involved in this period of development storytelling was not just a career but a mission, a performance art "with revitalizing potential for individuals, as well as for the culture as a whole" (Sobol 1994a:6). He suggests that the current revival has evolved (however erratically) in response to the cultural radicalism of the 1960s and the personal growth movement of later decades (Sobol 1994a:43). While Sobol focuses on the recent resurgence of storytelling in the United States and particularly on the role of the National Storytelling Association, many of his comments, as well as those of the tellers he interviewed, are relevant to the movement in Canada as well.

The dramatic rise of organized storytelling is not only a North American phenomenon, of course. Organized storytelling, both as a child-centered activity and as a performance art for adults, has continued to flourish in countries of continental Europe (see Görög-Karady 1989 and Calame-Griaule 1991) and the British Isles (see Harvey 1987, 1990), and in other parts of the world, most notably in Asia (especially Japan) and Australia.

When I began exploring this topic in 1989 few folklorists considered organized storytelling worthy of scholarly attention, due largely to a narrow use of the term "oral tradition" that excluded revival storytellers. At the same time, many tellers regarded themselves as heartfelt descendants of a vague oral tradition and failed to understand why folklorists were so disdainful of their claims. Often when I introduced myself as a folklorist I heard stories about how teller after teller had been firmly chastized by one folklorist or another for describing themselves as "traditional storytellers." It seemed to me that it would be more useful to look at the reasons behind such conflicts than to prove either folklorists or storytellers right or wrong. After all, the invention of tradition is not new, but arises as part of romantic nationalism in eighteenth-century Europe (Dundes 1985; Hobsbawm/Ranger 1983; Wallace 1956). The folk revival on this continent is yet another expression of the hunger for an imagined era of lost simplicity. Today there are dozens of masters theses and doctoral dissertations in preparation, as well as books and articles in various stages of completion by folklorists and others interested in this phenomenon. The "revival" has indeed come to life, not only for tellers and listeners but for scholars as well.

The continuing development of organized storytelling has brought dramatic increases in the numbers of tellers, groups, and events. A directory of storytellers published by NSA (then called NAPPS) in 1984 listed fewer than two hundred performers, only a few dozen local groups, and a handful of events in only half the states of the U.S. and just two Canadian provinces.[11] Little more than a decade later these figures leapt dramatically; the 1995 NSA directory listed more than eight hundred individuals, almost three hundred local and regional groups and centers, and nearly one hundred and fifty events in thirty-five states and five of the ten Canadian provinces (and two territories).

	Tellers	Groups	Events	State	(Prov.)
1984	174	68	39	24	(2)
1995	800+	240	147	35	(5)

Many of these groups now publish newsletters and local directories, offer workshops and other educational opportunities, and present concerts, festivals, and other storytelling events. As the figures reveal, most of these groups came into existence in a single decade. Some, however, originated from storytelling guilds and leagues established by librarians and teachers many years earlier.

In the 1970s, however, revival rhetoric portrayed organized story-telling as a new phenomenon, a spontaneous arising of like minds devoted to reviving a supposedly lost oral art. Joseph Sobol suggests that such idealistic viewpoints provided an important source of energy for many tellers who saw themselves as pioneers in new territory, as performance artists for adults. Yet many of the "pioneers" of the newest wave of revival storytelling began their careers in library and educational contexts. Despite the increase in adult audiences and the decline of formal storytelling programs in schools and libraries these child-centered institutions still provide the most steady source of activities and incomes for contemporary tellers.

We can see that organized storytelling arises from many sources. People with different interests, training, and goals have long been attracted to storytelling; in addition to those already mentioned, poets and writers, mimes, puppeteers and dancers, museum guides, radio and television performers, and many others contributed to the evolution of organized storytelling. In this myriad whirl of activity, I see four broad streams as the major forces shaping the movement of this continuing flow: traditional, library-educational, theatrical, and spiritual-therapeutic storytelling.[12] They cut the parallel channels that continue to feed the wide and winding course of organized storytelling today, providing a steady wellspring from which tellers continue to draw energy and experience.

Notes

1 For example, Ruth Sawyer's classic work, *The Way of the Storyteller*, commemorates her childhood nursemaid Johanna. Sawyer felt that "Thrice blest is that child who comes early under the spell of the traditional story-teller, one who holds unconsciously to the ancient and moving power of her art" (Sawyer 1942:16).

2 Cristina Bacchilega explores the literary creations of a number of fairy tale re-writers in *Postmodern Fairy Tales* (Bacchilega 1997). Wolfgang Mieder edited a collection of modern poetry inspired by fairy tales (Mieder 1985). Anne Sexton's classic collection of poetry, *Transformations*, was also inspired

by the Grimm tales (Sexton) 1971). Since oral and written composition are quite distinct in the contexts of creation and performance I do not include such works here, though I certainly acknowledge their significance in keeping the stories alive, even in altered form.

3 These include two widely read best sellers: Robert Bly's extensive exploration and retelling of a single Grimm tale in *Iron John* (Bly 1990), and Clarissa Pinkola Estés' exploration of her own literary versions of supposed folktales in *Women Who Run with the Wolves* (Pinkola Estés 1992).

4 Max Lüthi, in his classic study, *The European Folktale: Form and Nature* eloquently describes how these stories hold "lasting truths" that transcend time and place, and how these truths were expressed through the stable form and the flexible content of the wondertale (Lüthi 1982:xv).

Bengt Holbek, in his exhaustive study of Danish tales, *Interpretation of Fairy Tales* speaks passionately about the need for retaining "the earthy humour and cheerful, frank sexuality" of these stories, which are all too often adapted or edited, "wrapped in many layers of careful verbiage, sentimentalized, obfusticated or even obliterated" (Holbek 1987:606).

Hermann Bausinger, in *Folk Culture in a World of Technology* (Bausinger 1990), makes an eloquent case for the continuing creativity of oral lore in modern society—not despite increasing urbanization and technology but precisely because of these forces.

Lutz Röhrich's *Folktales and Reality* investigates the many ways these fantastic stories achieve plausibility by constantly adjusting to the "real" world around them, an on-going process among traditional narrators in all periods of historical development. He uses hundreds of examples to demonstrate how wondertales "have always, at all times, adapted to the current picture of reality" (p. 215). His work provides convincing evidence for the continuing appeal of fantastic narratives. Röhrich mentions the popularity of books written by those untrained in folklore; he eloquently urges folklorists to ask "why and with what justification 'their' field is now so successfully cultivated by those who harvests there without having sown" (Röhrich 1991:9).

5 Linda Dégh's classic study of a storytelling community in post-war Hungary, *Folktales and Society* (1969, 1989), is still a model of narrative scholarship. It explores in detail the social, geographical and political history of the community; the tale-telling contexts and the variety of narratives told; and the individual tellers who are recognized as master narrators by the community. Dégh broadens the perspective by exploring the vital connections between the stories, the tellers, and the social setting in which they existed.

Her consideration of individual narrators as artists within that particular society is a model for the study of traditional oral societies in general. Many of her observations are relevant to organized storytelling, especially those concerning personal connections between narrators and their stories. In organized storytelling professional performers were less dependent on their communities as a source of stories and of support, but they were not free of societal influences. Dégh's assertion that tellers "can develop only with the cooperation of the community" and that "every narrator is the vessel for the tradition of the community which he represents" (p. 52) expresses the intricate connections that existed at least in part for many modern tellers, even within their fragmented and specialized storytelling communities.

6   In his detailed study, *Passing the Time in Ballymenone: Culture and History of an Ulster Community*, Henry Glassie explores how and why stories remained alive for particular people in a small community in Northern Ireland, where tales might arise from ordinary conversation as people "face the long night together" (Glassie 1982:33). He also broadens the notion of context from the tellers' rather than from the observers' viewpoints:

> Some of the context is drawn in from the immediate situation, but more is drawn from memory. It [context] is present, but invisible, inaudible. Contexts are mental associations woven around texts during performance to shape and complete them, to give them meaning (p. 33).

7   Mark Azadovskii's monograph, *A Siberian Tale Teller* (Azadowskii 1974) focuses on master narrator Natal'ia Vinokurova. This is an excellent example of the biographical approach; he explores her personal esthetic style, and the psychological motivations that inspired her interpretations.

Robert Adams, following Azadowski's lead, wrote a doctoral dissertation entitled *Social Identity of a Japanese Storyteller* (Adams 1972). He describes a woman who, in addition to her own traditional tales, mastered many of the Grimm tales and transformed them so thoroughly into her own Japanese context that Adams did not at first recognize them as European tales. He describes the challenging personal and economic factors that led to her development of a social identity as a narrator.

Dégh devotes an entire book, *Hungarian Folktales: The Art of Zsuzsanna Palkó* (Dégh 1995b), to her primary narrator, Zsuzsanna Palkó, and included 35 of her tales. Palkó only began telling stories publicly, outside her circle of family and friends, when her storytelling brother died. She was 70 at that time, already a master teller. Dégh describes the details of Palkó's difficult life and her development as an artistic teller in *Folktales and Society* (Dégh 1969, 1989), but was unable to include Palkó's stories in that study.

The life and stories of Joe Neil MacNeil are reported in *Tales Until Dawn* (MacNeil 1987), translated and edited by John Shaw. Joe Neil describes his own early days, while John puts this into the broader context of Gaelic storytelling in Scotland and on Cape Breton Island.

8 A key article by Robert Georges, "Toward an Understanding of Storytelling Events (Georges 1969), introduces the term "storytelling event" to describe the full vibrant context of the process, not just the text and the teller as if they were two-dimensional. Similarly, Richard Bauman, in *Verbal Art as Performance* (Bauman 1977), attempts to catch the living art of storytelling in mid-flight as "a mode of spoken verbal communication" in which performers are responsible to their listeners "for a display of communicative competence" (p. ll). This treatment of the storytelling event, or performance art, includes tellers, listeners, and the overall context of an immediate storytelling session. In these storytelling events, oral presentations adapt to the changing contexts. Bauman describes this as "emergent quality" (p. 38). He discusses oral narrators in a more confining milieu than that of professional performers, but his basic concept of "communicative competence" and "emergent quality" capture the dynamics of narrating in general, for modern artists as well as traditional narrators.

9 Some very fine explorations have been written by those involved directly in the storytelling movement. See, among others, for example: Baker and Greene (1987); Livo and Rietz (1986); and Pellowski (1994).

10 Alvey defines this as storytelling "from an adult to children occurring within larger organized activities with children, particularly libraries, schools, and religious and recreational contexts" (lxxiv). Organized storytelling is more flexible than the currently popular term "professional storytelling," because it includes people who tell or read stories as part of teaching, library work, or other professions as well as those who are full-time performers.

11 These directories have been published annually since 1981. I have used the second edition (1983-84) because it established a pattern for future listings. The National Association for the Preservation and Perpetuation of Storytelling (NAPPS) has since changed to its name to NSA, the National Storytelling Association.

12 Storyteller Ruth Stotter conducted a survey in 1986, asking tellers to identify their backgrounds in storytelling, and their main sources of stories. She received 162 responses from the 182 questionnaires she sent to tellers listed in the 1986 National Storytelling Directory. Of those who replied, her four largest categories were (in order): "significant theatrical experience;" "degree in library science or library work experience;" teaching credentials or certificates;" "religious leader/educator." Another major category in her survey was harder to interpret, since it included theater, speech, literature, psychology, storytelling, and library science all together.

Stotter also noted that 59% of the respondents listed printed material as their main source, and the remaining 41% identified oral material—original creations, family and personal experience stories, and stories from other tellers—as their major sources. (Stotter, private communication, 1991).

TWO

FOUR STREAMS, ONE RIVER: THE STORYTELLING REVIVAL

I DESCRIBE this "revival" impressionistically, since it is not my intention to give firm definitions, or to create rigid models of actual communities. Instead, I hope to delineate the most obvious features so that each stream can be more easily compared, and so we can later appreciate the variety and the backgrounds of individual tellers.[1]

Oral Tradition

Folktales by their very name reveal their origins in oral traditional communities. Here stories were learned as part of one's heritage in a particular family, within a community united by ties of language, culture, religion, history. In Canada traditional narrators of European folktales have survived to the present day in French-speaking Quebec and in the Maritime Provinces, in particular. For example, Joe Neil MacNeil (included here in Section II, Chapter 2) was a narrator from Cape Breton Island in Nova Scotia, who retold Gaelic tales that connected him with families whom he remembered in detail decades after hearing their stories. In the United States the oral tradition thrived in the semi-isolated mountainous regions of the south and northeast, where the old European tales lasted well into the twentieth century. The Harmon-Hicks family of North Carolina is the most frequently cited example.[2] Their stories and traditions have been the subject of numerous academic studies and have been widely popularized by Richard Chase, who rewrote and published their tales for his own profit (Chase 1943, 1948).

There is also a rich and ancient tradition of aboriginal narration still very much alive on reservations in the United States and the reserves of Canada, and in urban centers as well. I have worked informally with two such tellers, Nathaniel Queskekapow of Norway House,

Manitoba, and Louis Bird from Peawanuck, Ontario, though I do not include their material here.[3] There is a very strong feeling about the importance of cultural identity as expressed in traditional narratives. One such teller who now performs professionally in an urban area emphasized community connections in describing herself:

> I am a woman of Inuit background. I grew up in Greenland listening to and appreciating the Inuit stories from my maternal grandmother. Teaching at the University of Saskatchewan in the College of Education, I have used my skills to entice my students to an understanding of the depth of Aboriginal storytelling. These relate to how we see ourselves as human beings (Karla Jessen Williamson, *Canadian Storytelling Directory* 1997/98:52).

In areas of both European and Aboriginal traditions tales might be told ceremonially during certain seasons or times of the day, or more informally at any convenient time or place. But no matter how formal the setting there was no equivalent of an established "storytelling hour," nor a stage that separated tellers and listeners; nor was there a set length of time since the duration of each storytelling event was determined by interactions between tellers and listeners.

While there were certainly some tales that were appropriate for adults or for children, many were fitting for all ages, since traditional narratives had many levels of meaning depending on the listeners' experiences and comprehension and the teller's skill at adapting stories to different audiences. The same story might be told by a mother to her children or by a master teller performing at an evening gathering, though each variant would be told differently. That is, the text (the basic story) and texture (personal style of expression) were in a constant state of emergence through performances in different contexts. Within the family or in small gatherings of friends women could be active narrators, but in larger and more public gatherings men were usually featured. For example, when the traditional tellers from the Harmon-Hicks family from North Carolina took to the stage in festivals that began in the 1970s, the men—Ray Hicks, Stanley Hicks, Marshall Ward, Frank Proffitt, Jr.—were much more active than the women—Hattie Presnell and Maud Gentry Long. Linda Dégh describes in detail the Hungarian masterteller Zsuzsanna Palkó who began narrating publicly only when the male narrators in her taletelling family had died (Dégh 1989:187-234; 1995b).

For traditional narrators, adults were the listeners on both the festival stage and in home own communities, except of course in the home where women narrated for children. Traditional audiences were relatively small and intimate, a few dozen at most and often much smaller, and tellers and listeners were part of the same geographic and cultural community. (This did not preclude the welcome visit of wandering narrators, who introduced new material to the local treasury of stories.)

Traditional narrators are so highly regarded at festivals today that their actual skill (or lack of it) as artistic narrators is often disregarded. Some have been unable to adjust to the concert stage while others—notably Ray Hicks and Joe Neil MacNeil mentioned above—have succeeded in adapting themselves and their stories to this new context.[4] There are also many people who are not so easily identified as either traditional or non-traditional tellers. Some—Donald Davis and Jackie Torrence of North Carolina, for example—grew up in oral milieus but were also influenced by the self-conscious setting of festival stage performing. Others who have claimed traditional backgrounds are on more tenuous grounds. Still, what unites all of these people is a real or an idealized connection to storytelling as a respected artistic expression.

Library and Educational Storytelling

Storytelling gradually became an important pedagogical tool as universal education spread across North America in the nineteenth century. The innovative kindergarten movement inspired by German educational concepts brought storytelling into the schools, and from there into public libraries, where it became established in regularly scheduled "story hours" for young children. As women came to dominate library and educational professions, they also became the storytellers—with notable exceptions, of course. These storytellers learned their tales from books rather than from an oral community, and also had to find their own means of preparing the stories and themselves for public performance. Storytelling workshops and classes, lasting anywhere from an hour to several weeks or months, were and still are offered through schools and libraries, though less so today.

Eventually formal library and school storytelling began to decline, but this did not happen all at once.[5] For several decades the school classroom and the library story hour continued to take place on schedule. Audiences tended to be larger than in a more spontaneous traditional context; there were often from twenty to forty children, with one or more adults as caretakers rather than as full audience members, thus maintaining storytelling as a child-oriented activity. While in traditional societies stories were often told to mixed-age or all-adult listeners at night when daily work was completed and the setting was informal and usually intimate, organized storytelling usually took place during the day and in a pre-designated place with a somewhat formal arrangement; children sat on the floor or in chairs and the storyteller stood or sat alone in front of them, more firmly separating the single teller and the many acquiescent listeners. These sessions often lasted from thirty to sixty minutes and were scheduled in advance. Thus tellers in schools and libraries had much less flexibility than traditional narrators, since their performances were scheduled and timed rather than arising at the moment. Also, the separation of teller and audience often discouraged spontaneous interaction, though not in all situations. I am not suggesting that tellers were not spontaneously creative or that their listeners were passive; if this were so, storytelling would not have gained and held its great popularity in the first four decades of the twentieth century. I am only trying to show a contrast between the two streams of oral traditional narration and library-educational storytelling.

Even at the peak of school and library activities, the public at large did not give storytelling the same respect it had in traditional communities; it was not regarded as a significant artistic expression for adults, nor was it part of the broader culture. Despite this, librarians and teachers who continued to tell stories regularly and enthusiastically were able to develop into skilled and artistic narrators who could bring the printed word into full and vibrant life. Such tellers kept storytelling alive and very dynamic for more than a century, and provided the firm base on which organized storytelling continues to grow and blossom.

Alice Kane, a retired Toronto public librarian and master storyteller, has noted with pleasure that in the closing years of the twentieth century storytelling began to return to schools and libraries, though in a changed form: "Now there is a difference. Now there is an experiment in having the pupils listen to stories and then try telling their own." And, she added, "The results have been spectacular and beyond [the educators'] wildest dreams" (Kane 1990:68). This innovation brought library-educational storytelling closer to an oral traditional context, though only partially, since it was children and not adults who were learning and telling the stories they heard.

Given the strong role that the library-educational stream played in the development of organized storytelling, it is no accident that many festivals are still dominated by tellers who are or have been teachers and librarians. Here is a description of one such teller, who is part of these innovations in telling:

> As a children's librarian, I tell stories to children under 12. I have over 12 years of experience telling stories to children at festivals and other festive events. Generally my stories include audience participation and often I use puppets. Most of the stories I tell are folktales (Linda Lines, *Canadian Storytelling Directory* 1997/98:17).

This teller emphasizes that she works with younger children and that she strongly favors folktales in her repertoire, which was the library-educational "tradition." Her use of puppets and audience participation is now more common for those who work mainly with children, a departure from earlier techniques that focused entirely on the story.

Alice Kane laments the turn away from "pure" storytelling as it was traditionally practiced in schools and libraries, that is, the old folktales told "without gimmicks" (her words) or anything else that might interrupt visualizing and internalizing a story, taking it in so completely that it would remain a part of one's life even into adulthood. She asks:

> Where then will children hear of King Arthur and Kostchei the Deathless and Kate Crackernuts and that doughty lass Molly Whuppee who defied a giant, and a two-faced giant at that. And if they don't hear of these heroes, how will they, in their time, stand up against the mighty powers that contend against us?" (Kane 1990:66).

We will return to these challenging questions when we reach the conclusion of this book, since her words point to the heart of the wondertale, its potency in struggling "against the mighty powers." But first let us look at how the theatrical stream presented its own challenges in organized storytelling.

Theatrical Storytelling

Storytelling developed as a dramatic art early in human history, and thus storytelling and drama shared many techniques and devices to project stories out to listeners through voice and movement. The close connections between these two performance arts made it difficult to distinguish clearly between them. It was not a matter of personal style, since many tellers perform stories quite dramatically, while actors can use an understated style of narration. There were notable differences, however, which can be viewed on a continuum: narration, at one end of the performance continuum, featured one person telling a story with few dramatic devices; acting, at the other end, involved one or more actors and often an entire cast who performed scheduled plays and employed dramatic voice changes and movement, costumes and props, set designs, and a rehearsed script. Theatrical storytelling rested somewhere between these two extremes, perhaps involving a single actor without theatrical props and sets but still using dramatic voice and movement, and often a costume of some sort—as minimal as a hat or a scarf. Though they might not present a fully staged play, their performance was still more one-person theatre than simple storytelling.

Most notably, differing concepts of distance and of interaction between performers and audiences created a different performance context: in an ideal storytelling event there was no "fourth wall" separating teller, tale, and listeners even when the event took place on a formal stage. I overheard an audience member at a New England conference in 1982 sum up these two contexts in words that remain with me years later: "When I watch theater I'm looking at the world they create on stage but when I listen to a story I'm right in the middle of it."

Non-theatrical tellers did not take on the role of any single character but moved in and out of all the characters in a story, consistently assuming only one "role," that of the storyteller. In contrast, a theatrically trained teller assumed dramatic roles and might have told a story from the personal view of a single character; or a story was enacted by an entire cast of characters as in the Story Theater model, in which each part was both dramatized and narrated by the actors. Often the stories and the individual roles in them were prepared from scripts, which were memorized and rehearsed. Depending on the production, there might be a large formal stage with lighting and sound systems, costumes, props, and stage sets, which took this kind of storyteller closer to the theatrical end of the continuum. In a theatrical setting performers and listeners were usually more distant than in school or library settings. In addition, the scheduling of theatrical storytelling was even more fixed than in classroom and library story hours, as these events often involved a great deal more preparation and depended on more advance publicity since tickets and money were involved.

In contrast to libraries and schools where women dominated as tellers, both men and women were equally involved as performers in theatrical telling. Their audiences were considerably larger, anywhere from fifty to five hundred (or even more) depending on the size of the venue. This further separated tellers and listeners though it did not preclude the possibility of interaction. That is, a folktale retained its power to stimulate imagination whether told in a school classroom for children or in a large theater for adults. One theatrically trained teller emphasizes the variety of venues in which stories can be dramatically told:

> My theatre training, which provides background for oral interpretation of literature, and a family tradition of storytelling, plus formal training in 1992, brought me to professional storytelling. I tell stories in English to any audience of any age that wishes to hear, in schools, libraries, festivals, meetings, special events, self-help groups, teachers, camps, hospitals, and other gatherings (Carol Leigh Wehking, *Canadian Storytelling Directory* 1997/98:45).

This teller clearly claims theatrical training and style and is available to any age and many venues. She underlines her training as background rather than foreground to storytelling, and augments this by mentioning family storytelling. Like Bob Barton, whom we will meet in the first chapter of Section II, she was drawn into storytelling from theater, instead of the other way around. In contrast, here is another performer who seems to be using storytelling within a theatrical framework, even giving himself a name and providing an accompanying photograph of himself in costume holding a puppet:

> For more than 25 years this "imaginer extraordinaire" has been dedicated to bringing his special style of folk art, story theater, puppetry, and educational entertainment to adults and children all over the world (John Byrne, Professor Ed U. Gator's

Humorous Humanities Theater Company. *National Storytelling Directory* 1995:28).

This write-up stresses theatrical background so strongly that story-telling is not even mentioned. Also, individual style of this "imaginer extraordinaire" is stressed over family or community connections. These two descriptions reveal subtle but telling differences in the continuum of theatrical storytelling.Again, I want to stress that this is not a criticism of one or the other. Though my personal preferences would inspire me to choose, in fact what I really want to show is the variety of possibilities. In Section II, Chapter 1, I mention a very theatrical performer, Brother Blue (Hugh Hill), who dances so elegantly back and forth between theater and storytelling that I gave up all attempts to define his unique and profoundly engaging style. Though he uses a theatrical name and appears in costume, and is indeed an "imaginer extraordinaire" like the performer cited above, he is also very much a storyteller who engages listeners directly, leaping through the fourth wall to address individual listeners personally, then leaping back again into his "Brother Blue" persona.

I deliberately do not address the interesting question of performances crossing the flexible border between theater and storytelling. I can only suggest a few guidelines for recognizing such a border as it exists for you, as a teller or as a listener.

Therapeutic and Spiritual Storytelling

This is the most difficult of the four streams to delineate with certainty, since it is more an outlook than a performing style or background. If we keep in mind the image of a stream or river, this particular current weaves back and forth like a prairie tributary braiding its way across the flatlands. Its strongest current is the favoring of emotional connection over education or entertainment. So many performers, especially now, describe themselves in either spiritual or therapeutic terms (or both) that it will be a challenge for me to make meaningful patterns clear. Brother Blue, for example, is a theatrical performer who is very firmly immersed in spiritual-therapeutic storytelling. It is interesting to note that he does not list himself in the *National Storytelling Directory*, much less display the advertisements or promotional photos customary for theatrical performers. Where does he "belong" in my scheme of streams and rivers? As you can see, the borders of this wandering stream will be a challenge to discover.

I begin in the most obvious place. As I mentioned earlier in this section, storytelling had long been a part of religious activities for children, in Sunday school classes, summer vacation Bible schools, and religious events such as Bar and Bat Mitzvahs and other coming-of-age ceremonies. Sermons for adults also relied heavily on storytelling to convey religious messages. In therapeutic contexts, psychotherapists such as Bruno Bettelheim (1976),[6] Sigmund Freud (1958), Carl Jung (1969, 1976, 1989), and Marie Von Franz (Franz 1970, 1972, 1974, 1977), among others, explored traditional tales as deep expressions of the unconscious and subconscious. Some of these explications, particularly those of Freud and Jung, inspired popularizers such as Joseph Campbell, Robert Bly, and Clarissa Pinkola Estés to reach wider audiences through their writing. Educational movements such as the Waldorf Schools brought a therapeutic-spiritual approach into teaching.

This stream of storytelling is a challenge to characterize because it has so many different forms of expression, of which formal performance is sometimes the least important. That is, in both spiritual and therapeutic settings stories are told more for their deep meaning than for entertainment. Notably, even mediocre tellers can be effective in this context since emphasis is not on performance techniques but on human understanding, and the emphasis is on "speaking from the heart" rather than putting on a good show. These are not mutually exclusive, of course. American entertainer Ed Stivender came to storytelling with a strong theatrical training, and his performances were considered by many to be one-man theater rather than storytelling. He also worked from a committed Catholic background that imbued his performances with both moving spirituality and diverting merriment, even when he wildly parodied well-known folktales or performed a monologue dressed in the brown robes of a Christian monk. His directory entry plays down theatrical background; in his own words he "tells Anglo-American folklore, literary tales, and personal narratives with an accent on the humor of life and legend" (Ed Stivender, *National Storytelling Directory* 1996:45).

If tellers in this stream are difficult to pin down, the contexts in which they present stories are even more elusive. It cannot be so easily defined by the times or places where it might occur, and in this it is closer to traditional narration than to the other streams. Spiritual or therapeutic storytelling could arise at any time or in any place that inspires it to break through into performance—in private therapy sessions or in a rabbi's, minister's, or priest's private study; in group therapy sessions or in the pulpit of a religious building; with a few friends in the kitchen or on a stage with hundreds of listeners.

Nor is this stream easily identified by the kinds of stories favored. For example, spiritual storytelling might take the form of a narrative sermon based on sacred texts, a recitation of a sacred text itself, or a personal experience with some spiritual content. Most listeners would be connected by a common religious bond with at least some knowledge of the material and the person offering it. Presentations of stories would be relatively informal, not a staged performance, no matter how polished and dramatic the minister/preacher/priest/rabbi might be; also, the listeners' responses often played a significant part in such presentations. Audience sizes might vary from a handful to a multitude. Listeners and tellers would have a firm bond beyond the context of the storytelling as entertainment. Similarly, therapeutic narratives might take form as personal stories, original compositions, written literature; Robert Coles (*The Call of Stories*, 1989) and Jerome Bruner (*Actual Minds, Possible Worlds*, 1986) used literature in their therapeutic practices.

In the last two decades of the twentieth century, both therapeutic and spiritual storytelling have taken on a broader role in organized storytelling, moving out of their usual settings and onto concert and festival stages. Storytelling publications listed workshops that lasted anywhere from an hour to a week (or several); you might find such events every month of the year somewhere in Canada or the United States. For example, while looking randomly through an issue of a storytelling magazine I found three spiritual workshops (one Jewish and two Christian) listed in the schedule of events for a single month. In the same issue there is a bold half-page advertisement for "Your Mythic Journey," described as "a three-hour preconference intensive workshop" led by Sam Keen, *Storytelling Magazine*, May 1997:46). Such workshops often straddled the line between therapy and religion, using popular phrases about "finding the inner storyteller." A personal advertisement in that same issue features a woman who describes herself as a teller of sacred and spiritual stories (Onawumi Jean Moss, *Storytelling Magazine*, May 1997:42). On the next page a teller asks, "How is my life a reflection of mythology?" (Jim May, *Storytelling Magazine*, May 1997:43).

Many American tellers interviewed by Joseph Sobol stressed the importance of both the healing and spiritual aspects of their stories. Sobol suggested that spiritual storytelling provided a central force, "the defining fervor of the revival," for many tellers who began their career in the 1970s (Sobol 1994a:73). As I read through storytelling directories and festival programs I found many tellers who described themselves in vaguely spiritual and "healing" terms. For example, one directory entry described a teller who "tells original and world tales, dream stories, and fairy tales for all ages. Specialties include healing stories, imaging the body mythologically; native American and dream stories; and stories for a world beyond weapons (Elaine Wynne, *National Storytelling Directory* 1983-84:43). Another teller wrote: "As a hypnotist, I use stories therapeutically and am interested in using story in this way with seniors, abused women and children" (Linda Siegel, *Canadian Storytelling Directory* 1997/98:20). The emphasis in these and other spiritual-therapeutical listings had quite a different tone from those that emphasized storytelling primarily as entertainment. For example, Professor Ed U. Gator, quoted earlier, changed his listing in the next directory. He was no longer "imaginer extraordinaire" but "an award-winning humor therapist," now offering workshops to educators and therapists (*National Storytelling Directory* 1996:31).

The hunger for stories as healing narratives was keenly felt as the twentieth century drew to a close. How, indeed, as Jim May asked above, were our lives reflections of mythology? Could stories be used therapeutically, to heal abuse? These notions are central to Susan Gordon's storytelling, as we will see in Chapter 4 of Section II, and it also echoes in the comments of other tellers mentioned in most of the following chapters.

There is a frustrating tension in these attempts to pin down the complex dynamics of actual storytelling, but despite the problems, I find it helpful to give some shape to this living art, however impressionistic my categories. I know, too, that tension is a key element in creativity; it keeps things alive and moving. And certainly that is the case with these four streams, since individual tellers began to interact more and more frequently as storytelling spread across the continent through concerts and festivals. These events brought all four together into a river that ebbed and flowed with increasing force and regularity.

As more people became involved in storytelling, groups and informal communities began to form in local areas, many of them inspired by the two major centers in the United States and Canada: The National Storytelling Association (NSA, formerly NAPPS) in Jonesborough, Tennessee, held its first festival in 1973 and established itself as a center two years later; The Storytellers School of Toronto was founded in 1979, at the same time that the regular weekly story-sharing events began. Their first festival took place later in that same year. In addition to festivals, the two centers in Jonesborough and Toronto offered workshops and classes throughout the year, which brought increasing numbers of people into active participation as tellers and as listeners. In later chapters we will look at groups and individuals that were inspired by these kinds of activities.

Any storytelling community, whether traditional or revival, draws a range of participants from active to passive, from those who appreciated stories but rarely told them to those who were regular public performers. Linda Dégh described several ways of classifying narrators;[7] but any such attempts were always complicated by the fact that storytelling was a natural form of human expression in both casual and formal contexts. Who was not a storyteller, in one way or another? However, at the very least, some sense of conscious intent is necessary for describing those involved in organized storytelling and viewing their range of commitment on a continuum that moved from casually conversational to formally professional.

Folklorist William Wilson has suggested the terms "Situational," "Conscious Cultural," and "Professional" (performance-oriented) tellers. (Storyteller and librarian Carol Birch reported Wilson's categories in a phone conversation on February 14, 1995.) We are all, at one time or another, "situational" tellers, able to relate brief jokes and anecdotes or longer personal adventures in casual conversation. Many of us are also "conscious cultural" tellers who preserve the stories of familial, ethnic, racial, and cultural heritage. It was Wilson's last category, "Professional" performance-oriented tellers, that I found most relevant for our purposes here. This term covered a wide range of possibilities, implying conscious intent but not necessarily differing levels of skill and experience (beginning tellers are often eager to perform when given the chance) or different contexts in which stories might be artfully told by practiced narrators—anywhere from the kitchen table to the festival stage. What I mean to emphasize is that some people, but certainly not all, made a conscious move from casual telling to formal, conscious performing. For such people this move altered the very concept of what storytelling was for them, no matter where they performed—at home, as part of another profession, or on stage.

Carol Birch refined Wilson's ideas by adding the term "Platform Performers," which she considered more appropriate than the widely used term "professional storytellers." She noted that many tellers told stories as part of an occupation rather than as an independent profession and often hesitated to describe themselves as professional storytellers. In this sense, platform performers might be tellers who were both intentional and experienced (echoing Wilson's terms) but did not devote their entire career to story performances outside the context of their other vocational activities (phone conversation, February 14, 1995). I agree that Birch's term is more flexible; hence I have used "platform performer" in place of "professional storyteller" as a more inclusive concept based on the background of the tellers, the physical setting of storytelling events, and the complex and elusive relationship among tellers, tales, and listeners.

Because tellers, tales, and contexts vary so widely, Birch favored the idea of a continuum of platform performers in place of rigid categories, since this would cover a full range of styles: from low-key recitations to dramatic theatrical productions, from brief humorous anecdotes to lengthy tales, from stand-up comedy to sacred storytelling. Also, the contexts of storytelling events varied from small, informal venues to large auditoriums and concert halls. I have kept in mind Birch's idea of a continuum as I followed the course of the four main streams of storytelling. I found that it allowed me to expand and refine the metaphor rather than contradicting it. That is, within each of the streams we could find a continuum of platform tellers, from situational to conscious cultural to performance-oriented.

I have discussed how performance situations for traditional oral narrators and for platform storytellers offer quite different challenges. In oral societies the community as a whole took part actively or passively in the telling and sharing of traditional narratives. The tale treasury was shared by all, though skilled tellers were fully recognized by the community and were most often called upon to perform. Stories associated with specific tellers or families of tellers might not be retold by anyone else.

In contrast, platform performers often did not have a steady group of listeners familiar with their tales even in their own wider communities; often they performed for audiences who had little if any experience with storytelling at all, much less with the tales of that particular teller. Specialized storytelling groups familiar with tellers and tales were often limited in size and experience, and focused on storytelling as an isolated activity rather than as a part of the community at large. In addition, as storytelling became increasingly popular as an art form, competition between tellers grew accordingly; this created serious challenges to community cohesion.[8] In the next chapter we will see how groups and communities met these challenges in order to function creatively within the limited social context of organized storytelling.

As festivals and other events continued to proliferate, the defining boundaries weakened between the various streams. This can be seen in directory listings in which tellers described themselves: for example, how might we identify the following performer?

> I like food, I like people. I am heard on radio and seen on television. I am an engineer, a physicist, a teacher, a sailor, and the host/author of *The Urban Peasant*. Most of the stories I tell are from my life and perspective (James Barber, *Canadian Storytelling Directory* 1997/98:12).

While such eclectic listings became more and more common in both Canadian and American directories, the four streams still held their own firmly enough to provide a useful framework for considering the complex dynamics of platform storytelling today.

Festivals and other events continued to bring together tellers from the four major streams, as well as those from a wealth of other backgrounds: writers, folk musicians, dancers, mimes, clowns, puppeteers, radio and television broadcasters and performers, and people with a rich ethnic or racial heritage who have brought their "conscious cultural" storytelling to concert stages. In addition, a number of academics with specialities in oral performance or narrative scholarship have carried their stories out of the lecture hall as platform performances.[9]

How do the four streams converge in actual festivals? In all of the festivals I have attended, even small local festivals such as those in Winnipeg and Saskatoon, I heard tellers from all four, as well as those with other backgrounds. Every one of these festivals highlighted tellers who claimed connections with oral tradition, however tenuous, reflecting the notion of organized storytelling as rightful heir to an "ancient art," as many described it. Fully authentic oral narrators such as Ray Hicks and Joe Neil MacNeil were featured tellers at national festivals as well as local events, and received featured billing and solo stage time instead of a shared stage with other tellers; and their traditional ties were clearly stressed in program notes. For example, the description of Joe Neil MacNeil in the 1987 Toronto festival program established his ethnic and linguistic roots, his long ties with narrating, and the traditional context in which he learned stories:

> Joe Neil MacNeil comes from Middle Cape, Cape Breton County. He was raised speaking the Gaelic of Barra extraction and learned traditional tales from an early age from local storytellers, especially at wakes.

In terms of numerical strength, library-educational storytelling is still often the most strongly represented category at festivals, since tellers with this training already had a wealth of experience before storytelling events became popular in the 1980s. Festival programs often stressed experience and training, as in the case of Helen Armstrong, a venerable teller with long experience in the Toronto public library system, as she is described in the 1981 Toronto festival program:

> As children's librarian she did in-service training in epic and romance for the Toronto Public Library, later teaching the same courses at the University of Toronto faculty of library science.

Because she was already so highly respected, Helen Armstrong was a featured teller in the very first Toronto festival, but more usually local library-educational tellers rarely received "star" billing. It would be easy to overlook their importance in the storytelling movement. Local festivals relied on area tellers, and since many of these people were experienced in schools and libraries, their participation provided the firm basis for any festival.

Tellers from a dramatic or theatrical background were also increasingly well represented at festivals, reflecting their strong ties with storytelling through children's theater and, more recently, adult-oriented monologues. Some tellers began in one form of theatrical performance and developed into the other. For example, one teller, Mariella Bertelli, was listed in the 1987 Toronto program as "a storyteller, puppeteer, and author," but then performed literary stories from Boccaccio for adults. Theatrical tellers had always been well represented at festivals, especially child-oriented events, but they became increasingly prominent as storytelling became more popular as adult entertainment.

The number of people who described themselves in therapeutic or spiritual terms also increased as adult-oriented festivals and other events spread across North America. However, it was often difficult to discover what, if any, professional background such tellers might rightfully claim in either religious or therapeutic training. Some simply alluded to the "healing power" or the magic of stories and storytelling, or were even more nebulous, as in this excerpt from the Toronto program of 1979:

> These are tales of mystery and delight, humor and seriousness— two ends of the spectrum. Who is the trickster? He is you and me, laughing, crying, and wondering (Robert Bela Wilhelm).

In contrast, another teller in the same program is more precise:

> For more than thirty years I have been telling stories professionally. In the 1960s I started telling stories on street corners in New York, and in the same period began using stories in therapeutic settings. Nowadays I use stories in my Gestalt practice [mostly with adults] (Joan Bodger).

I gained only a general sense of the first teller's actual connections with either spiritual or therapeutic backgrounds, though he was a nationally known spiritually-oriented teller and workshop leader. With the second teller there were no doubts.

Obviously, the hothouse context of storytelling festivals transformed the four streams as tellers with varied interests, styles, and backgrounds interacted. How was this expressed in festival programs? What would we expect as a description of performers, let us say, who had initial training in teaching or in library science, then might have taken some theatrical training, and later were inspired by the spiritual or "healing" aspects of storytelling? For example, in what category might we place the following performer from the 1995 Toronto program?

> Jo-Ann Ras is a storyteller and creative arts therapist in the schools. Along with music/drama she has performed stories in the schools, at the Royal Ontario Museum, and recently at the Celtic Roots festival in Goderich, Ontario.

Even in this brief description we see that the teller crosses ethnic and professional boundaries, performs for both children and adults, and uses storytelling in her therapeutic work as well as in stage performances. Because "creative arts therapist" comes first in this description, the teller would seem to fit into the spiritual-therapeutic stream; "music/drama" indicates theatrical connections; her school experiences imply the library-educational stream. For experienced tellers like this, a firmly delineated category is too narrow a means of identification. To state this more positively, more than two decades of organized storytelling events allowed performers like the one quoted above to interact, to exchange ideas and stories, and to expand their self-image considerably. Appendix I offers a brief schematic look at how the four streams appear over several years of the annual festival in Toronto. Other community festivals would make an interesting comparison.

The exciting variety of contemporary stories and performance styles has brought a constant flow of creativity into organized storytelling events across the continent, as we will see in the following chapters.

Notes

1 Part of this section is considerably revised from an earlier article, "Oral Narration in Contemporary North America" (Stone 1986:13-31).

2 A number of people have written about various Harmon-Hicks family members; for example, Joseph Sobol (Sobol 1994b), Cheryl Oxford (Oxford 1987, 1991, 1994), and, most notably, W.F.H. Nicolaisen (1978, 1980, 1994) who has explored the entire Harmon-Hicks family tree, and includes several of the contemporary tellers (Ray Hicks, Hattie Presnell, Frank Proffitt, Jr., Maud Gentry Long, Marshall Ward) in his studies.

3 Nathaniel Queskekapow insisted that his oral legends not be printed, since this removed them from the teller and from the culture. Louis Bird is working on his own material.

4 Patrick Mullen describes a Texas narrator who also managed the change of context from local storytelling to festival performing (Mullen 1981).

5 Alice Kane, a Toronto librarian and storyteller for many years, notes that library story hours declined after World War II; she thought that this was due largely, though not solely, to the technological advances that brought television into homes, especially Saturday morning television. Saturday morning was the time when children would have been lining up at library doors for the story hour, but now they did not have to leave home to be entertained. As Alice Kane comments, "No longer did one have to imagine

the enchanted wood or the ugly witch or the sultan's palace. The [television] picture told you what it looked like" (Kane 1990:66). Schools and libraries themselves also began to use more technological aids, replacing story times with films and film strips.

6   While Bettelheim's book, *The Uses of Enchantment* (Bettelheim 1976) is widely known, Julius Heuscher's study, *A Psychiatric Study of Fairy Tales* (Heuscher 1974, 2nd ed.), preceded it and deserves to be better known.

7   Linda Dégh explores a number of categories in *Folktales and Society* (Dégh 1969, 1989), beginning with Russian scholar K. V. Chicherov's four-part classification of Russian narrators: "Bearers of Tradition" could recall and repeat stories but did not develop them; "Performing Artists" could recall and repeat and also embroider stories for entertainment; "Poets" would recall, repeat, and embroider, but in ways that transformed a tale poetically rather than for amusement; "Improvisers" could masterfully reform a story so that it became a personal artistic expression (p. 173).

Dégh also mentions Romanian scholar Leza Uffer, who suggested three categories of traditional tellers: "Passive Narrators" recalled childhood tales but did not retell them; "Occasional Storytellers" could retell a story when urged to do so but did not actively seek out opportunities; "Conscious Storytellers" deliberately and artistically recreated the stories they heard and remembered (p. 174).

8   The controversial issue of "stealing" stories fuelled a hotly contested debate on storytelling ethics in the late 1980s (see, for example, Marvin and Lipman 1986).

9   For example, English professor Robert Creed performs *Beowulf* and other poetry in Old English. Toronto teller and educator Dan Yashinsky narrates "The Miller's Tale" in Middle English. Folklorists who perform professionally include Ruth Stotter, Jo Radner, Margaret Yocom, Susan Gordon, and myself, among others. The number of folklorist/storytellers increased in the 1990s. Some, like Barre Toelken, use narratives regularly as part of lectures and workshops as well as performing outside of academic contexts.

THREE

INTENTIONAL STORYTELLING COMMUNITIES

THE proliferation of personal advertisements in storytelling publications in the 1990s seems to verify that this is a performance art that thrives mainly on the creative energies of individual tellers. However, a closer look into the situation reveals that, with few exceptions, it is the existence of groups and communities that form the vital base of the movement. As we have seen in the previous section describing the four streams of storytelling, the number of groups has increased almost as dramatically as the number of individuals.

Since groups may have many members, we can assume that the jump from 68 to 240 groups and centers listed in the NSA directories from 1984 to 1995 (and from 174 to more than 800 individual tellers) is an even more dramatic increase in total numbers of those actually telling stories.[1] Every group may have anywhere from a dozen to a hundred or more members, many of whom do not list themselves in national directories since few members of any group are known well enough to make a living "on the circuit," that is, travelling from one local festival and event to another across the continent. The majority find most of their opportunities closer to home. The modest, low-key events supported by local and regional storytelling groups and communities keep the movement as a whole alive. I found this to be true of the several groups I visited in the 1980s and 1990s as well as from interviews, correspondence, and research in newsletters and journals and from Sobol's detailed survey. His chapter on storytelling communities is particularly thoughtful and relevant in clarifying group dynamics, which can be complex in their social and artistic relations, and emotionally laden in their struggles for survival.

For most tellers a storytelling "community" is a shifting group of people who meet more or less regularly to tell and hear stories. A group might vary in size from a handful to fifty or more (perhaps hundreds in major centers), and might exist for a short space of time or for a number of years. Joseph Sobol suggests "scene" as an alternative term to a short-lived group, noting that "scenes assemble, play themselves out, and change when their part in the human comedy is done. Communities, by contrast, generate traditions precisely to protect themselves against change—they replay the same scenes over and over with changing casts" (Sobol 1994a:321). Sobol's term is more flexible than "group," and while it can also apply on a broader scale, as in "the storytelling scene" or "the folk music scene," I use it here in his narrower sense as a smaller element in the organization of storytelling groups and communities.

Consciously formed organizations have different levels and degrees of formal structure and interaction. Let me clarify the terms as I use them in this section: a scene is an informal group often centered around one or two founding members and may or may not last longer than a year or so; members of a group make a more constant commitment and can survive shifts of fortune and personnel for a number of years; a community is a more firmly organized and extensive entity that may merge several scenes and groups into a more stable social unit. All three levels of organization are included in my concept of "intentional community." In this section I examine how these levels of organization touch the reality of the storytelling communities I have visited or whose members I have been in touch with in Canada and the United States since 1983. There are hundreds of changing scenes, groups, and communities in North America, so no survey no matter how detailed could capture their fluid realities.

These intentional associations are not entities in a strict sociological sense. They are not stable geographically or historically based societies with long established social customs and relations; nor do they possess extensive stores of traditional narratives like the "tale treasuries" found by Linda Dégh in the Hungarian Szekler community she has studied over the years, or in Henry Glassie's research among Irish narrators in Ballymenone. Yet a successful intentional community can (and perhaps must) develop a viable regional personality and also a recognizable tale treasury after a few years of existence. Some stories are associated with the group as a whole, others come to be identified with individual performers. For example, members of Stone Soup Stories of Winnipeg occasionally related their local variant of "Stone Soup," a folktale that functioned as part of the founding legend of the group; in Toronto, Stewart Cameron's "The Three Feathers" and Carol

McGirr's "Rosy Apple and Golden Bowl" were recognized by members of that community as "their" variants, and would generally not be told by anyone else without permission.

Groups such as Stone Soup Stories in Winnipeg and similar small gatherings in Saskatoon and Regina are barely known beyond their own members, as would be true of many such groups in the United States. But even the extensive and well-established organizations like those in Toronto, the Bay Area in California, and in Boston/Cambridge, while prominent in storytelling circles, may be little known in their communities at large. The wider community is generally ignorant of or indifferent to platform storytelling. In many cities and towns storytelling is at best familiar as an activity for younger children, as we have already seen; there may be story hours at some libraries or in children's sections of book stores or in a school library or classrooms, and at child-centered events (children's festivals or museums, for example). This is where storytelling began early in the twentieth century, as noted in Chapter 1. As a result, many people outside the storytelling community (and many inside as well) still firmly associate storytelling with children.

Storytelling guilds founded by librarians and teachers early in the century were the first groups to provide time and space for adults to come together and practice stories for children's performances. Such guilds set a pattern that still influences organized storytelling today, no matter how earnestly individual tellers might strive to free themselves of earlier conceptions. These early leagues and guilds were the first intentional communities.

The high regard for oral tradition in early library-educational story-telling circles arose at least in part from idealized notions of traditional narration as a high art. With this vision in mind tellers gathered in storytelling guilds to practice this art. These notions of oral narration were strongly influenced by European romantic nationalism, an important historical and political movement in the early nineteenth century that found popular expression in the publication of the Grimm collections and their translations. (The first edition was published from 1812-1815.) The steady popularity of the Grimm tales in North America provided an abundant source of traditional folktales. Folklorists now know that many of these stories did not in fact come from traditional sources; still, the Grimms' romantic notion of "the folk" as communal participants in a homey oral tradition still lingers enticingly in the rhetoric of the storytelling revival.[2]

Like the leagues and guilds of past decades, the rhetoric of the contemporary revival movement has idealized imaginary "folk"
communities on which they idealistically model their own. In fact, the
term "storytelling community" has become almost a sanctified description. Sobol asserts that it "expresses the romantic revivalism at the
movement's heart. It is an affirmation of desire, a courtship of community" (Sobol 1994a:320). Such ideas fuelled the rise and development
of intentional communities, many of which felt a sense of mission to
carry on storytelling as a face-to-face, personal form of expression to
the world at large by offering a venue for local tellers and listeners to
experience the art directly. Oklahoma teller Fran Stallings used the
term "village storytelling" to describe this kind of venue, in contrast to
the performance-oriented situations of many large concerts and festivals (letter, 1988).

Toronto teller Marylyn Peringer suggested that the ideal is more
than romantic revivalism. She felt that modern performers were not so
much "continuing an unbroken chain to the past" (as some claimed)
but "picking up the threads here and there and doing our best to connect the stories with our own lives;" Marylyn found a fictional rather
than an historical link for her own storytelling, and raised issues that
will be further developed in the next chapter on individual identity:

> I for one don't feel as though I'm serenely following in the steps
> of the great *conteurs*; I've undoubtedly reshaped all those French-
> Canadian stories by my own contemporary English-Canadian
> sensibilities, my education, my exposure to literature. Somehow
> I feel more comfortable saying I am following in the steps of
> Shaharazade [Scheherazade]; is it because she is a fictitious char-
> acter? Or because she had to tell stories to keep alive? (letter, July
> 7, 1995).

The issue of having "to tell stories to keep alive" is an immediate
issue for Marylyn and anyone else whose livelihood depends on regular performance opportunities.

For Marylyn, like other platform tellers in Toronto and elsewhere,
literary rather than folk connections were behind the initial establishment of intentional communities. This does not contradict the
egalitarian image of professional and amateur tellers coming together
to share their art. Some tellers might be inspired by thinking of storytelling as an ancient art from some undefined, romanticized time and

place in the past. Others share an interest in stories and storytelling as they exist now, and are not preoccupied with past oral traditions. Whatever their inspirations, many individual performers align themselves with some kind of communal, supportive group. Some tellers choose to work in isolation, either because they have grown beyond their community or because they never took part in one except as a means of promoting their activities. At the other end of the continuum are tellers who, by choice, rarely perform outside of their own local group, viewing their community as central to their identities as storytellers.

Two examples illustrate these opposite extremes, one from a private publication and the other a personal letter. In 1992 I was sent an unsolicited newsletter, produced not by a group but by a single storyteller who listed his activities for that year, and the five cassette tapes of stories he had available for purchase. On the first page of this four-page newsletter he naively commented: "Is my imagination working overtime or are there song and story circles, roundrobins, and informal gatherings popping up all over the place? Shades of the '60s!"[3] By 1992 story circles and other groups had been "popping up all over the place" for almost two decades, though he was apparently unaware of this and was not connected to any local or national group. He mentioned that he had begun to attend "a couple of groups close to home" but did not name them or declare any commitment to them. For performers like this who begin on their own and only belatedly discover that groups of tellers already exist, community association is understandably less important than their individual career. They would be more likely to look to a group for promotion rather than support since they are already independent.

In 1991 I received a personal letter from a teller who took the opposite view; for her the group was so central that she altered her retirement plans and remained in the city in which this group met instead of moving away. She described stories as "hanging over her cradle," where throughout childhood she listened to her grandmother, mother, father, and elder brother. She attempted to tell folktales in the junior high school where she was a librarian and found this "a valuable, if painful, part of my learning." She did not really feel comfortable with storytelling until she became part of a small local group of adults (Stone Soup Stories of Winnipeg) that met monthly: "No doubt such experience is useful [individual storytelling in her school], but nothing like what a group such as ours can do for one.

There one can listen *and* tell. Surely story tellers are made by example, and by appreciation and practice. I have found it so" (letter, Elisabeth Nash, May 1991). For this teller storytelling was less an individual accomplishment than a communal activity, beginning with her own family. A storytelling group provided her with the support she felt she needed to fully develop her art. She has since told stories as part of the group at a number of modest evening concerts and on CBC radio.

The two tellers might be seen as coming to similar realizations from opposite directions: one starts in isolation and has the possibility of moving toward community associations; the other centers herself in a community and has gradually moved toward public performance (though within the group). These examples illustrate the primary benefits that communities offer: a place to expand professional contacts and promotional opportunities, and a place to find nurturing, support, and new stories.

In the first decade of the new revival there were relatively few active and experienced tellers. Nor were there groups beyond the few guilds that had survived for decades and that tended to be small and specialized, often not known outside their immediate professional circle. Newer tellers were usually unaware that guilds existed at all and thus founded their own groups that attracted participants from various backgrounds, not only from the library-educational stream. Many of these new groups arose after, and were stimulated by, the establishment of major centers in Jonesborough, Tennessee, and Toronto, Ontario. Each of these national centers sponsored its own annual festival as well as frequent workshops and classes. These events drew more and more people who in turn were inspired to return home and start local festivals and organizations, each with its own local history of development.

There have been two general patterns of evolution, which I will call "Grassroots Development" and "Festival Development." The Grassroots pattern typically begins with a small group of individuals (as few as two or three in some cases), in other words a "scene," who decide to meet informally and tell stories. If this scene attracts other members it may become increasingly organized and may offer regularly scheduled meetings (once a week, once a month). At this point the scene becomes a group that might eventually offer occasional public storytelling concerts and perhaps a small annual festival that attracts tellers from outside that group. If activities and members continue to expand, the group may become a community, with a regularly published newsletter and perhaps a directory listing local tellers and events, and one day a festival that draws listeners from the community at large and perhaps even from surrounding areas. In Festival Development the pattern of evolution is reversed: a few people decide to organize an annual festival that attracts tellers and listeners from outside the area, and from this a local group might be inspired to start informal scenes that might become groups and then communities.

Some festival organizations never develop into "scenes" at all, putting all their energy into one annual festival. As only one example, there is a major international festival in Whitehorse, Yukon Territory, that draws performers and audiences from Europe as well as North and South America, but there is not even a scene, much less a story-telling group or community, that meets regularly to exchange stories. I am sure there are many other festivals that, for whatever reasons, do not inspire the formation of regular groups (other than the on-going planning groups, of course). Local tellers in such a place work independently, not relying on a group to further their career.

I should point out that major festivals like the annual events in Toronto and in Jonesborough became models for smaller festivals, giving strong impetus to Festival Development rather than Grassroots Development. Sobol described how the pattern of the Jonesborough festivals became "traditionalized" over the first decade, and how this traditionalized pattern became a model for festivals throughout the United States. He identified, among other things, the ritualized telling of ghost stories as a separate and very popular event; "swapping grounds" where, ideally, anyone could take the stage (in fact participation was by necessity controlled at least to some extent); "olios" where the festival performers opened and later closed the event with brief stories; sacred storytelling on Sunday mornings; the use of tents that evoked earlier American traditions like religious revivals, circuses, and Chautauqua shows; and finally, the canonization of traditional oral narrators (Ray Hicks for the Jonesborough festival, Joe Neil MacNeil for Toronto) who, by their mere presence, provided a sense of authenticity, a direct link in the chain of storytelling.

The influence of the Jonesborough festival could be seen at many events in the United States from the 1980s on. They were structured similarly and featured similar events, inspired by the model of the national festival in Tennessee, and many stable groups and communities developing from such festivals looked to NSA as their paradigm for expansion.

In Canada, Toronto was closer to the Grassroots model; the group developed first, drawing on a local base of experienced tellers and an established tradition in the library-educational model. The founding members first organized a weekly Friday night event that emphasized storytelling shared within the community. The festival came only after the several founding members decided to create a formal organization, The Storytellers School of Toronto. True to its name, the school began offering regular classes in storytelling, with community outreach rather than performance training or promotion as the main goal.

The Toronto festival also differed greatly from the Jonesborough event, which is hardly surprising since they were not historically linked: there were never any ghost story events or sacred tales on Sundays. There were no "olios" but rather evening concerts in which local and out-of-province tellers shared stories. There were no tents since Toronto has always been an indoor festival; the very first festival, held in a church basement on April 1, 1979, set the pattern of this event.[4] There were swapping sessions but these were more informal and open than the NAPPS model, guided by local tellers who encouraged all participants, even the most inexperienced tellers, to take part.

The Jonesborough and Toronto models have influenced the overall pattern of organized storytelling in their respective countries. In most parts of Canada storytelling has been consistently less high-powered, less competitive, and less commercialized, and more community-oriented than is the case in many parts of the United States. Obviously this overgeneralization has many exceptions, since every scene, group and storytelling community in either country has followed its own pattern. Within the limited format of a single book, however, generalizations provide a broad image of interactive patterns between individual tellers and communities.

There are now hundreds of groups in cities and towns in the United States and Canada that consider themselves to be communities, in contrast to the professional associations of other performance arts. They might begin as small, informal scenes and grow into large and active communities that stimulate the establishment of other local groups, as happened in Toronto or other vigorous centers in both countries. Or they may choose to remain more intimate and informal. The following description of a group in southern California might apply to many that came into existence in the past two decades:

Our local group, Community Storytellers, was founded by a woman named Peggy Prentice, who, after about a year of a group struggling to come together, invited me to be co-founder. Fifteen years ago [1980], it was quite difficult to get people to come to our meetings, but through the help of workshops, news articles and the like, it's grown to a really thriving group of between 25 and 30 people who meet once a month for a $3 donation. Sometimes we have a guest teller, sometimes not. We swap stories. It's a very nourishing part of my life and, and for everyone concerned (letter, Kathleen Zundell, 12 May 1995).

This is a fairly typical pattern for many groups in the Grassroots pattern of development. They meet regularly, often asking a small fee to cover costs; they attract a moderate number of participants who are encouraged to take an active part, even if they have never told a story publicly before. An Oklahoma teller says of her group, "I'm delighted when I can get people to recognize themselves as storytellers and make some moves toward retelling new tales that appeal to them" (letter, Fran Stallings, March 17, 1992).

In contrast, larger communities such as those in Toronto, the Bay Area, and Boston/Cambridge areas, for example, attracted many more people and had to develop a more formal structure. In Toronto the 1,001 Nights of Storytelling drew as many as 60 to 100 people in its weekly gatherings as it became well established. It was set up in cabaret style, with people seated at small tables rather than sitting in an informal circle or in rows of seats in an auditorium; participants stood in front of the group, creating more distance between themselves and their listeners than in a more casual setting, but still close enough for everyone present to feel actively involved in the event.

It is inevitable that success leads to growth and growth leads to increasing diversity, which in the end strengthens the community—but this same diversity is also a challenge. Tellers who were shy one year might try to become more active the next and feel rebuffed by those they regard as holding a privileged position. Such a situation anywhere might eventually give rise to jealousies and resentments if people feel frozen out of what they rightly or wrongly perceive as the established order. Long-standing groups and communities generally weather many storms of protest and, like any other kind of community, make room for new members and new ideas in order to survive.

In addition to actual local and regional communities, there is also a sense of a greater storytelling community, an ideal to which existing groups and organizations feel committed.[5] This sense of community for tellers in the United States, as described by Joseph Sobol (Sobol

1994a), differs in many ways from that of Canadian tellers and groups, but both countries share in a general belief that an overall storytelling community does indeed exist that goes beyond national boundaries, and certainly beyond individual tellers. This panorama, or network, as Sobol terms it, covers the whole of modern organized telling.

Certainly it was individual performers in Canada and the United States who sparked the fire of organized storytelling, but it was only when tellers began to form intentional communities that storytelling burst into full conflagration as a serious artistic profession on its own. Individuals alone could not have accomplished the task of spreading storytelling across the continent and to all age groups. What has developed is not only a community of tellers but a community of listeners, some of whom eventually become tellers themselves. In this way groups continue to arise, develop, and flourish—or decline and disappear.

The very success of this art and its steady propagation to more and more people in wider and wider areas also gives rise to inevitable growing pains. Unlike organic communities that are united by history, geography, and day-to-day social interaction that build shared ideas and experiences, the artistic organizations called "storytelling communities" by their constituents are specialized, sporadic, and geographically separated. Even in relatively small communities like Winnipeg and Saskatoon, members are geographically scattered and have commitments to any number of other specialized interests. Also historical development might divide rather than unite members, as newcomers feel themselves to be ignored by those who have been part of the initial founding of the groups.

Many established performers even remove themselves from the regular activities of their original communities, citing in-group conflicts as the reason. Stories like this can be told by communities across Canada and from all corners of the United States. In one such community I visited, some tellers would not attend an event if certain others were going to be there. Community members everywhere usually regard in-fighting as a negative aspect of the growth, yet even the most apparently detrimental occurrences might eventually contribute to overall cohesion if we accept growing pains as an inevitable part of maturity. As more people become involved, the diversity and challenge they introduce can lead to a healthy dialectical development. As we have seen, the first stage occurs when individuals initiate a local event or group that becomes a focus for storytelling. When a broader community is established it continues to expand and to draw in new people, who bring in new ideas; these may become a challenge to the "old order" and, after conflict and resolution, the community is renewed and continues to evolve—or it rigidifies into inertia or falls into chaos and dissolution.

As we have seen, intentional communities vary greatly in size, vitality, and organization. It would be impossible to give an accurate portrayal of the range of organized groups in the United States where they number in the hundreds. Even in Canada where the national community is considerably smaller (in 1997 there were twenty-five groups and ninety-eight tellers listed in the national directory), a generalized description can hardly do more than hint at the variety and vitality of intentional communities, which have begun to expand with the establishment of a national networking organization, Storytellers of Canada (S.O.C.). I draw on the 1997/98 edition of *Canadian Storytelling Directory* for figures.

		Groups	Individuals*
Western Canada:	British Columbia	7†	34
	Alberta	4	13
	Saskatchewan	1	2
	Manitoba	1	3
Eastern Canada:	Ontario	10	21
	Quebec	1	10
Maritime Canada:	New Brunswick	1†	2
	Newfoundland	—	3
	Nova Scotia	1	5
	Prince Edward Island *not listed*		
Territories:	Northwest Territories —		2
	Yukon	—	1
Total		26†	96

---

* As noted earlier, this figure is considerably lower than it would be if every teller were listed. For example in Manitoba there are only three entries, but there are at least a dozen people who tell stories with some frequency and many more who do so sporadically. This is not a criticism, merely an observation. Some do not list themselves because they do not wish to pay the fee and others because they do not see themselves as "professional." Presumably this is true of other areas as well, since there are certainly a great many more than 96 tellers in all of Canada.

† These are not all actually on-going sharing groups: The Vancouver Society of Storytelling publishes the Storytelling Directory and produces the Annual Vancouver Storytelling Festival; Storyfest Unlimited, Inc. plans and produces the annual Storyfest.

I could write an entire chapter just on these figures and what they reveal beyond bare numbers, but that goes further than I wish to move here. Instead, let me describe a typical scene, group, and community as described in the *Storytelling Directory*.

The Saskatoon Storytellers' Guild sounds imposing but in fact it is more a scene than a group, though it has remained in existence (due largely to its founder) for several years:

> Story swaps are held approximately once a month, September through May. Once a year there is usually a concert, and other special events happen sporadically with local musicians. There is no newsletter yet, but maybe someday (*Canadian Storytelling Directory* 1997/98: 51)

The tentative nature of this listing is a good description of a storytelling scene, though it is longer lived than most.

The Storytellers' Guild of Montreal is an example of a stable group, having grown steadily since its founding:

> The Storytellers' Guild of Montreal, formed in 1990, has presented story events for libraries and has given a concert, Montreal Mosaic in Story, including music, dance and story, to celebrate Montreal's 350th anniversary. Individual members offer storytelling workshops and tell stories in schools, museums, retirement centres, churches, synagogues, and concerts and festivals. The guild offers an evening of storytelling for adults the first Friday of each month from October to June. Tellers and listeners are welcomed. A small fee is asked from those who are not members (*Canadian Storytelling Directory* 1997/98:47).

This is obviously a solid group with regular meeting times, a variety of group and individual activities, and formal membership entailing modest fees.

Many groups also have newsletters which cover a broad area that includes several different regional centers.[6] For example, *Taleteller* covers events and tellers throughout Alberta. The latter publication is sponsored by T.A.L.E.S., a clever acronym for "The Alberta League Encouraging Storytelling," initially founded in Edmonton and now encompassing groups in Lethbridge, Calgary, Strathcona, and other Alberta regions.

Storytelling is well established in British Columbia where there are several major communities as well as many smaller ones. The following entry describes a large, active community:

> The Victoria Storytellers' Guild is a group of professional and non-professional tellers and listeners brought together by a need to restore the human component to communication. The group acts as a resource for other individuals and groups requiring tellers, workshop leaders, or background information for artistic, theatrical or educational purposes. The Guild also runs a community outreach program where there is a need. The Guild meets bi-monthly: on the third Monday of each month for a public sharing of stories with an open mike; on the first Monday of each month is Stories-in-Between, a working session for members. The newsletter *Tell Me A Story* is published quarterly (adapted from the *Canadian Storytelling Directory* 1997/98:10).

Even without knowing the size of this community we can sense that it is very firmly established and very active, with bi-monthly meetings and a variety of activities. It is influential beyond its membership, as indicated by both outreach programs and the existence of a regular newsletter.

The Vancouver Storytelling Circle and the Vancouver Society of Storytelling function together to sponsor regular events and a major national festival, as well as having published three editions of the *Canadian Storytelling Directory* since 1991. They also offer *The Storytelling Circle Newsletter* which covers local events and tellers. The Vancouver community has a vibrant social and artistic history and active relations with other B.C. scenes, groups and communities. It is a much younger organization than the Storytellers School of Toronto, and has a quite different artistic, social and geographic history within the storytelling communities and in the community-at-large. As a fast-growing association it is assuming a role as a second national community.

As I have said, the wider Toronto community does function as both a provincial and a national center. Many if not all of the six Ontario groups listed in the 1997/98 *Canadian Storytelling Directory* were inspired by the Toronto model, either indirectly or directly. Despite differences in size and level or organization, these groups began from the grassroots level, with a few people who were interested and willing to set up times and places to meet and exchange stories. In many of these groups the emphasis has been on participation rather than on performance.

Even in Toronto, which has sponsored a national festival since 1979 featuring national and international tellers, the emphasis has always been on creating a storytelling community that encouraged local tellers to participate on a regular basis. That is, even with a major festival that draws listeners and performers from across Canada and parts of the United States, the vitality of the community at large consistently encourages day-to-day storytelling: the 1001 Friday Nights of Storytelling has been a venue for both experienced and inexperienced tellers and has always tried to give special attention to visitors from outside of Toronto; regular workshops and classes in and outside of Toronto emphasized developing one's own personal approach rather than emulating that of teachers and workshop leaders. Thus both workshop/classes and the Friday night circle encouraged people to take their first steps into storytelling, and some of these people returned home to found the many local groups that carry on their own activities and interests throughout the year. Grassroots groups continue to spring up throughout Ontario, keeping alive this web of interaction initially created in the Toronto community and its networking throughout Ontario.[7] I want to end this chapter with a closer look at the wider Toronto community in order to provide a more vibrant background for the tellers we will meet (at least in print) in Section II.

Toronto as an Example of An Intentional Community

In the mid-1970s several people who had been telling stories separately in the Toronto area began to discover each other. This was the first step toward the formation of a storytelling community that would eventually organize a major festival and offer regular courses that would draw hundreds of people into storytelling. The community has grown steadily and substantially since its beginning in 1978 and now extends to outlying areas. I have visited the Toronto area numerous times between 1984 and 1995, and have met and become friends with many local and out-of-province tellers. In 1989, as I began work on this chapter, I realized that I needed to formally interview the people I had been informally conversing with in previous visits. Several of the most active members consistently reported that those involved in the development of the Toronto community decided early in their history to establish a group that would publicize and promote storytelling in the community at large, and did so through regular training classes that produced hundreds of beginning storytellers. The resulting enthusiasm carried the group with unexpected speed through the stages from scene to group to community, always with the ideal of promoting storytelling rather than individual tellers. This community also had the advantage of the coming together of several experienced tellers who were already telling stories regularly in their various professions. It is more common for a group to be founded by one or more tellers who are usually less experienced.

The founding of the Toronto community has become an historical legend, told and retold at the Friday night gatherings and the various festivals I attended. I wondered how personal accounts might amplify and verify the story. In order to find out I interviewed four of the seven founding members (Lorne Brown, Bob Barton, Celia Lottridge, Dan Yashinsky), and several other people who have been part of the community for many years.

Lorne Brown was a school principal and a folksinger in the 1970s when he met the other people who had begun to gather in a small restaurant in Toronto's Kensington area. He commented that Toronto was well suited for the development of a storytelling community because it was "a city of neighborhoods, and this was a very conscious decision as the city developed. There is still a lot of neighborhood feeling in different parts of the city, large as it is." Lorne felt that this lent itself to a stronger sense of community for storytellers in the area. He also noted that the Kensington neighborhood was a particularly agreeable place for this to take place: "Kensington was a multi-ethnic area, very centrally located and vibrant. The Kensington school [where Lorne was principal] already had regular Friday afternoon gatherings for the entire school—'Friday Afternoon in the Library'—complete with fireplace. We experienced folk and classical music, theater and dance, and storytelling, of course. And, of course, there was Gaffer's Restaurant, where it all began."

He named the seven tellers who came together by word of mouth in 1978: Alice Kane was a retired children's librarian already known as a skilled teller for children; Joan Bodger was a therapist and long-time storyteller who was already performing elsewhere; Rosemary Allison was a children's writer who had since left Toronto; Bob Barton had been a teacher and was an educational administrator who gave workshops as well as performing; Celia Lottridge managed a children's bookstore where she also told stories; Dan Yashinsky, who was then performing regularly at Gaffer's Restaurant, was consistently identified as the catalyst, the person who began to bring people together. As Yashinsky reports, "I remember I jokingly opened those first evenings with 'Welcome to Gaffer's, the home of the world renaissance of storytelling,' and everyone including me would laugh."

It was Yashinsky who suggested that they all begin to meet at Gaffer's on Friday nights. They agreed to call these events "The 1001 Friday Nights of Storytelling," a name that captured both the literary and the oral aspects of storytelling—and, Dan Yashinsky emphasized, "the most famous storyteller in the world—Scheherazade." He, like Lorne Brown, insisted that "none of this happened in a vacuum," because there were already well established events at the Toronto Public Library as well as in the schools: "And Gaffer's was already a place for musicians, an ideal place for storytelling to develop. All that was needed now was a regular time and a regular place to do storytelling and bring people together. And that is what happened next."

Celia Lottridge recalls one of the events that led to "what happened next" as she describes her early encounter: "We went to hear Joan Bodger at the Underground Railroad Restaurant, Dan and I and Rosemary and some other person I can't remember. While we were listening to her there was a blizzard, and when we came out the city was just dead still, stopped. There was about a foot of snow on King Street where we were, and what I remember is walking up King Street in this totally silent city and talking about how we had to, how we were going to meet again and get something going about storytelling. So I have an image of us walking through the silence. It must have been the winter of 1977 or 1978, because I was working at the bookstore then."

Within a year they had established weekly storytelling at Gaffer's and had begun to organize a center for storytelling. Lorne Brown recalled suggesting the term "guild" because for him the term evoked medieval guilds with their emphasis on fine craftsmanship, and also because storytelling guilds were already familiar in school and library contexts. But other organizers wanted a name that was different: "Most of us were involved with education in some way, but it was someone else—not me, the principal—who said, 'Why not a *school* of storytelling,' and that's what we became eventually."

The founding of the Storytellers School, which has offered regular courses at various levels since 1978, was a decisive step in bringing people into storytelling. It was conceived of as a way of encouraging people to develop their own style rather than setting up model to be followed. Celia Lottridge felt that the courses taught were meant to "help people find out where they are in their own storytelling." She added that traditional narratives were strongly favored, reflecting the fact that founding members were educators and librarians, or involved in children's books in some way. All, including therapist Bodger, were accustomed to using folktales: "We emphasized the importance of starting with existing oral tradition and using that as your model, and then if you want to go on to other things you can use that as your grounding, of what has been done in oral storytelling."

From the very beginning participation was emphasized over performance, despite the number of experienced tellers who were involved. This is not to say that competence was not valued (Alice Kane, for example, provided an inspiring model for careful and precise storytelling), but that accomplished tellers chose not to dominate the evenings. Audience members were encouraged to take the stage with their own stories at the Friday night events. Lorne Brown and Dan Yashinsky stressed that storytelling in the Toronto area developed from a community of peers. That is, from the beginning this group evolved with communal ideals. Dan Yashinsky noted that "storytellers here develop their skills within the community rather than on and for the concert stage." When I asked him to expand on this he said, "When I see performers from elsewhere, I sense that they have worked mainly for a concert setting. What I feel is that their stories were just that— somebody else's story with no openings for the listeners."

The community that developed was an ideal rather than a contiguous geographic entity (though the Storytellers School and its activities did provide a physical center); like other such groups, it was a constantly evolving assembly of people. Marylyn Peringer was one of many tellers who heard about the 1001 Nights of Storytelling through a friend. She finally appeared one night and was immediately urged by Dan Yashinsky to tell a story: "It was wonderful to have a whole group of people who thought that what I was doing was valuable, because nobody else at that time told stories in French and in English, at least in the Toronto area." Marylyn described having a sense of community even when she was away; "All storytelling presupposes community, even if you're telling to only one person," Marylyn observed, and later added, "And oh yes, the story is more than the story, more than the words." She felt that the fuller the commitment and comprehension of the interactions of tale and teller and listeners and, by extension, the community, the more is it evident that "the story is more than the story."

The stress on community context rather than a concert stage context worked well for the informal weekly gatherings, but it was much more of a challenge when the organizers decided to put on a festival in 1979. The festival was unique because, like the Friday night gatherings, it developed gradually from a community of peers rather than from a group of organizers. The combination of weekly storytelling and regular classes brought hundreds of people into storytelling, many of whom returned to their own areas and started local events. As storytelling expanded there was less "cloning," not so much copying a Toronto pattern but letting regional ones evolve.

Carol McGirr was a school librarian with long storytelling experience when she discovered that people were meeting on Friday nights to tell stories, and that adults and not children were the listeners. She recalled the unexpectedly rapid rise of storytelling in the Toronto area and the problems that success brought with it:

> Over the years we've encouraged so many people and we've had courses and everything, so we've developed a lot of tellers. The community has grown, and now there are so many people who want to be in the festival. You know, in the early days of the festival, we were all running around doing all these things, telling and hosting and organizing, but now we have so many people involved. I think it's very healthy growth—but then the problem is, how do you fit all those people in?

Despite the steady progress of the festival and its growing reputation as a major event, Toronto struggled to maintain its character as a grassroots festival that expressed the interests of a larger community rather than that of a few organizers; local performers continued to be the backbone of the festival, unlike some festivals in which "star" performers with national reputations are centrally featured and promoted. Jim May, a teller from Illinois who performed at the festival in 1993, remarked that it was a different experience for him. When I asked why, he said that it seemed to be a more active local event, with people in the community taking part as first-class rather than as second-class participants. "There's no star system here, everything seems to be more equal."

An early participant in community events, Lynda Howes, said that the festival probably reached its optimum audience size in the late 1980s: "The audiences had not grown substantially in size since this time, though the festival continued to attract new listeners every year, as did the Friday Nights." Size is not necessarily as significant as the ability to attract new listeners. Many newcomers to both the festival and the regular Friday night gatherings have since become involved in storytelling, and carry their interests and activities back to their own communities and neighborhoods. Thus storytelling communities in Ontario continue to develop and mature.

As with all communities, development here did not come about without struggles. A few years ago the Toronto community suffered through "growing pains" that seemed, at the time, to be a crisis. Howes commented that "the same people had been involved in the organization from the beginning, and we knew things had to change." Originally the board of the Storytellers School was responsible for organizing the festival and the yearly courses, and many board members were also active in the 1001 Friday Nights. Others thought that duties and responsibilities should be shared more democratically. There was also some feeling that there was a "Toronto style" of performing that favored a certain kind of storytelling. Bob Barton, for example, noted that "in many instances there has been a kind of aura surrounding the Storytellers School," which meant that other viewpoints were not readily accepted, which threatened to polarize the community.

Inevitably feelings were hurt; some people felt their ideas and support were not being fully recognized. There was apprehension that the comfortable feeling of community might be lost in the shuffle. This has not happened, as evidenced by the continuing success of both the l00l Friday Nights and of the festival itself, which, despite steady evolution, retains a firm sense of friendly communality as well as of high-level professionalism. Change did occur, and it was beneficial to all involved.[8] As Barton explains: "Now you can look at styles that encompass everything from a more theatrical style to a laid back library style, and to everything in between. And that mix is what I think is extremely important for storytelling, and for people to have access for listening to all that."

I asked those I interviewed to comment on their own sense of what a storytelling community was, what it had to offer for both tellers and listeners. Lorne Brown emphasized the contrast between storytelling groups and other artistic organizations: "It's not the same as, say, the musicians union or any other artistic organization that's made up of separate individuals with their own particular interests. A community is an on-going gathering with a real place in time and geography, not just coming together for an annual event or for occasional workshops or classes."

Dan Yashinsky raised the issue of "authorization," specifically, the right of certain tellers to tell certain tales. He felt that "the Toronto community in general has managed to place less emphasis on authorization than on reaffirmation. This accounts for the overall lack of competitiveness at the festivals and the Friday Night gatherings."

Bob Barton observed that "you could do storytelling in isolation, but it helps to have a lot of other voices." He also stressed the importance of support, especially but not exclusively for storytelling in education: "That's where I think that the community of storytellers— the notion of communal support and encouragement—has really paid off."

Celia Lottridge was particularly thoughtful about this aspect of the community as supportive to the individual:

> Well, I have found in my life that you can be a storyteller on your own. But if I hadn't met the other people, I would have just done it on a much lower level in my life, and I wouldn't have learned how to be more effective. I would have done it, because to me it seems to come naturally. But what was so exciting for me was when I met others, like Dan and Lorne. And I was quite surprised, because it hadn't ever occurred to me that anybody else would be particularly interested in this.

Like many tellers in the 1970s Celia was telling stories within the context of children's literature and would have gone on doing it without the community, and felt enriched rather than disturbed by learning that others were also telling stories. Like the other tellers I interviewed, she felt that "growing pains" were a healthy sign of maturity: "It means that you have to keep thinking about what and why and who. That, to me, is what this kind of community means."

Marylyn Peringer also stressed the way the community sustained her and other tellers:

> It [storytelling] gave me a way to use that knowledge, and I've been reinforced by having a storytelling community, people that I

can break bread with. It feels very comfortable now. I don't get the sense of competitiveness with them at all, and we stay together all year 'round. We get together, do our little bit, then go home, which is what I understand happens in some other places, where storytellers come, but they just wait for their moment to tell, and they don't seem as interested in listening, just in telling.[9]

In summary, Toronto evolved into a full community that reached beyond the immediate area. It offered both support and promotion to its participants through weekly gatherings, concerts, regular courses, and the annual festival. The positive result was a sense of community that continued to be both deep and broad. The negative aspect was the constant concern with organization and finances, and the occasional criticism of people who felt themselves to be ignored by those at the center of the action. This was inevitable in a large community where not all people knew each other, and in Toronto it led to positive growth as new voices came to be heard and included. Challenges continue to be met and crises addressed as I write these words.

The dynamic tension between individual tellers and their groups and communities is a source of innovation for both the groups and the individuals. Henry Glassie, speaking for tellers in the area of Northern Ireland he studied, commented that "community is not a thing of territory or law or blood." He challenges conventional assumptions about traditional communities struggling to survive in the changing times in terms that are useful in understanding the survival of intentional storytelling communities as well:

[The idea of] "our district of the country" shifts, forming and reforming itself through endless negotiation during ceili and work. Here is a challenge: community is the product, not of tradition but of personal responsibility, yours to build or destroy (Glassie 1982:583).

It is easy to forget that a community is indeed created by the people who view themselves as its members. It is not a supercultural entity that exists as a platonic ideal. This is no less so for storytelling scenes and groups and communities than for any other form of human gathering. In Section II we will see how this is lived out by tellers in the Toronto community. Some are local participants who take on "personal responsibility" as an on-going commitment, while others come from the outside to contribute new material and ideas as they take part in the festival or other events sponsored by the community. But before we meet these tellers, we will explore how and why performers choose the stories they favor in their repertoires.

Notes

1 These figures cannot take into account groups that do not appear in the annual NSA directory. For example, the 1995 directory lists only nine groups in five Canadian provinces, while a 1992 survey completed by the Vancouver Storytellers Circle names eighteen. Even the Canadian survey is incomplete, as not all Canadian groups responded to the Vancouver questionnaire.

2 Folklorist Charles Briggs observed that romantic notions of traditional culture still exist in folklore as a scholarly field, though these notions have gone underground where their existence is more difficult to discern, and they are often obscured by scholarly jargon (Briggs 1993).

3 Quoted from *Let It Shine!*, a personal newsletter published privately by Reid Miller, fall/winter, 1992:1.

4 For the first several years the festival rented space in a downtown church. In 1988 the festival outgrew this facility and had to move to a larger public institution, and has since moved to a still larger and more central location.

5 In Canada the situation is further complicated by the recent establishment of an informal network, Storytellers of Canada, that has met for the past three years in different cities. The commitment to decentralization has been very strong, as well as the wish to avoid formal dues. As of this writing, S.O.C. is an informal communication network linking groups and individual storytellers across the country. How long it can exist in this loose form is a question that can only be asked and not answered at this point.

6 There are a multitude of publications from groups and communities in the United States; the 1996 *National Storytelling Directory* listed more than 70 newsletters and magazines, and this was only a portion since many local groups did not list their publications. Major regional centers covered tellers and events from several regional groups and communities. For example, *The Territorial Tattler* reported on centers throughout Oklahoma, *The Illinois Storytellers' Guild Newsletter* did the same for Illinois, and so on (*National Storytelling Directory* 1996:87).

7 I should mention that it goes beyond Ontario as well. I cannot speak for other provinces but I know for certain that Manitoba's storytelling group, Stone Soup Stories, was indirectly inspired by the low-key, participation-centered Toronto model. Before we became a group we decided to write to

Dan Yashinsky, whose name one member had heard from an acquaintance; Dan's encouraging response influenced the development of this group over the years, as we can see from the opening of the *Directory* entry: "We have been holding informal storytelling circles since 1983. Our greatest interest is in encouraging participation rather than emphasizing performance" (*Canadian Storytelling Directory* 1997/98: 24).

8   Several letters I received from Toronto tellers in 1995 indicated that another crisis was brewing. Yashinsky, for one, described it as "a state of rather dangerous flux," and "that community feelings are about to be severely tested" (letter, October 1 1995). By 1997 the community had, once again, weathered the storm.

9   Melissa Heckler described listening to Kunta, a traditional narrator in Namibia, tell stories most of one day and night and still get up to make morning coffee for friends, in contrast with a hypothetical platform performer: "Kunta's modern counterpart in our culture, after reconfirming the community of humanity, often retires to the nearest hotel room, stranger to those in the next room, with as storyteller Gerald Fierst puts it, 'only the stale smell of the previous occupant's cigarettes for company.' Forget making coffee for anyone" (Birch-Heckler 1996:31).

FOUR

ONCE UPON A TIME TODAY: TELLERS AND TALES[1]

MANY storytellers I have heard have an understanding of the dynamics of oral composition; they do not merely repeat tales from a set text or script but recreate them at each performance, thus giving us the possibility of observing the correlations between text, texture, and context (see Dundes 1964 for a full discussion of these terms). The text is the story itself, the texture is the characteristics that develop as the story is told by particular tellers at each telling, and context encompasses the internal and external circumstances of an actual storytelling event. In oral communities individual tellers are often too immersed in their art to answer the endless questions academics are capable of asking, so it has been a great pleasure to talk with articulate platform performers who, while equally absorbed in their art, have had to learn it consciously rather than taking it in as part of an entire culture; thus they retain a self-consciousness that allows them to respond to academic queries with great patience. Also, storytellers love to talk about their art of word-weaving.

I have questioned a number of urban tellers about their understanding of the oral process, and in particular how this understanding contributes to the continued life of folktales as they tell them today. Many who responded spoke of their interest in the kind of folktales popularly known as fairy tales, what I call here wondertales. I have been very curious to discover how the sophisticated metaphoric genre of wondertales come to life for those who knew them first as children, largely from popular selections of the Grimm tales in English and from the films of Walt Disney Productions. It excites me that wondertales have gained appreciation from modern adult audiences. At least some listeners, and many of the tellers, recognize and are moved by the transformational and cathartic powers of this sort of narrative. Sweep away all the nostalgic trifles written today about quaint old tellers whiling away the hours before a comfortable fire—still a popular sentimental notion of oral narration—and you will find many listeners and tellers who understand that these old tales do indeed retain an ancient and uncompromising power that is anything but sentimental.

In this chapter two streams of thought flow along in their own channels and eventually merge into the same river. The first is my folkloric search for the place of traditional folktales in modern repertoires; I acknowledge that, though there is now a much greater wealth of world folktales available to tellers than in past decades, I use the Grimm collection as a model since it is still so central in North American childhood reading as well as in the repertoires of many contemporary performers. The second stream of thought, which insists on continually flooding its banks here, is my storyteller's quest for the elusive muses of narrative artistry. How and why do people continue to tell and listen to old and seemingly outdated tales; do these carry the same expressive weight now, in an age where written literature is regarded as the supreme form of narrative expression and where other technological playthings tempt us away from old "magic"? I know that many other explorers have been guided by a similar curiosity and each has an answer. Some have taken a psychological perspective, others political (particularly gender-based), and others have looked at tales and tellers as within a societal or communal framework. In general many who have written about the wondertale have done so from the outside in—that is, looking at the stories themselves and interpreting these according to their own particular models. What I want to do here is look at what the tellers themselves have to say, especially about the Grimm tales that have been the center of attention for so many scholarly and popular interpretations.

I was bemused to hear, while conducting my dissertation research in the early 1970s, that one woman assumed that the Grimm tales she read were English folktales because her German-born mother had told her German stories in German and she did not understand that these were also the Grimm tales (Stone 1975a:314). I was surprised to find this was true of many of those I interviewed at that time; they did not think of the Grimm tales as Germanic, but rather as world folktales that belonged to everyone. English translations of these stories began almost as soon as the first Grimm collection appeared in the early 1800s, which made them more widely accessible as children's reading. The original intention of the Grimms was to examine old oral tales as expressions of archaic culture but when the stories became increasingly popular as children's reading the brothers seemed to split their interests: Jacob continuing his investigations into archaic language and custom while Wilhelm went on preparing the various editions that became increasingly acclaimed as children's tales, despite their darkness, violence, and irrationality.

Despite the continuing popularity of this collection and its perceived position as a world treasury, I have heard only a few Grimm tales told by professional storytellers, and these were often the lesser known stories. For example, the murderous tale called "The Juniper Tree" was favored by several tellers, among them Susan Gordon whom we meet in Section II, Chapter 4. Because the tales had been so central to the dozens of people I questioned in the 1970s I wondered if these tellers were deliberately avoiding them, or if the Grimm collection had lost its hold on North American readers. In order to find out, I selected a number of professional urban performers across North America, all but one of whom I had heard in performances at storytelling festivals and concerts in the United States and Canada and at smaller and more informal sessions closer to home, in Winnipeg and Saskatoon.

I sent out a questionnaire to twenty-five experienced tellers and received seventeen responses.[2] The questions I asked were meant to discover the place of the Grimm tales in their repertoires and also to uncover their understanding of the complexities of oral composition. I chose tellers whom I knew to favor traditional stories (though not necessarily Grimm tales) and who treated them as serious literature rather than as something to parody. One teller said specifically: "I prefer not to fracture fairy tales to make them more palatable to contemporary values" (Lynn Rubright, letter January 5, 1988). This is worth noting since some contemporary performers who claim to tell traditional stories do "fracture," performing well-known tales (Cinderella, the Frog Prince, Hansel and Gretel are favorite choices) as parodies or as modernizations based more on stereotypes of fairy tales as "happily ever after stories" than on a deeper understanding of the *Märchen* as a genre of literature for adults.

I must note that many tellers would disagree with me here by pointing out that parody and satire, and theatrical storytelling in general, are legitimate literary expressions. This is certainly true with some experienced tellers, for instance, Brother Blue (Hugh Hill) and Ed Stivender, both notable examples of performers whose innovative retellings of familiar tales do deepen rather than cheapen. Also, The

Folktellers, Barbara Freeman and Connie Regan-Blake, have evolved from library storytellers to dramatic artists, scripting an original dramatic production based on folktales. But more often than not I have found that theatrical presentations and modernized stories are superficial and empty if entertainment is the primary motivation for story adaptations.

The responses of the seventeen tellers revealed that the Grimm collection was certainly familiar to them and had played a central part in their repertoires in the early part of their performance careers. Many had since chosen to draw on less familiar material, though some admitted that Grimm tales still provided a prototype. Many of those who did continue to interpret Grimm tales chose little known texts. Others retained many of tales, popular and unfamiliar alike, as part of their repertoire because they still considered them to be a meaningful literary expression.

The questionnaire I sent to tellers began with the query, "What part (if any) have the Grimm tales played in your repertoire, past and present?" Most responded that as children they had read the Grimms avidly and later found them to be important models for oral narration. Barbara Reed, from Connecticut, said: "I consider these tales at the heart of (folk)fairy tales, and folktales at the heart of storytelling. Some I have told so long I don't remember when or where I first met them" (letter, January 2, 1988).

Another professional performer, Lynn Rubright, of St. Louis, described her early experience in strikingly similar words when she recalled not only the tales themselves but the human context in which she told them: "Grimm tales played an enormous role in developing my love of story as a child. My grandmother used to tell me 'Red Riding Hood,' 'Jack in the Beanstalk' [not Grimm[3]] and 'Hansel and Gretel' while I was nestled next to her warm body under the featherbed in the back bedroom during nap time when I was about four years old. It wasn't until years later that I recalled the warm and loving environment in which I was introduced to the Grimms' tales" (letter, January 5, 1988).

Elizabeth Ellis, a southern teller with knowledge of traditional Appalachian tales as well as childhood familiarity with the Grimm collection, identified several Kentucky tales as being local variants of Grimm tales: "I tell some Grimm-based fairytales. I grew up hearing Appalachian Mountain versions of some of those stories. I still tell some of them. I've messed with some of them, but others I tell pretty much the way I heard them" (undated letter, 1988).

Another woman, Ruthilde Kronberg, of German birth, found the Grimm tales even more central in her childhood: "As a child in Nazi Germany I used to get in trouble because I didn't do my homework. I read fairy tales instead. I think they saved my sanity because they taught me that the evil which was taking place around me would burn itself out. Which it did" (undated letter, 1987).

Not all contemporary tellers retained the Grimms as part of their active repertoire, however. Washington State storyteller Cathryn Wellner commented: "Though I do not tell tales from the Grimms, they have influenced me enormously. To call them favorite childhood tales is to ignore the fact that they were very nearly the only folktales I heard then. They taught me the pattern which still provides the frame on which I hang a tale: introduction, problem, development, denouement, conclusion. From them I learned that good triumphs over evil, that the weak can outwit the strong, that industriousness leads to success, that loyalty and honor are among the highest virtues" (letter, January 7, 1988).

It was interesting to me that the storytellers I questioned in 1987 remembered the Grimm tales with similar ease as did many of those I questioned fifteen years earlier as part of my dissertation research. The stories had not lost their popularity, as I guessed they might have. Quite the opposite; those I talked with in both the 1970s and the 1980s not only remembered the collection in general, they were able to name specific tales and, in many cases, could provide full plot summaries.

I discovered those who were now storytellers listed a greater variety of tale titles (even when they were no longer telling Grimm tales) in response to my second question: "Can you describe any specific Grimm tales you've favoured either now or in the past, and can you describe why these appealed to both you and to audiences?" Some mentioned only a few, others offered many titles. I quote Elizabeth Ellis in full because her response was so concise and detailed (I provide the Grimm titles for her southern variants):

"The June Apple Tree" ["The Juniper Tree"] I tell a lot. I love telling it because it helps people focus on those things in our culture that devour the lives of our children. "Three Golden Shirts and a Finger Ring" ["Seven Ravens"] I enjoy telling, I guess because I have felt mute most of my life with my family. "Don't Fall in My Beans" ["The Lad Who Went Forth to Learn What

Fear Is"] is a perfect opening story—a scary/funny ghost tale. One of the most used tales in my repertoire. "Beauty and Her Aunts" ["The Three Spinners"] never fails to get a laugh. Useful with adult audiences. Everyone appreciates a good scam. "Jack and the Devil's Grandmother" ["Devil With Three Golden Hairs"] I used to tell, but not so much now. I really enjoy riddling stories. People seem to enjoy them a lot too. They bridge the gap between funny stories and seriously plotted tales. "Mr. Fox" ["The Robber Bridegroom"] I tell a lot. I like its haunted quality. I also enjoy the spunky heroine (undated letter, 1988).[4]

Barbara Reed named a dozen traditional tales as part of her regular repertoire, commenting that she included "all the old favorites, in "Barbara Reed" versions suited to the occasion."[5] She was one of the few tellers who incorporated "old favorites" instead of seeking out the lesser known tales.

The desire to find less commonly known tales was so strong that even a teller who favored the Grimms said, "I stay away from the ones popularized in this country such as "Little Red Riding Hood," "Hansel and Gretel," "Cinderella," "Sleeping Beauty," etc" (Renate Schneider 1988). Similarly, Marvyne Jenoff, a Toronto writer and occasional storyteller featured here in Section II, Chapter 4, avoided some stories precisely because they were well known; she commented that this "spurred me quite energetically in pursuit of more unusual materials" (letter, December 1987). A Winnipeg teacher and teller who also preferred more unusual stories observed that the Grimm collection was only one of many available today: "There are so many stories to draw from that often I choose something else—eg. Nanabush, Anansi, Jack Tales" (Mary Louise Chown, letter, November 1988). Cathryn Wellner was even more specific in her rejection of the best known Grimm tales: "Another of the problems in using Grimms' tales is that their adaptations and commercial uses have set up certain expectations for them. Children hearing "Hansel and Gretel" or "Rumpelstiltskin" have pre-formed images that skew the way in which they listen to the tales. I prefer to tell stories that do not set off an automatic reaction" (letter, 1988).

Of the seventeen tellers who responded to my questionnaire, only five identified Grimm tales as forming a significant part of their current repertoires and only two of the five, both German-born, had built their repertoires around them. Ruthilde Kronberg told about fifty

Grimm tales over several years, including well-known and obscure tales, while Renate Schneider said that twenty of the fifty tales she told regularly were less commonly known stories from the Grimms and many of the others were German tales from other sources: "Grimm tales play, of course, a big part in my repertory since I grew up with them and for me they represent and express the German countryside, where these particular versions were shaped. I tell only certain ones which to me give the special flavor of German philosophy and mood and myth" (letter, 1988).

For these two German-born narrators the Grimm tales were not just a collection of world tales but an intimate part of their cultural identity. As already noted, others regarded the texts in a more universal light. For example, Elizabeth Ellis had more general, but no less committed, reasons for regarding these tales as central: "I include the Grimm tales because they are rich and opulent sources of meaning. I can tell them over and over without tiring of them because there is always something there I never noticed before, always something powerfully parallel to my own life. I figure that must also be true of my listeners"(letter, 1988).

Barbara Reed named less than a dozen Grimm tales that she tells regularly but still felt that these were important to her as a storyteller: "I look back at the Random House/Pantheon edition [of Grimm tales] as my source, but I feel quite free and entitled to do my own versions of 'The Fisherman and His Wife,' 'The Frog Prince,' 'Snow White'— fun to undo Disney—'Cinderella' when requested, 'Sleeping Beauty' when I find a class of children so tired I want to put them to sleep. And 'The Wolf and Seven Kids,' 'Rumpelstiltskin,' 'Rapunzel,' 'Hansel and Gretel' (letter, 1988).

Maryland storyteller Susan Gordon, whose text of "The Juniper Tree" is included in Section II, Chapter 4, wrote that she often did not know why a particular story appealed to her but had learned that when a story, particularly a Grimm text, caught her attention it usually had something deeply personal to offer her and would therefore have the potential of touching others as well. In speaking of two of her Grimm favorites, "The Juniper Tree" and "The Handless Maiden," she said:

The stories seem to be touching needs and areas of growth which I would not have named myself. My desire is to tell them a story that is, in some way, their story, which will provide them the opportunity to reflect on their own lives. In each of these instances the storytelling becomes very mutual, with the listeners not only helping you tell the story by their presence, but recreating the story and deepening it for both listeners and teller (letter, Dec.-Jan., 1987/88).

Even though Gordon listed only four Grimm tales ("The Handless Maiden," "The Juniper Tree," "The Boy Who Set Out to Study Fear," and "The Golden Goose") in her repertoire of fifty to sixty stories, she insisted that these were key narratives: "All of these stories make a whole for me, none is more important than the other" (letter, Dec.-Jan, 1987/88).

Like others, Gordon noted the absence in her repertoire of the more popular titles that she identified somewhat disdainfully as "the typical female stories, 'Snow White,' 'Cinderella,' 'Sleeping Beauty,' etc.," meaning that popularizers relied on these stories to maintain a stereotypical view of women as passive and helpless.

When I compiled a full list of the stories named by these tellers I found a rich variety of titles mentioned. I also noticed that while three of the more popular tales did still appear at the head of the list, their positions were far less prominent than they were with the listeners I interviewed in the 1970s. The titles are listed according to how many times they were mentioned (including multiple references by a single teller). Frequency of response is in parentheses, followed by Grimm (KHM) and Aarne/Thompson (AT) numbers:[6]

Tale Titles	(Responses)	Grimm	Aarne-Thompson
Cinderella	(5)	KHM21	AT510A
The Juniper Tree	(4)	KHM47	AT720
Snow White	(3)	KHM53	AT709
Hansel/Gretel	(3)	KHM15	AT327A
Rapunzel	(3)	KHM12	AT310
Rumpelstiltskin	(3)	KHM55	AT500
King Thrushbeard	(3)	KHM52	AT900
The Goosegirl	(3)	KHM89	AT533
Wedding of Mrs. Fox	(3)	KHM38	AT 65
The White Snake	(3)	KHM17	AT673
The Frog King	(2)	KHM1	AT440
The Seven Ravens	(2)	KHM25	AT451

Snow White, Rose Red	(2)	KHM161	AT426
The Robber Bridegroom	(2)	KHM40	AT955
The Three Spinsters	(2)	KHM14	AT501
Gifts of Little Folk	(2)	KHM182	AT503
Maid Maleen	(2)	KHM198	AT870
Rich Man, Poor Man	(2)	KHM87	AT750A
Boy Who Went Forth...	(2)	KHM4	AT326
Mother Holle	(1)	KHM24	AT480
Brother and Sister	(1)	KHM11	AT450
Jorinda and Joringel	(1)	KHM69	AT405
Three Little Gnomes...	(1)	KHM13	AT403B
The Three Feathers	(1)	KHM63	AT402
The Water of Life	(1)	KHM97	AT551
The Star Coins	(1)	KHM153	AT779
The Singing Bone	(1)	KHM28	AT780
The Twelve Brothers	(1)	KHM9	AT451
The Two Brothers	(1)	KHM60	AT567A
The Strange Musician	(1)	KHM8	AT151
The Turnip	(1)	KHM146	AT1960D
Old Man & His Grandson	(1)	KHM78	AT930B
Three Golden Hairs ...	(1)	KHM29	AT930
The Golden Goose	(1)	KHM64	AT571
Maiden Without Hands	(1)	KHM31	AT706
Bremen Town Musicians	(1)	KHM27	AT130
Three Sons of Fortune	(1)	KHM70	AT1650
The Queen Bee	(1)	KHM62	AT554
Three Green Twigs	(1)	KHM206	AT756A
Spindle, Shuttle, Needle	(1)	KHM188	AT585
Fisherman & His Wife	(1)	KHM19	AT555
Brier Rose	(1)	KHM50	AT410
Wolf & Seven Kids	(1)	KHM5	AT123
The Tailor in Heaven	(1)	KHM35	AT800
Mother Trudy	(1)	KHM43	AT334

We can see that even the widely-known story of "Cinderella" was only cited five times, and the other favored tales had only two or three references. "Little Red Cap" did not appear at all, except as a tale that was avoided because of its very wide popularity (Marvyne Jenoff and Renate Schneider mentioned it negatively). Of the forty-six titles mentioned, forty are "romantic" or "magic" tales. There are only four animal tales (AT65, 123, 130, and 151) and two humorous anecdotes (AT1650 and 1960D). Interestingly, the latter are named by male tellers. We can see that these titles reflect the exaggerated position romantic "fairy tale" texts hold in most popular English translations (many collections feature only thirty to sixty of the full Grimm collection).

Seven tellers maintained that the Grimm tales were not a regular part of their performing repertoire, six of these explaining that they preferred lesser-known sources. Only one, Elisabeth Nash of Winnipeg, rejected the Grimms completely on the basis of their violence, thought she did recall a few childhood favorites: "I don't remember ever telling a Grimm story. That was not the result of a conscious decision. The brutality of some of the stories shakes me even now: the community that drove spikes into a barrel, forced an old lady into it and rolled it down the hill; the gang that heated iron shoes red hot, jammed them on an erring woman's feet and made her dance until she died. This child was distressed to tears by them on more than one occasion, and possibly that's why this adult has not told Grimm stories" (Elisabeth Nash, letter, December 10, 1987). I note that she listed "Hansel and Gretel" and "Rumpelstiltskin" as former favorites though both have violent resolutions. She also remarked that, as a result of completing the questionnaire, she decided she might try to tell "King Thrushbeard" despite its poor treatment of the wife.[7]

John Harrell was another teller/author who told very few Grimm tales; he named only "The Bremen Town Musicians" and "The Three Gifts of Fortune" ["The Three Sons of Fortune"], but these were important stories for him: "'Bremen Town Musicians' was a favorite tale of my wife's and when I would tell it to her, it always made her laugh heartily. It was good therapy. I [also] liked 'Three Gifts of Fortune' because, like 'Bremen,' it is so easy to tell, so basic" (undated letter, 1988).

Harrell identified an essential quality of folktales in general that he felt accounted in part for their longevity: "they are easy to tell because they are so basic, not because they are simplistic." When I questioned him later that year he said that he thought of folktales, and most particularly wondertales, as masterful metaphors that "could carry great potential weight in a consistent and sequential plot with clearly defined characters." For him this profound simplicity of form allowed even poor tellers to learn and retell the stories. This has certainly contributed to the survival of such tales, since skilled narrators have always been in the minority and thus the burden of passing on the tradition frequently falls to narrators with weaker talents and less experience. Of course, a few of these tellers will eventually become skilled themselves, but master tellers will always be in the minority whether in traditional narration or in platform performing.

The Grimms claimed to have taken their tales from gifted narrators, but in fact the brothers (notably Wilhelm) reworked many of texts without sufficient regard for the "unadorned style" they claimed as characteristic of the stories they gathered "from the lips of the tellers." There may have been a handful of truly skilled tellers, but even from these individuals only the bare outlines of stories were taken, rarely a full text. So there really are no "authentic" oral variants of Grimm tales for tellers to rely on, only their printed reworkings. In any case, oral tales are always multi-textual. That is, unlike written literature they have as many texts as there are tellers—more, in fact, since each retelling is somewhat different. Traditional narrators, skilled and unskilled alike, have the advantage of hearing different tellings of the same stories and enriching their own understanding of any story's potential.

Because of this immeasurable diversity, the search for an authentic original was a futile quest of nineteenth-century scholars. While this approach was eventually abandoned it left a still-valuable tool for comparing the variants of hundreds of basic folktales: the Aarne/Thompson index lists and summarizes variants of most of the Grimm tales as well as many others across the broad range of the Indo-European tradition (Aarne/Thompson, 1973). Many storytellers, notably those with library training, use this index to broaden their knowledge of any given story. We saw that, for example, in Elizabeth Ellis' describing Kentucky variants of Grimm tales.

Almost two centuries have passed since the first edition of the Grimm Tales was published in 1812. Germany in the nineteenth century was not North America today, yet despite this distance in time and place many of the tales have maintained their vibrancy and relevance as world folktales even though hundreds of other collections are now available, as reflected by the tellers considered here.

All of these narrators had a clear idea of their reasons for telling tales orally, Grimm and otherwise in response to my third and last question: "Why do you either include or exclude any Grimm tales in your repertoire now." As we have already seen, several indicated that whether they told them or not, the Grimm tales were still meaningful, still offered a framework for viewing the human condition. Susan Gordon commented on storytelling as a human expression that goes beyond theatrical diversion: "When I entertain, it is my intent to just tell the story absolutely alive and let it do and be whatever it is supposed to be—funny, mysterious, scary, etc. That same thing holds true in any setting, but in therapeutic, educational and religious settings, the story is chosen with care to the occasion, with some knowledge of the people I'm telling it to. In those settings, often I have developed some ways to help us reflect on the story, think about it, and feel it more deeply, as well as providing a way for people to respond creatively" (letter, 1987/88). Gordon, like others in this survey, learned this through her own direct experiences as a teller.

Several reflected on this sense of oral narration as an emergent exchange between narrators and listeners brought together during storytelling events. John Harrell, for instance, highlighted the difference between narrating and reading: "I prefer to tell tales rather than to read them because the communication is direct between me and the other person. With reading, the story is in the book. With telling, the story is part of me and I'm giving that part of me to you" (letter, 1988).

Toronto performer Marylyn Peringer, featured in Section II, Chapter 3, similarly underlined the direct power of spoken rather than read or recited words: "I don't ever write out a text that I am learning. Writing freezes it, and then it freezes me. I just talk to myself when I'm alone—out loud, of course, getting through the story part by part until is sounds right" (letter, January 10, 1988).

Jane Yolen, who both writes and tells stories, emphasized that finding one's own "voice" is important: "I keep defining and then redefining what stories mean to me and how I can transmit that feeling (and those stories) in the best possible manner to others. When I listen to others tell, I realize that as good as they are, they are not me. I have to take the story again into my own mouth" (letter, February 7, 1987).

Each of these tellers had their own firm idea of what the oral process meant in terms of audience responses. California artist Ruth Stotter, for example, asserted that she found her personal connections while preparing and telling a story and often was able to give her listeners a chance to discover and reveal their own: "At present I tell just a few stories from the Grimms—those that fascinate me by their symbolic interpretations and my psychological reverberations—giving me a chance to step back and ponder life. I often tell Grimm tales to adult audiences and we usually have a discussion afterward" (Stotter 1987).

Susan Gordon makes this kind of discussion a regular part of almost all of her performances and workshops.

Most of these tellers considered their storytelling role as potentially transformational for the listeners as well as for the story. Cathryn Wellner was most eloquent on this issue: "Though I avoid moralistic and didactic stories like some dread disease and squirm when I am forced to sit through one, I nevertheless perceive the storyteller's role as that of moral and spiritual bellwether in a secular society. The first task of the story is to entertain, for only entertaining stories will be heeded. But once the attention is focused we must ask ourselves, 'To what end?' I want my stories to be affirmations of hope, of belief in humanity's basic goodness" (undated letter, 1988).

These words seem to echo the declaration Zipes makes in the introduction to his recent translation of the Grimm tales:

> Today we have inherited their [the Grimm brothers'] concerns and contradictions, and their tales still read like innovative strategies for survival. Most of all they provide hope that there is more to life than mastering the art of survival. Their "once upon a time" keeps alive our utopian longing for a better world that can be created out of our dreams and actions (Zipes 1988: xxvi).

Indeed, these tellers would agree that the Grimm tales offered them, as children if not still as adults, "innovative strategies for survival." However, since storytelling as a dramatic art takes place in the ethnographic present, I suggest that their "survival strategies" are not primarily utopian, not dreams of the future but observations and aspirations for the world as we live in it now. In the hands of skilled tellers, these old stories have the capacity they have always had to identify and address the most basic human concerns and contradictions as they manifest themselves today.

A more concrete example will be bring this immediate aspect of told stories more clearly into focus. "The Juniper Tree" was mentioned by four of the tellers who responded. This is one of the very few Grimm tales in which a victimized protagonist, in this case the boy murdered and served up in a stew by his stepmother, avenges himself directly rather than having the villain punished obliquely.[8] In this odd tale the boy returns to life as a bird and rewards his loving sister and father by dropping down gifts, but punishes his mother by dropping a millstone on her. He then regains his human shape.

Each of the four respondents expressed their immediate reasons for finding this particular tale so compelling. Marylyn Peringer was moved by the simplicity of the story as told by French performer: "I heard Bruno de la Salle tell it simply, movingly, and [he] sang the song of the bird as composed by one of the musicians in his storytelling troupe" (letter, 1988).

Marvyne Jenoff, whose radically reworked version of "Snow White" is found in Section II, Chapter 4, commented on the current popularity of "The Juniper Tree" with adult and mixed-age Toronto audiences as a result of the performances of two particularly influential tellers (Alice Kane and Joan Bodger). She attributed the story's local popularity to a vicarious experience of violence: "Both [Kane and Bodger] seem to feel that children need the violence in folktales to help them understand and articulate their own lives, which include at least the awareness of violence" (letter, March 2, 1989).

Elizabeth Ellis, who said that she usually told the Appalachian variant ("The June Apple Tree"), still placed it first among the stories she identified as "Grimm" tales. She viewed it as a deep metaphor that is very much relevant today: "I love telling it because it helps people focus on those things in our culture that devour the lives of our children" (letter, 1988).

Susan Gordon also said she told this tale frequently, and was considerably more expansive on her reasons for so doing:

"Juniper Tree" is a story which I told initially at a conference on the existence of evil. I had never told it before, but had developed the song for it. I planned to tell other stories, but the types of evil people were discussing—rape, batterings, sexual abuse, etc.—just seemed to call for that story. I talked to the fellow who hired me to tell, and he remembers the story as being as frightening as Stephen King is frightening, but offering hope (Gordon 1987/88).

Gordon and the other narrators return "Juniper Tree" fully to life, like the murdered boy who returns as a bird and eventually gets his own shape back. The same text, then, is ever emergent for each teller and every audience. With this in mind we can say that the Grimm text is no more authoritative than any of these modern oral variants.

We can see that the vibrant balance between stability and innovation is at the heart of the creative process in oral composition, as much for many professional performers as for traditional narrators. In the context of a storytelling event the texture of the story emerges as narrator and audience participate in the recreation of the text, directly and indirectly. Cathryn Wellner described in detail what many tellers experience, the actual birth of the story when it is first told to an audience:

> I used to nearly work a story to death before testing it on an audience. Now I lay the framework and then begin telling it. There are a few things with which I am comfortable at that point: I know the story line, the nature of the characters, essential details, places in which I want to use a chant or a song, and something of the culture. The audience teaches me what the story is about, and each audience teaches me something slightly different. Through their reactions, I see where the story takes wings and where it is earthbound. Eventually, after many tellings, the story takes a shape which I tend to return to each time. It will always be fluid and unrepeatable. Sometimes an especially attuned audience will give me a moment of such clarity that I am stunned (undated letter, 1988).

The immediacy of the storytelling experience as described by Wellner and others quoted here emphasizes the fact that for them storytelling is not primarily a theatrical event with a rehearsed script or story text and confined by the convention of the fourth wall. Instead they address themselves candidly to the audience, and in some cases (particularly in more informal contexts) the audience responds with equal directness, and thus becomes part of the ongoing recomposition of the story.

We have seen that the Grimm tales have lost their primacy in terms of quantity; very few tellers feature Grimm texts in their current repertoires. Still, the variety of titles mentioned by these tellers is much greater than those recalled by the listeners I interviewed in the early 1970s. Also, several tellers identified the Grimm collection as having provided a valuable model for their early repertoires.

I asked the tellers described here to mention and discuss a specific kind of story in order to reveal how living tales function even when they arise from old stories preserved in print. Many were able to identify a number of their favored tales, but one teller did more than this. I asked Toronto performer Carol McGirr if she could record the titles of all the stories she remembered telling. A recently retired school librarian with more than three decades of experience and a very fine memory, Carol was able to recall, enumerate, and comment on more than one hundred titles of stories she had told; these included literary stories for children and adults as well as anecdotes, fables, folktales, wondertales, and lengthy myths and epics. She wrote them down in chronological order (as well as she could recall), which allows us to see her pattern of development as well as her story preferences. Carol wrote out these titles over a two-hour period as we ate lunch at a Greek restaurant in Toronto in February, 1995. I reprint the list as Carol wrote it. She used asterisks to identify material as traditional, and also noted stories she had learned orally. Carol attempted to list the titles chronologically, beginning with "Peter Rabbit" which she told regularly to her friends at age six. Carol noted the length of her longer pieces, mostly epic material that is presented to adult audiences. If this were a list of literary readings rather than oral presentations, she might have included the number of pages rather than the length of performance. Carol's list is impressive for its length and variety. It also clearly identifies her as a teller with library training because of the emphasis on children's stories still favored by tellers with this background. Narratives from traditional sources figure heavily in Carol's repertoire, accounting for seventy of the 102 titles. These include not only folktales such as "The Rosy Apple and the Golden Bowl" but also the more challenging sagas from Scandinavian tradition and tales from the Arthurian cycle. In both these story titles and in program descriptions for several years of Toronto festival performances, we see her evolution from a public school librarian relating stories for children to a teller of lengthy myths and epics performed for adults.[9]

Stories Recalled by Carol McGirr

Peter Rabbit (literary)
*Rosy Apple/Golden Bowl
*Budulinek
*Golden Arm
*Three Sneezes
*To Your Good Health
*Gunniwolf
Grandma's House (literary and oral)
Loudmouse (literary picture book)
*Tale of Tales
*Man Whose Trade Was Tricks
*Elephant's Bathtub
Tiger Skin Rug (picture book)
*Maui & the Sun
*Maui & the Kite
*The Black Crow

*Too Much Noise
*Indian Cinderella
*Ti-Jean & the White Cat
*Master Thief
*Golden Brothers
*The Just Man
*Name of the Tree
(book/oral)
*Fair, Brown & Trembling
*Ashpet
*Jack & the Bean Tree
*Old Dry Frye
*No-So-What
*Mighty Mikko
*The Cat on the Fell
*The Farmer Builds a Church
*Deacon of the Dark River
*The Chapel in the Hillside
*The Berserks
*Earl of Orkney
*Magnus the Good
*Skadi & Njord
*How Thor Got His Hammer
*Iduna's Apples
*Hymir's Cauldron
*Freya's Necklace
*Loki's Flyting
*Norse Creation Myth
*Ragnarok
*Balder's Dream
*Death of Balder
*Night Troll
*Saemund the Wise
*Laxdaela Saga
*Gudrun's Dreams (part of
Laxdaela)
*Hoskuld's Story
*Olaf & the Peacock
*Gautrek's Saga
*Saga of Hrolf Gautrekson

*Havelock the Dane
The Werewolf (Boccaccio)
Kunafa Cakes (1001 Nights)
Jake & the Kid (W.O.Mitchell):
    You Gotta Teeter
    A Voice for Christmas
    Auction Fever
    A Deal's a Deal
    Gentlemen Don't Chaw
    Franken Cents & Meer
    Golden Jubilee Citizen
    The Princess & the Wild
        Ones
    How Jake Made Her Rain
Stories by Jack Finney:
    Third Level
    Of Missing Persons
    Home Alone
    A Dash of Spring
    The Love Letter
    Prison Legend
Secret Life of Walter Mitty
(James Thurber)
Stories by Rosemary Sutcliffe:
    Merlin
    *Finn M'Coul
    *O'Carolan the Blind
    Harper
    Grace O'Malley (various)
    *Taliesen (Welsh sources)
Stories by Hans Christian
Andersen:
    The Twelve Windows
    The Ugly Duckling
    The Nightingale
    Marsh King's Daughter
*Brave Mary
*Lass Who Could Not Be
Frighted
Stories by Farley Mowat:

Stranger In Taransay
Countess of Dufferin
The Privilege of the Limits
*Blind McNair (literary)
*The Baron & the Traveller
*The Lazy Boy
*The Foolish Young Man (oral)
*The Fixer (oral)
*3 Golden Hairs of the Devil
*Song of Orpheus

*Eye of the Tail of Peacock
*Greek Creation myth
The Zodiac
The Jade Emperor
*Lakshmi & the Washerwoman
*Mouse With Seven Tales
*Hanuman the Monkey King
*Rama and Sita
Aida (adapted)

Let us briefly compare Carol's list of stories with another, this one from the table of contents of a collection of oral tales told by traditional narrator Joe Neil MacNeil, featured in Section II, Chapter 2. Joe Neil was able to recall dozens of stories of all sorts: folktales, wondertales, original fabrications, jokes and anecdotes. He remembered them in the context of his growing up as a Gaelic speaker on Cape Breton Island, Nova Scotia. The list of fifty-two stories included in *Tales Until Dawn* (MacNeil 1987) represents only a fraction of the more than four hundred narratives that Joe Neil dictated to John Shaw from 1976 to 1980. They are listed according to the families from whom Joe Neil learned them, since that was how he was able to bring them to mind. This way of presenting the stories stresses Joe Neil's view of community and individual: it was the families that he identified, not himself, as the sources of most of the tales that he learned and told. The tales are listed as they appear in the table of contents of *Tales Until Dawn*.

Stories Recalled by Joe Neil MacNeil

The Kennedys:
The Man in the Light Grey Coat
O Croileagan of the Horses
Iseadal Son of the King of the
    Hunts
How Oscar Got His Name
Oscar and Mac a'Luin
Fionn & Strange Adversaries
How Conan Got His Name
Diarmaid and the Slim Woman in
    the Green Coat
The Death of Diarmaid

The Amhas Ormanach
Jack and the Master
Great Brid of the Horses
The Death of Cu Chulainn
The King and the Foal
The Castle that Boban Saor Built
Working with the Adze
Did You Ever See the Like of Me

The MacLeans:
Duanach the Widow's Son
The Man with the Long Tales

The Strong Woodsman's Son
The Woman Who Was Awarded a
    Pair of Shoes by the Devil
The Three Knots
How the Fairy Suitor Was Tricked
The Night It Rained Porridge
Stirling Castle
The Miser and the Tailor
The Two Misers

The MacIsaacs:
Jack Fury
The Man Who Received the Three
    Counsels
The Forgetful Minister
Monday, Tuesday
Angus MacIsaac's Trip to the
    Moon
The Big Pig

The MacMullins:
The King of Egypt's Daughter
The Fair-haired Doctor
The Bad Mother's Daughter
The Lad, The Girl in the Cradle,
    and the Ring
The Widow's Son and the Robbers
The Golden Bird

Angus MacKenzie:
The Soldier Who Was Refused a
    Drink of Water

Joe MacLean:
The Shirt of the Man Without
    Worries

John MacNeil:
The Young Lad Who Quit School

Mrs. Michael MacNeil:
The Little Old Man with the
    Grains
The Fox, the Wolf, and the Butter

Neil Campbell:
The Journey Boban Soar Made
    with His Son
How Boban Soar's Son Found His
    Wife
Boban Soar: The Chalk Line

Dan MacNeil:
Boban Soar: Barley Bread & Milk

Roderick MacNeil:
The Tub That Boban Soar Built
Crazy Archie and the Hen

Anonymous:
Crazy Archie and the Minister
    Sutar
The Farmer's Big Lad

Personal Anecdotes:
from Dermot MacKenzie
from Michael MacDonald
from Martin MacInnis
from Alexander MacIsaac
from John MacIsaac
from Mrs. Roderick MacIsaac
from Neil MacIsaac
from Roderick MacNeil]
from Joe Neil MacNeil

A narrator who learns from other tellers in the social context of an
oral community will obviously recall and identify stories in a different
way than one who depends largely on individual training and on

printed sources. Joe Neil connects his stories with people, Carol recalls many of hers from printed sources—and also from her own actual performances. I do not mean this contrast as an evaluation of traditional and nontraditional narration, but as an underlining of what we have already seen in the introductory comments on the four streams of storytelling. Carol's and Joe Neil's lists of stories provide another way of delineating the two streams of oral traditional narration and library-educational storytelling.

Any experienced performer from any background who could enumerate the stories they told over a long period of time would see the patterns of their own artistry revealed. Their choices of stories at various points in their development would present an overall image of what was most important to them as performers: their favorite kinds of stories, their preferred audiences, and the evolution of their styles and techniques.

We have explored how traditional narratives have figured in the repertoires of contemporary tellers. In the following chapter individuals describe how they came to regard themselves as storytellers, and how their identities developed with experience.

Notes

1 An earlier version of this chapter appeared as "Once Upon a Time Today: Grimm Tales for Contemporary Performers" in *The Reception of the Grimms' Fairy Tales* (Haase 1993). I am grateful for the careful editing of the original text by Donald Haase and his assistants, and I acknowledge Wayne State University Press for allowing me to reprint it (much adapted) here.

2 Two separate questionnaires were sent out to the 25 selected tellers in the fall of 1987. The first was a complicated form with several questions, to which I received only a handful of responses. I sent the second, with only three questions, to those who had not yet responded. Over the next few months I received a dozen more replies, and these form the central portion of this chapter. The respondents are: Elisabeth Nash, Mary Louise Chown, Joyce Birch, Gerri Serrette (all from Manitoba); Elizabeth Ellis (Texas); Susan Gordon (Maryland); Jane Yolen (Massachusetts); Ruth Stotter and John Harrell (California); Marvyne Jenoff and Marylyn Peringer (Toronto); Renate and Robert Schneider, Barbara Reed (Connecticut); Lynn Rubright and Ruthilde Kronberg (Missouri); Cathryn Wellner (British Columbia).

3 "Jack and the Beanstalk" is, in fact, an English story printed in Joseph Jacobs (Jacobs n.d.). I discovered that many people did not distinguish

between the tales of the Grimms, Andersen, Perrault, or Jacobs. That is, the Grimm tales were so dominant that any folktale might be remembered as a "Grimm tale."

4 Several of the titles Elizabeth Ellis mentions are from Marie Campbell's collection of Kentucky folktales, *Tales From The Cloud Walking Country* (Campbell 1976) and from Richard Chase's two reworked collections (Chase 1943, 1948).

5 Barbara listed "The Fisherman and his Wife," "The Frog Prince," "Snow White," Cinderella," Sleeping Beauty," "The Wolf and Seven Kids," "Rumpelstiltskin," "Rapunzel," "Hansel and Gretel," "The Goose Girl," "The White Snake," all from the Grimm collection.

6 The Grimm numbers refer to their position in the full gathering of 210 tales; KHM is the original German title, *Kinder und Hausmärchen*. The AT number identifies the basic tale type as it is listed in the Aarne/Thompson index (Aarne-Thompson 1973) that identifies the classic Indo-European folktales.

7 Elisabeth eventually did tell this story at a small informal gathering at Stone Soup Stories, in the winter of 1988. Her story was well received and she enjoyed the experience thoroughly, but has not told the story since.

8 In the three most popular wondertales the protagonists have nothing to do with retribution or revenge: it is the doves and not Cinderella who punish the stepsisters; unknown wedding guests and not Snow White force the stepmother to dance to her death in heated iron shoes; the angry old woman who curses Sleeping Beauty is not punished at all—except, of course, in the Disney film.

9 Carol's description in the first program (1979) reflected the poetic nature of almost all of the entries for that year: "I am a school librarian at East York. Stories help us imagine and dream, and from our dreams come our lives" (Storytelling Festival of Toronto, 1979). Two years later she placed more emphasis on her library training and educational experiences: "[Carol is a] teacher, librarian and storyteller. Has taught courses for the Ontario Ministry of Education in various county boards. Has given lectures at the Faculty of Education, University of Toronto, and conducted workshops for groups of teachers, librarians, and clergy" (1981 festival program).

For the next two festivals Carol returned to a more whimsical style, dropping her description as a librarian: "[She] has travelled from the misty coasts of Iceland to W.O. Mitchell's baldheaded prairie to 'see' her stories" (1985 and 1986 programs). In 1995 she returned to a matter-of-fact description, but emphasis was on her activities as teacher and performer for adults, since she had retired early from her long-time profession as a school librarian-storyteller: "Carol McGirr teaches a course in storytelling at the Summer school of the Arts, Canadore College (North Bay, Ontario). She recently founded Fireside Epic to promote the telling of ancient tales in a series of small informal concerts" (1995 program).

By 1997 she had trimmed her description down to a single sentence that reflected her shift into epic recitations: "Carol McGirr is the founder of Fireside Epic dedicated to the promotion of epic storytelling" (1997 program).

FIVE

SOCIAL IDENTITY IN ORGANIZED STORYTELLING[1]

NYONE present at an organized storytelling event would no
doubt hear performers recount how they discovered when and
why they had become storytellers. These narratives are not as
simple as they might seem since they involve on-going perceptions of
emerging social identity by both tellers and listeners. Oral accounts on
stage, along with written descriptions by tellers in directories and festival programs, reveal how tellers express their artistic and social
decisions. How they describe themselves is often an indication of the
performance style of the tellers, as well as their formative connections.
For example, this Ottawa teller, who favors epics, writes almost as she
speaks:

> I began telling stories as a result of organizing a program at Expo
> 86, hearing some of the great all-time tellers and marvelling at
> the depth and power of their work. A professional storyteller and
> children's writer, I prefer traditional material and have a particu-
> lar interest in epics (Jan Andrews, *Canadian Storytelling Directory*
> 1997/98:38).

I have heard Jan Andrews present eloquent versions of long myths and
epics in an effective low-key style, influenced by other tellers in the
library-educational stream. Her self-descriptions in Toronto festival
programs were similar in tone and style.

Toronto teller Dan Yashinsky's entries reveal a different approach to
self-description. In many of the Toronto festival programs Dan focused
on his primary position as the initiator of the 1001 Friday Nights of
Storytelling and as one of the founders of the Storytellers School and
its annual festival. For several years his entries were variations on this
theme. A reader would not guess from these entries that he was a stim-
ulating performer with a dramatic style of presentation. His directory

entry offers a striking contrast; here his role as founder disappears and he reveals a different kind of energy: "Born to a crossroads heritage, I tell traditional stories from around the world. I call my approach 'Scheherajazz'—a mix of wonder tales, personal memory, and of-the-moment stories" (Dan Yashinsky, *Canadian Storytelling Directory* 1997/98:46). Unlike Jan Andrews' description, this entry does not relate how Dan came to storytelling, but it does hint at his performance style by referring to both Scheherazade and to the legendary crossroads as a place of magical transformation.

Another contrast in the self-descriptions of these two tellers is that Jan Andrews emphasizes her connections with other tellers, with a community, while Dan Yashinsky focuses on his own work as an original creator. Yet both are equally committed to, and identifiable by, their storytelling communities. The development of self-identity is a complex and exciting process, one that continues as long as a teller continues to perform. In this chapter I explore tellers at various stages of self-discovery as they struggle to find their place within specific storytelling communities and events.

Folklorist Robert Georges described storytelling events in a way that emphasized the social and communicative, whether events took place in traditional or in organized contexts (Georges 1969). His inclusive statement is an effective position for examining organized story-telling:[2]

> There is nothing especially authentic or traditional about the messages of storytelling events generated by the actions of the nonliterate or the preliterate, for storytelling events constitute one kind of communicative event within the continua of human communication and one kind of social experience within the framework of social interrelationships among people, irrespective of their relative social, educational, and economic statuses (Georges 1969:323).

Storytelling in all of its contexts is a dynamic experience in which participants assume social identities as tellers and as listeners. In organized storytelling the social roles of tellers and listeners are often more rigidly defined than in casual "kitchen table" telling where conversation and stories flow back and forth. In contrast, as we have seen, platform tellers perform formally, often on a stage separating them from listeners, while audience members listen without interrupting.

Both Jan Andrews and Dan Yashinsky, mentioned above, have become experienced tellers after some years of stage experience, but of course they began more modestly, as all tellers do.

Organized events may take the form of hour-long concerts featuring a few tellers or festivals with dozens of performers, each of whom has found their own way to establishing a personal and social identity through direct experience in whatever venues and contexts they were able to find. That is, it is not enough to call oneself a teller; you have to convince others that this is so. The social and personal dynamic of organized storytelling is not unlike that of traditional narration in this case. Folklore scholar Robert Adams, who studied a Japanese woman (although he uses a masculine pronoun here), observed that:

> In order for an individual to become identified in his community as storyteller, he must have sufficient opportunity to practice the craft, both in order to perfect his technique and to gain the recognition that only comes from wide exposure to an entire community (Adams 1972:355).[3]

Adams underlined social identity as a dynamic process, a continually evolving perception that unfolded as narrators participated in events and evolved personal style and technique.

Self-definition is central to artistic development. In the case of organized storytelling, perhaps more than in traditional narration, there is often a confused sense of what it means to be called or to call oneself a storyteller. The term is vague enough to cover a multiplicity of performance arts: reciting memorized pieces or reading from books, relating personal anecdotes, satirizing and parodying folktales, doing one-person drama or stand-up comedy, or mime, dance, and puppetry. Obviously any teller's previous training will affect how they see themselves as performers, but as we saw earlier the boundaries of professional identities are fluid. A teacher becomes an actor, an actor becomes a spiritual teller, a traditional narrator shifts from folktales to personal anecdotes (as Ray Hicks has done in recent festival performances).

I have been curious to learn what stages tellers mark as memorable in the process of their development from telling stories casually, as we all do, to taking on an identity as a storyteller. Not surprisingly storytellers often communicate their formative experiences in narrative form, both orally and in writing. Joseph Sobol, who interviewed almost one hundred American tellers, called these stories "vocational narratives" (Sobol 1994a).[4] He claimed that experienced tellers have at least one and usually more stories that mark the stages of their conscious development as performers and that they regularly repeat these anecdotes as part of their performances. I report a number of these kinds of stories from my own explorations as well as examples from Sobol's work.

I began to wonder how tellers defined themselves after hearing formative stories told both on stage and informally at the first festival I attended in 1982, but my formal quest began only in 1989 when I took part in a weekend retreat sponsored by the Storytellers School of Toronto. I noticed that one topic that kept arising spontaneously in conversation was the ways in which these people had come to recognize that they were storytellers in more than the casual sense of the word. I wanted to know how they had come to perceive and accept this social identity.

When I began to question participants at the 1989 retreat, I expected to hear variations on a typical statement I overheard many times at festivals and other events; these were usually delivered in a tone of awe and often concluded with the phrase, "... and that's when I knew that *I* was a storyteller." The speakers often spoke the words as if they had a conversion experience, which is appropriate phrasing for a movement described as a "revival." I continued to eavesdrop, fascinated with these assertions. Some of the tellers had been listeners at an event and said to themselves, "Well I could do that too" and consciously began to develop a new identity. Or they had been inspired by a teller and decided that they had been "called" to become a teller. Here are three brief examples quoted from Joseph Sobol's work, in the words of tellers who could name the moment when they assumed their identities:

"And at that moment I came to the notion of storytelling as my lifework" (Sobol 1994a:384).

"The most wonderful thing happened to me today: I have found out who I am! I'm a storyteller" (Sobol 1994a:132).

"And that's when I knew. I just told people, 'I'm a storyteller.' And that's what I've been doing ever since. I've never turned my back on that. I haven't had a regular paying job with benefits since" (Sobol 1994a:335-336).

Most of the responses I heard at the retreat, however, were not phrased in such a dramatic way. When I asked participants if there had been a particular moment when they recognized themselves as story-tellers, they did not make the pronouncements Sobol and I were familiar with. Their "vocational narratives" were less focused on partic-ular moments, more introspective. I guessed that the more intimate context of the retreat setting influenced the nature of their replies so I broadened the base by putting notices in storytelling newsletters in both Canada and the United States. All those who answered had already assumed their identities as tellers. Their responses, like those I had heard at the retreat, were retrospective rather than dramatic, look-ing back to the experiences they identified as formative moments. Some found these moments in childhood storytelling experiences and others recalled later periods of their development. All understood that they had been storytellers for some time and that their identity had evolved with their artistic (and life) experiences. It is clear from the replies that these particular tellers had undergone lengthy apprentice-ships before becoming fully conscious of themselves as public performers.[5]

Mary-Eileen McClear, from West Baden, Ontario, recalled taking her older sister's white mittens at age eight. She told her friends that her own mittens had turned from black to white because they were made of the fur of ermines, who turn white in winter. She saw with some surprise that she had become a storyteller in their eyes and explained: "I wasn't trying to impress them, or to lie. I remember thinking of it as a challenge: how much would they believe, how well could I convince them?"

Nan Brien remembered friends begging for stories when she was twelve. "They would chant, 'Nan! Tell us a story,' and she complied. "At that time of my life, I knew that I was a big sister, a babysitter, a camper, and now best of all, a storyteller."

As a teenager Celia Lottridge decided on her own to entertain a group of children in wheelchairs at an afternoon party, but at this time she was already an experienced raconteur from having entertained her younger sister with stories when they were twelve and five, respective-ly: "I often told stories to her in the back seat of the car as we drove somewhere. I have no idea whether anyone else listened but Lucy cer-tainly did."

Carol McGirr, a Toronto school librarian specializing in lengthy sagas and myths whose words and story appear here in Section II, Chapter 4, told me an epic tale about discovering the essence of story-telling when she decided, at age six, to memorize *Peter Rabbit* so that she would still have the story even when she no longer had the book: "I'm sure the kids in the neighborhood were sick of Peter Rabbit. We'd be out in the yard playing ball and then we'd sit down to rest, and I'd start, 'Once upon a time there were four little Rabbits who lived with their mother under the roots of an old fir tree, and their names were Flopsy, Mopsy, Cottontail, and Peter.' And it would go on and on until I finished the whole story" (taped interview in Fredericton, New Brunswick, February, 1994).

Childhood memories framed the later development of Mary-Eileen, Nan, Celia, and Carol, providing them with the first of many other moments of recognition as storytelling became part of their professional lives. In contrast, George Blake grew up surrounded by stories in Jamaica but his early storytelling background did not at first come to mind when he emigrated to Canada. He says, "I never heard the term 'storyteller' when I was a boy in Jamaica, though I was exposed to hearing many stories from 'elders,' teachers, and my contemporaries." He could not understand why urban tellers were so concerned about calling themselves storytellers, until he experienced his own moment of recognition, as an adult in Canada: "Some weeks after I had told stories at my local public library (to an adult audience) a woman approached me in a store and asked, 'Aren't you the storyteller who was at the library?' That was when I received my identity as a storyteller."

Others reported similar responses that fostered their self-recognition. Lynn Williams was surprised at the effect her first story had when she told it as part of her job as interpreter at an historic house in London, Ontario: "I had learned a suitable version of the legend of the Blue Willow and told it at the next opportunity. The children were captivated and I was overwhelmed at the intensity of their attention to the story. I felt the power of storytelling as a teller and it was an inspiring sensation."

Several people could recall specific individuals who not only recognized what they were doing but named it. Canadian writer and performer Robert Munsch, for example, described an incident in 1979 in which he was entertaining two children in a car on the way to the airport. He reported the boy, Otis, saying, "You're a storyteller. You're a *fancy* storyteller." He had considered storytelling to be hobby but began to take it more seriously: "From that point on I decided that that's what I had become and that's what I was going to be" (letter, February 15, 1991). This was the kind of anecdote I had heard from various American tellers describing how the title "storyteller" had been conferred on them by a listener, usually told in legend style.

Yet even after experiencing such an affirmation of the potency of directly related narratives tellers still mentioned a sense of inadequacy once the actual storytelling event ended. Carol Howe was initially thrilled by her first performance but then expressed ambivalence: "Several people came up afterward to tell me how much the story meant to them—and for the rest of the evening I felt like a storyteller. The next day I knew only that I could tell stories." She added, "The response is crucial—you can't be a storyteller with no audience."

For Mary-Eileen McClear the immediacy of storytelling events influenced her sense of social identity: "It's not something I consciously think about or question until someone questions me and then I begin to wonder. Am I really a storyteller, am I fooling myself, cheating the people who come to hear a 'real' storyteller?" The doubt can run riot until the next time I tell a story."

Paula Graham, a high school math and science teacher, said she had been using stories in class for years yet still felt uneasy calling herself a storyteller, though her listeners, in this case her high school students, saw her as one: "It's gradual. I'm becoming aware. I sometimes feel like a pretender to the title of storyteller. Even though the 'nature of the beast' is to be a storyteller, I don't usually see myself as one—but my students do."

Indeed, listeners play a role even when they are not at all aware of it. This is central in oral societies where narrating is still highly regarded and storytelling events still offer ample contexts for human creativity. In organized storytelling, however, the teller assumes (often by default) more responsibility than the community in developing a social identity because storytelling is not widely regarded as a performing art. This means that the opportunities for formal narration are limited and must be sought out or even created by the performers, who cannot simply wait for spontaneous storytelling events to occur. Even though more tellers and listeners now recognize storytelling as a performance art, self-recognition is still problematic. Social identity does not arise from the community as a whole as it does in a more traditional context. Instead, tellers develop their sense of vocation from their experiences in a series of storytelling events. They are led to self-definition by different groups of listeners who may not, in a meaningful sense of the word, form a community at all and who may be quite inexperienced about the esthetics and the dynamics of oral performance.

As we have already seen, those who tell stories as part of their occupation are often confused about their possible identity as tellers. Alice Bur from Mississauga, Ontario, began to use storytelling to develop new teaching techniques; she was comfortable narrating in her own classroom, but ambivalent about regarding herself as a storyteller outside of it: "Sometimes I think I'll give up teaching and perhaps go into classrooms in a new capacity—as a storyteller! But then once again I come back to the reluctance I feel about moving in that direction. I don't want to be a storyteller/performer. I don't feel ready."

Her sense of not being prepared is a part of the challenge of developing a social identity. Since the community at large does not offer what Adams calls "sufficient opportunity to practice the craft," which is how storytelling is learned in traditional contexts, urban tellers must learn in other ways. They can take workshops and classes but this does not guarantee performance opportunities. Identity comes only from on-going direct experience, constant interaction between listeners and tellers. Despite statements to the contrary, no one can confer the title of "storyteller" on anyone else, though such pronouncements may help tellers see themselves in a new light.

The growth of storytelling as a money-making profession has caused full-time tellers to rethink their social identities. As Mary-Eileen McClear put it earlier, she was worried that she was not, in fact, a "real" storyteller. I heard similar responses from other retreat participants who did not want to lose their initial exuberance for storytelling in order to become self-supporting professional performers.[6] Furthermore, some people who opportunistically describe themselves as professional storytellers in directories and publicity brochures may not have much experience in storytelling events at all. As Ruth Stotter, a performer who also heads a certificate program in storytelling, notes: "Anyone who takes a class or sometimes even a single workshop can declare themselves a storyteller and begin to charge for their service. How do we distinguish between amateurs and professionals then, especially since there are many misconceptions about what storytelling is and is not?"[7] This was not the case in the earlier history of the profession, when both library and educational professions offered training programs that prepared students for storytelling in a disciplined way.

While my formal interview sample here is small, I have supplemented it with material found in other sources; interviews conducted by Joseph Sobol, past issues of the journal and newsletter published by the National Storytelling Association, performer directories and festival programs, and my own experiences with many tellers and listeners. Directories and programs portray tellers in a less ambivalent light than have the personal letters quoted above, since they are usually self-descriptions intended to publicize the performer. Thus dilemmas in the development of social identity seem to disappear in such writings. For example, we learn that Marylyn Peringer began her two-decade career as a teller gradually, through her teaching experiences and an interest in French: "[I am a] former high school English teacher; later studies in French language and literature, including a year in Paris, paved the way for my interest in French-Canadian folktales and legends which I now tell bilingually or all in French" (*Canadian Storytelling Directory* 1997/98:44). Her earlier experiences in teaching encouraged Marylyn to be sensitive to the educational aspects of stories, as we will see later (Section II).

In the same directory Bob Barton wrote that storytelling "grew out of my experiences as a classroom teacher (English/Dramatic Arts)" and added that "now, as a full-time teller, I am still committed to supporting classroom teachers in their work with stories in the classroom" (*Canadian Storytelling Directory* 1997/98:39). He seems to down-play his background in drama here, though we will see in Section II how central this was in his development.

Librarian and storyteller Alice Kane described her reluctant beginnings as a storyteller as part of her career:

> This was not for me; I was shy, I stammered. Suddenly the time [of training] had passed, I had been to library school. I was a children's librarian. I had well defined duties, and one of them was to learn and tell stories (Kane 1990:63).

Despite her resistance, Alice Kane gained experience (along with her colleagues), telling stories "with dry mouths and shaky knees." She became a mainstay of library storytelling in the Toronto area for many years, an inspiration to countless numbers of tellers and listeners.

For others, storytelling was a less predictable vocation. Canadian writer and teller Joan Buchanan described an experience similar to one reported by many of the tellers interviewed by Sobol—that of being unexpectedly challenged to tell stories. Joan, who wrote, "I can remember distinctly the moment I became a storyteller," described going to an Australian storytelling event where the invited storyteller had not yet arrived and children were waiting. A friend said, "Joan, you're a writer, you can do some stories for the kids, can't you?" She did not hesitate long, and later reported enthusiastically: "I found that I could do it. I was a storyteller!" (letter, 10 Dec. 1990)

Oklahoma teller Fran Stallings reported a similar challenge when early in her performing career she was invited by a teacher to tell the entire *Odyssey* over a span of several months. She already had a number of years of experience, "but those months with *The Odyssey* put me in touch with something more huge, more powerful, and old than any little story I had played with before. It was certainly not the first time I was called 'a storyteller.' Better perhaps to say that it was the first time the storyteller called to *me*" (letter, 5 Dec. 1990). Joan and Fran were certainly not novices when they were "called," in this case literally, to take the floor, but these experiences did set them on a firmer path toward platform storytelling as a more regular activity.

Storytelling directories and festival programs are a key source of expressed identity, as we have seen above. In addition to providing descriptions most often written by the tellers themselves (even when this is expressed in third person) these entries allow us to observe the evolution of tellers' identities over time as they emphasize different aspects of their professional persona—and also the stability of those identities. Here are Toronto festival program write-ups for Bob Barton, who has appeared at many of these annual festivals.[8] In the 1979 festival program he provided an expansive entry:

> Thanks to the early advice and guidance of Bill Moore, who was at that time Supervisor of Oral English for the Hamilton Board of Education, I learned how to involve children in stories in an active, oral way. A decade later as an English Consultant involved in assisting teachers with the teaching of dramatic arts, I discovered that story was one of the most valuable structures available to the teacher as a starting point for drama. Re-enacting a story was not the point so much as finding ways to approach the story which would help to deepen the children's understanding of the original story (Toronto Storytelling festival program 1979:3).

Bob's role in "assisting teachers" was such a strong theme for him that it was repeated almost two decades later in his directory entry, where he emphasized that he was "still committed to supporting teachers in their work with stories in the classroom" (*Canadian Storytelling Directory* 1997/98:39). After his lengthy entry in the 1979 festival program, Bob became consistently more succinct, identifying himself simply as "a teacher ... of dramatic arts" (1981) and as "a founding member of the Storytellers School of Toronto" (1985 and 1987 and later programs). In 1988 he began to move more regularly beyond his local community after the publication of two books on storytelling and to "travel throughout Canada and the United States as a storyteller and language arts consultant." By 1991 he was on the Board of Directors of NAPPS (now NSA) and was travelling so frequently that he was often not in Toronto for the festival. In 1995 he described himself as travelling "widely to offer workshops and tell literary and traditional stories," and as "the author of children's books and books on storytelling." This festival featured Bob and another author at a major book-launch, underlining his growing identity as an author. In the 1997 program he said, simply: "Bob Barton has been performing in festivals and schools since 1979. He is also the author of several books for children and adults."

It is not surprising that we saw no dramatic changes in his write-ups. Bob had already been an experienced performer for more than two decades, and was firmly established in his identity as author, educator, and teller. We might expect to see more fluctuation in the self-description of a teller who was just beginning, trying to find new ways of expressing a developing identity as it evolved over the years.

Not all experienced tellers settle into such a comfortable sense of identity, however. For example, here are descriptions of Joan Bodger, written over a period of several years in Toronto festival programs:

(1979) For more than thirty years I have been telling stories professionally. In the 1960s I started telling stories on street corners in New York, and in the same period began using stories in a therapeutic setting. Nowadays I use stories in my Gestalt practice (mostly with adults). In my other, secret life I accept straight storytelling gigs all over North America.

(1981) Author of "Clever-Lazy, The Girl Who Invented Herself," she [Joan] weaves folklore into her life and writing.

(1985) Comes from the kind of family that would make a story out of a shopping list. Founding member of the Storytellers School.

(1988, 1989 and 1991) Joan Bodger "turned professional" in 1948. Ten years ago she helped create the Festival and The

Storytellers School of Toronto. She has told stories in Australia, Japan, Jordan, and the British Isles and the U.S.

(1995) Joan Bodger has been a storyteller for almost fifty years. She is writing a book about the life she has lived and the stories she has told, how they interact.

She emphasized a different aspect of her storytelling persona with every entry, except for three years when she repeats the same write-up with minor changes (she adds "and the U.S." to her storytelling travels as an afterthought, since she had certainly done a lot of workshops and performances there before 1989). In 1979 she was a street performer and a therapist, in 1981 an author, in 1985 a member of a creative family and a founding member of the Storytellers School, in 1988-91 she was a pioneer and a traveller, and in 1995 she was summing up her life. Of all the entries I have read, Joan Bodger's came closest to narrating the life of the teller in short bursts of prose, each one revealing a different place on her map of experience.

I noted earlier that these moments of recognition are often told as narratives that recount experiences from specific storytelling events. These "vocational narratives," as Sobol called them, frequently enter tellers' repertoires as preambles to their performances, then spread as legendary narratives to other tellers. Sometimes these accounts may even be associated with traditional stories, making them stories within stories within stories. Canadian teller Ted Stone wrote to me about American teller Cynthia Orr, for whom the fable of "The Grasshopper and the Ant" was a formative metaphor: "She would remember that story and then would be afraid to try because she didn't want to starve like the grasshopper. One day she told a friend, who said 'But Cynthia, that story was told by an ant.' So she became a storyteller, and made a rather nice story out of how she became one" (letter, January 14, 1991).

The grasshopper, not unlike free-lance storytellers, is in danger of starving because he does not behave like a practical ant. Many performers mentioned here are understandably hesitant, even after some years of experience in storytelling events, because storytelling is an uncertain profession that does not guarantee a steady income—or a safe cache of winter food. One such teller observed that "very few of us in this evolving role of storyteller are paid enough money to live on, which makes issues of financial reimbursement even more complex—

and brings us back to the confusing modern role of storyteller" (Birch/Heckler 1996:34).

Such ambivalence about assuming a social identity as a teller is rarely found among those growing up in an oral milieu, where narrating was—ideally—a more casual event. Here money was not usually a primary motivation, even when collectors offered to pay for what they took away. In a society such as ours, however, formal storytelling is less spontaneous, and also less respected as an art than in traditional oral milieus; opportunities for telling stories professionally often have to be sought out. Also, professional training is less developed than for other performing arts. It is not surprising that many feel unsure of their social identity as tellers.

Yet despite the problems and challenges, or maybe even because of them, the number of people who identify themselves as tellers continues to rise steadily. Alice Kane, who began as a library storyteller in the first quarter of the twentieth century, commented on this continuing vitality:

> In a day of highly efficient communication such as the world has ever known before, storytelling remains the most effective form of communication. Through storytelling strangers can converse. Even the shyest and most reticent can speak from the heart, and the listener, even the silent listener, responds completely—and no two in exactly the same way (Kane 1990:68).

The ever-emergent quality of face-to-face experiences is a powerful characteristic of actual storytelling events. Within the social and artistic context of these events tellers begin to establish and develop their identities. In a positive light, the hesitancy of tellers cited here reflects the on-going evolution of storytelling as a developing profession, with constantly changing means of establishing standards and limits. In Section II we will meet several tellers whose individual identities and storytelling preferences have unfolded over years of experience in one or the other of the four major streams, and within a recognizable storytelling community.

Notes

1 A brief version of this chapter was presented as a paper at the American Speech Communication Association in Atlanta, Georgia in 1991 and later printed in *The Appleseed Quarterly* published by the Storytellers School of Toronto in 1994 (vol. 4, no. 1, pp. 14-19). A fuller version was prepared for a special issue of *Western Folklore* in honor of Robert Georges, to appear in 1998.

2 I stress this inclusiveness because many folklorists did not considered organized storytelling to be a proper subject for academic research; Georges was one of the first folklorists to offer a path of investigation that opened the way for such an approach.

3 Robert Adams, in *Social Identity of a Japanese Storyteller* (Adams 1972), devotes much of his dissertation to the lifetime development of Mrs. Watanabe, a skilled oral narrator who learned to read Japanese when she lost her hearing at age 67 so she could continue learning stories from books. Adams was intrigued to discover that she had taken the Grimm tales into her repertoire, though they were not immediately recognizable as European tales because Mrs. Watanabe adapted them very successfully to her own narrative traditions.

4 Joseph Sobol's interviews provide a wealth of this kind of information in both breadth and depth. He cites numerous instances of formative identity stories ("And that's when I knew I was a storyteller"), for which I have only anecdotal information.

5 Those who answered my published request by letter are cited by letter and date. Uncited material is from the oral and written responses gathered at the retreat.

6 In fact, there seem to be only a handful of self-supporting tellers from among the hundreds of people who list themselves in the National Storytelling Directory. Sobol estimated that about 50 tellers he knew actually supported themselves through storytelling. In Toronto there are only a handful who draw most of their livelihood from storytelling engagements. Others either tell stories as part of another vocation (most notably teaching and library work) or have another source of income so that they need not rely on performing to support them.

7 Ruth Stotter was the discussant on a panel at the American Speech Communication Association in Atlanta, Georgia in 1991. Her comments were in response to four papers describing how people assumed their identities as storytellers,

8 The *Canadian Storytelling Directory* had published only three editions as of this writing in 1997, so I supplemented self-descriptions from program write-ups from the Toronto festival from 1979 to 1995. *The National Storytelling Directory* (from the National Storytelling Association) printed its first directory in 1984, so this was a rich source of comparative information for American tellers.

SECTION II: INDIVIDUAL TELLERS AND TALES

I N the previous section we saw how important organized gatherings have been for individual tellers and for the continuing development of storytelling. In this section we meet several experienced tellers loosely representing the four major streams of organized storytelling: traditional, theatrical, library-educational, and therapeutic-spiritual.

For example, Joe Neil MacNeil was a traditional narrator from a Gaelic-speaking community on Cape Breton Island in Nova Scotia who adapted oral narrating to the contemporary concert stage. In contrast, Bob Barton's experiences evolved from his use of the techniques of creative drama in his school classes and Stewart Cameron was a professional performer with dramatic style.

Marylyn Peringer and Carol McGirr began telling folktales as part of their teaching careers and their performance style was much more low-key and conversational, a mark of their place in the library-educational stream. Similarly, Susan Gordon developed her storytelling in therapeutic contexts that privileged story over performance. It is more difficult to place Marvyne Jenoff, writer and poet, who frequently works with fables and folktales, and myself, a folklorist specializing in traditional tales; we represent the "other" category into which many tellers might place themselves.

Each chapter concludes with a full story text from these tellers; I suggest enjoying these stories before reading the interviews, in order to read the commentary in perspective.

ONE

CREATIVE DRAMA
AND STORYTELLING

S CHOLARS interested in folktales have pondered the nature of
stories and storytelling since the Grimms first attempted to rein-
terpret oral tales. Written literature was the paradigm from the
beginning, a model against which "folk" creativity was compared and
contrasted; the literary ideal continues to influence narrative scholars,
even those who broke away from the text-oriented studies of earlier
decades and worked directly with traditional oral narrators.

A literary approach puts stress on the mode of expression, whether
poetry or prose; on genre, whether anecdote or epic, fable or tale,
myth or legend; and on the "authors" or tellers, and their relationship
to their stories and to the community in which they live and perform.
Written literature is still used as a paradigm, even by folklorists. For
example, Henry Glassie's careful study of Irish narrators in
Ballymenone observes that "two modes make stories," and that these
modes are the literary genres of prose and poetry (Glassie 1982:43).

Glassie and other scholars would certainly agree that storytelling is,
in addition to poetry and prose, a dramatic art. This aspect was most
strongly emphasized by folklorists who considered storytelling events
in the context of living performances, where the interaction between
tellers and listeners was central instead of incidental (Georges 1967,
Bauman 1984). When stories are seen in this setting, the teller who is
performing, however casually, is "on stage," and the dynamics of creativity shift from literary to dramatic. It is not only the story that is
essential, but the whole rich scope of its momentary existence for
tellers and listeners. A dramatic approach considers the multi-dimensional action of an on-going event: movement, sound, and
interaction—between characters as well as between teller and audience.

There is a difference, of course, between dramatic storytelling and
storytelling as a dramatic art. The first describes a style of narration,

while the second encompasses all storytelling regardless of performance style. These two arts are also closely intertwined, of course, and in the Toronto community are well represented by performers like Leslie Robbins and Helen Carmichael Porter. Leslie was instrumental in founding Jewish Storytelling Arts, and Helen founded the National Storytelling Theatre. Each teller mentioned in this book is engaged in a dramatic art, though not all are distinctively dramatic in style.

Organized storytelling and creative drama both gained their initial momentum within school and library contexts, and both experienced a rush of activity in the 1970s as they began to grow beyond child-oriented milieus. In order to find a more personal view on the connections between creative drama and storytelling, I sought a storyteller with a background in creative drama. Bob Barton, one of the founding members of the Storytellers School of Toronto, was an ideal model. As an early participant in the fast growing Toronto community, he was thoroughly immersed in an artistic environment in which an understated "library" style of performance was strongly favored over dramatic storytelling.[1] I was curious to learn how Bob Barton was able to grow and flourish in these circumstances.

I had observed Bob in performances and workshops in Winnipeg and Toronto and read his two books on storytelling techniques, and over the years we had casually discussed stories and storytelling.[2] I interviewed him once in 1993 about his role as a founding member of the Toronto storytelling community, where I learned more about his background in dramatic arts. He was an obvious choice when I was looking for a storyteller with theatrical interests, and he agreed to a second interview in 1995. Both interviews were taped in his Toronto home.

I had asked Bob when he heard his first platform performer, that is, someone telling stories outside of a school or library context. He described his initial experience with Brother Blue, a flamboyant street performer turned concert-stage teller.[3] This was in 1976, years after Bob had been working with stories and creative drama as a teacher. By coincidence, Brother Blue was also the first platform performer I had seen, when he was a featured storyteller at the national meeting of the Canadian Library conference in 1974. I understood why he caught Bob's attention. He was dressed in colorfully patched blue clothing from head to toe, with butterflies painted on his hands and bells that chimed with every movement and a harmonica that he used to punctuate his stories. He danced, sang, and told his own personal stories along with his unusual reinterpretations of folktales. His version of "Little Red Riding Hood" was set in the streets of Philadelphia and featured a resourceful little girl who used karate on the "wolf" who pursued her. Some of the librarians and teachers in attendance were intrigued, but many were dismayed by his idiosyncratic presentations. One commented, "Well, this is certainly interesting, but is it really storytelling?" Since I had never seen a "professional" teller before, nor did I know that there was a long tradition of library storytelling, I was not sure what she meant.

I still pondered the question as I began to ask Bob Barton about storytelling and drama. Was this really storytelling? Bob began by describing his first appearance on a public stage where he had an audience of adults instead of the children he was used to entertaining. This event took place in 1976 during a week-long artists' residency at Art Park in Lewiston, New York. He had been recommended by Joan Bodger, another Toronto-area teller who had heard that Bob was working with storytelling as part of his teaching. He had never performed for an adult audience before, nor had he seen a professional performer like Brother Blue before—or since. As he recalled the moment that still echoed as a turning point in his life, his conversational tone took a new cadence, becoming almost a rhythmic chant:

> The first summer I would be there
> I would share the stage for seven days
> with Brother Blue.
> And that was my "Baptism of Fire."

Bob understood, as had the librarians at the Winnipeg conference, that this very theatrical performer was not to everyone's taste: "At times he scared away more of his audience than he ever held," Bob said, "but I saw him tell some quite remarkable stories, and I saw an incredible spirit that I would not ever see again, anywhere."

This auspicious beginning was one in a series of unexpected adventures in Bob's long journey in dramatic storytelling, which he described as "following my nose, and just stumbling into the most wonderful situations." It is coincidental yet significant that a highly dramatic American performer influenced Bob's view of what storytelling was and could be. Another American performer, Diane Wolkstein, also provided steady support and guidance. Bob Barton's long career as teacher, storyteller, workshop leader, and author is a living example of the overlapping boundaries between narrative and theatrical arts.

His storytelling is a response to the librarian's appraisal of Brother Blue: is it "really storytelling" when a performer acts out unconventional stories, complete with costumes, props, musical instruments, dramatic voices, and other tools of the dramatic arts? The bias hidden in this question grows directly from the strong influence of library/educational storytelling and its idealization of a traditional style that downplayed theatricality; the exemplary model in the library tradition favored "pure" storytelling that used only the voice as the medium of presentation with no facial expressions or bodily gestures, and certainly no costumes or props. The effects of this tradition are still strong. An American teller commented on theatrical storytelling after attending a New England storytelling conference:

> The rapid growth of festivals fosters Storyteller-as-stage-performer. In Boston I was astounded at the number of folks who not only didn't "discover" storytelling until late in professional life, but who came from a background in theater, mime, and/or contemporary literature. They excel in presenting polished performances of original postmodern personal experience stories, akin to small press academic fiction. I found it interesting to see just how far the boundaries of "storytelling" could stretch (letter, Fran Stallings, March 17, 1992).

When I raised the issue of this "stretch" of storytelling as a theatrical production with Bob Barton, he suggested politely that I was going around in circles and missing the point: looking at a style of performance out of context would not reveal the close connections between storytelling and creative drama; both arose as expressive forms that were, at first, utilized to lead children into fresh and imaginative ways of experiencing literature and drama. Both storytelling and creative drama evolved within and then moved beyond educational contexts as the revival gained prominence in the 1970s. Bob offered his own personal story as a living example of the parallel growth of storytelling and creative drama, which he did not regard as separate artistic genres.

Throughout the interview Bob described the unexpected events that serendipitously drew him into storytelling, "flying by the seat of my pants," as he described it. This kind of personal narrative is common with tellers whose now-successful careers took sudden flight in the

1970s when storytelling as a serious art form was just beginning to blossom. Bob, like many others, found himself being described as a storyteller and put on stage to perform before he was quite certain "what this storytelling thing was all about."

In both performances and workshops Bob used the dramatic techniques of voice modulation, facial expressions, and enthusiastic gestures and body movement to bring his stories to life. He acted out his stories instead of just telling them, stepping in and out of the roles of the characters without losing his essential role as narrator. It was clear to me from observing him in performance that his long experience in the educational field of creative drama took him along a path quite different from the more reserved "library" style of the Toronto storytelling community—and indeed many other communities in North America.

Bob challenged my assumptions about theatrical telling when he pointed out that creative drama and dramatic storytelling are not the same; creative drama focuses on the process of story-making while dramatic performances work toward a scripted, rehearsed, and polished final production. "In the schools drama had become too focused on staging something," Bob observed. School productions of scripted stories did not allow full participation; once roles were assigned and rehearsals began, only the few students chosen to participate got direct benefit from the productions. Creative drama developed in the educational field as a challenge to the staged theatrical productions: "We shifted the emphasis away from putting stuff on, getting that final product." It was the actual process of spoken creativity that became more central. Using the techniques of creative drama, a story was explored from many different angles: retelling it from the point of view of other characters or even objects (for example, the bean in "Jack and the Beanstalk"); telling it in a group using shifting narrative perspectives; drawing a rough map of the story and walking through it.

My own direct experience with creative drama and storytelling came in a workshop Bob conducted in Winnipeg in the fall of 1994. At his instructions we divided into small groups and chose roles in an historical legend Bob had just told. He handed us printed texts but we were told not to work from the script or to act out the story; instead we were to retell it from another point of view. This opened up further potential depths of meaning and interaction. We also sang parts of the story, changed the ending, and pretended that we were going to perform it as a group for different audiences—children or adults, for example. If we had been in one of Bob's school classes instead of at an afternoon workshop, we would have taken the next step and begun to act out our roles, continuing to play with them in order to see fresh possibilities of interpretation. After this brief experience I began to understand how such tactics for enriching stories might allow tellers to experience at least a taste of what traditional narrators might encounter through hearing stories told over and over, in varied contexts and from the viewpoints and personal styles of different tellers. Bob recognized this himself when he commented: "I don't have the good fortune to be getting that—hearing lots of different versions of a story—so I have to give it out and then get it back." He tells a story, has people work with it, and is able to, as he puts it, "get it back" in as many different versions as there are people in attendance. While this does not offer the depth and breadth of hearing a story and its variant tellings in oral tradition, it does break a story out of the rigidity of the single text concept we are accustomed to from the printed page.

When I saw Bob in Toronto later that year I asked if he would discuss storytelling as a dramatic art. He agreed. When I appeared with tape recorder in hand we began to talk casually about storytelling and different performers we had met. Bob said that he had begun to use storytelling from the very beginning of his teaching career, before he was aware of either storytelling or creative drama as expressive arts:

> In the early days I wasn't so much telling the stories as reading the stories, but then as I began to know the stories I would narrate them. I'd hold a book in my hand but I'd tell them. And I can't remember that day when the book went down and would never be picked up again. It just evolved.

This gradual "evolution" began with one of the many unexpected challenges early in his teaching, when he was asked to set up a program for intermediate students:

> I was sent to an inner city school. It was an intermediate school, grade seven and eight students, something like 600 students in all. The instructions from the superintendent were: "These children do not like to read. Your job is to make them love it."

When I asked how he came to use storytelling—that is, not just reading stories aloud but bringing them to life—he repeated that he was "stumbling along," just "following his nose." He insisted that he had been given no further direction about what he was to do other than to "go in there and make them love stories," which has been his guiding principle ever since: "I had no philosophy, I had no pedagogy, I had nothing. I was a pretty inexperienced and ignorant person but I had enough drive, and some sort of sense, of what worked and how to keep it going."

He began by doing dramatic recitations from Chaucer in Middle English, which intrigued his students because they had never heard anything like that before. They were surprised at the story, at the language, and most of all at the dramatic manner of presentation: "'Well,' I said, 'that's how stories were told hundreds of years ago, and that's what English sounded like.' 'You're kidding!' 'No.' And so that was the beginning."

He continued with Chaucer until he told all of the stories, at first reciting them word-for-word "because I didn't know anything about storytelling then." Eventually Bob began to tell them in his own way: "These kids just ate it up. It was the most unusual thing that ever happened. And I realized that as soon as I went anywhere near those readers, these text books of stories, the place just deadened like a pall of gloom fell over it."

As Bob's reputation as an innovator spread, he was asked to introduce other imaginative programs. He was inspired by the influence of William Moore, Oral English Supervisor in the Hamilton school district, who "made language come alive out loud." This was Bob's first training in dramatic techniques: "We would all eventually learn from him how to do choral speaking, quite dramatic choral speaking. I think it was in the sharing of words out loud with the children, reading from poetry, reading from scripts, from texts, that I began to develop my own interests and my own skills in using words."

He was still following his nose and using, he says, "everything I could—the radio, records, everything that had an oral dimension." As a result, the students in his classes were participating fully in what his was doing instead of passively sitting, taking notes, or answering study questions. "I wasn't very good with the teaching, but I was learning a great deal about oral literature and literature in performance," Bob observed.

Two years later he was asked to teach speech and drama, and though he still felt unprepared he accepted the task and began to use the plays written for school productions. After trying several he decided that the plays were not good enough, and decided to try doing original scripts. "And that's when we started to do stories. We would take a story and say, 'Now how can we bring this story to life?'" Their production was so successful that it toured the city. At that point Bob decided that elaborately staged presentations of scripted plays were not what he wanted to. He began to have his students look at folktales, asking again how these might be adapted for dramatic presentation. He continued innovative techniques that would come to be called creative drama, inspired by the work of Winnifred Ward in the United States. By the late 1970s he was working with David Booth and they found themselves moving away from Ward's view of creative drama as the enactment of a story's plot. They called this new approach "storydrama":

> By now our work focused on getting beneath the words to mine the rich subtext of the story. Instead of "doing the story" we were making new stories based on themes, characters or events found in the story. This would involve everything from elaborating moments not fully developed in the story to projecting beyond the story or borrowing a character from the story to examine in the light of a new situation (letter, August 1995).

As a result of his earlier work Bob was asked to teach in an experimental program entitled "The Teaching of English With an Oral and Dramatic Approach." In that program and in others that Bob would set up in coming years he focused on stories rather than plays: "stories were the heart of the work, the oral exploration and the relating of those stories in dramatic form." Bob not only kept this work centered on stories, but also on the participatory nature of the process of developing a dramatic event from a single folktale. This has guided him all along, and he warmly recalls his initial enthusiasm at understanding the creative nature of this approach to drama: "Some of the most exciting work was in the development and the build-up, and when we started with a story and we had to determine how we could retell that story in our own way, using 35 of us all together so that everybody had something to do—that's what turned me around." Bob quickly became known as a teacher who worked with storytelling; since Toronto already had a strong tradition of library and educational storytelling, Bob's reputation spread beyond the school classroom. What guided him into storytelling was a preference for folktales over scripted plays, an absorption with process over product, and a firm commitment to full participation for all performers rather than starring roles for a few.

Storytellers challenged Bob with the query, "But is this storytelling?" Actors and directors asked him, "But is this theater?" He always seemed to be on the edge of one or the other. The apparent contradiction between creative drama and staged theatrical productions was "a raging debate" for several years. It subsided eventually, when, as he notes, "people realized that what we were really talking about was actually a continuum and steps along a continuum; so there were no great divides, and no need to clobber people because you didn't like what they were doing that ran against your philosophy." What is true for theater is equally true for storytelling; it is more helpful to think in terms of a spectrum than an either/or polarity, as Carol Birch and other tellers have insisted (Birch/Heckler 1996).

Let us come back to Bob's observations that the lasting values of theater and storytelling are akin—that is, the active engagement of those present, performers and listeners alike. Both storytelling and drama immerse the audience in the artistic creation, guiding them into a world of imagination. In storytelling, participation takes place in the minds of teller and listeners; they provide the costumes, props, and scenery, as well as the voices, appearance, facial features, bodily movements, and all aspects of each character. In dramatic telling, the story takes place on the world of the stage, with everything already in place, yet the audience brings the production alive in their own minds. Creative drama is between these two, using theatrical tools to bring stories to life but stressing the spontaneity and changeability of the process; the on-going imaginative process is as important as a final rehearsed production.

It is difficult for folklorists to describe a multi-dimensional storytelling event; it is even more of a challenge to describe the elusive process of creative drama and storytelling. Bob Barton weaves a discussion of this process around his work with a little-known Norwegian tale, "The Honest Penny," from a nineteenth-century English translation.[4] Because it was an unusual story marked by interesting twists and turns, and because it was written in the elaborate literary style of the nineteenth century, it took Bob a year just to learn it well enough to use in workshops and performances. What excited him most was that people began to see, as he had, that this was a compelling story.

The story came to life through the interaction experienced in Bob's workshops, where participants were asked to draw parts of the story, retell it from other points of view, and play with different characters and their motivations. Bob credited this process with inspiring him to "go back and take a moment and completely rethink that story." I quote him fully here to offer a comparison for the complete text that follows this chapter.

Like in the "The Honest Penny" this boy is sent out by his mother to look for firewood, and he's collected it and is on his way home when he comes across this crooked stone that's all covered with frost. And he says, "Poor little stone, you're all white and pale. I believe you're frozen to death. And he throws down the wood and takes off his coat and he wraps his coat around the stone—and then he pops off on his way home. When his mother sees him coming without his coat she says,

"What on earth are you doing running around in winter without your coat?"

And he tells her, and he's very excited:

"I found this stone and it was all white and pale and I gave it my coat!"

And she says,

"You featherhead! Do you really believe that stones can freeze? Maybe this will teach you a lesson, you'd better pay attention. You look to thyself and take care of thyself. Nobody cares for thee. You've got to go back and get that coat."

So he goes back to get the coat and he's amazed to discover that the stone has lifted itself and turned itself, and where the stone was laying is a box of silver coins. He looks at that and he says to himself,

"Well, that's stolen money, no doubt about it. Nobody who comes by money honestly hides it under stones." So he picks up the money, takes it down to the lake and throws it in. As the money is sinking to the bottom of the lake, one penny floats to the top. "Now there," he says, "that's an honest penny, because what's honest floats."

Now when his mother hears about the money she throws him out!

"You're an absolute fool! I've tried to teach you and teach you, look to thyself and take care of thyself," and on and on she goes. And she throws him out.

Bob stopped at that point to observe that when he asked people in workshops to draw a scene from the story, they often focused on the stone, filling a whole page with it, remarking to him: "This is really the pivot for the entire story. Everything hinges on this moment." As he listened to their descriptions, he began to reexamine a puzzling place in the story where the boy throws away the treasure that the stone has revealed to him. This incident became more and more central for him as he continued to work with the story: "This is literally the moment of truth. The boy looks at the money and he says, 'that's stolen,' and he throws it away. He throws it all away." For Bob this was so central that he stopped telling me the story and began to summarize it instead.

> And at that point the boy is put to one side and the story continues without him. And this is a remarkable thing about this story—he does not go on the journey himself, he does not go on the quest. He sits back and waits for the results of the quest. All he does is to take that penny and give it to a merchant who has taken him in and asks him to buy him something, because he knows that it's honest money. And this merchant will have to go through temptation after temptation after temptation, each time getting himself in deeper and deeper trouble.

The process of recreating this story was so essential that Bob moved away from the story and into what he learned about it from his workshops and from his long years drama training in schools. He discovered that in the workshop process he could see the story from the divergent perspectives of the participants: "Until I begin to take a story into the audience and literally give it to them, and have them tell it back to me, I don't begin to know what's in it. I get the most amazing discussions as people see that they've missed something entirely. So I sit back and I just watch all this, direct it a little bit and guide it along."

He emphasized several times that this allowed him to learn "in ways I could never do just by myself." I mentioned to Bob that when he let himself "sit back and just watch," he instinctively emulated the boy in the story who "sits back and waits for the results of the quest." Until I pointed this out he was unaware how directly this story had influenced him, even though he understood that it had become so important to him that he sought out publisher after publisher trying to convince them that it was, in his words, "absolutely amazing."[5]

The story reflected his career as a drama teacher and storyteller in many ways. The boy, like Bob, ambled along good-heartedly ("flying by the seat of my pants"), not looking for fortune, not following advice to set out on a path of ambition; Bob was offered challenging situations throughout his career in education, and he accepted them for the challenge itself and not for the opportunity to advance in his profession. Both Bob and the story character fell unexpectedly into good fortune, and both refused the ambitious call to exploit it selfishly; when Bob suddenly found himself propelled into storytelling performances in the 1970s he was more intrigued than self-seeking, and allowed his dramatic training to continue to guide him in developing his stories. In the end, both character and teller sit back and observe how someone else deals with the treasure that they have found and passed on; in his workshops Bob learned that he had "to give it out and then get it back." That is, not control the outcome he hoped for.

Bob became aware that "getting it back" was a means of experiencing the variety and depth of stories for which he had only a single text. He understood that this allowed access to the multi-textual, emergent quality of oral tales. In orally-based society one might hear the same story over and over again, told over a span of years by different tellers with different styles and emphases, and in varied contexts.

"So," he concludes, "I never thought of storytelling as a solitary thing at all, because it's in those communities—sometimes communities of children, sometimes communities of adults, but never just me alone." He added, "Without drama I don't think I would have recognized that there was something in this story. I like the notion of creating a community. I guess that's what drama does. It brings all of our voices actively into play, and we can hear these many voices in ways that we can't hear unless we are willing to take on role. And that's the big difference—exploring role. You have to be in it, you have to be willing to suspend disbelief and step into role, and into that world for a few moments."

For a storyteller, to "take on a role" does not necessarily mean assuming the full persona of a character, but rather entering fully into the world of the story and providing a bridge for listeners to enter as well. This implies the theatrical concept of "presence," of being fully and unambivalently in the moment of the storytelling event. The teller is in the middle of the tale, not standing behind it and repeating the words, nor in front of it performing as The Storyteller. It is useful here to imagine narrative performance as a continuum, with "pure" storytelling idealized in library and school contexts at one end, theatrical presentations at the other. If "pure" narration is completely devoid of any dramatic devices it ceases to be effective as storytelling; if, on the other hand, the dramatic devices become more important than the story, then something other than storytelling is taking place. For example, the theatrical production of *Into the Woods*, by Stephen Sondheim, is often described as "storytelling," but it goes far beyond simple narration; it is a full stage production with consciously reworked folktales, props, costumed characters, scripted dialogue and songs, stage lighting, and sound amplification. Most organized storytelling lies somewhere between simple narration and full-scale theater, using the techniques and tools of each to bring stories to life in the minds of the listeners.

It is a delicate balance: a teller might gesture in "The Honest Penny" to indicate the boy's tossing the box of silver coins into a river while an actor would enact the full movement. In a storytelling event the box would be entirely imaginary, while in a theatrical production it would most likely be an actual box. The illusory penny, like the story being told, can be picked up and passed on by other tellers. It is more difficult to pass on a theatrical production.

Each of the tellers in the following chapters has found a place in this continuum. All have developed their own way of attaining a sense of presence in their stories. This is one of the ways their stories have come to life, through an effective use of dramatic techniques: gesture and movement, dialogue, and a deep sense of presence.

THE HONEST PENNY

(Bob Barton, 1995)

This is an interesting variant of "Dick Whittington and His Cat," listed as AT Type 1651 in the Aarne/Thompson Tale Type Index. Another variant is tale number 70 in the Grimm collection, "The Three Sons of Fortune." Bob told the first part of the story during our taped interview, using it to illustrate various aspects of his experiences as a storyteller. I wrote him later in the year asking if I could include the story. He enthusiastically agreed and sent me his printed text. You can compare his words here with the parts of the story he summarized earlier.

THERE was once a boy who lived with his mother in the far away northern lands. They were very poor and there was often little food for the table or fuel for the fire.

One day the boy was sent out to look for roots and twigs to burn. As he struggled along in the freezing cold, his little fists turned as red as the cranberries that he passed by and he had to run and jump and jump and run to keep himself warm.

When he had gathered all the wood he could carry, he started for home. Suddenly, he came upon a large, crooked stone that was white with frost. "Poor old stone," said the boy, "how white and pale you are! Why I believe you are frozen to death."

The boy threw down his load, took off his jacket and wrapped it around the stone.

When he got home his mother met him at the door. "What are you doing walking about in winter in your shirt sleeves?" she demanded.

The boy, all excited, told her about the stone white and pale from the frost, and how he had given it his jacket.

"You featherhead," said his mother, very angry. "Do you really believe that stones can freeze? Even if they could, here's a lesson for you:

> Look to thyself.
> Take care of thyself.
> For nobody cares for thee.

It costs me enough to keep clothes on your back without you leaving them draped on stones. Go back and fetch your jacket!"

The boy returned to the stone but was amazed to discover that it had lifted itself and turned itself. And where the stone had lain there was a box full of silver coins. "This must be stolen money," thought the boy, "no one puts money come by honestly under a stone."

He picked up the box of coins, took it to a nearby lake and threw it in. As the box was sinking to the bottom, one silver penny piece floated to the surface. "Now that," said the boy, "is honest money. What's honest always floats."

He scooped the penny from the lake and went home with it in the pocket of his jacket.

When his mother heard about the money thrown into the lake she burst out crying, "You're a born fool. If you had kept that money we might have lived well and happily all our days. If nothing but what is honest floats on water there can't be much honesty in the world. Even if the money was stolen ten times over, you found it. I've tried to teach you to:

> Look to thyself.
> Take care of thyself.
> For nobody cares for thee..

Well you'll stay no more in my house. Get out and earn your own keep!"

And she pushed the boy out the door and slammed it in his face.

For weeks the boy tramped the country far and long asking for work, but no one would put him to any use.

"You're too small," said some.

"You're too weak," said others.

One evening, footsore and bone weary, he found himself outside the house of a wealthy merchant. He went around to the kitchen door and tap tap tapped. The cook came out.

"Off you go!" he shouted. "There's no charity here!"

"I need work," pleaded the boy, "I'll fetch water. I'll chop wood, I'll stir the porridge. You don't even have to pay me."

"Mmm," thought the cook, "I could use a kitchen boy. Well, don't stand there gaping. In you come!"

After a time, the merchant announced plans for a trading voyage and he called his servants to him and asked every one of them in turn what he should buy and bring back for them. When it was the kitchen boy's turn to say what he would have, he held out his silver penny.

"What would I buy with this?" laughed the merchant. "There won't be much time lost over this bargain."

"Buy what I can get for it. It's honest money, that I know," said the boy.

The merchant gave his word to do his best and put out to sea.

At the first port of call the merchant exchanged fish oil for linseed and barley. At the next he traded for nutmeg and cinnamon. At another, he loaded up cotton and lace. Each time he dropped anchor, he would get off the ship, go into town and buy the items which he servants had requested.

At last his business was finished and he was about to return home, when he put his hand into his pocket and pulled out the kitchen boy's penny.

"Oh no!" he thought, "I forgot the boy. Must I leave the ship and go all the way up into town for the sake of a silver penny?"

Just then an old woman stumbled on to the wharf. She was dragging a sack.

"What have you got in your sack, old mother?" called the merchant.

"Oh, nothing else but my grimalkin. I can't afford to feed her any longer. I thought I'd throw her in the sea and good riddance."

Suddenly the merchant had an idea. "Would you take this silver penny for the cat?"

"I would," said the old woman, and she handed him the sack.

The merchant released the cat from the bag. The cat ran straight to the main mast and sat down to lick and groom her coat.

Now when the merchant had sailed a bit, rough weather fell on them. Thunder crashed, waves lashed, the rain came down in torrents. The ship drove and drove through the pounding seas.

At last the merchant was blown on to the shores of a land where he had never set foot before. He went immediately up into a town and entered an inn.

A large table was set for a meal and at each place was a stout stick for the person who sat there. "This is odd," thought the merchant, and he sat himself down to find out what everyone would do. By and by others joined him at the table. No sooner had food been served when he saw what the sticks were for. Out from the walls and down from the ceiling beams tumbled mice in hundreds, and each who sat to eat had to seize a stick and flog and flap about and nothing could be heard but thwack! thwack! thwack! Sometimes people accidentally flailed each other in the face and barely had time to say "beg your pardon" before they struck someone else.

"Hard work to eat in this place!" cried the merchant.

"Very hard!" shouted the others.

"Have you no cats here?" called the merchant.

"Cats, what are they?" exclaimed the others.

The merchant darted from the inn and fetched the cat he had bought for the kitchen boy. Instantly she ran among the mice raking them with her claws and scattering them to their hiding places in the walls.

All who ate there agreed that never in living memory had they enjoyed such peace at a meal.

"Sell us the cat," begged the people. And after much haggling they gave the merchant a hundred gold coins and much thanks besides.

The merchant sailed away again, but he had scarce got good sea room before he discovered that the cat was back. It was crouched beside the main mast. The merchant grinned at the cat. The cat did not grin back. Suddenly foul weather was upon them. Thunder crashed, waves lashed, the rain came down in torrents. The ship drove and drove through heaving seas. When finally there came a calm, the merchant found himself on the shores of another land where he had never set foot before.

Immediately he went up to the town and entered an inn. As before, a table was set for dinner and at each place there was a stick twice as long and twice as thick as the ones in the inn the night before. And they had to be, for at dinner that evening, the mice that attacked the food were twice as many and twice as large. Once again the cat was fetched and the mice dispatched to their hiding places in the walls. This time the merchant sold the cat for two hundred pieces of gold with no haggling at all.

The merchant had just cleared the harbor when he spied the cat. It was back by the main mast. The cat narrowed its eyes and the merchant shivered and shook, for he knew what would surely follow.

Suddenly foul weather was upon them. Thunder crashed, waves lashed, the rain came down in torrents. The ship drove and drove through rolling seas. When the storm died, the merchant found himself on the shores of yet another land where he had never set foot before.

He made his way quickly to the town inn and there was a table set for dinner and the sticks beside each place were thick as brooms and twice the length of your arm.

When dinner was served that night, rats the size of small dogs swarmed the room. The fighting was so thick that it as only through sore toil and trouble that one could get a morsel of food into one's mouth. The merchant scurried from the inn, fetched the kitchen boy's cat and sent it into the fray. In no time at all, the rats were running for their lives. Before the merchant could say a word, three hundred pieces of gold had been collected and offered to him and the cat was sold again.

The merchant returned to the ship, weighed anchor, and thought happily about all the money he had made out of the kitchen boy's penny. "Why this is more money than I've earned on this entire voyage," he exclaimed. Suddenly a thought crossed him mind. He frowned. "No, why should I? It's me he has to thank for the cat. And besides ... there's an old saying:

> Look to thyself.
> Take care of thyself.
> For nobody cares for thee.

Yes, I'll keep the money."

No sooner had he said this than he felt a small chill at the back of his neck. He turned. The cat was back. It was sitting beside the main mast glaring at him.

Suddenly the sea grew angry; the sky got dark; the terrified merchant cried out, "I'll give all the money to the kitchen boy, I swear it!"

Instantly the sky brightened. The swell subsided. And the ship was blown home on a soaring breeze.

As he promised, the merchant counted out every gold piece into the boy's hands. The boy was now richer than the merchant, and he and the cat became fast friends. Together they lived well and happily all their days.

But the story doesn't end here. The boy sent for his mother and shared all of his fortune with her.

"How is this happening?" she would say. "After the way I treated you, how can you do this for me?"

"Because," smiled the boy, "I never did believe that I should look to myself, take care of myself, and that nobody cared for me."

Notes

1 The library tradition was so firmly rooted that theatrical storytelling was looked down upon by many Toronto tellers. This became an issue that seriously divided community members in the 1980s.

2 *Tell Me Another* includes specific information on using creative dramatic techniques for developing stories. Bob's next book, *Stories in the Classroom*, co-authored with dramatic arts teacher David Booth, is even more direct in its use of "storydrama" techniques.

3 Brother Blue (Hugh Hill) grew up in Philadelphia and later studied dramatic arts and theology at Harvard and Yale universities.

4 Bob discovered this little-known story in *Tales from the Fjeld*, (Asbjørnsen 1874) and found it too fascinating to ignore.

5 As of December, 1997, its potential remained unrecognized by the commercial presses Bob had approached.

TWO

OLD TALES, NEW CONTEXTS[1]

O N a February morning in 1986 I sat with dozens of other people at the annual Storytelling Festival of Toronto listening to a frail, elderly man reciting a long story in Gaelic. After a few minutes he stopped and sat down while a younger man stood up to translate a summarized segment of the story into monotonous English. "This isn't going to work," I thought to myself; "It's too tedious." We had heard the two men tell a livelier story the previous night and had come in anticipation of being entertained once more. Instead I was beginning to get a headache from trying to follow the complicated story in two languages, only one of which I understood.

I forgot my discomfort half way through the lengthy tale of a good-hearted young sailor and his encounters with pirates, a corpse, and the King of Egypt's Daughter. The chanted cadence of the Gaelic, the gentle intensity and non-theatrical style of both performers, and the story itself, were compelling enough to hold me and the rest of the audience for most of an hour. Also, it was obvious that the man speaking to us in an unknown tongue relished the tales he was telling—and eventually he also came to enjoy us, his uncomprehending but patient listeners, as the festival weekend progressed.

Later when I spoke with Joe Neil MacNeil, the narrator, and John Shaw, the translator, I learned that they had not faced a formal audience together before and had no idea what to expect.[2] This was surprising, since they seemed entirely competent despite the occasional awkwardness of balancing narration and translation. I spent the remainder of the weekend following Joe Neil and John from one performance to another and talking to them informally about stories and storytelling. I learned that Joe Neil had heard stories in his own community as a young man but had ceased to be an active narrator when the Gaelic language declined. John found Joe Neil's earlier stories recorded on archival tapes and sought him out. Their work together over the next few years eventually led them to the Toronto festival, and here my story begins.

My interest is in Joe Neil MacNeil's return to active storytelling in the late 1970s and John Shaw's indispensable role in this personal revival. Joe Neil's memories of his own community are described in the book he and John Shaw published together, *Tales Until Dawn: The World of a Cape Breton Gaelic Story-Teller* (MacNeil 1987). John has been so directly involved in Joe Neil's success in reaching listeners beyond his own community that to describe just one of them is to tell only half of the story. What they have accomplished together is, in my experience, a unique approach to "tandem" storytelling.

My initial contact with Joe Neil and John was as an eager listener and not as a folklorist-researcher engaged in a careful study of narration. I emphasize this in hopes that others will find in my comments some useful information for their own work. My observations are based on attending every performance Joe Neil and John offered at three of the annual Toronto festivals, from conversations with them during the festivals, and from letters exchanged with John Shaw over the past five years. I have been curious to know how they evolved from the more usual roles of informant/researcher into dual performers; why they chose to take their traditional art to a major professional festival; how this change of performance context has affected both the tellers and the tales. Joe Neil and John offer a manner of performance that touches on issues relevant to organized storytelling.

Joe Neil MacNeil—Eos Nill Bhig—was adopted into the MacNeil family of Middle Pond at the age of six months. At this time Gaelic was still a fully vital language in Cape Breton, and the only language spoken by Joe Neil's adoptive parents. He says of himself: "I spoke only Gaelic when I was young. I used to make some effort to pick up a bit of English here and there, though I spoke only the odd word" (MacNeil 1987:3). His curiosity with language, and eventually with storytelling, was to lead him into a life-long diversion that eventually caught the interest of scholars studying Canadian Gaelic.

Like Ray Hicks of Beech Mountain, North Carolina, he was not a casual teller of tales but a master performer with innumerable lengthy stories learned within a traditional oral community. Both men succeeded in bringing an ancient body of oral literature to new audiences unfamiliar with the stories, the language, and the culture in which they were developed. However, neither teller initiated this on their own; both were "discovered" by outsiders who appreciated their stories and saw the potential for carrying them to a wider audience. In the case of Joe Neil, it was John Shaw, a Gaelic researcher, who "discovered" him in 1975. John was working in the archives of the College of Cape Breton in Sydney, Nova Scotia, when he heard a tape of a lengthy Gaelic tale and was impressed with the linguistic abilities and esthetic sense of the storyteller:

> A recording that caught my attention was a version of "Nighean Righ na h-Eipheit" ["The King of Egypt's Daughter"], delivered with a sureness of detail and a command of Gaelic that I recognized as the work of a master story-teller. The same command of language—without apparent effort or limitations—impressed me again when I met Joe Neil some weeks later (MacNeil 1987:xv-xvi).

After this meeting Shaw recorded whatever Joe Neil could call back to memory of that story and others. The two men worked together for the next few years patiently reconstructing fragments of tales that gradually returned to life as full, vibrant oral compositions. One concrete result of their collaboration was a book (actually two, one in Gaelic and the other in English) containing Joe Neil's wealth of oral lore arranged according to families and individuals from whom he had first heard the various items. Of the fifty-two narratives recorded in the book (not the whole of his repertoire) there were only two for which he could not remember sources. He claimed not one of them as his own, saying modestly in his preface:

> Please do not regard me as deserving of any special praise but see this book as a tribute to those living in times past who were gifted, kindly and sensible, and generous with their store of tales (MacNeil 1987:ix).

Joe Neil was so modest that you might not guess from his own words that "their store of tales" were a challenge to learn since they were told only in Gaelic. He was in a rare position to hear and learn the stories because he began his schooling later than other children in his community. Children caught speaking Gaelic in school were vigorously punished by the teachers, and also publicly embarrassed in front of their peers. Shame was a most effective weapon, so much so that many gave up speaking their own language in public, and gradually it died out in private as well. Joe Neil, however, clung tenaciously to his language despite retribution. He noted that an illness kept him out of school for the first year: "I am sure that is the reason even until today that I have such an interest in Gaelic, for Gaelic is my first language and it is still the language that I prefer" (MacNeil 1987:4-5).

There was no hint of bitterness in his words, rather a quiet pride in the beauty and strength of the language. He went on to suggest that he was somewhat different than other children in that he sought out older people instead of avoiding them, and this of course gave him even stronger connections to well-spoken Gaelic—and to the old stories. But as the older tellers died Joe Neil was left without sources for stories, and also without an audience, since many of his own generation could not speak the language well enough. Fortunately Joe Neil had an excellent and active memory, which allowed him to call back the wealth of tales he had learned years earlier once he had a reason to do so.

In the years of careful work with John, Joe Neil regained his role as an active rather than passive tradition-bearer. He not only recalled and described what he remembered from earlier years, he was able to return it to life. Still, he no longer had any listeners—other than John—for whom to perform. There were still a handful of Gaelic-speaking contemporaries very eager and willing to listen to Joe Neil, but they could not function as a regular audience because they were too few and too scattered to form an actual community of listeners. John understood that such an audience was necessary for Joe Neil and began to seek out performance occasions in which Joe Neil might be comfortable.

In 1986 they travelled to the annual storytelling festival in Toronto to seek their fortune, in the manner of the folktale protagonist and a magical helper. Shaw comments on their debut in a letter I received in the fall of 1990:

> You may have seen our first performance ever, in Toronto, in, I think, 1986. This was for an English-speaking audience. The manner felt, at least, to be *ad hoc*. I doubt this had ever been tried before, but this was the only way I could think to present the stories, Joe Neil, and the language to a mainstream audience. This was also the only active way that presented itself to bring the material to a larger audience (undated letter, Fall 1990).

At their first night as participants in the pre-festival storytelling concert, some seventy-five people sat around small tables in a former synagogue now an art school by day and a performance space by night. Candles burning on each table provided the only source of light. Joe Neil and John were the first performers, invited by host Dan Yashinsky to take the stage as the honored guests of the festival, which began officially the following day at a large old church on Bloor Street several blocks away.

The setting was anything but elegant and perhaps this was for the best, since Joe Neil seemed very much at ease in the casual setting. There was no formal stage, just a small space on the bare wooden floor, and no microphone to separate him from his listeners. After they were introduced, Joe Neil and John came to the front and sat down in grey metal folding chairs, bringing the chairs closer and turning them slightly inward so that the two men could see each other as well as their listeners. After exchanging glances and looking out to greet us with shy smiles, Shaw stood up and briefly introduced them and described what they intended to do: MacNeil would narrate in Gaelic and Shaw would summarize in English. They nodded to each other, a shared signal that was repeated each time I saw them perform; then Joe Neil stood up and began to speak in Gaelic. His focus was inward rather than out to us, though he acknowledged our presence with occasional nods in our direction. He told the story with a minimum of movement, facial expression, or voice changes, though his personal involvement in the story events was apparent from the calm intensity of his voice. Sometimes he looked out over our heads as if he were seeing the action of the story in the distance; other times he looked intently at John, the only one who understood his words in this audience of non-Gaelic speakers.

Despite the seeming distance between us, it was obvious that something interesting was taking place, as there were none of the usual signs of audience restlessness. There was a cadence and a power to his tales that seemed to break through the language barrier; and there was Joe Neil himself, so unselfconsciously immersed in his story that even an uncomprehending audience was no hindrance to his flowing words.

After a few minutes he stopped abruptly and smiled out at us, nodded to John, and sat down. John took the floor and began a brief summary of the exploits of the legendary carpenter and trickster Boban Saor, who exchanged clothing with his inexperienced apprentice in order to fool some strangers who had come to see if he was as masterful as people believed him to be.[3] John sat down and Joe Neil continued the story of Boban Saor's clever prank with greater enthusiasm, responding to our growing interest in the story now that we had some clues to its progression. By the time John had summarized the final segment the audience as a whole was completely attentive, including the few youngsters, who had ceased fidgeting.

It was an excellent choice of stories; we, like the strangers who had come to test Boban Saor, were curious to know if this legendary master, Joe Neil, was as good as we had been told—and if his "apprentice" was worthy of his mentor. Translation alone would not have been sufficient to hold our attention. What John had accomplished was transformation, not merely translation. We, like the strangers, left convinced that we had indeed been in the hands of experts who were equally skilled in their work.

"Boban Saor" was much briefer and lighter than other stories Joe Neil and John told during the formal part of the festival over the next two days. The much more complex story of "The King of Egypt's Daughter," mentioned at the beginning of this chapter, seemed at first to be far less engaging than "Boban Saor." As a wondertale it was it much longer and apparently more serious; both tellers were so caught up in the intricacies of the tale that they seemed less aware of the audience. At times we felt distant from them, cast adrift like the young sailor in the story. But like him, most of us found our way to solid land and were rewarded for our perseverance by following the adventures of the tenacious young protagonist.

Joe Neil was delighted by the warmth and receptivity of the listeners, and responded by coming further out of his stories as the weekend progressed. Instead of focusing on John, as he had been doing, he looked out at his listeners to note the reactions, both when he was narrating and when John was translating. As the weekend progressed, both men were able to test their abilities as effectively as had the characters in their stories. One would not have guessed that Joe Neil's fine tales had been largely dormant for years and that John himself had no performing experience. John stated: "Joe Neil, as far as I know, was not an active storyteller before I met him, although he clearly had the capability to be so. He recorded some stories for an archive in 1975, and had recorded earlier for at least one Gaelic-speaking fieldworker" (undated letter, 1990).

In my letter I had also asked John how they came to work together as actual performers rather than as informant and collector, which is the more usual relationship. He replied that he gradually realized that

Joe Neil deserved a good audience, and the only way to find one was to agree to accompany him as a translator, since Joe Neil felt that the stories had to be told in Gaelic. Shaw understood that it was necessary to take Joe Neil and his stories into a new context. On his part he was willing to do the necessary work, including learning to face an audience himself, in order to do so:

> The crux of it is that this is the only real audience going for Joe Neil's material. Dealing with this new audience, I feel, has been an important experience for Joe Neil and has had a constructive effect on his understanding of the importance of his own tradition and the larger context of which it was a part. Now that nearly all of his own generation is gone, along with their acuity of mind and ability to listen well, the mainstream may be the source of people who are broadminded and thoughtful enough to relate to the material (undated letter, 1990).

Since both men are by nature modest and reserved, it was an even greater challenge to brave an unknown audience in Toronto. John described the difficulties of his own situation:

> I felt very much the mediator here between Joe Neil's very high standards of content accuracy/verbal skills and a well-disposed, expectant audience with no previous exposure and who knows what expectations. At first in my job there was not much room to move: It was all I could do to keep the details straight and put them into some kind of coherent English. My verbal understanding of the stories had always been as I had heard them in Gaelic, and giving them in English, especially at first, felt like trying to play a tune you knew on a fiddle left-handed (undated letter, 1991).

Learning to perform together required a great challenge for both men. Joe Neil would have been accustomed to an intimate setting where both stories and language would had been familiar; Shaw was not a storyteller at all and had to develop the basic skills of presenting a coherent narrative accurately and engagingly without imposing himself on the story. By the end of the 1986 festival it was obvious from the enthusiastic responses of listeners and the growing ease of these two tellers that they had accomplished their daunting task.

One of the festival organizers, Dan Yashinsky, recalls Joe Neil's comments at that first festival:

> I remember Joe standing up at a brunch at the Festival a few years ago and talking about how even he thought he'd forgotten all of his stories until John came around and started listening to him. His own community had stopped giving his story tradition much value, at least publicly, and had certainly stopped providing a continuity of listeners with whom he could exercise his powers of memory and performance. And as Joe tells it, they were both surprised by what came forth. "We were scraping the bottom of the barrel," Joe said—and then they seem to have turned the barrel into one of those magic fairy tale vessels which provides abundant, and always replenished, stores of good stuff (undated letter, 1991).

As his experience as a platform performer developed (not only in Toronto but also at the large Vancouver festival), Joe Neil continued to respond to the challenge of attentive but non-Gaelic-speaking listeners. Since he had no living oral sources he began to seek stories out in print in order to increase his repertoire. He read collections in both Gaelic and English, though until the 1990 festival he performed only in Gaelic. At this festival he chose to relate a 45-minute tale in English that he had found in a published Scottish collection. His task was doubly difficult: not only was he drawing from less familiar material in written rather than oral form, he also chose to tell the story in his second language, and without John's help.

I sat directly in front of Joe Neil in the first row, eager to take in every word. At first he was obviously anxious about standing up there alone, without John sitting beside him ready to help. But once he had launched into his story he displayed the same unselfconscious concentration that he had in his Gaelic presentations—a calm intensity that demonstrated his deep involvement with the story and its characters. We now had the great privilege of hearing his eloquence and precision firsthand. Though he called it "reciting," the story was in his own words.[4]

John Shaw notes, in *Tales Until Dawn*, that all narrators had their own artistic techniques for bringing a story to life, some relying on language and style, others on elaboration of detail or vivid imagery, while some delighted in lively dialogue between characters.[5] Joe Neil,

Shaw says, was particularly talented in both imagery and dialogue, as was apparent when we were able to hear him perform his own story in English. My handwritten notes scribbled on the festival program capture one of the many vivid phrases used in his lengthy story of a heroic quest. Here is a description of a threatening ogress his hero has encountered in a mountain cave: "She had one great eye in her head like a pool of deep dark water, and her gaze was as swift as a winter mackerel."

His very fine, dry humor was also apparent in his choice of words and phrases as well as in occasional glances at his audience to see how listeners were responding. For example, he commented on the raven who wanted a quid of tobacco as payment for helping the hero: "I guess he wasn't afraid of the cancer."

John emphasized that along with Joe Neil's artistic skills, his deepest interest in the stories was with the characters and their interactions: "his main concern is with the psychology of the story, using the relations between events to elicit the pathos or humour from the characters' situations with a frequent emphasis on the moral implications of the tale. This is all expressed through language which, although not ornate, is slightly formal" (MacNeil 1987:xxxii-xxxiii).

We were able to experience Joe Neil's involvement with the tale firsthand, and to appreciate more directly the consummate artistry of his performance. The "slightly formal" language did not detract in the least from his involvement with each of the characters. In this way Joe Neil resembles the skilled Siberian narrator, Natal'ia Osipovna Vinokurova, studied in depth by Russian scholar Mark Azadovskii (Azadovskii 1974).

I questioned Shaw about Joe Neil's response to his experience of narrating a complex tale in English; Shaw wrote that he thought it had been as significant for Joe Neil as it was for us:

Joe Neil viewed telling a full-length story in English as a challenge, and it took some courage to do this. I had encouraged him in this, and after an instant's confusion when I left him on his own, he went about the work quite naturally, as I knew he would. It seems to me that telling stories in English ("translating" is what Joe Neil calls it) is part of a constant effort to stretch himself and extend his skills. Since he was 80 Joe Neil has worked on and mastered, from books, at least two of the truly big Gaelic stories which to my knowledge have not been told anywhere for close to 40 years now (including Scotland) (undated letter, 1990).

John Shaw, too, has been willing to take up the challenge of stretching himself by learning and occasionally telling stories in a second language, one he learned as an adult, and not as part of his own background. He set off for Scotland as a young man, wandered about the more isolated regions learning Gaelic as he went. When he returned to the United States he began to study the language and culture formally, and in the 1970s succeeded in finding a research job in the only Gaelic-speaking region on this continent, Cape Breton Island.

With his knowledge of Gaelic and his deep respect for Joe Neil and his stories, Shaw would seem to be the most obvious person to carry on MacNeil's tradition, but when he was asked by someone in the audience if he considered himself to be MacNeil's apprentice he said that he did not, that he *could* not. Later when I pressed him further he responded: "In order to be a true apprentice to Joe Neil a person would have to be training to be a full-fledged Cape Breton Gaelic storyteller with Gaelic as the primary language. Although I would view this as one of the more worthy and productive intellectual pursuits this part of the world has to offer, to do so would be unrealistic because these days there is no real audience for this" (undated letter, 1990).

He went on to say that while the tales might be taken into an English language tradition they would, in his opinion, eventually lose their power:"The long tales, which are the heart of the tradition, have been unsuccessful at crossing the language boundary as active material" (undated letter, 1990). In their book he comments further that the longer narratives have not "crossed over into English," though some of the shorter and more humorous genres as well as a few belief legends (stories of strange happenings) have been more successful (MacNeil 1987:xxv).

While the future of Gaelic storytelling in Cape Breton is in doubt, at least for a brief but significant time MacNeil and Shaw managed to breathe literal life into a great narrative tradition. Both men together achieved what neither could have accomplished separately. As Dan Yashinsky noted: "The thing is not to merely record the stories in a mechanical way, but to put yourself directly in the path of the tradition. What John's up to is the affirmation of oral tradition not only as an "artifact" but as a living source of value, something in need of live practitioners" (undated letter, 1991).

John had no intention of becoming a performer himself but saw himself mainly as translator and as cultural broker between Joe Neil and "mainstream" audiences. He did, however, recognize improvements in his own presentations:

> Our performing has been sporadic, but within the last year or so [1989-90], due to practice, I've been able to do my part more easily, describing in English the visual scenes that Joe Neil gives through Gaelic. The feeling is one of more freedom in bringing across the nuances that I hear in Joe Neil's telling while giving the content of the tales. This is all easier and more comfortable than it was at first. In many ways my mind is able to work very easily with Joe Neil's; I think if I did the same kind of summarizing with another storyteller it would take some time before I felt comfortable (undated letter, 1990).

It was the experience of actual performances before living audiences, after ten years of working together to reconstruct the stories, that allowed John Shaw and Joe Neil MacNeil to return an old art to full vitality. This is certainly a storytelling revival in the most complete sense, though both Joe Neil and John might have argued that the tradition and the stories had never quite died at all, and were in need of a healthy transfusion rather than full resuscitation. New listeners provided exactly that.

Traditional communities almost everywhere have undergone rapid and radical transformations that have resulted in the loss of such artistic forms and expressions as oral narration. We should remember, though, that changes in social and technological patterns have always been a natural part of human existence; tellers who wished to keep their art fully alive have met challenges with innovative responses, certainly including the use of "book" stories in their oral repertoires. I emphasize this to avoid the stereotype of oral tradition as an unchanging, "pure" expression that suffers from innovation. Quite simply, active narrators cannot survive without good listeners, and when their audiences change they must respond without losing the rich heritage on which they depend. It may even be necessary to seek out new audiences in unfamiliar contexts.

An example of narrators actively pursuing their own audience is described by narrative scholar Linda Dégh. She worked with two aging Hungarian women who had been active tellers in Hungary and then in their former ethnic neighborhood in Gary, Indiana, but now lived alone in separate suburban areas. They managed to keep their stories alive by telephone calls to each other but resourcefully sought out new listeners as well, regaling delivery men, canvassers, postmen, or anyone else who turned up on their doorsteps. The fact that their hapless listeners could not speak Hungarian did not discourage the women, who were determined to maintain their legends and tales (Dégh 1969b).

It is not so surprising, then, that skilled artists such as Joe Neil MacNeil, and Appalachian teller Ray Hicks, succeeded in accommodating themselves and their stories to new audiences and new contexts. Listeners could not always follow the language of their tales, since Ray Hicks' Beech Mountain English was often as incomprehensible as Joe Neil's Middle Cape Gaelic; but the proficiency of these artists was compelling enough to carry over linguistic boundaries, to captivate audiences unfamiliar with the oral communities in which the tellers and their tales originally blossomed—even when listeners could not follow the words of a story.

They succeeded by meeting the challenge of entertaining new listeners in performance contexts quite unlike the more intimate settings of their original communities. (For another example of a traditional teller adapting to a platform performing context see Mullen 1981.) These tellers certainly had to make adjustments to unfamiliar situations, but their listeners also had to adapt; they had to relax their expectations of platform performing in order to appreciate understated performance styles and to follow stories that were difficult to understand. Both Joe Neil MacNeil and Ray Hicks blossomed by meeting the challenges and enjoying the stimulation of festival audiences. Rather than maintaining the material with which they were most comfortable they sought out other sources for narrative material. Ray Hicks has added more biographical content to his performances while Joe Neil MacNeil, with John Shaw's help, sought out traditional Gaelic material from printed sources. In other words, they did not passively maintain oral tradition as they initially experienced it, but found new ways of keeping their rich legacies fully alive. Joe Neil had the benefit of John Shaw's generosity, perception, and good judgement.

Folklorist William Wilson's useful continuum of situational, conscious cultural, and professional storytellers, mentioned in the introduction, is especially useful here. While less experienced situational and conscious cultural tellers might be easily discouraged by the loss of supportive and familiar listeners, active and experienced tellers are more ready for any opportunity to perform and are willing to adapt to new situations.

However, innovation is not subordinate to tradition. The sense of stories being part of a wider inheritance, not merely one's personal possessions, inspires a balance between traditional stability and individual innovation. Respect for the community of tellers and for the tales themselves is paramount. As Shaw notes, Joe Neil's only audiences for a while were the occasional academic collectors who came to listen respectfully and to record his tales. Joe Neil was willing to comply because he sensed this respect. John notes that "characteristic of outstanding Gaelic informants is their willingness to record for the serious collector. Once the informant's confidence is gained, such a task is perceived as a duty growing out of their unspoken role as guardians of their people's tradition" (MacNeil 1987:xvii).

Ray Hicks, too, was more than willing to share his wealth of traditional and personal stories with collectors as well as large festival audiences. Like MacNeil, he regarded himself as an heir to a rich local tradition. Folklorist Cheryl Oxford, who has worked extensively and intensively with Ray Hicks and his relatives Marshall Ward and Stanley Hicks, emphasized Ray's conscious sense of responsibility: "Perhaps because of his long apprenticeship in the communal wisdom of his mountain kin, Hicks is unwilling to relinquish his patriarchal role as storyteller to just anyone. He believes that these stories impart the collective memories of a kindred people" (Oxford 1991:6).

Both MacNeil and Hicks were so completely immersed in their art that they sometimes seemed oblivious to their listeners, while at other times they responded directly and engagingly. Oxford described Hicks' penchant for fixing his total attention on specific listeners:

> In contrast to these moments of reverie, however, are examples of Hicks' flair for showmanship and comic relief. He may emphasize a point in his telling by holding a member of the audience with a wide-eyed stare, leaning closer while watching for a reaction, as if daring her to laugh or express disbelief (Oxford 1991:13).

While MacNeil was less aggressive than Hicks, since he was well aware that listeners could not understand his tales, he was still very aware of his audiences; he looked out at them with occasional smiles and nods as his narratives progressed. Both MacNeil and Hicks were also eager to talk about stories and story telling before or after performances. They did not regard storytelling as an activity separate from other parts of their lives, nor something to be guarded as a personal treasure. They were fully aware of themselves as skilled artists and retained a keen sense of obligation to those from whom they learned their stories—and the art of telling them.

Part of this feeling of guardianship is a deep understanding of the inherent timelessness of the stories, a continuing relevance that goes beyond specific historical community and individuals. As Joe Neil remarked about some of the stories he remembered:

> They were exceedingly lengthy tales and their subject matter was so strange. In a way they were just as strange as some things that could happen today, but at the same time so understandable; you could understand everything that was there—every misfortune and hardship that they encountered (MacNeil 1987:16).

Toronto storyteller and author Celia Lottridge recognized what Joe Neil and John had accomplished, and acknowledged their impact on her as a storyteller:

> You know, when we had Joe Neil here, it was significant. He does come out of oral tradition, and he's made himself a person who takes that tradition he really grew up with and the stories he heard orally, and he's seeing himself as the lone person who's really doing that. I mean, he's gathered up stories that maybe he wouldn't have told if he had just gone on in an oral culture. But he still comes out of that background. I've found that listening to those people [Joe Neil and John] to be extremely illuminating, and it puts what I do into a much broader context (taped interview, Toronto, June 1993).

As Celia and others have noted, both men were so fully engaged in the stories as lived experiences that their sense of presence invited audiences directly inside their tales. I overheard one listener remark to a friend:

"Well, now I know stories aren't just something you tell or hear—they're something that happens to you when you tell or hear them."

In the three years I observed Joe Neil and John at the Toronto festival (1986, 1987, 1990) it was apparent to me that they had altered the context as much as they had been altered by it. This is significant in a performance milieu where many modern tellers feel that traditional material needs to be dramatically transformed (often through parody) to suit contemporary listeners. On the other end of the scale are those who feel that traditional tales are to be told in their "original" form (that is, word for word as they exist in print) in order to retain their purity. For Joe Neil, stories, even those he sought out in books, were always alive and relevant and authentic. They did not require purist preservation or heavy-handed modernization.

Joe Neil MacNeil reflected thoughtfully on storytelling as an immediate experience, even when he was speaking nostalgically of his own difficult early years. What he remembered most clearly was the immediate personal face-to-face exchange:

> You were alive with them [the tellers he recalls by name] there in the flesh and participating in the whole event. You could talk to them right there, but if you ever chose to address the gadgets I mentioned [radio and television] they could never answer you. So there was the pleasure and a sense of unity. I think that people felt very united, united physically and united in spirit (MacNeil 1987:10).

For Joe Neil, of course, unlike most of us who bring stories to a stage setting, storytelling grew from a communal base rather than from individual efforts. He modestly stated, as Shaw said earlier, "My own experience was ordinary enough," meaning that he had been only one of many narrators who felt a deep connection to their tales as part of a much larger whole. His devotion as a "conscious cultural storyteller" inspired him, when the opportunity presented itself, to evolve into a fully skilled "platform performer"—with the help of a scholar who wanted to record as well as to bring to full life the verbal artistry of master narrator.

This chapter is an attempt to recreate in words what has been only partially verbal. Anyone who has tried to transform spoken words into print will understand my sense of dissatisfaction with the one-dimensional results that can only hint at the exhilarating reality of being there at the re-living of a traditional art.[6] I learned more deeply from my experiences with Joe Neil and John that both scholars and storytellers are professionally engaged in a revival, each in their own way trying to bring life to stories that originated in another medium. Scholars, in this case folklorists and anthropologists, try to replicate the event as accurately as possible by describing it in ways that capture the actual spoken words so they can, if it is desired, be measured, weighed, compared and contrasted. The highest ideal is to present in words—sometimes with the addition of charts, graphs, and other statistical methods—what existed orally for a few fluid moments, not only for the scholarly viewer but for the participants, both tellers and listeners.

It is easy to forget that measuring and weighing can get in the way of appreciating artistic creativity. Linguistic anthropologist Del Hymes, who spent much of his career exploring the complex narratives of Northwest Coast native traditions, counseled readers to remember that whatever the other function of stories they were also entertaining: "Scholars are sometimes the last to understand that these stories were told and told again, not simply to reflect or express or maintain social structure, interpersonal tensions, or something similar, but because they were great stories, great fun" (Hymes 1981:22).

Storytellers have another challenge, being attuned to the living storytelling event in a different way—as a model for presentation within their own experiences and interests as platform performers. They recreate an oral experience by retelling the story they have heard to another audience in a different context, instead of attempting to describe it accurately and objectively as an event. The danger here is that ignorance of the rich soil in which any given story took root and flourished can lead to misunderstanding, unless a teller has taken care to do a bit of research on a story and to appreciate and respect the generations of actual (not idealized) people who contributed to this continuing artistic creation. An anti-historical perspective can result in egocentric claims that a story "belongs" to them simply because they have recreated it in their own words.

Any story text is only a part of actual creation, one link in a long chain of human interaction and reflection that does not stop with any individual teller. Joe Neil, a master of the art, did not claim a single traditional tale as his own; he recalled them as belonging to the families in which he had first heard them, and that is how the tales were presented in his book, as we saw in Section I, Chapter 4 (MacNeil 1987).

I have learned a great deal from the combined performances of Joe Neil MacNeil and John Shaw. As a folklorist I was impressed with their dedication to storytelling as the living legacy of both a community and an individual artist, and also with the careful way in which they brought this art into a new performing context without losing the integrity of the tales or the telling of them.

As a storyteller I gained new perspectives on issues now central to platform performance contexts: that is, conscious standards of excellence in training and expression; the ethics of public presentation (notably "ownership" of tales); relations between tellers and listeners before, during, and after performances; the individual artist's commitment and responsibility to a wider community as well as to the stories themselves. Any one of these topics would require another full chapter (if not an entire book) so I only mention them here to suggest further possibilities for exploration.

The last words belong to Joe Neil MacNeil. In describing one of the tellers remembered from childhood, he echoed his own joyous approach to storytelling:

> Angus [MacIsaac] was full of a kind cheerfulness. He used to tell stories and he could make them up as well. He made them up in great numbers and with ease. And he could invent long ones, too; some of his tales were extremely long. He knew himself that they were not true and when he was finished telling one of these big stories, after he had let out a little laugh, he would say, "And that's no lie" (MacNeil 1987:95).

Joe Neil was well aware of his deliberate ambivalance here; wonder-tales are both true and false at the same time, and both teller and listeners must find their own way to solve this apparent dilemma. In the following chapter we find storytellers Stewart Cameron and Marylyn Peringer meeting this challenge in their own ways.

THE KING OF EGYPT'S DAUGHTER

(Joe Neil MacNeil, 1978)

This was one of the Gaelic stories recorded by John Shaw in 1978 which he later translated for Joe Neil's collection of stories in Tales Until Dawn. *John's notes to the story identify it as having been told by Angus MacMullin and Alexander MacLean. Joe Neil remembered hearing it from the MacMullin Family years earlier. As I noted earlier, this is the story I heard them tell at the Toronto festival in 1986. It is AT type 506, "The Rescued Princess."*

THERE was once a young man in a certain part of the world and, since employment was scarce and work could not readily be found, he decided one day that he would go down to the pier to see if there were any sailing vessels in hopes that he would be able to strike a bargain with a captain. And it happened that there was a sailing vessel in at the time, so he went to talk with the skipper of the vessel and was hired on. He was to stay on the vessel for a certain number of years—some years and a day—and a wage was settled, conditions were agreed on, and when they were ready they sailed.

And however many years he had sailed, when that number of years and a day had passed, the sailor said that his tour was now completed and that he wished to leave. Well, the skipper was unhappy to see him leave because he had been so good on board, but he would not oppose him. But he asked him how he intended to leave now that they were out at sea.

"If you give me," said the sailor, "the longboat with a sail, a compass, and a little food to put on board, I will be able to sail right from here." So everything was fitted out and the sailor was given his wages, and he took leave of the skipper and the others on board and set sail.

Whether a storm arose or he went off course, whatever happened, he sailed for some time before he reached an island; I'm certain that he did not know at the time that he was on an island. He landed and beached the boat, pulled it up, and went walking around. He climbed up in the mountains, noticing then that he was on an island, and he saw a hut on the other side of the island and made his way down to it. When he reached the hut he beat on the door and a young woman opened the door and looked at him.

"Isn't it an unlucky thing for you," said she, "to arrive here!"

"Yes, indeed," said he. "And what is the reason for that?"

"The reason," said she, "is that this is a sea-pirates' lair. The ship on which we were sailing was caused to founder and they took everything that was on her and took me along with the rest. All the others on board were put to death, and they sent the ship down to the bottom. I'm the King of Egypt's daughter and I'm being held a prisoner here by the three pirates. Right now they are out at sea, but when they return you are not going to be safe at all."

"Well, be that as it may," said he, "I'll stay here until they return."

Whether the passing time was long or short, one of the pirates came down to the hut and saw the man sitting inside and asked him where he had come from. The sailor replied that he had come off a wrecked ship which was torn apart in a storm, and that he had been fortunate enough to cling to a piece of wood that was floating on the surface. He had kept hold of it and was driven around the ocean until at last he came to rest on this piece of land.

When the second pirate came home, he questioned him, and the sailor gave him the same story that he had told the first pirate, and when the third pirate arrived he had the same story for him. So they agreed that since he had come to them in those straits he could stay. So one of them said that they were going out to sea to plunder and that he was to stay on land and was to walk the shores to see what he would come upon there.

"And we have," said he, "a rule here on this island: the man among us who does best during the week becomes lord or king of the island until someone else does better than he. And whoever does, the title goes to him."

The pirates took off on the ocean, and he was going around on the shore and I'm sure with what he had hidden—the little bit of money that he had—when they returned home in the evening he had gathered more along the shore than they had out on the ocean. And by virtue of this it was agreed that he would become king of the island for the week.

So they continued going to sea and he remained on land. But one day he began thinking that the time was right; he had begun to reckon the length of time they were out at sea, so he said to the young woman that it was time for them to be taking off. They got ready, though she wasn't all that eager to take this opportunity in case they might be captured, but at last she agreed to go. They were only a short distance out to sea when they heard the stroke of an oar, and when they looked the pirates' boats were coming after them. Well, she began crying and lamenting, saying that they were now worse off than they had been before.

"Never mind," said he, "we are not lost yet."

And before the pirates caught up with them they entered a bank of fog and he put the boat onto another course; he changed course when he entered the fog patch, and they could no longer find him. But the young woman was even worse off once they entered it; now they were lost and she thought they would never get out. He told her not to worry at all about finding their way out and that he would continue on course with the boat.

Whatever length of time they sailed, they reached a seaport. He brought the boat into the wharf and went up to an inn to spend the night there. They intended to stay there until they could see whether they would find a chance to go to Egypt. Anyway they went to the inn and engaged rooms and, as they were on their way up to their rooms, they noticed a corpse hanging up there. The woman took to yelling and crying loudly.

"It was bad enough," said she, "to be with the pirates, but isn't it terrible to be with murderers now?"

"Never mind," he replied, "I will find out the meaning of this before we go a step further." He went down to the proprietor of the inn and asked him what was the meaning of the corpse hanging there.

"Well," said the proprietor of the inn, "it is always the custom in this town—it has been a rule for some time—that the body of anyone who leaves the world with debts is to be hung in the inn for so many days as a visible example to those passing back and forth so that they will be sure to settle their own debts before they leave this world."

"And," said the sailor, "would it be permitted or regarded as correct for another man to pay those debts off?"

"Oh, yes indeed," replied the innkeeper. "That would be all right."

"Well," said he, "we will take it upon ourselves to pay the debts that this man has incurred, whoever he may be."

"Very well," said the innkeeper, "I will send for the merchant to come here tomorrow morning and we will settle the matter."

They retired that night and on the morning of the next day the merchant was sent for and arrived at the inn. The sailor asked him what debts were owed by the man, the merchant told him, and the sailor agreed to pay them. "Very well," said the merchant, "I am well satisfied."

So the sailor settled the debts owed by the poor man and sent for a grave-digger and told him to clothe the body and to give him a gentleman's burial, and that he would pay the costs. That was done, and however long they stayed in the town, he would go down to the wharf daily to see if there were any sailing vessels coming around. One day a great sailing vessel came in and he went to speak to the skipper. He found out from the skipper that they were about to sail, and he obtained passage to Egypt on the vessel, mentioning that there was someone accompanying him. And that was all very well, they were to set out on their journey the next day.

He and the King of Egypt's daughter went down to the wharf, and when the skipper of the vessel saw the girl, he thought that he ought to recognize her. He went down to his own room where he had a picture of the King of Egypt's daughter, and sure enough it was she. But he did not let on at all.

They went on board and set sail. But the skipper gave an order to one of the sailors on the vessel to throw him overboard at the first opportunity. It was not advisable for that sailor to challenge the skipper, but he conveyed to the other man what was supposed to happen, saying that he would not do what had been asked.

But in the end, Jack the sailor went overboard, and down he went. He caught hold of a connecting rope that was underneath between the boom and the bow of the vessel, and there he remained. And the story went around that the sailor had fallen overboard, and when she heard the news, didn't the girl take to screaming and complaining, but the skipper told her not to be upset at all.

But the boat became becalmed. It was not moving—there was a dead calm—and Jack was seen swimming alongside the vessel. Right away the skipper gave the order to throw him a rope to try to bring him aboard. And sure enough he managed to grasp the rope and came aboard quite smartly. So that was settled. But one night when he and the skipper were up on the top deck keeping watch, the skipper saw his chance. The ship was tacking back and forth and on one of her tacks across, the skipper gave Jack a shove and out he went into the sea. He knew then that there was malice behind the skipper's actions so he did not attempt to return to the vessel, he struck out from it, calling out to the skipper, "I will be in Egypt before you."

And he kept on swimming. Whether the time was long or short, he kept on at his own pace until at last he gave up. He couldn't swim any further; he was just trying to stay above water as best he could. It looked as if he had just about given up completely, lying on the surface between two waves.

"Is my plight not a pitiful one!" said he. "All the big waves I have surmounted during my time at sea, and now it seems my lot to sink down between two of them right here."

Then he heard a blow or a noise as if from a boat, and when he looked, there was a black longboat beside him and a middle-aged man sitting at the oars. "It seems to me," said the man, "that you're in a fix."

"Oh," replied Jack, "I am in a fix. My time has come."

"Oh, I don't know," replied the older man, "that your time has come yet. If you were to make an agreement with me," said he, "I will take you safely to harbour."

"It is difficult for me to make a deal with anyone in my present circumstance."

"Well, if you promise to do what I ask of you, I could see that you were at a harbour in time."

"Well," replied Jack, "how can I promise something that is neither there nor within my power?"

"Well," the man replied, "the promise I'm asking is to give me your son on the day that he is three years of age."

"It is difficult for me," said Jack, "to give someone my son or my daughter at any age since my life is at an end and I have no wife, son, or daughter."

"Well," the older man said, "if you promise we will see about the rest."

So Jack got into the boat and stretched himself out on the deck, so exhausted that he fell asleep. And however long a time he slept or however long their journey took, at last they reached Egypt. They came into port and Jack was there a number of days before the skipper landed. He had found employment and was working at the shore around the wharf when the big vessel came into harbor. The King of Egypt came down with his servants and they went down to the wharf, and the skipper of the boat came in with the king's daughter, and she was received with great pleasure.

"I see," said the king, "that you have found my daughter."

"I have," replied the skipper.

"We will go up now," said the king, "to the castle, for there are agreements to be kept. I promised that whoever should find my daughter would have her in marriage."

"May I," said she, "say a few words?"

"Yes," replied her father. "You have my permission to speak at any time at all."

"This is not the man who found me. I was found by the man you see working over there."

"Oh, indeed. We would require some proof of that."

"There can be no such thing," said the skipper.

"Oh," said the king, "we must settle the matter somehow."

"Go over there," said she, "or call him over here, so that he may give you a little of his life story, and you will learn that things are different from what you believe at present."

The man was called over and was asked where he hailed from and the way the world had treated him, and he began telling his story, I believe, from the time he went on the sailing vessel until he was thrown off the vessel by the skipper. When the King of Egypt heard what had been done to him and all the rest, he ordered that the skipper be shackled and deprived of his freedom for the rest of his days, and that the sailor be taken to the castle, and that he be dressed in garments suitable for a person of his quality. A great wedding was arranged, and Jack and the King of Egypt's daughter were married.

But, with the passing of time, she grew heavy with child and gave birth to a baby boy, and there was much more happiness and rejoicing. But time passed and passed swiftly, and soon the period of three years had run its course. And the day arrived at last when the young lad was three years of age. The older man came around, he knocked on the door, was invited in, and entered. When the older man had been sitting inside for a while, the sailor told his wife the conditions to which he had agreed in order to save his own life while he was at sea.

"Well," said she, "hard as it is, a promise must be fulfilled."

So the lad was brought to the older man. And he lifted him up and placed him on his knee and said, "You have been as good as your promise, which promise has been fulfilled tonight. It is in fact a long time since you paid me."

"I don't understand," said the sailor, "how I could ever have paid you."

"Oh," replied the older man, "you may remember when you were at the inn and took down the corpse that was hanging from a rope and gave it a respectable gentleman's burial and paid off the debts. Now the lad is going back to you as he should. And he has my blessing that every good fortune will meet him and the rest of you."

And there you have the story that I heard about the sailor and the King of Egypt's daughter.

Notes

1 An earlier version of this chapter appears as "Old Stories, New Listeners" (Birch/Heckler 1996), and is used with the permission of August House Press. I am grateful for the helpful editorial suggestions of Carol Birch and Melissa Heckler.

2 I also did not know that Joe Neil's story, "The King of Egypt's Daughter," was the same narrative John Shaw first heard on tape and recognized as the work of a master storyteller.

3 John commented on this story in a letter he sent me in 1993: "The Boban Saor story we told on the first night was one of two that did not appear in *Tales Until Dawn*. As far as I know it has been recorded only once in Scotland, and nowhere else in Cape Breton. Summary: Boban Soar hears that people were coming to put him to the test and see whether he is equal to his reputation as a carpenter. He sees them approaching from afar, exchanges place and role with his apprentice, begins planing an adze handle. He uses his eye to measure the handle for the adze head lodged in a vice at the other end of the work table. When ready he throws it and the handle fits perfectly into the eye of the adze head. The strangers walk out, saying to each other: 'Did you see what his apprentice just did? Well, if the apprentice can do that, imagine what the master can do.' They never returned to test Boban Saor."

4 Master narrators, like the Yugoslav epic singers studied by Parry and Lord, do not build their stories by rote memory, word-for-word, but rely on formulaic phrases and images around which they recreate their narrative anew at each performance (Lord 1970).

5 John elaborates on this: "Within the carefully transmitted framework of the tale, the story-teller was an active, frequently vigorous 'shaper of tradition' whose personal, creative role in telling the story was known to Middle Cape story-tellers as *Eideadh na Sgeulachd*, 'The Raiment of the Tale.' The devices used to achieve this differed from person to person, depending on a narrator's ingenuity and talents" (MacNeil 1987, xxxii).

6 This problem is disquietingly familiar to folklorists and ethnographers. Two particularly thoughtful and challenging books on the topic are: *"In Vain I Tried To Tell You:" Essays in Native American Ethnopoetics* (Hymes 1981) and *The Spoken Word and the Work of Interpretation* (Tedlock 1983).

THREE

THE TELLER IN THE TALE[1]

I T is widely understood that fictional characters are often patterned, wholly or in part, on actual people. Features, forms, voices, motivations, and the general demeanor of familiar acquaintances find their way into imaginative stories. The preferences and judgements of authors also guide their stories. This is no less so for folktales than for any other kind of story. It is no secret that fact and fancy are not as distinct in the expressive arts as we think them to be in ordinary life. How does the process of actualizing fiction come about? I was curious to discover if this was a conscious decision or a spontaneous act. I wondered, too, how these choices might contribute to or detract from the effectiveness of a story, for the listeners and for the narrators.

I addressed these points through the responses of two Toronto area performers, Stewart Cameron and Marylyn Peringer, familiar to me as tellers and as colleagues. Over a period of several years we shared information in open-ended interviews and through casual conversations and letters. I had also observed them in a number of storytelling events, private and public. In order to keep their remarks closer to this creative context, our interviews took place around the telling of a story of their choice. Each approached the act of creation in different ways and with different degrees of consciousness. Stewart Cameron was aware that he was modelling Jack in "The Three Feathers" on his own son, but until I began to ask how and why, he had not realized how intricate and continuous this process had become. Marylyn Peringer was surprised to discover how familiar people and objects had come into her stories unexpectedly, and how much they enriched the stories for her. From the perspective gained in the interview context, both were able to comment on the subtle ways that their stories reflected their concerns about their own lives and convictions.

A formal interview has the advantage of placing a story in a different perspective for the teller by taking it out of the more natural context of the storytelling event, the platform performance. In the midst of repeated tellings in different contexts a story takes on a life of its own, but when a narrator is asked to consider an episode, motif, or character out of the performance context they must stop the story in midstream in their minds in order to sense what is happening as they tell it. In this way they might detect how the familiar waking world has suggested an intuitive interpretation that they are not aware of—or not fully so. They see for themselves how they awaken a printed story by breathing their own lives into it.

The interchange of reality and fantasy is not surprising to narrative scholars, who have long recognized folktales and wondertales as significant literary expressions.[2] These scholars all concentrated on oral material developed over generations in European communities. When traditional narration arises from the overall social fabric of a community even the most fantastic story is alive with local characters, settings, motivations, and other narrative attributes that reverberate for tellers and listeners. A story figure might have the face or disposition of a neighbor, a situation might arise from the teller's own experience, a house in the forest might be a familiar home. As we saw in the introduction, narrators who grow up listening to Märchen (wondertales), legends, and other stories of a community learn them in the context of personal associations that join the common reality of everyday life to the very uncommon reality of the stories in which trees speak and ants can help a heroine or hero succeed. This story-world that exists between what we call fantasy and reality has intrigued many who have explored wondertales. The observations of Linda Dégh (particularly 1995a: 93-151), Max Lüthi (1985, 1986) and Lutz Röhrich (1991) are invaluable in understanding this betwixt and between world of reality/unreality. Dégh explores actual tellers of tales, Lüthi focuses on the stories and their deep magic, and Röhrich comments on the abiding connections between the fantasy of tales and the waking world of reality.

For tellers of these tales it is a challenge to find their own feet as they balance between seemingly separate realities that are, in wondertales, one world. Their artistic innovation develops as they become increasingly experienced in drawing together their own real and fictive worlds. It is not only that the tales live in tellers' minds, but that tellers live within the stories—not literally as participants but as temporary visitors, walking along with their protagonists, as we will see in the stories and comments of Marylyn Peringer and Stewart Cameron.[3]

For many tellers in traditional and in organized storytelling, the story as they learned it from a person or a book is sufficient as a place to begin; they have only to remember the sequence of events and characters, the necessary repetitions, the opening and concluding phrases, and they can build their own story. But for some this becomes too rigid, too restraining. Folklorist Linda Dégh explored the issue of how traditional narrators with more than ordinary talent retained the storyline yet managed to rise above it to fashion an artistic composition; she affirmed what we will see in the case of Stewart Cameron and Marylyn Peringer—that creativity occurs in the skillful embroidery of detail. Dégh observes that this kind of elaboration is quite the opposite of the brief narratives (jokes and anecdotes, for example) so popular in our contemporary lives; in these kinds of stories detail is deliberately left out in order to put the weight of the story on the punchline. "In contrast," she states, "the good narrator of magic tales must prove his art within the framework of the tale by including his own thoughts and weaving his personal opinions into the tale" (Dégh 1989:224). And, I add, thinking of Marylyn and others, *her* thoughts and opinions.

In addition to elaborating on details and expressing their own viewpoints, tellers also deepen a story by connecting it to their own everyday lives. This might be true of only some parts of a tale, as when North Carolina narrator Ray Hicks identifies himself with the Jack character in his tales (Sobol 1994b; Oxford 1987). Or certain stories as a whole might echo themes from the teller's life, as in Bob Barton's story, "The Honest Penny."

Personal preferences of individual narrators are essential in understanding the dynamics of creativity.[4] In the dramatic art of storytelling we can find the artistry in the skillful interweaving of communal and personal interests. This is no less true in organized storytelling than in oral tradition. However, narrators in oral tradition feel a strong commitment to a community of tellers, as we saw in the case of Joe Neil MacNeil. Platform performers are freer to develop their storytelling repertoire and style in isolation if they wish. They can simply claim a story, lift it free from any relevant cultural context, and rework it as their own without reference it its traditional associations. This is all the easier since many popular folktale collections provide no context beyond a generalized source. They might mention the country of origin but there is often no contextual information that expands the story and offers possibilities for interpretation. Rarely, if ever, are the tale-tellers identified. Such stories are often regarded as "public domain" material, free to be used and manipulated as a teller sees fit. Some tellers respond by simply reciting the story as they learned it, adding nothing at all from their own experience; others go to the other extreme, modernizing and personalizing tales extensively, deconstructing the old and recreating "modern" (or "postmodern") tales in an entirely new context.

Between these two ends of the creative continuum there are tellers who respond by doing their own comparative research and trying to understand how stories arose from living narrators in a specific time and place. Marylyn and Stewart each found their own ways of seeking this kind of connection with the stories they tell here. I wanted to discover how they faced the challenges of modern audiences, how they found ways of bringing stories to life from printed texts without transforming them into postmodern literary stories. Their methods and motivations were different, but both had similar views of folktales as a enigmatic metaphors for modern life, and for adults, not only for children.

Marylyn Peringer and Stewart Cameron were active in the widespread Toronto area storytelling community for a number of years. Like many others I met they were aware of their personal preferences for certain kinds of tales as well as the place of the tales within particular oral traditions. Many of Stewart's songs and stories were of Scottish origin, while Marylyn had found that French tales and legends drew her strongly. Each sought out other variant texts of a story when they could find them, both in print and in oral tellings when possible. Marylyn did further research in order to gain a fuller sense of social and historic contexts as well as esthetic possibilities. They were also attentive to ways in which the tales reverberated from their own past and present lives and back again, as the stories developed through performances.

I met both Stewart and Marylyn during the 1985 Toronto festival, the first of several I attended. A few years later I asked if they would take part in individual interviews centered around the retelling of a favorite story, and if they would discuss how it reflected their experiences as performers. Both agreed enthusiastically. The story Stewart told, "Jack and the Three Feathers," was one I had heard at my very first festival, though I did not know then that it was a particular favorite of his because Jack had gradually taken on the character of his son Duncan. The interview and the narration of "The Three Feathers" took place in 1988; we exchanged letters the next year, which allowed Stewart to reflect on this story in particular, and on his storytelling in general.

Ten years passed between the time I met Marylyn in Toronto and our long-overdue formal interview on a park bench in the Yukon in 1994, though we conversed at several festivals and corresponded regularly in between. Marylyn chose a French-Canadian tale, "The Horoscope," that reflected a number of facets of her life, among them her love of the French language and her Catholicism.

By looking at these two tellers and their story examples I hope to show how reality enters the realm of the wondertale.

Marylyn Peringer[5]

In response to one of my questions about "The Horoscope," Marylyn said, with a hint of surprise, "Oh, the story is more than the story," meaning that she was aware that the basic storyline was only the framework for meaningful expression. I explore how she came to realize this after several years of telling the story.

Marylyn discovered "L'horoscope," an Acadian legend told by Benoit Benoit, in a collection by Luc Lacoursière.[6] In it a farmer asks an astrologer to predict the fates of his three sons and is told that the oldest will be hanged at twenty-one, so he decides to avert this by working his son to death. The son eventually leaves home, meets and befriends a mysterious stranger and they work together on various farms and then in a shipyard. Here he falls in love with and marries the owner's daughter; on their wedding day the horoscope prediction is revealed but the friend, actually a guardian angel, saves the young man from his fate.

After listening to Marylyn tell this story I asked her how her identity as a storyteller had evolved. Like many tellers I met, Marylyn's first public experience was accidental; she had decided to do her oral presentation in a French conversation class on the rich store of Quebecois lore and legends, not realizing how challenging this would be. As she described it, it was "the beginning of a whole long tale" that continues today after almost two decades of research and performances. Though her performing career has centered on bilingual tales, Marylyn is neither French nor Canadian; she grew up in New Jersey, the child of an English father and a Maltese mother. Her interest in French Canada that began in the conversation class blossomed as she told more and more stories from French-Canadian traditions.

Marylyn places high value on precision, loyalty, and integrity in her life and in her stories. "I've always liked creating order," she said, and expressed this in her careful preparation and telling of stories. She felt that the detailed research she put into each tale "informs your telling, and makes it more authoritative and more confident." This was, she thought, of utmost importance for professional tellers who relied on printed stories; that is, to recreate at least some of the social and cultural context.

Marylyn recalled how she rehearsed the story of "The Horoscope" several years earlier, pacing back and forth in a dormitory in Moncton, New Brunswick, where she was preparing to give a storytelling workshop. She learned and told it in French for her Acadian audiences, but told it to me in English. As she practised it aloud to herself she began "to smooth out the few inconsistencies in the original." She struggled with the scruples of changing a collected text, aware that a folklorist would say, "It has to be left that way, that's the way the story was told." She felt that there were "artistic decisions that I made in order to make the pattern clearer. I suppose that I felt that the pattern had to be as clear as some of the images in the story were to me." She carefully chose to make slight alterations that were appropriate for her as a performer rather than a researcher, responsibly aware of what she was doing and concerned about being faithful to the "the spirit of the story" rather than the exact word-for-word text. For example, she felt she needed a clearer motivation for the father trying to work his son to death, and thus had him overly concerned about family reputation (he would have been embarrassed to have his son hanged publicly). She increased the ties of friendship between the young man and the enigmatic stranger rather than emphasizing his mystery, as in the legend. She also portrayed the shipowner's daughter as livelier and more decisive, strengthening her presence in the story. She ended the story by describing the happy couple rather than focusing on the guardian angel as he disappeared. She was aware that these modest alterations, particularly in the conclusion, shifted the nature of the tale:

> The ending I added, because in the original he just walked away and they never saw him again. He just walked away and that was all, and I wanted to put, I don't know, I thought it deserved a more fairytale type ending—'And all the days of their lives...'—a happy-ever-after type of ending which was related to their marriage in some way.

This seemingly small change transforms the story from its original legendary form into a folktale, by emphasizing the happy union of the couple rather than the supernatural feats of the guardian angel.

In order to avoid arbitrary changes made simply for personal reasons, Marylyn began extensive research on French tales in the United States and Canada. She sought out comparative material from the Robarts Library at the University of Toronto, from publications of Laval University in Quebec, from back issues of *The Journal of American Folklore*, and from "all sorts of books and transcriptions of tapes, collections from here and there, folktales, fairytales, lore, commentaries on the stories." She discovered variants of the story from Spain, Czechoslovakia, and Ireland, not to mention a version from India called "Savitri and Satyavan." Since much of her material came from scholarly collections rather than from popular books she understood that the story was indeed more than the story, as she put it; that outside the context of a functioning community the texts lost some of their significance and that she had to work to recontextualize them:

> Most of the sources I got them from came from storytellers whose listeners were familiar with all the tales so not everything had to be explained. So of course I had to do so much preliminary work in just explaining the beliefs that had given rise to these particular stories.

By her own research Marylyn discovered that she needed to know more about the overall context of her stories from the viewpoint of their original tellers. In this way she was able to create a more relevant context for herself as well as for her listeners. She was interested to hear from our correspondence that this approach was favored by narrative scholars. I have mentioned Henry Glassie's work in Northern Ireland, and here his comments are most relevant:

> Context is not in the eye of the beholder, but in the mind of the creator. Some of context is drawn in from the immediate situation, but more is drawn from memory. It is present, but invisible, inaudible. Contexts are mental associations woven around texts during performance to shape and complete them, to give them meaning (Glassie 1982:33).

This elusive contextualizing was what Marylyn tried to sense in her own search. In order to become a more effective creator herself she tried to see into the mind of the creators with whom her stories arose.

In the long process of seeking out and preparing narratives from

French-Canadian sources Marylyn developed a sense of comparative research that is one of the invaluable tools of a folklorist. She was especially excited to find a version of "The Horoscope" from India, "Savitri and Satyavan" mentioned earlier. In this story a young woman falls in love with and marries a man even though she knows that he is fated to die on their first anniversary; she manages to trick Yama, god of death, into three promises that can only be kept if the husband lives. Marylyn said with wonder, "It's the same story! How did that story get half way across the world into some little French-Canadian fishing village in New Brunswick?" She occasionally told both together without commentary, allowing them to echo from one to another. This curiosity led her to appreciate comparative work on folktales, and in particular the value of indexes that listed the titles of variant texts, and of the motifs within stories (Aarne/Thompson 1973; Ashliman 1987; MacDonald 1982; Thompson 1955-58).[7] Any teller using these indexes could find comparable stories and story motifs from a broad range of cultural areas.

One of the aspects of both texts that attracted Marylyn was the central place held by promises that were made and kept. In "The Horoscope" the astrologer promises that the son will be hanged on his twenty-first birthday, but he is saved because he promises his mother that he will pray to his guardian angel—who eventually saves his life; the son is faithful in his promises to his mysterious friend, to the shipyard owner for whom he toils, and to the owner's daughter whom he pledges to marry. In the Indian variant the daughter extracts promises as well as keeping them: she compels her father to promise that she can choose her own husband, promises a young man's parents that she will protect him, later tricks Yama into promises that save her husband's life. Marylyn remembered another story that hinged on promises, a Quebecois legend in which the hanged corpse of a murderer is insulted by a young man and returns to life to avenge himself; the young man is saved by promising to have the corpse properly buried and to show respect for the dead—and he keeps his promises. None of these stories contain the deliberate disobedience and cunning capriciousness that we will see in Stewart's story of Jack.

The motif of faithfulness was one of the ways that Marylyn connected her stories to the world of experience, observing that such stories offer hope for "things coming around right" when we maintain our integrity. "I always try to keep my promises, and I'm so grateful when I find that reinforced in a story." It is not the rigidity of morals she found compelling but the fact that the characters demonstrated "so much love, so much faithfulness." She also expressed an interest in stories featuring angels and devils, at least in part because such stories stress the constant human struggle with good and evil. These figures are particularly favored in French-Canadian tales of all sorts, humorous folktales, legends, and wondertales. Thus it is not unusual that the guardian angel in "The Horoscope" takes the place of the fairy godmother or other typical folktale helpers. She commented that this was particularly true for French-Canadian Catholic legends; "you know, they give the devil so much time, so I can see them putting an angel in for a little bit more equal time for the other direction."

Marylyn found that as she told this story (and others) it gradually began to express aspects of her own life—people she knew, objects she was familiar with, situations she had experienced. The shipowner's daughter came to resemble a lively young woman in her choir; the mahogany table at the wedding feast was her mother's table, which Marylyn had often polished as a child; the keeping of promises and of creating order were a daily part of her own life. She remarked that such personal content was usually known only to her, that she did not "always say all the things I know about a story," but felt that what she understood might carry over to listeners:

I think it [personal details] always exists in an invisible sort of way—and it certainly clarifies the pictures you get of things. You see more clearly, and the more clearly you see, the more clearly your audience can get their own images.

Marylyn was puzzled at first that she could not "see" the young man as clearly as other characters, and realized that this was because she was viewing the story from his point of view: "In so much of the story I am him, I see everything through his eyes, and that's why I don't see him—and I have no wish to look in a mirror and see what I look like!" In other words, it is not personal ego that dominates the character but quite the reverse; Marylyn finds herself taken into the story instead of consciously placing herself there by identifying with the young man. She does not become the character, she moves through the story as if she were accompanying him even more closely than his guardian angel.

She realized as she was telling "The Horoscope" this time, to me, that it had grown so personal that she could hardly tell it without tears. "I'm starting to cry more and more every time I tell that story, and I think it's because of the people I'm telling it to. They all become part of it." She recalled times and places she had told "The Horoscope": to her young son while giving him a bath (she often practised first with her family), watching his eyes grow wide with fear as the rope descended; to a married couple celebrating their anniversary and thinking back to how they met; to a roomful of parents at a workshop in Manitoba who were all in tears at the end of the story; and to a group of friends at the wedding reception of the young woman in her choir who was embodied in the shipowner's daughter. "They've all become part of the story," she said, as she explained the tears that came as she concluded the story with me.

Because the story had become so personal, Marylyn said that she did not tell it casually but always waited to "sense out the reaction of listeners" in order to guess how they might respond. When I asked what indications she looked for she replied that listeners might indicate readiness by the kind of attention they paid to the other stories she had told—whether they were sitting attentively or nonchalantly, if there was fidgeting or giggling, or if listeners were simply not in the mood for a serious story. She was careful for herself as well as for her listeners because the story was so important to her: "I'm not really sure, but it's a very powerful story, and I know that it moves me very much."

Marylyn felt very strongly that her research and contemplation, her artistic decisions, audience reactions, and memories of the listeners themselves, all helped bring a story to life. Marylyn insisted, as I said earlier, "Oh yes, the story is more than the story," and now we can see more fully what she meant by her enthusiastic statement. But while she understood the work she put into her stories, she also seemed to downplay these contributions with her concluding statement, "What more can I say? The stories say everything." The apparent contradiction is clarified by understanding that the story becomes enriched through her research, her personal connections, and the responses from both Marylyn and the many listeners who have heard it; these all become a natural part of the narrative so there is nothing more for Marylyn to add, except to try and trace a few of the threads of her weaving for an inquisitive folklorist.

Stewart Cameron

Stewart began his telling of "The Three Feathers" with a familiar opening describing the family context:

> Once upon a time in Scotland there was a king, and he had a very, very prosperous kingdom, and he had three healthy, strong princes, sons, to look after—and to look after him. Now he was getting on in years and his mind was bending towards just who he was going to leave this kingdom to.

Stewart used his own son as a living model for unworldly Jack but when he spoke these words in Toronto in 1988, he did not know that he would find his own mind "bending towards just who he was going to leave this kingdom to." Barely a year after he spoke these words he died of cancer, a great loss not only to his family but to storytellers throughout Canada.

Stewart, of Sudbury, Ontario, began his performing career as a singer who favored "the ballads with their long and complicated plots full of blood and mayhem." (1979 program, Toronto Festival of Storytelling.) His fascination with "complicated plots" led him to traditional tales, which began to appear in his repertoire in the 1980s as he became a regular contributor to the annual Toronto Storytelling Festival and to many of their weekly Friday night gatherings. Stewart did not come to ballad-singing and storytelling from a traditional background in a rural community, though both he and his wife Dianne learned some of their songs and music from their respective "pan-Celtic" families. Dianne wrote to me the year after his death: "We were certainly exposed to people in our families and immediate neighborhood who could sing, relate anecdotal stories, or talk about family history. Stew played accordion and guitar as a child, and was very early involved in doing Scottish songs for his family gatherings" (letter, March 8, 1990).

Unlike many other urban, non-traditional performers, Stewart appeared most often with his family. Dianne was an experienced singer and son Duncan and daughter Moira were gradually brought into the act as they matured. Dan Yashinsky, one of the founding members of the Storytellers School, recalls Cameron performances at the weekly Friday night gatherings: "There would be singing, funny stories, ghost stories. The audience would join in—and I'd leave feeling like I'd been to a party in a very warm, friendly living room (*Appleseed Quarterly*, Volume IV, No. 1, Fall 1989: 5).

These performances were closer to the more intimate oral traditional model than to the more usual theatrical model of many urban storytelling events, possibly because they grew naturally from the family setting. Daughter Moira Cameron remembered that storytelling was always important:

> At home, storytelling came naturally to my father. Having two story-minded kids certainly gave him ample inspiration to learn and tell stories in the home environment. My father would tell me a story almost every night before bed. Often, because his stories were so long, he would have to tell them in several instalments—one each night—until the story ended. "The Three Feathers" was one of my favorites (letter, February 6, 1990).

Because storytelling and singing began at home, Stewart (and the Camerons as a whole) developed a strong sense of performance as a communal exchange in which tellers and listeners were not separated by a "fourth wall," and also in which the individual performers functioned as part of the ensemble. Stewart was always aware that any single story or song was only one link in a complex chain of artistry. He never viewed "Jack and The Three Feathers" as his own story, even though it became one of his favorites and took on unique features as a result of his frequent retellings—and came to be associated with him in the Toronto community.

I first heard Stewart tell "Jack and The Three Feathers" in 1985 at one of the Toronto festival "swap sessions," when he introduced it as his favorite tale. The next year I had the chance to hear his story again, to ask him about how he had learned it and why he loved it so. He said he had first heard Jim Strickland tell the story at one of the regular Friday night events in Toronto, recorded that performance, and got permission from Strickland to retell the story: "The story when I first heard it [from Strickland] had an immediate appeal. I won't bother to analyze why—it just did. When I began telling it, it developed a life and purpose all its own" (letter, January 29, 1988).

In 1988 I returned Toronto and was able to tape Stewart's retelling of the story as it had evolved after several years of performances at home and in public. The annual Toronto Festival of Storytelling, with dozens of tellers and large crowds of avid listeners, was taking place all around us, but we managed to find a quiet room with no one else present. We shut the door hoping for complete privacy, but as I turned on the machine and Stewart began to speak, three boys (I would guess their ages as eight, ten, and eleven) came in noisily and sat down at a table near the door, across from where we were sitting. I tried to ignore their presence, hoping that they would realize we were taping a story and would quiet down, but Stewart acknowledged them with a nod and launched into his story. They went on with their own loud conversations, pretending not to listen but casting glances in our direction. Stewart turned occasionally and addressed parts of the story to them directly and they began acting out the roles of the three sons among themselves.

Thus instead of being a distraction, the presence of these three boys inspired Stewart to add details that I did not remember from his earlier telling, and to act out more of the story with broad gestures, facial expressions, and changes of voice. These elaborations made the story much lengthier than the one I had heard in 1985, and considerably richer. Also, he told the entire story with an engaging Scottish accent that I did not recall hearing in 1985.

About half way through the story the door opened again and a man wandered in and sat quietly in the opposite corner, paying no obvious attention to what was going on. I was surprised to see that Stewart seemed, momentarily, to lose his concentration. The casual conversational tone and natural pace shifted into a more formal and elaborate style, which lengthened his tale even more. (In my memory the story as told in 1985 was not more than ten minutes long, but this telling took up the full side of a half-hour tape.) Stewart quickly recovered his balance, and when he finished the story he addressed his closing words to the three boys, who had stayed to the very end, each keeping in character within the story. He then turned to the man in the corner, who was, as it turned out, Jim Strickland himself. I understood why Stewart had become concerned with Jim's entry; telling a story in the presence of the one who "owns" it (in the teller's mind at least) is a daunting feat.

Stewart was aware of the effects of both the boys and Jim Strickland. He commented that the story "wasn't very tight," noting that he had not told it for a while. He admitted that Strickland's presence had affected his telling of the tale and seemed to feel that he had not "done as well" as usual. He did not discuss the three boys, though he had obviously enjoyed their presence and benefited from their participation.

The process of evolution is enlightening even when it is seen in the fleeting history of a single variant told by one person. Stewart, of course, was aware of the longer evolution of the story over the few years in which he told it. He was sensitive to the immediate effects of audience on performance and of his own response to the differing contexts of storytelling within his own family and in public performances. For example, he described how the motif of Jack's "mucking about in the mud" came to take an increasingly central part in his telling because both he and his audiences found it compelling. (Strickland's variant has Jack "puttering about in the back garden.")

> When I began telling it to my kids I found that it changed considerably [according] to my audience's response. My son Duncan was heavily into the wonders of mud at the time and spent many hours mucking around in our "back garden." I naturally enlarged the importance of this part of the story (undated letter, 1988).

Another memorable feature of the story is the convincing vitality of Jack and his opportunistic brothers, which also evolved as Stewart became more experienced:

> The characters within the story gradually assumed their own peculiar personalities as I told the story. Jack becomes not so much a fool as an absent-minded child, too full of his own world and imagination to be overly concerned with the "real world" around him. His brothers, on the other hand, are worldly wise and socially conscious. They do the right things, go to the right schools and generally excel at doing what princes are supposed to do (undated letter, 1988).

Stewart understood that such narrative developments were a natural part of the storytelling process and did not try to hold himself rigidly to Strickland's text, commenting in his letter that "other things have crept into my telling of the tale as well." His critical portrayals of the ambitious brothers and of the two somewhat pompous kings, human and frog, contrast with his sympathetic portrayal of Jack, who simply refuses to play the worldly game available to him through his position as prince in a royal family. Stewart was also fond of the frog princess who allows Jack to continue his adventures in the mud even after they become king and queen. Indeed, Stewart emphasized that even marriage and regal responsibilities did not squelch Jack's love of play. It was this conclusion that expressed his sense of the story most fully. He ended his letter to me by quoting it fully, and poetically. I quote it here as he wrote it:

The ending of my tale is different also. Jack ends up marrying the princess and inheriting the kingdom, but:

> She is as wise as he is foolish,
> As industrious as he is lazy.
> And she is quite understanding
> When he slips away from his kingly duties
> And putters about in the back garden;
> For after all, considering her background,
> She knows just how much fun that can be
>   (undated letter, 1988).

This written text can be compared to his closing words in the oral text of "The Three Feathers." It is obviously an important feature of the story, not just a convenient way to end it.

Tellers of tales in all times and in all places have always faced the challenge of making their stories convincing for their audiences and for themselves without losing the integrity of the story. Stewart understood that the creative balance between teller and audience was by its nature a risky venture in which the teller's interpretations were destined to be acclaimed by some listeners and rejected by others. He noted, for example, that he was sometimes faulted for digressions and anachronisms, such as his elaborately detailed descriptions of Jack "mucking about in the mud" as well as playing with Lego, and for "side allusions to the [British] Royal Family" that were not always complimentary. He felt that his responsibility to his listeners was to create an immediately entertaining story without denying his own faith in the deeper realities of the tale: "This approach is a tricky business. I do not require my audience to believe in what I tell, but I make damn sure they know that I believe in it. My characters are real and the story I tell is important, no matter how far-fetched, fantastic, or ridiculous" (undated letter, 1988).

In his desire to remain true to a story as well as to the audience, he struck a balance between stability (telling it as he heard it from Jim Strickland) and innovation (responding to his own esthetic sense, his own life experiences, and the immediate performing context). He believed in the inner truth of the story but he did not demand this of his listeners: "Anachronisms abound in all my telling. Some consider this a fault. They say a storyteller should create a self-consistent world conducive to a willing suspension of disbelief. I don't even attempt to do that in many of my tales. I find that I can draw more people into a tale if I don't insist on 'suspension of disbelief' as a prerequisite" (undated letter, 1988). Stewart was certainly willing to suspend disbelief, to see Jack as a convincing human being and not merely a character to be manipulated for theatrical effect.

Like the aging king in his story, Stewart passed on a living legacy, not only to his family but to those who heard and remembered his stories. Stewart's modern Jack retains his place as an ordinary hero, adaptable to challenges and adversity and utterly lacking in worldly ambition—even in modern urban life.

Like Marylyn, Stewart brought life to this story by allowing it to develop personal connections to his own life, sometimes aware and sometimes not that this was happening. Like Marylyn in "The Horoscope," Stewart found himself in his own story as it grew.

I began this chapter by asking how professional storytellers might "modernize" a wondertale without losing the balance between traditional stability and individual innovation. We have seen how Marylyn Peringer and Stewart Cameron were clearly conscious of their commitment to the stories as they first learned them, not because they were unwilling to make any changes but because they had a sense of connection with the wider tale-body from which individual texts arose. They developed the textures of their stories by reworking them for the different contexts in which they retold them again and again. In the continual telling of the tales their personal life experiences came naturally into the stories as reflected in characters, objects, and their own ethical views. They saw the reality of the stories, and this sense gave their performances a more compelling quality.

Narrative scholar Lutz Röhrich, speaking of the nature of reality in folktales, noted that among traditional narrators it was the younger and less experienced tellers who considered folktales to be unrealistic; older narrators found in them ample range for expressing the realities of life as they knew them. As he noted: "Unique personal experiences can supply a narrator with a lifelong stock of motifs and give his or her narratives their unique stamp" (Röhrich 1991:202). We have seen how these two tellers skilfully drew on their wealth of personal experiences to bring old tales to full life in the modern world. By understanding and developing the full power of metaphor, they offered what Röhrich described as "a link between the present and an archaic, magical predecessor of our world-view," one that was not bound by time and place nor by politics and history (Röhrich 1991:4).

It is obvious that a teller learns from experience what is effective and what is not; but what also comes with experience is the many subtle ways in which one's own telling of a tale comes to reveal one's own life. The personalizing of the stories by both Marylyn and Stewart was not entirely a conscious process; as often as not it was discovered after the fact, sometimes only during our interviews and correspondence.

The two texts here cannot be regarded as typical of the full repertoires of these two experienced tellers, but since each was freely chosen we can assume that these particular stories reflect strong individual preferences. Marylyn's choice revealed a partiality for protagonists who find themselves in impossible situations and must rely on help from an unexpected source. The young man in "The Horoscope" is a good-hearted and somewhat naive protagonist whose integrity and devotion are rewarded by a guardian angel. Marylyn's involvement in the Catholic church, as an active participant and as a choir member, provided her with inspiration for re-visioning characters, objects, and situations.

Stewart's sense of the reality of the story was very clear. He insisted more than once that his characters and his stories were genuine for him even if they might not be so for all of his listeners. Stewart was aware of his conscious artistic reworking, but he also understood that the elements of deepest verity for him (the characters of the old king and his youngest son) arose gradually and were as much intuitive as deliberate. Stewart did not opportunistically adjust the story to fit his family, but told it in such a way that his life experience had a place for expression.

I also note that a firm bond between these tellers and the supportive Toronto community is implicit in the unfolding of these stories within the dramatic context of events sponsored by the Storytellers School; both were regular contributors to the weekly Friday night events and the annual festival as well as other local events, and these particular stories are still associated with them. They have become the tellers in the tales because they allowed the tales to live within them, and this continues to be recognized and honored by members of the Toronto storytelling community, and like-minded communities elsewhere.

THE HOROSCOPE[8]

(Marylyn Peringer, 1994)

Marylyn told me this story as we sat on a park bench overlooking the Yukon River in Whitehorse, where we were performing at the annual storytelling festival in the Yukon. The taped story has intermittent background noises from children playing behind us, a dog barking, the siren of a police car across the river, and the constant wind that almost drowned out the story at some points. Marylyn interrupted herself at the beginning to ask if I wanted her to tell it in French or in English. We agreed on English with occasional French phrases in order to retain some of the flavor. I have used poetic indentation to indicate the two points in the story where Marylyn breaks into almost a rhythmic chant when she is completely immersed in the story—so much so that conscious use of French disappears at these points. The story as she tells it is a variant of AT type 934B, "Youth to Die on His Wedding Day." Marylyn describes it from Luc Lacoursière's notes as "Hero Avoids His Predicted Destiny."

Il *était une fois,* Once upon a time there was a farmer, and he had three sons. One day, when these sons were almost completely grown up, he went to an *astrologue,* the astrologer, to have their horoscopes read. He gave the *astrologue* their birthdates and the astrologer consulted his charts, he consulted the stars, and then he said, "Monsieur, I have the horoscope for your three sons: *Le cadet,* your younger son, he's going to be a priest."

"Oh, wonderful!" said the farmer.

"And your middle son, *lui, il sera avocat,* he's going to be a lawyer."

"Oh, marvellous, *merveilleux!*" said the father.

"But your third son, Monsieur, I don't like to tell you."

"Oh tell me, tell me!"

"Well ... your eldest son, *l'âiné,* he ... well, when he's twenty-one years old, on the very date of his birthday, he is going to be hanged."

"He's going to be hanged? My son? That's impossible. My eldest son, he's a good lad, he's never done anything wrong!"

"I'm sorry," said the *astrologue,* "but he's going to be hanged. That is his fate. It is written in the stars. There is nothing we can do."

And so the farmer stumbled out of the house of the astrologer completely *bouleversé,* shaken. What was he going to do? His eldest son, hanged, at twenty-one! You see, the father had quite a bit of property, and he had made provisions that when he, the eldest son, was twenty-one, he would come into that property. Now did it mean that the government who hanged him could take the property too? And the disgrace upon the family ... oh, this could not happen, thought the farmer. This could not happen. The farmer's heart hardened. By the time he got home his mind was made up. "My eldest son will not be hanged on his twenty-first birthday," he said. "He will not be hanged because he will already be dead, from too much work."

So the next morning at five o'clock the eldest son was pulled out of his bed, thrust out into the fields, given a list of tasks that would be too much for ten men to do, and told not to come back until they were all done. And so the poor eldest son *travaillait, travaillait, travaillait,* worked on and on. He didn't stop to eat, he didn't stop to drink, he didn't stop to rest ... he wanted to please his father and he was obedient, so on and on he worked, and he didn't get home until two o'clock in the morning. He stumbled in half dead with fatigue and his father was still up, and he said, "*Papa, pourquoi me punis tu?*, why are you punishing me? What have I done?"

"Oh, you haven't done anything," said the father, "I'm just checking, to make sure you deserve that inheritance you're going to get when you're twenty-one." And the next day, the very same thing; *à cinq heures du matin, envoyé aux champs pour travailler.* And once again he came in more dead than alive, and again he said, "Papa, what have I done, why are you punishing me?" And again his father said, "*moi, je ne te punis pas,* but I'm not punishing you. I'm making sure you deserve that inheritance."

And this went on for a week, and by the end of the week, well, the poor eldest son, he was nearly dead, and he knew that he certainly would die if he stayed. He decided that he would leave the farm, and he went to his father and said, "*Papa, je quitte la ferme,* I'm going to leave the farm, I'm going to leave you. I'm going to go away, I'm going to go so far away that you'll never see me again. I can't stay here—I'll die if I stay here. But before I go, can't you please explain to me what this is all about?"

And his father said, "Given that you're going away, alright, I'll tell you. You see, I went to see an *astrologue,* I wanted to have your horoscope read, you and your brothers. And *il m'a dit,* he told me, '*le cadet,* the youngest, he's going to be a priest; and your older son, he's going to be a lawyer, *avocat*;' but you, *mon fils,* he told me that when you're twenty-one, on the very date of your birthday, you're going to be hanged." "*Il a dit ça! Moi?*" "Yes, *oui, voila ce qu' il a dit*—yes, you, that's what he said."

And for a long time the eldest son didn't say anything, and then at last he said, "Well, papa, if that is the case, I will go so far away that when it happens, no one here will hear about it. Thus no shame will be visited upon my family. You can give my inheritance to my brothers." And away he went.

But before he left, he said goodbye to his mother, and she cried, because he was her favorite. She wept, and she said, "*Mon fils, mon fils,* what's going to happen to you? You're going out into the world and I have no friends, no relations that I can ask to look after you. Look, you must promise me something. Wherever you go to find work, find the nearest church, go in, and say a prayer to your guardian angel, *ton ange gardien*. Because you know that each of us has an angel looking after us, and if you pray to your guardian angel, then I will know that someone is looking after you."

So of course he promised his mother that he would do this, and then he left. Now the only kind of work he knew was farm work, so he got a job at a nearby farm, and when he finished there he went to another farm a bit farther away, and always a little farther, farther. But he didn't forget the promise he'd made to his mother. Every time he changed locations, he found the nearest church, and he'd go in, get down on his knees, and say a prayer to his *ange gardien*.

And thus the summer passed, and it began to be fall, and the young man was walking along the road looking for another job. He passed a young man of his own age seated at the side of the road, and he [the seated man] said "*Bonjour, où vas-tu,* where are you going?" "*Bonjour,* he answered, I'm looking for a job."

"Oh, *moi aussi,* I'm looking for a job too. Let's go together." So they went together. They went together, and a farmer hired them for harvesting. Oh, about six weeks they were on that farm. A lot of work. They worked well together. They got to be good friends. Such good friends that when the farmer dismissed them because the harvest was over, they decided to stay together to get some more work. So they knocked at the door of another farm, but no, that farmer didn't need them. All the work was done. Who was going to hire someone in winter? At farm after farm the door was shut in their face.

So they decided they would stop looking for farm work and go to the city to see what work they could find, and they journeyed to a city that was on the sea coast. And there was a *chantier,* a shipyard, with a sign outside that said "Men Wanted."

"Oh," said the young man, "here they're building ships—I don't know how to do that." But his friend said, "Oh, don't worry, I have experience, I'll teach you." So the young man knocked at the door and the owner opened, and said, "Yes?" And the young man answered, "Well, we're looking for work." And the owner said, *avez-vous de l'experience*, do you have experience?" And the young man said, "*Non, je n'en ai pas, mais mon ami, il en a*, I don't but my friend does, and he's going to teach me."

"Well, I can really use some more help," said the owner, "so come on in and see what you can do."

The young man and his friend went in, and, oh, it was busy in that shipyard! There was a team of ten men working over here and a team of eight men working over there, and there were about fourteen men on another boat. But the owner took them to a place all by themselves, and there was a lot of wood there. So he said, "Start on the keel. Start on the keel—I'll let you two work all by yourselves and I'll see how good you are."

So the young man and his friend started all by themselves. And you know, that young man learned so well, and his friend taught him so well, that within three weeks they'd caught up to the other teams, even though there were so many more men in them and they'd had a head start. They caught up to them, and in another couple of weeks they'd finished the keel. Everyone was amazed at the quality of their work.

When it was finished, the young man's friend said, "You know what the next step is—the planking, *le bordage*, why don't you go to the owner's house and see if you can get it [the wood for the planking]." So the young man went to the owner's house, and he was just about to knock on the door when a window at the side of the front door opened wide, and the prettiest girl he'd ever seen, *une jolie demoiselle*, said, *Bonjour, jeune homme, es-tu venu me rendre visite*, You've come to see me?"

"Oh, *mademoiselle*," he said, "I wish I could, but I've come to talk to your father. It's business—I need the planking, for the shipyard."

"Oh, well," she said, "I'll go and get him." And she left.

The father was very, very pleased at what they had done, and gave him *le bordage*, the planking, and the young man got all of that material back to the shipyard, and he and his friend worked and worked for five more weeks and the planking was all in place. Then his friend said, "Alright, the next step is *les mâts*, the masts. Go and ask for the materials."

So the young man went back to the house, looked up at the

window, and sure enough, before he had a chance to knock at the door *la fenêtre s'ouvre*, the window opened, and there she was, that beautiful girl. She said, "*Bonjour, jeune homme*, this time have you come to see me?" "Oh," he said, "I would so love to, but it's business again. I, I have to get the materials for the masts." "Well," she said, "I'll go and get papa, but before I do, could I ask you a question? *Es-tu marié ou célibataire?* Are you married or single?" "*Oh, moi—je suis célibataire*, he said, "I'm single." "Oh! *Quelle belle réponse!* That's good! Now I'll go and ask papa."

The father came back, and was very pleased to find out what they had done, gave him the masts—or at least the materials for the masts—and the young man took them back to the shipyard, and he and his friend worked four weeks more and the masts were in place. Then his friend said, "*le dernier étage*, the last step of all, *les voiles*, the sails. Go and ask."

Oh, the young man went off with a happy heart towards the house of the owner, and sure enough, *la fenêtre*, the window was wide open and there she was again, that beautiful girl. "*Bonjour, jeune homme.*" "Hello *mademoiselle*, it's nice to see you again." "Ah, did you come to see me this time?" she asked. "Oh, *mademoiselle*," he said, "I do wish I could, but I've got to get the sails, that's what I've come for." "Alright," she said, "*je cherche papa*, I'll go and find papa. But before I do, can I ask you another question? Are you in love with anyone?" He turned red—"*Je n'y ai jamais pensé*, I've never thought about it." So she said, "I have, and it's you I love. Do you want to marry me? *C'est toi que j'aime. Veux-tu m'épouser?*" "*Ah oui mademoiselle, bien sûr*, of course I do—oh, wait a moment. I'd better go ask my friend's advice first. I don't like to do anything without consulting him. We're a team, you know. Wait a minute, don't go away!" And he ran back to the shipyard.

His friend said, "*Alors, les voiles*, aren't you going to bring the sails?" "Never mind the sails, this is more important! Guess what happened! The owner's daughter, she wants to marry me, what do you think?" "I think that's a good idea," said his friend, "She's a nice girl. You should marry her."

"Oh, wait until I tell her!" And he went running back to the window, and he said, "*mon ami, il dit 'oui,'*" my friend says 'yes'!"

"Wonderful," she said, "but now, what date?" "What date?" "What date shall we be married?" she said. "Oh—I'll ask my friend." So he ran back to the shipyard again. "*Où sont les voiles?* Where are the sails!" "Oh, never mind that. She wanted to know what date we should be married." "Well," his friend said, "I think we should get the boat finished first. So, if you got married ... if we launched the boat in the morning, you could get married in the afternoon."

"What a wonderful idea! I'll go and tell her." So he left the shipyard and ran back to the window and called, "*Après le lancement*—after the launching?" "Yes," she said, "after the launching. Now I'll go and get papa."

So her father came to the door, and found that not only did the young man want material for the sails, but also the hand of his daughter in marriage. And he gave it, he gave it joyfully! For, you see, she was his only child, and in those long-ago days women weren't allowed to run businesses by themselves so he knew that whoever married her would end up managing the shipyard. He wanted her to marry someone who was intelligent and honest and hardworking, and the young man was all three—so he gave him his consent, and he gave him material for the sails.

The young man carried them back to the shipyard, and he and his friend worked putting those sails up, installing them, and six weeks later, the boat was all ready.

It was a beautiful morning in spring when they launched that boat. Everybody at the shipyard was so excited—it was the first launching of the year. And everyone was excited too because they were going to be guests at a wedding that very afternoon.

But just before the ceremony that young man's friend said to him, "Now I have a favor to ask of you. I know that this is your wedding day and tonight will be your wedding night, and you probably feel like being alone with your wife, but I wonder—would you mind inviting me to dinner tonight? And could we eat outdoors in the garden? And could we eat, just the three of us, you, and your bride, and myself?" "I don't see why not," said the young man, "but I'll ask her, just to be sure." So before the ceremony he asked her, and she said, "Ah, *bien sûr*, he's your best friend, of course he can come for dinner."

And so they were married.

And all the people who were invited to the wedding toasted the health of the bride and groom and much happiness abounded. But then it became late, it became dark, the shadows lengthened, the guests left. Then the servants were instructed to carry a table out to the garden, three chairs were arranged around it, places were set for three, and there the young man and his bride entertained the man's friend at dinner.

And it was a lovely dinner. The servants came and went with different plates of food and they [the three friends] laughed and talked together, and it grew even later. And finally the meal was over and all the food was cleared away, and they still sat around that bare table. The young man smiled at his wife and she smiled back at him, and he took his chair and pushed it closer to her, then he bent down and he put his head on his wife's lap and he closed his eyes—and he fell asleep.

Now that was when his friend got up and said to the girl, "Don't be afraid. Just don't move and don't say anything." And she looked at him in surprise, because just a moment ago they had all been laughing together but now her husband's friend seemed so serious. He came over to her and he picked up her sleeping husband in his arms, and he put him on the table. And as he did so, the girl noticed that the night sky was opening a crack, and out of a hole in the sky was descending a rope, a thick rope with a noose on the end of it.

> She turned to her husband's friend
> but he cautioned her not to move,
> and not to speak,
> so she obeyed him;
> as the rope came down,
> the friend took the noose,
> and passed it around the neck of the young man,
> tying a knot,
> and when he let go,
> the rope began to ascend,
> pulling the bridegroom with it.

And the young woman watched in horror as her husband ascended into the dark sky.

How long she sat there looking upwards she had no idea, but she remained motionless, and she did not speak. Finally, she saw her husband coming down again—his feet, his legs, then the rest of him, and his neck was still in the noose—and his face still had the smile of a dreamer. And down, down, down he came, and the friend was waiting.

Once again he took him up in his arms,
laid him on the table,
slipped off the noose,
and the rope went up into the sky once more,
and disappeared.
Then the friend took the young man,
brought him back to his chair,
repositioned his head on the lap of his wife,
and then took his own seat,
at the table.

All at once the young man opened his eyes and he sat up and he looked around and said, "Oh, oh, I'm sorry. I fell asleep. I must have been dreaming. I had the strangest dream, and do you know what I dreamed? I dreamed that I was floating in the sky and there was something heavy on my neck."

"That is a strange dream," his friend said. Tell me, I have a question for you. Do you know what day this is?" "Of course," said the young man, "it's my wedding day ... Oh, wait a minute, wait ... this is my twenty-first birthday ... oh no, I'm going to be hanged today!"

"No you won't," his friend said, "I've already hanged you."

"You have!"

"Yes. You don't have to worry about that any more. But I do have another question for you. *Tu me connais?* Do you know who I am?"

"No," said the young man, "I don't know who you are."

"I'm your guardian angel," the friend said. "I brought you here, taught you your trade, and got you to meet your wife. Now you have a home, you have a future, you have a job, a trade, you don't have to worry any more. And God bless you both."

He got up, and he walked away, and they never saw him again.

But they prayed to him every day of their married life, which was long and happy.

THE THREE FEATHERS

(Stewart Cameron, 1988)

I listened enthusiastically as Stewart Cameron retold a Scottish variant of "The Three Feathers" (AT 402, "The Mouse (Cat, Frog, etc.) as Bride," taped at the 1988 Toronto Festival of Storytelling. Variant texts are in the Grimm collection, tales 63 ("The Three Feathers") and 106 ("The Poor Miller's Apprentice and the Cat"). We began the recording in an empty room but were soon joined by three boys, and later by one attentive adult who turned out to be Jim Strickland from whom Stewart had first heard the story. This variant is more than twice as long as the one I had heard in 1985, and certainly much longer than it might have been, due to Stewart's response at having an audience rather than just a machine and a curious folklorist. I have tried to capture Stewart's poetic phrasing at the end of the story. I also indicate his on-going responses to the other listeners—the boys and Jim Strickland—since these become part of his story.

Once upon a time in Scotland there was a king, and he had a very, very prosperous kingdom, and he had three healthy, strong princes, sons, to look after—and to look after him. Now he was getting on in years and his mind was bending towards just who he was going to leave his kingdom to. He wanted to leave it to the right man. Which of his three sons would do?

Well I tell you, two of his sons were everything you could expect as far as princes were concerned. You couldn't tell one from the other. They were great at all of the things that princes were supposed to do. They went to the polo and they went to the tennis matches and they went to the horse races, and one thing and another. And they always did well in their lessons, as far as courtly bowing is concerned, and politics and everything of that sort. A-one students they were. You couldn't wish for better. And they dressed to the teeth. No doubt about it—they looked the role of princes. And all of the girls were falling head over heels in love with them, vying for them right left and center.

But the third son, if you must know, was somewhat different. Jack was his name. Now the king would say, ah, somewhat easily [uneasily] that Jack spent most of his time tending to the back garden. But truth be told the back garden was nothing but a marsh full of muck from rain and drizzle, full of frogs, toads, bulrushes, and all manner of weeds. And that's where Jack liked to spend his time, just mucking around in the back garden.

Well, the king made up his mind that yes, he would have to decide, and he could not decide between his three sons—well, between two of them—just who he was going to leave his kingdom to. So, as all good kings do, he had a number of good advisors, some wise men, and he assembled them around him and asked the big question of them.

"How can I decide who I am going to leave my kingdom to?"

And they gave it some long and hard thought and came up with a solution:

"Just set your sons a quest."

"What's a quest?" said the king

[*Stewart is now beginning to tell the story to the boys off to our right, who still pretend to be uninterested, though they have become silent.*]

"Oh, just send them out to do something or find something in a certain period of time, and the one that does it to your fashion is the one that wins the kingdom in the end."

"That's a great idea," said the king, and he summoned his three sons in front of him.

He had an idea in mind, yes indeed. They stood in front of him, and the king said,

"I am going to set you three lads a quest. Each one of you is to go off, where the winds will take you, and come back with the most beautiful tablecloth in the entire world. And the one who comes back with the most beautiful, finely made tablecloth—that is the lad that will be the king after I go."

[*Here he turns and addresses the three boys as if he were the king, and at this they respond by giggling and pretending to take on the character of each brother. They actually leave the room briefly and return, still laughing.*]

Fair enough. The three lads were ushered up to the topmost turret of the castle and each one of them was given a white feather. The first lad, the oldest prince [*Stewart points to the boy on the left*], he was told,

"Go over to [the edge of] the turret and cast that feather to the winds. And whichever direction that feather goes, that's the direction you shall go to find the finest tablecloth in the entire world."

Well, the eldest son, he took the feather and he threw it over the turret of the castle, and it caught in the breeze—shhhwsh—and off to the east it went. Fair enough. He saddled and he bridled his horse, and he got his bags of gold and his suits of clothes up on his back, and enough provisions to last him a good long time, and he set off to the east after that feather and after that prize of a tablecloth.

Well, the second son [*Stewart points to the middle boy*], he came to the topmost turret, and he too was given a feather, and he too cast it to the winds and away it went—shhhwshh—to the west. He too saddled and bridled and dressed appropriately and away he went in search of the finest tablecloth in the west.

And of course Jack, too, must be given a chance at this. After all, you have to be fair about these things. So the king calls,

"Jack,"

[*Stewart indicates the remaining boy, who is already in character, acting silly and grinning foolishly.*]

and up he steps, and he was given a feather too. Jack took the feather in his rather grubby hands and threw it over the edge of the castle. Shhhwshhheeew, thunk—right down into the mud in the back garden.

[*The boy imitates Jack's actions.*]

"Oh well," says Jack, but he didna' mind.

Well, I tell you, a year and a day was the length of time these princes had to fulfill their quest. And just about that time—it was just about a year later, Jack found himself mucking about in the back garden. [*Stewart addresses himself to the boys again.*] You know, he had his rubber boots off to the side there, and he was mucking around in this little pool of brown, yucky water, squishing the mud up between his toes ... Ach, there's no more beautiful feeling in the world than to have the squishing up between the big toe and the little toes. Just marvellous. So he was squishing around, and trying to do a sword fight with a little bit of a bulrush he had in his hand, slicing back and forth and pretending he was the prince he should have been, when there, in front of him, he hears this little bit of a voice.

"Jack! Jack my man!" [*He uses a higher, lighter voice.*]

Jack looks around, you know, but there's nobody there whatsoever. So he says,

"Ach, it's just the wind."

But then as he's mucking around, squishing back and forth, he hears the voice again:

"Jack, Jack my man! You've no left us much time!"

And Jack looks down, and sure enough it's a tiny, wee frog talking to him.

"Jack, Jack my man, you've got to hurry. What about your quest?"

And Jack, he'd never seen a frog talk before, but he said in answer, quite amiably,

"Oh, I've forgotten all about my quest."

[*Stewart looks at the three boys, who are paying somewhat closer attention, waiting to see what will happen next.*]

"You've forgotten about your quest! Well your time is almost up. Follow me! Follow me!"

And the frog hopped over to the tail end of the garden and there was a great big rock. And the frog said,

"Tap that three times, Jack." And Jack took the bulrush that he was holding and tapped it three times, and—eeeaaaeee—the boulder opened right up and this great big tunnel went down, down down into the center of the earth. And the frog said,

"Come on Jack! Come on Jack!"

and leapt and hopped right down the tunnel.

Jack followed after, for what could he do, you know. He was curious. He went down and down and down, and lo and behold, this tunnel opened up into a great big huge cavern, filled to the brim with frogs and toads and lizards and snakes. They were writhing about like it was "Raiders of the Lost Ark" [*again, added for the benefit of the listening boys*], and there at the farthest most end of it was this great huge bullfrog sitting on a stone throne and with a tiny wee crown on his head. And he's shouting from the back as Jack enters,

"Jack, Jack my man, you've made it at last! You didn't leave us much time. Come here, Jack, come here."

So Jack steps forward, minding where he's putting his feet, and he bows before the king of the frogs, and the frog says, "Jack, what is your quest? How can we help you?"

"Oh, my quest," says Jack. "Ahhh ... well, I'm supposed to bring back a ... a tablecloth. Yes, a tablecloth." "A tablecloth," says the frog. "My my my, we don't use tables down here. But I tell you what—we have this wee bit of a rag over the top of the walls just to keep the moisture in, you know. You can take that—I'm sure it will do. Over there, Jack."

So Jack goes over to the corner of the great huge cavern and takes down this cloth, bundles it up, and shoves it inside his shirt. And away he goes, to the cheers of the frogs, the lizards, and the toads, up up up the big tunnel.

And as soon as he gets out in the air again the rock closes behind him. And he is just in time, I tell you, because his brothers at just that moment have returned. And in fact, his eldest brother was up there in the throne room in front of the father himself, and spreading out on this table the most beautiful piece of Holland linen you have ever seen in all your born days. Not a stitch out of place, perfect in every regard, with a little trim of lace around the edge, and embroidery all the way through it. The king was feeling the texture of it—as fine as silk it was—and he says,

"This is the best tablecloth I have ever seen. Ah, it's going to take a heap of beating. But to be fair, we must see what your brother has brought in."

Well, the second brother with much ceremony came forward and spread out the most beautiful piece of Irish linen—lacework like you wouldn't believe, in and out woven with little bands of silver and gold. It sparkled in the sunlight.

"Och," said the king, "Have you ever seen a tablecloth so beautiful! That's marvellous, marvellous! I don't know how I can tell the difference between them. What a choice. But, to be fair," said the king, "we must give Jack his chance as well."

Jack had just come into the throne room, and he had his boots on—he shouldn't have, of course, because they were caked with mud and were leaving a track like you wouldn't believe across the velvet carpet. But the king ignored it as he usually did, and he said,

"Jack, Jack. Have you managed to complete your quest?"

And Jack said,

"Ah ... I have something here."

And he opened up his shirt and took out the rag, and since all the tables were used he just sort of spread it out in front of the throne. And I tell you, it was beautiful! It had a picture on it like a mural, and every time you moved from one location to another, the picture seemed to move. The cloth was made of the finest, finest silk, never before seen in that land. Transparent, it was so fine. Not a stitch out of place. And the king stood transfixed. And the king said,

"Jack, my man, that's the finest piece of work I have ever seen. You've won!"

"Wait a minute! Wait a minute!" said the other princes. "No way is Jack going to win the kingdom! Now we've been away for a year and a day, and he ... we don't know where he found that piece of rag. We demand a rematch! Another quest!"

"Well, it does seem a little peculiar" said the king. "well, it's only fair. Ok. Another quest. Let me think now. Alright, alright. You three are to go out and find the finest ring in the entire world. The most beautiful, the most priceless ring. Right enough!"

Up to the topmost turret of the castle they went. Each of the sons was given a white feather. The eldest son [*Stewart again points to the tallest of the three listening boys*], the tallest one with the brown hair and the sparkling eyes, he went over there and very proudly tossed it over the edge [*the boy imitates the tossing*] and the wind caught it and —ssshhhwwwshhh—off to the north.

The second son, he took his feather and threw it over the turret of the castle and—ssshhhwwwssshhh—off to the south it went. [*The second boy imitates the first, and follows his imaginary feather out of the room.*]

And Jack, he took his feather and he threw it over the turret of the castle, and—ssshhwssshh, thunk—right down into the mud in the back garden. Oh well, Jack, of course, went down to muck about in the back garden. [*The third boy sits down on the floor and "mucks about in the mud."*]

Now it was almost a year later, and Jack was there making a tiny castle out of the dried muck, and he was putting little flags of grass in all the turrets, and he was making it like so when, what do you think happened? This tiny wee frog hops right up to him and says,

"Jack, Jack my man! You've no left us much time!"

"Oh," says Jack, "Is that you again?"

"Yes, yes, I'm here to help you."

"Oh great! Would you mind getting a stick and pulling it 'round ...'"

"No, no! Your quest, Jack, your quest!"

"Oh, my quest. I've forgotten all about my quest" he says.

"Oh sure, Jack, now follow me, follow me."

So they go, hip hip hip hop hop hop over to the big rock at the end of the garden.

"Hit that three times with your stick, Jack."

And Jack did, one, two, three, and—eeeehhhheee—the boulder opened right up, and this great big tunnel went right down into the center of the earth, and ...

"Come on Jack, come on Jack ..."

And down he went, and Jack right after, lickety-split. And there he was in that great big huge cavern filled with all the toads and frogs and snakes and lizards, and the great big bullfrog sitting on his throne says,

"Jack, Jack, my man, it's nice to see you. Now what can I do to help you on your quest this time?"

Jack sat himself down, and he said,

"Well, I'm supposed to bring back, uh, I'm supposed to bring back ..., what am I supposed to ... Och, a ring! A beautiful ring, that's what. Yes, I remember now."

"A ring," says the frog. "Well, I know just what to do now. See that big chest over in the corner? Bring it here."

So Jack goes and gets this great big heavy chest and carries it back.

"Well, open it up, Jack."

And Jack did. And oh, I tell you, the priceless gems, the rings, all of the things you wouldn't believe were there. And the frog says,

"Choose whatever you like, whatever you like."

So he dishes in to the backmost corner of the chest and pulls out a ring, which he can't see very well because they don't have too many lights down there, and he sort of rubs it off and puts it in his shirt pocket. And to the cheers of all the toads and lizards he goes up the tunnel and comes out into the daylight.

And when he gets out the rock closes up behind him and he's off, up to the chamber of the king. And sure enough the eldest brother had just come back, carrying a velvet cushion, and was just kneeling in front of the king and saying,

"I've got the ring for you."

And the king picked it up and looked at it and said,

"That's a beautiful golden ring, it's marvellous." It was all inscribed with fine Celtic knot-work. "That's going to take a heap of beating."

[At this point I notice someone has come into the room and sits in the back, well behind us. I'm watching Stewart and do not realize that it is Jim Strickland, the man from whom Stewart learned the story, but I observe that Stewart seems to be searching more carefully for words and momentarily stops playing to the boys on my right.]

"You ..." [the second son]

And with much ceremony, the second prince came forward and opened up this little jewelry box. And there, sitting on a piece of velvet, was the most beautiful silver ring, with a great big pearl sitting right in the center. It was beautiful, and the king looked at it and said,

"Och, I don't know," he says, "I don't know which is more beautiful," he says. "My my what a decision."

Just at that point Jack comes through the door, and the king catches his eye and says,

"Jack, my man ..." just to be fair, of course ... "Have you got anything for me?"

"Yes, I do," says Jack.

[*Stewart resumes the easy conversational flow of his story and is again including the boys in his audience.*]

And he takes out this ring, polishes it off on his shirt and hands it to the king. And I tell you, it was the most beautiful ring the king had ever seen. It was a band of gold, true enough, but it was studded and encrusted with diamonds and pearls, and the inside edge of it was inscribed with the most beautiful flower pattern you've ever seen. The workmanship—why you'd need a magnifying glass just to see the detail in it. The king was struck dumb. Then he says,

"Jack my man, you've won again!"

"Wait a minute! Wait a minute!" shouted the two princes. "There's no way we're going to have the kingdom go to Jack just because he— we don't know where he found that ring down in the muck and mud in the back garden, but that's no fair at all! We demand another quest!"

"Wait a minute yourself," said the king. "For heaven's sake! I'm getting on in years and I'm going to die before you guys come back with your quests! No!"

"Yes!"

"No!"

"Alright, just one more quest. Just one. And that's it! I've had enough! I want you and you and you [Stewart points to each boy] to go out and find yourself a wife. [They giggle at this.] Yes, and the one that comes back with the most beautiful princess ... after all, when you inherit the kingdom you're going to need a wife and the kingdom is going to need a queen. Therefore I give you one week."

"ONE WEEK!"

"One week to go out there and find yourself a wife, come back here and I'll decide."

Up to the topmost turret of the castle they went, and the eldest son he threw his feather—sshhwshh—and off to the east it went, and the second son he took his feather and—sshhwshh—off to the west it went. And Jack he took his feather and—sshhww—right down into the muck in the back garden.

"Oh well."

Well, Jack, of course, he was about to go down into the back garden, but he was a little bit hungry, you know, so he spent his time in the scullery of the castle—because he, you know, well the people of the castle didn't mind having him there, he was an alright sort of chap, you know. And if they were making up some cakes and pies and what-not they'd let him lick the spoon, and clean out the stuff from the bottom of the bowl [*He winks at the boys and says, "Hey, have you ever had that? Great."*] And when he was getting in the way they'd say,

"Go away, go away Jack!" they'd say, and they'd shove him out the door.

Well, no problem for Jack. He went out to the back garden to play a little bit further. He was going to make an entire village. And just when he got something interesting going ...

"Jack, Jack my man!"

And sure enough, it was the frog, the tiny wee frog. "You've no left us much time! Come on, Jack, come on. Hurry! Hurry!"

So Jack, he goes over to the rock, taps it three times and it opens up and he goes down the big long tunnel and there is the bullfrog sitting at the back of this hall. And he says to Jack, "Jack, what is your quest this time?"

"Och, I don't think you can help me this time," says Jack.

"And why not?" says the bullfrog.

"Well. I'm supposed to come back with the most beautiful bride, the most beautiful princess in the entire world."

"No problem," said the bullfrog. "Ah, my daughter happens to be the most beautiful woman, the most beautiful princess you could ever care to marry. And I would be more than happy to grant my consent to your marriage."

Now Jack was sort of taken aback at the king's kindness, and said,

"Well ... where is this princess?"

"Why Jack, my man, she's sitting right there in the palm of your hand. Isn't she the most beautiful princess you've ever seen?"

Sure enough, he had to admit that she was really beautiful—for a frog. And they left to the cheers of all the toads and frogs and lizards all the way up. They almost picked them up bodily, he and the princess, as they went up the great big long tunnel. And all Jack could think of was that he wasn't even sure that his father approved of mixed marriages. [*Stewart smiles at his own wit.*]

So he got outside to the tumultuous roar of turtles and lizards—do they roar tumultuously? Well they did this time! Sure, you wouldn't believe it. And Jack, as he turned around ... this great big huge turtle turned into a coach and four. A coach and four! He was dumbfounded! And then that tiny wee green frog turned into the most beautiful princess that he had ever seen. Why she was beautiful! His mouth dropped open and his tongue hung out. She says,

"Come along Jack" as she steps into the carriage, in her green gown.

And Jack followed her in and closed the door.

Well I tell you. Just at that time the king was up in the throne room, and the two elder brothers had come back with the most mean, miserable women you could ever imagine. They, being princesses, wanted to buy all sorts of things and wanted a big fancy wedding to invite their hundreds of relatives, just as you would want. But in one week? You cannot do that in one week! It takes that amount of time just to get the invitations printed, to say nothing about ordering the trousseau—so in one week they had to elope. And here they were, already arguing with their husbands. And married only one week, for heaven's sakes. And just then the butler said,

"Och! Stations everyone! I think we've got visiting royalty. Hurry! Hurry!"

And the king and the princes and their wives looked out the window, and what did they see but this huge, great emerald carriage pulling up to the front gate. And weren't they dumbfounded when out should come—Jack. Jack, little tiny Jack with the most beautiful woman, the most beautiful princess, anyone had ever seen.

Well, there was no doubt about it—no doubt about it at all. Jack won the day. And in time Jack became the king. And a good thing it was, too,

for his wife was as smart as Jack was a little bit—soft.
She was as industrious as he was, well maybe a tiny bit lazy.
And besides that,

every time when the affairs of state got a little bit beyond his control he would nip out the back door and go play in the mud in the back garden.

But she let him do that because, you know,
considering her background,
she understood how that might be a nice thing to do.

And that's the end of the story.

[*The three boys applaud and Stewart bows to them, then turns and addresses Strickland, who joins us as we talk about the story for several minutes.*]

Notes

1 Part of this chapter appeared in brief form as "Jack's Adventures in Toronto," in *Jack in Two Worlds* (McCarthy 1994), and is used here with the permission of The University of North Carolina Press.

2 See, for example, Bottigheimer, 1987; Dégh, 1989, 1990, 1994, 1995a, 1995b; Haase, 1993; Holbek, 1987; Lüthi, 1976, 1985, 1986; McCarthy 1994; McGlathery, 1988; Röhrich, 1991; Tatar 1987; Warner 1994; Zipes 1991.

3 I have questioned tellers and listeners about their own place in a story; those who were able to imagine themselves actually inside found that they were moving just behind the protagonists and often a little to the left so they could see where they were going. Some could even estimate the distance, usually from one to three feet. One teller suggested that this distance might even indicate how close she actually felt to a particular character.

4 Lutz Röhrich is most eloquent in his comments on the relations of tellers their tales in his detailed study, *Folktales and Reality*: "Psychological analysis of narrators reveals that informants always prefer certain themes and rarely go beyond the bounds of their personality. Although tradition provides the materials for the plot, the folktale nonetheless allows for individual differentiation" (Röhrich 1991:204).

5 All quotations are from our interview unless otherwise noted.

6 Marylyn found the published story in *Culture vivante* (*Living Culture*, 9:37-43), collected by Luc Lacoursière from Benoit Benoit in 1955. In his brief commentary Benoit said that he did not recall where or from whom he had learned it, but that "he had known it all of his life." Marylyn noted that Lacoursière said he knew eleven variants from Acadia and one from Quebec.

7 The index of tale types gathered originally by Antti Aarne and revised by Stith Thompson lists the basic folktales known from India through Europe, identifies them by number (for example, "Cinderella" is AT Type 510, "Beauty and the Beast" is AT Type 425) and identifies archival and published collections where variant texts can be found. Thus you can compare different texts of these and other stories from many different areas.

8 Benoit was 75 when he recorded the story for Lacoursière on July 10, 1955 in Tracadie, New Brunswick ("Chemin des Basques, to be exact," Marylyn added). "L'horoscope" is listed as #2454 in the collection of Luc Lacoursière in the Archives de Folklore at Laval University, Quebec, Quebec. Marylyn noted that Benoit Benoit had contributed 22 folktales and 185 songs to the archives there. I thank Anne Thau for checking and correcting the French phrases in my transcription of Marylyn's text.

FOUR

DIFFICULT WOMEN
IN FOLKTALES[1]

W
HEN a story is retold it is the teller's choice whether to hold closely to the story as they learned it, or to use it as the basis for their own reweaving. In traditional oral communities skilled narrators maintained the vibrancy of old stories by seeing them in the light of their own ever-changing experiences and also through the variable contexts of actual storytelling events. In organized storytelling the situation was more complicated because of storytellers' reliance on printed rather than narrated stories. Some felt that a printed story could be repeated but not substantially reinterpreted by individuals. Others decided that because a folktale text was isolated in print and seemingly unbound by cultural context, it was thought to be in "public domain," potentially free for any kind of reinterpretation; a teller could lift the story from the page and refashion it at will. (There is a rich tradition of old tales transformed into new written literature, but I do not consider such stories here.[2])

In the case of female characters who were either victims or victimizers the impulse for tellers to alter stories was often very strong, given the popular stereotypes about wondertale heroines as passive and powerful older women as vicious. Popular wondertales were justifiably criticized by feminists for their narrow portrayal of women as passive objects, romanticized innocents, and victims of mental and physical abuse; women of power, in contrast, were typically portrayed as the perpetrators of such abuse. There have been many critics of gendered wondertales, most notably Ruth Bottigheimer (1986, 1987), Maria Tatar (1987, 1992), Jack Zipes (1979, 1983, 1993, 1994), and Marina Warner (1994). Like them, I first challenged the passive princess stereotype in popular fairy tales (Stone 1975a, 1975b, 1980, 1985c). My view expanded as I continued to examine and write about—and tell—many of the stories and came to see more potential in passive heroines (Stone 1988, 1993a). This chapter is a considerably expanded reworking of my last two writings, in which I have been compelled to revise my views even more radically, to regard persecuted heroines as active, heroic, in charge of their positive destinies (Stone 1996b, 1997). How this came about is, in part, a central theme in this double chapter on victims and victimizers. I was not willing to give up without a fight. What I learned arose from re-viewing the stories, however reluctantly, from readers' and tellers' perspectives instead of looking only at story texts.

Maria Tatar characterized the wondertale as a melodramatic "account of helplessness and victimization" (Tatar, 1987:xx-xxi). Her reminder that heroes were also victimized downplayed the fact that heroines suffered more violent and extended persecutions and that they often depended on rescue by someone else. This passivity was underlined by Ruth Bottigheimer, who detailed the many and varied ways that heroines were made to suffer, most often in silence, often at the hands of another woman: a mother/stepmother or sister/stepsisters, a jealous mother-in-law, servant, or false bride, a threatening witch figure (Bottigheimer 1987). The maid who replaces the princess in "Falada" is one of many examples. My first articles agreed with this view of stereotyped women in folktales, but my later work challenged it. This change of view made it all the harder to write this chapter on difficult women.

The contrast between good girls and bad women is a familiar motif in wondertales, and has been further emphasized in many popular interpretations, especially in the films of Walt Disney Productions. Many girls and women I interviewed as part of my dissertation interviews in 1973 remembered only the stereotypical women, good and bad, from childhood books and from popular films. For those I interviewed and many other contemporary readers of wondertales, stereotypical good and bad women faded into vague memories, losing any vibrancy they might have had as effective story characters. However, performers who chose to relate wondertales had to confront the issue of difficult women—those who were either too passive or too aggressive. They had the choice of accepting or rejecting stereotyped portrayals, and, if rejecting them, the challenge of doing so without destroying the essential fabric of the stories. This chapter describes three tellers who addressed the stereotypes of victimized protagonists and murderous mothers/stepmothers. After several attempts to unify victims and victimizers into one very long chapter (was I struggling for reconciliation?) I gave in, and divided the chapter into two sections so that the tellers and their stories would be more comprehensible.

Based on the responses of those I had interviewed in the 1970s and on my own biases, I had classified victimized heroines as "Persecuted Women" in my dissertation and some of my later writing. Ten years after my dissertation interviews I met an American teller, Susan Gordon, who surprised me by going beyond stereotype in her subtle reinterpretation of the mutilated heroine in the Grimm tale, "The Handless Maiden." Susan saw this victimized young woman as heroic because of her determination not to be overcome by her fate, while I had viewed her as one of the most abused of the "Persecuted Women." Coincidentally, another decade later, in 1994, Toronto teller Carol McGirr told me a story as part of an interview I was conducting with her. Her narration of one of Afanasyev's Russian tales ("The Rosy Apple and the Golden Bowl") features a woman who is murdered and buried by her sisters, found by a shepherd, resuscitated by her father, and married to the tsar. Carol, in contrast to Susan, never regarded this heroine as victimized at all; she saw her as dynamic and resourceful in her efforts to live happily ever after.

I was curious to know more about how and why these tellers saw so much more promise in these unpromising heroines than I had, and wrote asking if I could query them on their stories. Susan Gordon's response inspired me to consider another aspect of stereotypical portrayals of female characters when she suggested another Grimm tale. She was already writing her own article on "The Handless Maiden" (Gordon 1993:252-288) so I could not use the text as my main focus; she suggested in its place "The Juniper Tree," in which a stepmother murders her young stepson and cooks him up in a stew. This dealt with persecution in quite a different way as Susan struggled to deal with the woman as villain instead of victim. Since my focus was on the reinterpretation of difficult women I accepted this substitution. This choice became even more fitting shortly afterward when I met a Toronto writer, Marvyne Jenoff, who was working on her rewritten version of "Snow White" in which the stepmother (in Marvyne's story, the natural mother) was in the process of becoming a helper rather than a destroyer of her daughter. These tellers offered excellent contrasts in the varied ways they re-figured their difficult women, the good and the bad. Let us begin with the "good girls."

The Victims

When I met Carol McGirr in 1984 in Toronto at the annual storytelling festival, I was impressed with her calm sense of strength in person and in performance. Carol, one of the featured tellers, was a school librarian with extensive experience and also training in storytelling. She had been active in the Toronto circle of storytellers from the 1970s on. As I attended festivals over the next decade I heard Carol perform long stories from the Arthurian legends, episodes from the Icelandic sagas and from Norse mythology, and lengthy folktales. Her strongest interest seemed to be in heroic protagonists, both male and female. I wanted to know more about her preference for strong women in particular and her development as a storyteller in general so I asked if she would be willing to be interviewed some time in the future. She was most willing. We finally managed to carry this out in Fredericton, New Brunswick, where we were both performing at the annual Storyfest in February 1994.

I taped two sessions with Carol over that week, the first a sixty-minute discussion of her storytelling in general and the second a ninety-minute conversation that developed around her telling of the "The Rosy Apple and the Golden Bowl," a Russian folktale she had learned from a book (Riordan 1976:138-143). In this story a wealthy merchant asks his daughters what gifts they want when he returns from market. The first two want velvet and silk but the youngest wants a rosy apple in a golden bowl, which she had heard about from a beggar woman she had been kind to. Each gets what she asked for. The older sisters mock the younger until they see the beautiful images that form in the bowl when she rolls the apple in it and chants a song. They contrive to steal the bowl; they take her to the woods to pick strawberries where they kill her, bury her under a silver birch tree, and return home with bowl and apple. A shepherd passes by the tree where he sees reeds growing there and makes himself a flute, which reveals the murder in its song. The father later hears the flute, finds where his daughter is buried and goes to the king for the healing water. She is revived, marries the king, and begs him not to kill her sisters. Instead they are exiled to a distant island, and the king and queen live on happily.

Carol described this as her "keynote story," a favorite of hers and of many listeners in the Toronto area. It had been one of the first she told, and one she was still most often asked for and enjoyed telling. I asked why she was so fond of it and she said she was first attracted to the story by the wondrous golden bowl that filled with moving images, and by the silver birch tree where Tanya, the heroine, is buried.

I was surprised as I listened to the story and the heroine became increasingly more put-upon. Her only response seemed to be to escape with her golden bowl. She seemed to be the very opposite of the bold heroines in Carol's lengthier stories. When I asked why she had chosen to tell that particular story, she responded that she wanted to tell a relatively brief narrative and one that she knew she could control the length of time it needed for a full telling. She did not regard it as substantially different from her other stories in terms of character portrayal. She did not see her heroine as a helpless victim at all.

She also considered it a profound story, one that offered a positive metaphor for human endurance under impossible conditions. Also, because it did not follow the usual "happily ever after" pattern, it struck her as more convincing as well. She recalled one of her students who wanted to hear the story over and over again because it was "more real," because the heroine "was really dead;" in other words, it wasn't Disneyesque escapist fantasy.

I thought about the story, about Carol's stated reasons for telling it, and this particular student's reaction to it, and I wondered what I was missing. Tania was "really dead," and was later saved and resuscitated (unlike less fortunate counterparts in ballads[3]). But how was she heroic? She did not say a word to her parents about mistreatment by her sisters. Nor did she exhibit much mental acuity when she followed her cruel sisters into the forest to pick strawberries and then foolishly took out the golden bowl and sang the magic chant that caused it to fill with beautiful images. How could she not know that her sisters were listening and that they coveted this wondrous bowl? It was only after she was murdered that she began to assert herself enough to have her story told.

I asked Carol how she felt about Tania as a heroine. At first Tania seemed to be of lesser importance to Carol, who gave me a cursory answer and went on to what she found more engaging—the evocative images of the golden bowl and of the silver birch tree. I pressed her a bit, suggesting that Tania seemed very placid to me, not the sort of woman I would expect Carol—a single, independent, assertive woman who favored bold heroines in sagas and legends—to prefer. Carol seemed surprised:

Actually I see her as being very much her own person, where some people would see her as taking all that from her sisters...But she does it all without complaining, because I think she's in her own world. She knows what she wants, and eventually she gets what she wants. She gets the king and the kingdom, and the rosy apple and the golden bowl.

I suggested that Tania avoided the intolerable situation of her own "real" life by escaping into the fantastic world of the golden bowl instead of standing up to her covetous and cruel sisters. Only in death did she manage to speak out—and even then indirectly, through a reed pipe played by someone else—and at last reveal how she had been mistreated and finally murdered by her own sisters. Carol saw these same elements as the proofs of Tania's dauntless nature, so much so that she was surprised when I asked her to look more closely at Tania's situation and apparent lack of control over herself. Carol thought about it, but did not agree that Tania was a hapless and persecuted protagonist with little control over her fate.

Carol's reaction reminded me of some anomalous responses from women I had interviewed years earlier. When I returned to Winnipeg after the Fredericton event I reread the words of two women who were as insistent as Carol that their favorite heroines were indeed heroic, though I had placed the stories they mentioned in my "Persecuted Women" category. The first respondent was a lively and articulate seventeen-year-old who was working as a summer volunteer at a daycare center; she recalled with delight Hans Christian Andersen's "Little Mermaid," not the Disney version but the dark and unhappy original in which the mermaid gives up her immortality for a prince who does not accept her love. The young woman I interviewed pointed out the mermaid's strong will: "One of the most aggressive women I remember was 'The Little Mermaid.' She actually did something, she went out to get a prince and she almost got him" (Stone 1975:378).

The second woman was in her late twenties and worked as a live-in counsellor in a group home for disturbed adolescents. She frankly rejected the more popular heroines as too passive but saw her outcast heroine in a Grimm tale as bold and resourceful: "Those two, 'Cinderella' and 'Snow White,' were pretty much the same type of character, but the sister in 'The Seven Swans' was different. They [Cinderella and Snow White] just sat around, more or less, and let things happen to them. But *she* went out actively, like when she had to pick the nettles, and she won their freedom" (Stone 1975:313). It was not clear which of three Grimm tales she meant since her title neatly combined two of them ("The Seven Ravens" and "The Six Swans" and her description implied the third—"The Twelve Brothers"—where the sister is slightly more active.[4] For this reader the sister was clearly heroic because she disenchanted her brothers; her imposed silence, pain, and near-death were proofs of her strength and her determination to endure.

One significant motif connected all three Grimm versions: the sister was forbidden to speak or even to laugh for several years while she wove the magical shirts needed to disenchant her brothers. Thus she was almost executed because she could not tell her own story. In all three tales she was rescued—by male characters, of course—only at the last moment. The women I was interviewing mentioned neither the imposed silence nor the impending death, but focused instead on the girl's decision to go out and seek—and eventually to disenchant—the brothers no matter how difficult it was for her. This woman connected the story with her own life: "As I said, the story I remember particularly is the one with the girl and the seven brothers, or 'The Seven Swans,' probably because it fitted my life. I was the oldest and responsible for the other kids. I really remember that girl, how she worked to free her brothers" (Stone 1975:313).

For these two women interviewed in the 1970s, the beleaguered sister and the love-stuck mermaid were favorites because they were active. This seemed more memorable to them than the heroines' self-inflicted pain. This was the key—not their suffering but the fact that they accepted the challenge instead of "just sitting around and letting things happen to them." In recalling the stories, these two women highlighted the contrast between action and inertia rather than victimization.

This seemed to be the case for Carol as well, though Tanya in "The Golden Bowl" was even less active than the protagonists in the stories mentioned above. She took no action on her own beyond asking for the golden bowl. She was, however, aware of its existence, managed to obtain it, however indirectly, and knew how to use it. Her sisters failed to do this even when they possessed it. For Carol, like the other two women, silence, abuse, and even murder were cancelled out by firm resolve and—most important—by eventual victory.

Another woman who found heroism in a victimized protagonist was Susan Gordon, who used folktales in therapeutic contexts. In her article on "The Handless Maiden" she discussed the boldness of the woman who was mutilated by her father and then set out on a self-imposed exile, married a king who provided her with silver hands, and after a second exile gained her own hands back and was reunited with her husband. Susan, like the other women mentioned here, did not dwell on the woman's suffering but on her decisive acts of self-salvation—her refusal to remain in her father's house, her commanding a tree to feed her, and finally the miraculous restoration of her hands, not by a divine act but by her own action—reaching into the water to save her child from drowning. For Susan this heroine was clearly valiant, not passive; the protagonist refused to accept her victimization from the beginning to the end of the story. This attention to detail, to active transition from victim to heroine, is the thread weaving through all the examples discussed above.

Susan, and to a lesser extent Carol, transformed the stories by giving silenced heroines more to say. This seemingly superficial change took on a great deal more significance for me in the light of Ruth Bottigheimer's observations on the many ways in which heroines were silenced. She examined a number of Grimm tales (notably the "Twelve Swans/Seven Brothers/Six Swans" variants) to show how each edition silenced the heroines even more. She detailed how, in the three variant tales, the sister became progressively less active, increasingly silent, and more beleaguered with each edition of the Grimm collection (Bottigheimer 1987:37). "The Six Swans," being the last and most melodramatic, featured many of the motifs Bottigheimer identified as negative features of the Grimm tales: an innocent, powerless and silent good girl, a powerful and wicked stepmother, the threat of death, and last minute rescue by male characters (Bottigheimer 1987:39). In contrast to feminine silence, Bottigheimer found that many male characters were given more dialogue in each edition (Bottigheimer 1987:53). She pointed out that while many of the hapless heroines were able to call up forces of nature to help them solve impossible tasks they were unable to defend themselves from acts of cruelty by their own families; for example, she noted that "Cinderella was an effective conjurer, but as a daughter and sister, she remains conspicuously silent in the face of verbal abuse from her stepsisters and stepmother" (Bottigheimer 1987:58).

I agreed with Bottigheimer that silence was an important element of passive characterization, and compared how Susan's and Carol's stories shifted subtly but decisively with alterations in speaking patterns.

Susan, who recognized and challenged the victimized situation of the girl in "The Handless Maiden," gave her more direct dialogue and also changed the nature of that dialogue. The daughter did not dutifully submit to her father, as in the Grimm tale, but challenged him to take responsibility for his actions. When he failed to do so she boldly rather than meekly refused to remain with her parents for fear that she might "become just like you." In the forest she did not merely "think" (as in the Grimm tale) but spoke, not prayerfully but commandingly, calling out, "My god I'm so hungry! Give me some fruit." The tree obeyed, without the intervention of God or an angel. In fact the angel disappeared from Susan's story altogether. During the daughter's second exile (in which the Grimm tale had her almost completely silent) she taught her young son about the natural world around them. Later when her husband found her again and wondered how she had regained her hands, she answered by instructing her son to get the silver hands as proof of her identity. We hear the daughter's voice clearly throughout Susan's story.

Carol's method was less obvious because she did not see her protagonist as a victim, and thus did not dramatically alter the text of the story by giving her a stronger voice. Following the library tradition in which she was trained, she stayed so close to the wording of the printed tale that at first I could not see any difference. I listened to the taped story several times before I caught two seemingly small but pivotal ways in which Tania's voice was strengthened: first, Carol brought her chant to life as an evocative song, while in the printed text it seemed hardly more than a secretive whisper. Also, Carol had her utter a resounding "No!" when her sisters asked her tauntingly if she would use the golden bowl to feed the ducks. This "no" continued to echo through the story, coming to full fruition when Tania's voice spoke through the reed to tell her story to the shepherd and to her father, and then commanded the father to go to the tsar to obtain the healing water that would revive her.

In addition to these changes, the manner in which Carol spoke the story invoked a heroine who did not passively submit to her sisters' cruelty. As I noted earlier, Carol often told explicitly heroic tales in which both women and men faced the difficulties of their lives with bravery. Her style of narrating was much the same for the heroic tales as for "The Rosy Apple and the Golden Bowl." That is, she was firmly and unambivalently centered in her stories, telling them from a position of comfortable authority in a strong, calm voice that sometimes verged on a chant. She was not merely repeating the words but calling them fully to life. Also, many of Carol's stories emphasized individual action over co-operation. The heroic model was so familiar that it influenced her storytelling as a whole, if not in explicit content then in her own implicit interpretations.

Carol was still intrigued with the issue of Tania's character when I saw her a year later in Toronto. She had read a first draft of this chapter and was eager to say more about why she considered Tania to be heroic. She pulled me aside at a reception before the annual Toronto festival and expanded enthusiastically on her earlier remarks: "I see it now. It's because she never relinquishes hope! And she's not made to work—she does it for joy. Her sisters are lazy so she does her work and theirs. No one asks her to do it, she does it because she wants to." She repeated what she had said earlier, that Tania was "just biding her time. She has her visions in the bowl. She always knows what she wants." She also observed that it was "a very lean story" with little time spent on description, motivation, or moralizing, "So that audiences have space for their own images" (conversation, Toronto, February 24, 1995).

While Carol and Susan had different perceptions of their two protagonists and used different means of underscoring the heroic qualities of their characters, they both succeeded in challenging the narrow stereotype of passivity without substantially changing the stories.

The Victimizers

If re-viewing passive heroines as heroic was a challenge, the confrontation of murderous mothers was even more so. Marvyne Jenoff and Susan Gordon dealt with these villainous figures in "Snow White" and "The Juniper Tree." Their versions of these stories were carefully considered, not casual or contrived interpretations inspired by a desire to be "modern."

Marvyne Jenoff is a Toronto poet and author whose postmodern variant of "Snow White" shifted between oral and written composition as she struggled with it for several years. She had been working on a collection of traditional fables and folktales which was to include this story, but she was not satisfied with the romantic resolution.[5] I asked why she used folktales and fables, and she responded that she found traditional material to be a challenging contrast to her more autobiographical poetry and prose.

Susan Gordon is a folklorist, oral performer, and workshop leader who lives in rural Maryland. She devoted several years to a handful of traditional tales, including "The Juniper Tree" and "The Handless Maiden," telling and retelling them in a variety of contexts.[6]

Susan and Marvyne used disparate means to accomplish similar objectives. Marvyne deconstructed the traditional tale of "Snow White" to create a postmodern story in which the cruel stepmother is excised and the natural mother is transformed into a figure of wisdom and compassion; Susan remained close to the printed text and found extra-narrative ways of challenging stereotypes of the vicious step-mother in "The Juniper Tree." Marvyne transformed the text through direct interaction with the story, recreating all of the characters—not only the queen, but also the king, the dwarfs, and Snow White herself. She also shifted the focus from Snow White to her mother, who became the central character. Susan's reinterpretation was far less direct; she made only the most subtle changes in the story, but after it was told she brought her audiences into the act of interpretation.[7] Let us look at each woman and her story individually, to follow their process of recreation.

Marvyne Jenoff

Marvyne was already a published poet when she began to take an interest in telling stories. I heard her present some of the darker Grimm tales at Toronto storytelling festivals in the 1980s, and read several of her original stories based on folktales and fables. In preparing to work on "Snow White" she searched for all English versions she could find; though she used occasional details from these sources, she based her story on what she felt to be the most familiar elements so general readers would recognize her references.[8]

In one of the earliest printings of "Snow White" the mother wished for a lovely child but later regretted this as her daughter matured. The mother herself, not a cruel stepmother, took the girl out to the woods to pick flowers and abandoned her there, not knowing that the girl eventually found her way to the helpful dwarfs. After consulting her mirror and finding Snow White still alive, she tried to destroy her (disguised as a peddlar, not a hag) using the familiar motifs of the poisoned comb, strangling bodice, and fatal apple. In this variant it was Snow White's father and not the prince who found and removed her coffin, and ordered his royal physicians to revive her by tying her body to ropes connected to the four corners of the room. After her resuscitation the prince appeared and the story proceeded (as in the later editions) with the cruel queen attending the wedding and dancing to her death in red hot iron shoes (David and David l964:303-315).

The fact that the natural mother retained her central place in this variant instead of dying at the beginning gave Marvyne more scope for a positive transformation. She also used the father's expanded role in the story to develop his character more fully in her own story. Marvyne began her story with a dream, rejecting the stark red and white imagery of blood and snow in favor of a contrast of human-made and natural worlds:

> One winter morning the Queen was embroidering the scene outside her window. The King was looking beyond her at the steel city in the distance. Their sad eyes met, and the Queen pricked her finger. That night the Queen dreamed of colors, her own red blood against the black wood window frame. She dreamed of a daughter... (Jenoff 1993:1).[9]

The father too had a dream, one that inspired him to ban all mirrors in order to keep his wife young when he left her to go off to war. Without the magic mirror, the motif of vanity disappeared; the queen did not become jealous of her maturing daughter, thus they developed a loving relationship rather than a deadly enmity.

Snow White's curiosity about the world, encouraged by her mother, led her unintentionally away from home and into the steel city which replaced the threatening forest of the Grimm story. On her way to the distant city she was found by the seven dwarfs, misguided urbanites who turned her into a fashion model. Her mother's incessant searching finally resulted in Snow White's rescue from the impersonal steel city and the foolish dwarfs, who were interested only in image and facade. On their return home, Snow White's mother gradually reintroduced her to a more natural life in which birds sang, the seasons passed, and love between human beings could develop.

Marvyne's involvement in the story was with the mother. This shift of focus from the daughter to the mother fundamentally altered the balance of the story; if the mother's character was positive then the threatening forces had to be found elsewhere. In Marvyne's tale these were embodied in the overbearing father and the materialistic, opportunistic dwarfs who threaten her daughter—and by extension, the queen herself. However, these antagonists were more misguided than evil or destructive. Instead, a vague evil was embodied by the anonymous, impersonal steel city and its inhuman technology that created the contrived world of fashion modelling—and also the helicopters that carried men off to war. The mother's expanded role created a problem for the story's conclusion, however; Snow White still met her prince and the mother had to disappear. Despite two attempts to rework the ending, Marvyne was still dissatisfied with the result. The story remained unresolved, and unpublished, until its appearance here.

Marvyne employed both a shift of viewpoint from daughter to mother and the introduction of a contemporary setting to create her postmodern fairytale. Her personal identification with the characters, not just her literary skills, gave this text its vibrancy. She described how she developed her stories: "In a story I have to consider all the characters and their relations to one another and to what happens, and I'm bound firmly and complicatedly to the text" (letter, March 2, 1989). Her emphasis on character more than action or motivation underscored the message she wished to express: that sinister forces unfold when we forget our personal connections to the natural world and other living things.

Marvyne's approach took this well-known tale in very different directions that reconstructed instead of rejecting an old genre of storytelling. By re-figuring the "bad" mother as helper rather than destroyer, Jenoff offered a transformed text that spoke specifically to those for whom "steel cities" are not only dehumanizing but dangerous. She effectively challenged the woman-against-woman conflict found in many popularized folktales where daughters are threatened by mothers and stepmothers, "bad" fairies and crones, elder sisters, and false brides. Instead she developed the connections between women that led to freedom for both instead of competition and control.

Susan Gordon

I first heard Susan Gordon at a week-long storytelling retreat in 1982, when she was working on the Grimm tale of "The Maiden Without Hands."[10] This tale, along with "The Juniper Tree," had been a central story in her workshops and performances for some time. "Maiden" dealt with violence *against* women, "Juniper" with violence *by* women. Her reasons for choosing to work on "Juniper Tree" were applicable to "Maiden" as well: "I initially came to the story seeing it as a depiction of great depravity and evil, which it is. But I think that the process [of storytelling] is one of balance, that guilt and self-hate alone will not allow one to really achieve personhood (letter, May 2, 1989:2).[11]

"The Juniper Tree" begins with the familiar motif of parents longing for a child. As in "Snow White" the mother cuts her finger, sees blood on the snow, and wishes for a child "as red as blood and as white as snow." Susan slows the story at this point by describing seasonal changes at each month of the woman's pregnancy. Finally a son is born, the woman dies, the man grieves but then finds a new wife with her own daughter. Motivated by jealousy she entices her young step-son to put his head in a chest to find an apple and then plunges the lid down, decapitating him, and putting the blame on her own innocent daughter. She cooks the boy in a stew and serves it to her husband when he comes home, claiming that the boy has gone to visit a rela-tive. After the grisly meal (eaten only by the unknowing father) the grieving sister carefully gathers the bones and plants them all under a Juniper tree; the boy is reborn as a vengeful bird, returning to punish his stepmother with death and to reward his father and sister with gifts,and in the end, reverting to his original human form (Grimm 1988:186-95).

Unlike Marvyne, Susan chose to stay with the Grimm text so faith-fully that she carefully reproduced the sounds described: the chest closing on the boy's neck, the turning mill wheel, the twenty millers cutting a new millstone, and, most importantly, the singing of the bird. She made no significant alterations in the plot, no changes in charac-ter, no shifts of the point of view. Instead of transforming this mother into a nurturing woman, as Marvyne did in "Snow White," she tried to illuminate how the story struggled with evil in ways now relevant to modern listeners. "Maybe a real confrontation with this story pulls a person up short and makes them realize the level of human depravity, but I think a real integration of the evil aspects and the good aspects in us only takes place over time (letter, May 2, 1989:1).

Because she remained so close to the text, Susan found it problem-atic in terms of contemporary expression. In particular she began to find some of the most gruesome parts of the story almost ridiculous: "I must say that when I went to tell the story for you on tape parts of it did seem harder to tell without laughing, basically the parts that are the most horrifying—the cutting off of the boy's head, the setting of his head on his body and its knocking off by his sister. While I know full well the horror of them, they seemed almost ludicrous and slapstick" (letter, May 2, 1989).

Though Susan held to the text as she learned it, her personal involvement with the story gave it vibrancy; she did not merely repeat the words of the story by rote but managed instead to subtly extend it while remaining faithful to the Grimm text. She narrated in her own words rather than reciting it word for word, which gave her the opportunity to suggest delicate shadings of character and motivation. She also centered on the song with which the bird serenades the other story characters, giving this gruesome tale a more lyrical tone. Most important, she engaged her listeners very directly by asking them to reflect on their own interpretations of the story and its characters.

Since her telling was so faithful to the Grimm text, even the smallest deviations were significant. The younger sister as portrayed by Susan was even more pitiful in her guilty weeping for her murdered brother, and more melancholy when she buried his bones under the juniper tree. The father's insensitivity was heightened by Susan's tone of voice when she spoke his brusque demands for his dinner and his sharp words expressing his greed in keeping it all to himself—"All of this is for me. None of you may have any of this." The Grimm text was softer and more ironic: "Give me some more! I'm not going to share this with you. Somehow I feel as if it were all mine" (Grimm 1987:89). The stepmother, too, was portrayed somewhat more tragically. She alone understood the true meaning of the bird's song and went out to meet her fate, saying mournfully, "Then I will go out and see what the bird has for me" (tape transcript).

Susan made her own compassionate identification more explicit when she stated how she came to understand the story as "unrelentingly patriarchal, both in its depiction of the woman as solely responsible and in the solution to kill only her" (letter, May 2, 1989); that is, because of its failure to implicate the father in the tragedy. Because she made only minor modifications to the Grimm text, these might easily go unnoticed without her explicit comments—particularly her insistence that each character was responsible for the outcome: "It was when I finally had her [the mother] and didn't diminish her, just let her be who she was, that I then began to—the story began to de-focus off of just her and began to move to look at the other characters. A very simple thing to notice is, where is the father?" (letter, May 2, 1989).

Susan found her own storytelling voice most clearly in the bird's song, which had to be exactly right before she could tell the story. "I worked for a long time trying to learn the song, which I felt was so important to the story" (letter, May 2, 1989). Since the bird was the teller of the boy's tale, Susan, as singer of the bird's song, was bound by her identification with son rather than mother. The bird unrelentingly punished the murderous mother but rewarded the devouring father, making it all the more difficult for Susan to resolve her own doubts in her retelling.

Many of Susan's performances were for very specific audiences whose interests she was aware of in advance.[12] These were often specialized groups in a workshop setting, not general audiences who expected an entertaining story. Thus audience context was even more influential on her own understanding of the story as it came back to her from their responses. She divided her listeners into small groups and had them retell the story from other viewpoints. They were asked to portray the mother as sympathetically as they could and to reconsider the daughter and father as accomplices in the crime rather than as innocent bystanders. She explained some of the situations in which she told the story:

> In therapeutic, educational, and religious settings the story is chosen with care to the occasion, with some knowledge of the people I'm telling it to and the desire to tell them a story that is, in some way, their story, which will provide them the opportunity to reflect on their own lives (letter, Dec./Jan., 1989).

She modestly felt that such audience responses, rather than her own artistry, helped to expand the meaning of the story. By encouraging her listeners to interact directly with the story through their own reinterpretations, she allowed the story to deepen, even when her retelling did not change greatly from one storytelling event to another.

Stories such as "Snow White" and "Juniper Tree" retain transformative power because they function both literally and figuratively. For example, many of those who listened to Susan's performances had themselves experienced the reality of childhood abuse. When real violence is treated at a comfortable distance, as in a seemingly unrealistic folktale, both teller and listeners create their own space for making personal connections.[13] These stories also function as an emotional release for the stresses of ordinary day-to-day parenting or from childhood fantasies of feared abuse and abandonment.[14] Story interpreters such as Susan and Marvyne are effective because they perceive and respect the archetypal nature of the material they choose to work with.

In their stories, literal and figurative come together; actual and imaginative worlds meet and interact, as they have for centuries.

These two tellers consciously chose old stories with the clear intention of finding new meaning for them, seeing in them symbolic expression of human actualities. Both women found personal connections rather than intellectual explications. In contrasting ways they reconstructed "old" new stories for today, allowed them to function as both reflections of lived reality and as a means of transforming it. They challenged us to avoid narrow responses to negative stereotypes. The dreadful mother figures in "Snow White" and "The Juniper Tree" were not cardboard characters with no sense of three dimensionality; Marvyne's queen was more fully fleshed out within the story itself, while Susan encouraged her listeners to find new perspectives for viewing the stepmother after they had heard her story. Both tellers alluded to alternative destinies without turning away from the stark realities of human existence. They did not sugar-coat the tales to bring about an unconvincing happily-ever-after resolution, nor did they parody or satirize them. By treating these very real difficulties within the artifice of fictional folktales, they addressed the issues of actual violence and urban alienation, while at the same time providing artistic distance for their audiences.

Also, Susan and Marvyne identified themselves directly with their stories instead of taking a more objective critical stance. In this way they paralleled the creativity of Hungarian narrators described by Linda Dégh:

> The personal text not only shows the narrator's ability in formulating a story from available plot episodes, his or her way of making the world of fantasy palpable by connecting it with the world of everyday reality: the told story also mirrors the narrator's specific conceptualization of the world and its affairs: his [or her] cultural and personal meanings (Dégh 1990:48).

The "cultural and personal meanings" for Susan and Marvyne centered on the figure of powerful women who—in the Grimm variants—were incapable of using their strength for creative purposes. What Marvyne and Susan expressed in personal letters reveal that they were very aware of their own involvement and of the transformational potential of these stories in contemporary life. Susan in particular used her storytelling—not only in this particular text but in others—to encourage listeners to tell their own difficult stories and to reflect on their own lives. She concluded her own article on the Grimm tale of "The Maiden Without Hands" with these words: "I hope that you [the reader] will hold 'The Maiden' against the fabric of your experience, as I held the Grimms' tale against mine, and note where the story informs your life, and where your life informs the story, and create it anew" (Gordon l993:285).

In their personal struggles with these stories, holding them against the fabric of their own experiences, Susan and Marvyne attempted to transform stereotype to archetype.

I began this chapter as an examination of the ways in which three tellers interpret difficult women in four folktales. Two of the women (the daughters in "The Rosy Apple and the Golden Bowl" and "The Maiden Without Hands" were protagonists who rose from a state of victimization to mature independence; two were mothers\stepmothers who were a threat to their children (actually in "The Juniper Tree" and potentially in "Snow White: A Reflection"). The tellers of these tales were self-conscious reinterpreters of folktales, not traditional narrators, but they were not casual or careless in their treatment of traditional material. All began with a regard of the wondertale as a serious literary expression with its own integrity and its place in traditional narrative. That is, they did not simply lift the text from the printed page and treat it as their own private property. This was as true of Marvyne Jenoff, who played liberally with both mother and daughter in her "Snow White: A Reflection," as it was of Carol McGirr and Susan Gordon, whose modifications were very subtle.

Folktales do not come to life on the printed page; they need the breath of tellers and the imagination of listeners. Marvyne and Susan have lifted their texts from the "literary amber" that Cheryl Oxford used as a metaphor, cited in the foreword. Change is necessary for life, in stories as well as in the natural world. Literary authors accomplish this by editing and re-editing until they arrive at a compelling written text; narrators do so by telling and retelling a story until it gains a sense of full resolution. Both kinds of artists "listen" to responses from others as they proceed.

In the case of retelling traditional folktales, it is useful to look at this balance on a continuum rather than as an either/or situation. In this hypothetical continuum, rigidity, or unchanging texts, rests at one end. Here context (the situation in which any story is retold) and texture (an individual artist's interpretative words and non-verbal expressions) do not affect the story text. It is told exactly word-for-word each time. Fragmentation occupies the other end of this imaginary continuum, actually and theoretically. A book aptly entitled *Fractured Fairy Tales*, for example, literally and wilfully takes apart well-known folktales for humorous effect (Jacobs 1997). Humor, resting on the surface story and not its depths, is a popular fracturing device (see also Arnason 1994, Gardner 1994). Other writers have used horror and eroticism to deconstruct and recreate literary fairy tales (Carter 1979, 1990, 1993; Lee 1983).

The three tellers and their tales described in this chapter range themselves along this continuum. Susan and Carol were closer to the rigid end of the scale though they opened their stories to new life, Susan by bringing listeners into an ongoing interpretation that changed with each storytelling event and Carol by letting her own imagery deepen the story for her. Marvyne, in her radical transformation of the Grimm text, came closer to fragmentation, but her research on the story and her care in reinterpreting significant elements to move her own plot along kept her story balanced and unified; it did not fly away from the Grimm tale completely, nor did it treat it at all lightly.

The first audiences for performed stories are the tellers themselves. We have seen how each of these three tellers offered personal "audience" responses—their own association with their story and its characters. They viewed controversial heroines as heroic rather than victimized and opened new prospects for understanding destructive mothers/stepmothers because these issues were personally significant to them. If nothing else, such responses inspire other tellers to rethink their stories and to look at possibilities for answering such challenges creatively, without falling immediately into either censorship or didacticism. We will see another example of this struggle in the final chapter in this section, where a girl encounters a dangerous witch-figure in the Grimm tale of "Frau Trude."

We should not forget the center of the story as the tellers see it, the place where the story comes alive for them and where they will bring it most fully to life for listeners. For Carol this center was not primarily the heroine, whom she accepted without question as heroic; it was, rather, the imagery of the story—particularly the golden bowl and its rosy apple, and the silver birch tree that reminded her of the Ontario birches from her childhood. Marvyne was as fascinated with the mother in her "Snow White: A Reflection" as with Snow White herself, which created a new equilibrium in the old story (and an imbalance at its conclusion). Susan was torn between sympathy for the murdered child in "Juniper Tree" and some pity for the cruel mother; this ambivalence came through in her telling, and was addressed when she urged listeners to consider other possible interpretations.

The balance between teller, tale, and listeners is always a delicate one that needs constant renegotiation. This is one of the many ways that old stories continue to be renewed, to meet the needs and interests of changing audiences and the ever-changing perceptions of the tellers themselves. In told tales, as opposed to folktales in print, the story is always emerging anew. In the following chapter we will follow the evolution of a story as it emerges.

THE ROSY APPLE AND THE
GOLDEN BOWL

(Carol McGirr, 1994)

We recorded this story sitting across from each other in our hotel room in Fredericton, New Brunswick. Carol did not look at me but stared over my head. When I asked, she said she was focused on an imaginary audience behind me. Tunes for the two songs are Carol's original compositions. This story, AT 780, "The Singing Bone," is found throughout Europe in both story and ballad form. Carol's text is from James Riordan (1976, 138-143), translated from Afanasyev's collection of Russian tales. In the unhappy Grimm variant (number 28, "The Singing Bone") brother kills brother and there is no resuscitation.

ONCE there was an old man and an old woman who had three daughters. The older two were stupid and lazy, but the third one worked very hard, and without complaining. The first two were arrogant and haughty in their ways, but the third was modest in all she did and said.

One day the old man had to go to the village to sell a load of hay, and he said to them, "What would you like me to bring from the village?" The older one said, "Oh father, I would like a length of red velvet, and the second one said, "I would like a length of blue silk." But the third said not a word. And so he looked at her and he said, "Well, what do you want, Tanushka?"

So she thought about it, and finally she said, "I would like a rosy apple and a golden bowl."

Well, the sisters burst out laughing. They nearly split their sides. "What are you going to do with an apple," they said, "when we have orchards and you can pick all the apples you like? And what are you going to do with a golden bowl? Are you going to use it feed the ducks?" "No," she said, "I'm going to say magic words over it, magic words an old beggar woman taught me once when I gave her an Easter cake."

Well, the sisters began to laugh again, but their father said, "That will be quite enough. I will bring each of you what you've asked for." And so he went off to the village to sell his hay. And when he came back he gave the oldest daughter a length of red velvet, and the next daughter a length of blue silk. And for Tania he brought a rosy apple and a golden bowl. Well, the two sisters set to work at once. They cut themselves dresses from the velvet and the silk, but Tania just sat in the corner with her apple and her bowl. So after a while they said to her, "What are you going to do with the bowl, Tania? Are you just going to sit there all night?" "No!" she said. And she began to roll the apple and sing:

> Roll apple roll, in the golden bowl,
> Show me forests and leas and ships on the seas,
> And mountains so high they touch the sky.

And all at once the whole house filled with light and there was a sound like the pealing of bells, and in the bowl you could see forests and leas, and ships on the seas, and soldiers in fields with golden shields, and mountains so high they touched the sky. And when the sisters looked in the bowl they grew very envious. They wanted that bowl, but they could never get it.

All through the day when Tania did her work, she carried that bowl with her. She had to feed the chickens, she had to milk the cows, she had to do all the work in the garden, and then she had to do all the chores her sisters had left undone. And at night she held the bowl in her arms.

So the sisters began to plot how they could get that bowl. And one of them said, "Let us ask our sister to go into the forest with us. We'll tell her we're going to pick strawberries, and then we'll get the bowl." Now when they asked Tania, they said, "Come, sweet sister, we're going into the woods to pick strawberries." Now they didn't always take Tania with them and sometimes she felt left out, so she was very happy to go along with them. But when they went to the woods they didn't pick strawberries, and they didn't find wild flowers. They walked a long way, and at last Tania sat down on a log and she began to roll the apple:

> Roll apple roll, in the golden bowl,
> Show me strawberries red, cornflowers blue,
> Poppies, daisies, and violets too.

And the most beautiful flowers appeared in the bowl, flowers of every colour, and Tania sat gazing down into that bowl. And as she did that, her sisters crept up behind her and they killed her. They buried her in a shallow grave, under the silver birch tree. And they took that apple and that bowl and they went home.

It was very late and very dark when they got home. They said to their parents, "Tania ran away from us in the forest. Maybe a wild animal has eaten her. Maybe a wolf or a bear." And the father said, "Bring the golden bowl and the apple. They will tell us what has happened to Tania." And the two sisters grew cold with fear because they knew what they had done. But they couldn't make the apple roll because they didn't know the magic words. And the old man and the old woman sat down and wept for Tania.

Now the very next morning a young shepherd was going through the forest and he came to the place where the silver birch tree grows, and he saw some fresh green reeds springing up from the earth. He took one, thinking he'd fashion himself a pipe. He began to cut the holes in the reed. When he finished he put the pipe up to his lips, but before he could play a note, the pipe began to sing all by itself:

> Play pipe play for the shepherd to hear,
> Play pipe play for the shepherd to cheer;
> By my sisters I did die,
> Under the silver birch I lie.

The shepherd was terrified. He ran into the village and he told people what the pipe had said. Now Tania's father was in the village, and he said, "Let me see that pipe." And he took it in his hand, but before he could play a note, the pipe began to play:

> Play pipe play, songs sad and gay,
> Listen, father, to what I say:
> By my sisters I did die,
> Under the silver birch I lie.

And Tania's father said to the shepherd, "You must take me to the place where you cut this reed." And they all went out into the forest, and they dug down. And there in the shallow grave beneath the silver tree they found Tania. She was very beautiful, and very pale, and quite dead. And the sisters fell on their knees and confessed.

Now I don't know how long a time it was or how short a time it was, but Tania's father went to see the king. And he begged the king for some of the living water from the well, and the king told him he could take it. And he said, "If your daughter recovers, bring her here. And bring her sisters as well."

And Tania's father went back to the silver birch tree, and he sprinkled a few drops of living water on Tania's fair brow. And she awoke. It was as if she had been in a faint. And they all rejoiced. And then they went to see the king, and Tania wept all the way. She wept at the cruelty of her sisters and what they had done to her. And when they came to the king's castle, she was still weeping.

And the king when he saw her, fell in love with her. He said, "Tania, I would like you to marry me and be my wife and my queen." And then he said, "Show me the golden bowl." Tania twisted the apple in the bowl, and she sang, "Roll, apple, roll, in the golden bowl ...," and the whole castle filled with light, and there was a great pealing of bells, and there in the golden bowl you could see all the great cities of Russia, one by one. And then there was the sound of battle, and the sound of cannon, and soldiers marching and generals galloping on ahead with flags flying. And then the sounds of battle died away, and there in the bowl were white clouds, like white swans swimming against a blue border in the bowl.

And the king marvelled at what he had seen, and he said to Tania, "Will you marry me?" And she said, "Please don't harm my sisters, please don't put them to death even though they've been cruel to me." And the king said, "I want you for my wife, and as for your sisters, they should be harshly punished. But since you asked me to spare their lives, I will. But they will be banished to a bleak island at the far end of my kingdom."

And so the sisters were banished, and Tania married the king, and the people had a queen as fair as the realm had ever seen.

SNOW WHITE: A REFLECTION

(Marvyne Jenoff, 1993)

Marvyne sent me two printed variants of her text. The first one, done in 1989, had been put aside, but after reading an early version of this chapter Marvyne was inspired to work on it further. This is the final text, previously unpublished. It is AT Type 709, and in the Grimm collection it is number 53; both are called, simply, "Snow White."

THE King and Queen were sad because they had no child. The King was chagrined that the Queen's beauty was marred by her sadness.

In the harsh winter light at the castle window the Queen sat with her embroidery. As she worked, she let the old folktales come to mind, tales which had encouraged her before she met her Prince. Now, in the happily ever after, she comforted herself with their familiarity. In other seasons she would go and sit with the crones who told these tales, crones old beyond sadness. What was there for a childless Queen to do but endure the wait to become a crone herself and join them in the dark forest where they lived? This was the scene she embroidered. Grimly she worked her needle in and out.

The childless King, disillusioned by the natural order, liked the idea of the man-made. He looked beyond the Queen, out the window of the crumbling castle. Over the snow beckoned the shadow of the city, the tall, steel city of his own kingdom. To its neon pulse he tapped his foot. A King could live there if he decided to. But the years he spent as a prince dreaming of kingship prepared him mainly for a life of dreaming. He let himself be content with the glimpses of urban life he caught on TV, though reception was bad in the castle.

One day as the King sat watching the flickering TV screen, a great longing came over him. A longing that only a child could fill. He looked over at the Queen. She looked up from embroidering yet another blade of grass. As their sad eyes met she pricked her finger. A moment of pain, her finger soothed in her mouth, then joy at what she understood would happen. The King had never seen the Queen so beautiful. He sat up. He reached for her other hand and held it. That night the King and Queen dreamed of their child.

In the Queen's dream she had to search for her child through interminable summer. No matter where she turned, between her and the child was the singing of seven harsh voices, seven pairs of menacing footsteps, seven grotesque faces in and out of focus. And where was the King, to help?

The King listened to the Queen's dream and said nothing. In his own dream he was reigning from a TV studio in the city. Beside him was a beautiful, steel-coloured woman, who chanted rhymes to her mirror and was pleased with what she saw there. He had dreamed this before, and didn't want to spoil it in the telling. But this time the dream went further. When the woman looked into her mirror she hissed in shock. For in the mirror was the image of a little girl. The king knew it was his child, his and the Queen's—where was the Queen in his dream?—and he woke afraid.

They named the child Snow White, for the peacefulness of winter before their troubling dreams. They would let nothing prevent her from growing strong and beautiful in their care.

A second time the Queen dreamed her dream, of searching for Snow White. But the King's dream progressed. This time in the mirror he saw Snow White, grown a little. The steel-coloured woman, now grimacing, would have dashed the mirror to the floor, had he not restrained her.

And so the King hovered over the Queen and Snow White, particularly in summer. Outdoors the Queen held Snow White's hand as the child danced in circles around her, the King, with his back to the city, holding a parasol over them to guard their complexions. Snow White wished there were more to life than her parents' fretting.

Once more the Queen dreamed of the long, summer search for Snow White. The King dreamed Snow White in the mirror was half-girl, half-woman. The steel-coloured woman ignored the King. She sat with pharmaceutical manuals, making notes and cackling to herself. The King couldn't get near enough to stop her.

He woke in a fearful dilemma: to remain in the castle, where his dreams would progress, or pursue the matter in the city, where the dreams might come true? He decided to go to war and be too busy to dream. He summoned soldiers from the surrounding fields and the city, and they came! He ordered a helicopter, and it was delivered! Encouraged by these successes, he thought of a plan to foil his terrible dreams—as long as Snow White didn't grow to resemble her image in his dreams, he reasoned, the dreams could not come true. And so the King issued an edict that banned the years and the seasons with them. No sooner was the edict signed than the earth shuddered to a stop on its path, spun out of control—dark, light, dark, light—then settled into a succession of long summer days.

At first the Queen was anxious having to face her dream alone. Snow White danced in wider and wider circles on the field, and the Queen at first tried in vain with one parasol, then with two, to keep up with her and protect her. But when she realized that under the King's edict no harm would come to their complexions, she put away the parasols and joined Snow White in play. They ran, they shouted, they sang songs. They tended the castle gardens, where in the space of days the same summer flowers bloomed, died, and bloomed again. Happy outdoors, happy with her mother, Snow White thrived. But her burgeoning energy, the energy of growth, thwarted by the King's edict, made her movements frenzied. She tossed more and more in her sleep.

When the Queen felt the need for the thoughtful pursuits of a darker season, she sought the relative cool inside the castle. There she embroidered, this time with a bright array of colours to tempt Snow White. But Snow White was too agitated to learn and she burst outdoors. The Queen, in the solitary rhythm of her work, sought comfort in the old tales and repeated them aloud to herself. She paused often to let the phrases resonate and be absorbed by the castle walls. A child, if she were ever still, could hear the old tales and be guided.

Snow White danced aimlessly over and over the castle grounds. The open gate was unattended with the men at war. She was standing there, restless, taking in the view of the gleaming city that her father had so carefully avoided, when a dwarf came by. He was a sprightly creature, oddly shaped, and small like herself. The way he walked, so earnestly—she could do that, too. Swinging her arms in imitation, joining in his boisterous song, she followed him into the city.

She felt small and shabby among the perfect, high, steel buildings. Fascinated by the expanse of streets and the people—a few strangely-dressed women and one dwarf—she was still.

The dwarf had no idea what to do with a young girl in an ermine robe and diamond tiara alone in the city. Taking his time, smiling secretly at her attention, he led her to the penthouse where he lived with his six brothers. Dwarfs could think more effectively when all seven were together.

In the presence of the King's daughter the dwarfs were charmed to a man, and they boasted to her of their arts. Among other things they were glaziers: they took her to the windows to point out their handiwork—the buildings were made of glass as well as steel. In a certain light was it not a city of mirrors? They showed her the mirrors they had made for themselves, individually distorted so that each dwarf could be satisfied with his own handsomeness. They had mounted the mirrors at an angle, tilted away at the top, so that the dwarfs appeared tall and grand. When their age began to show, they clouded the glass surfaces. But now, in the presence of a child, the King's child, they saw themselves as they really looked. They would henceforth use their arts instead to make something of Snow White.

Even with the lack of men, the dwarfs did not fit into urban life in the way they wished. And so they took an interest in trends. They would turn Snow White into a fashion model, and her success would reflect on them. All seven of them went out to arrange modelling assignments for her. They left her in the penthouse and forbade her to let anyone in: child-soft as she was, smiling unnecessarily might wrinkle her skin.

Far above the relative activity of the city, the stillness of the sealed penthouse permeated Snow White like a spell. She felt she could have sat up there forever surrounded by photographs of herself, dabbling in make-up in front of the perfect mirror the dwarfs had given her. How kind they were! But at night, in her sleep, she hated them. She dreamed of her mother dancing toward her with entreating motions, wanting her home.

The Queen went searching through the city for Snow White. She looked down hoping to see a sign—a small footprint in the dust of the pavement, or a lost jewel. Then she came across a page of a glossy magazine with something familiar about the photograph. Before she could pick it up a breeze lifted it toward the penthouse, and she knew where she would find her daughter.

The Queen had brought a sash which she had woven herself of silk and cotton in the colours of the fields. When she wrapped the sash around the child's waist, Snow White fell into a swoon of pleasure. By now Snow White was accustomed to wearing what the dwarfs required, and she couldn't remember ever feeling anything as soft as her mother's sash. The Queen sat next to Snow White and held her hand—how good the warm hand felt! She would take her daughter home, at last. But Snow White told her about the seven dwarfs. Remembering the menace in her dream and afraid to encounter them, she left Snow White, more or less safe, where she was. Returning to the castle the Queen hoped she wouldn't dream about the dwarfs. She wanted to dream about the King carrying Snow White home to the castle.

When the dwarfs revived Snow White she was so sparkling and wistful that they had to warn her very sternly not to let anyone in at all. Snow White tried to obey, though she couldn't help but wish her mother were beside her. As soon as the dwarfs were gone she skipped a little. Sealed in the fluorescent room, she longed for the light of the castle garden, softened by green. For at night as she slept there was the feel of grass in her hands and the scent of her own skin in the sun.

The Queen soon returned with a wooden comb she had carved herself. Snow White's hair, treated with many processes, had never been combed with wood, and never so gently as her mother was now doing. Snow White once again fell into a swoon. The Queen, feeling the seven pairs of footsteps coming closer, left Snow White once more where she lay, and retreated to the castle. This was the second time she had failed to rescue Snow White, and she was uneasy. She went to the crones for their wisdom. But they had never heard of a real mother in this kind of story. The Queen didn't like to hear that.

This time when the dwarfs revived Snow White she was animated, and her simplest movements held them fascinated. They repeated their warning more strongly. Angrily. For each of them fervently, secretly, recalled his mirror-image and hoped, to a man, to find out what husbands did and marry Snow White himself. Why would she want a visitor? Did they not provide well for her? Were they not fine fellows, the best of company? Snow White was beginning to doubt she could obey them much longer. She dreamed they had grown larger, and were fiercely folding their arms to block her dreams. But she also dreamed of summer flowers, and these dreams were stronger.

The Queen brought an apple, which she had picked green and ripened in the castle. At first Snow White couldn't remember what an apple was for—her working diet was bland liquids. But at the unaccustomed tartness of the first taste she fell again into a swoon. The Queen, afraid of the dwarfs, retreated once again without rescuing Snow White. She knew the finality of the number three in folktales. With the failure of her third attempt, she feared nothing more could be done. She paced and fretted, trying to come up with a plan.

When the dwarfs found Snow White lying there for the third time, they made no attempt to revive her—they, too, knew the intractability of number three. They carried her gently up to the roof of the penthouse. They laid her out in the shade of the trees in the roof-garden, and, holding hands, sat around her in a ring.

As loyal supporters of the King's edict the dwarfs never once believed Snow White was dead. Indeed, they saw a higher purpose for her in her present state. Having always fancied the sky as a kind of mirror, the dwarfs were now in a position to offer up to it a creature of beauty. Snow White, though motionless, glowed with life. To point up this contrast they designed a coffin-like structure for her. They invented a special kind of glass that would both show her and protect her from the sun. For their dear Snow White they built the coffin straight and true—they loved her even more now that she could no longer disobey them. Up on the roof they worked with great clatter and sang as they worked, so that nothing else, not even a would-be visitor, could be heard.

Snow White was aware of the coffin being built around her. Unable to move, she dreamed. She dreamed she had grown tall as the city, one huge hand reaching in vain for her mother and the other for her father. She dreamed of covering her little penthouse mirror with coloured bits of cut-up photographs arranged in a scene she remembered from the castle, but her own face showed through and she was bored with it. She dreamed the dwarfs were digging underground, farther and farther, digging for diamonds and finding only coal. This was her favourite dream, hearing the retreat of their raucous singing. She liked to repeat this dream and extend it—herself at the entrance to the mine shoving them one by one toward their fate. As she dreamed in the coffin her muscles tensed and eased, and refreshed her.

The seven dwarfs carefully lowered the transparent lid and admired the completed glass coffin. Yes, Snow White was shown off to good advantage. They brought the TV up to the roof, and stayed and watched over her until the King returned from the war.

*   *   *

The King looked down from his helicopter over his satisfyingly vast domain. Successful in war and confident now that he could deal with the natural order, he was ready to restore the years to the kingdom. But when he caught sight of Snow White so still on the roof, his first thought was to cure her. And so, scattering the dwarfs, the King had the helicopter brought down on the penthouse roof.

The King had once travelled with poets, then philosophers, then jesters. With him now in the helicopter were three physicians, who were eager to help Snow White. As the King watched over her, the physicians researched modern cures. But hers was not a modern affliction. Gently the King himself removed the child from the coffin and had her airlifted to the castle. He laid her down on a bed in a room facing away from the city while the physicians researched ancient cures. They read old folktales until they found the cure in which string was wound around the afflicted person and then fastened to the four corners of the room. To find enough string, the kind that had already been used to wrap parcels, they had to search even beyond the castle, for no one saved string any more. Their search took them as far as the city, and the King, fancying himself a scientist, went with them. Snow White might have lain there forever, and the kingdom might have waited forever for its years, if not for the intervention of the Queen's heart.

The Queen bathed the unmoving child. She rubbed scented lotions into her skin. She dressed her in different kinds of cloth so the variety of sensations would tempt her to wake. Snow White stirred with pleasure. She sat up, then walked a little. As her energy came back she ran in the remembered fields, ran gracefully at first, but soon, her growth-energy once more thwarted, she moved instead in a wearied frenzy.

Watching once again the frustrating effect of the King's edict, the Queen was angry. This was not the life she had in mind for her daughter, and she would not allow it to continue. In a window on the forest side of the castle the Queen tried once again to teach Snow White how to embroider. This time Snow White learned, with earnest fingers. With their coloured silks they depicted flowers of every season. And in their shared delight, as they sat threading their needles, the Queen taught Snow White one more thing. She taught her daughter how to prick her finger.

At that moment there was a great shudder beneath them as the earth spun forward on its path, sped on by the pent-up years, the seasons hot and cold as they flashed past. The child Snow White, dizzy with unfamiliar motion, soothing her bleeding finger in her mouth, grew tall, bewildered. Love for her mother surged through her unfurling body. She became a woman, then a woman of a certain age. Her hair turned grey, then white.

The Queen looked long at the trembling woman who was her daughter. Then she looked further through the open window. There was a second child, the Prince. The Queen embraced her daughter and left the room.

The Prince had been searching ever since he could remember. That's what Princes did. But though he had searched, he was never old enough to know what he was seeking. When he felt confused, he wandered in unlikely places for a change of scene. When downhearted, he slept.

As a city Prince he had been exposed to only the finest of popular culture and had consequently never seen anything old. The castle with its unfamiliarity had never appealed to him. Only in an extreme of despondence did he happen to be wandering near the far side of the castle at the time of the great shudder. Exhilarated by the motion, thinking the castle had something to do with it, he was drawn to the open window.

At first he thought he was imagining the white-haired woman, for he had never seen an older person. He stood there pondering. So this is what youth comes to! The smell of blood was in the air, and the chill of winter with its challenge. He climbed in over the windowsill. You must be Snow White, he said. And he reached up to touch her hair.

An ancient mirror reflected them both against the dusk, the wide-eyed Prince now tall as a man, his hair on end and whitening. And he was weary, so weary. He looked around for rocking chairs and blankets.

Snow White and the Prince strolled through the novelty of seasons. They rocked and dozed. From the castle walls folktales emerged into their dreams. When they woke they repeated the tales to each other.

How strange those lives were! And how strange their own! And thus, in wonder, they lived out their days.

THE JUNIPER TREE

(Susan Gordon, 1989)

Susan sent me a tape of her telling this story which I have transcribed fully. The "oral voice" is clear, in contrast to Marvyne's story, which was composed in writing. I have indicated dramatic voice changes (for example, when the sister is shouting) with italics. The song was a central feature of the story for Susan, and the tune to it is her own composition. "The Juniper Tree" is AT type 720, and number 47 in the Grimm collection. The motif of the bones that come to life as a singing bird echoes the motif of the singing reeds (E631, "reincarnation as musical instrument") in the earlier story told by Carol McGirr.

THERE was once a wealthy merchant who was married to a woman who was kind and good and they had everything they desired, except for the thing they desired most—and that was a child. And although the woman prayed and prayed for one, still they did not get one. And one day in the winter she was standing out in her yard beneath the juniper tree and she was peeling an apple when the knife slipped and it cut her finger. And three drops of her blood fell upon the ground. And she thought, "If only I had a child as red as that blood and as white as that snow." And suddenly she felt as if it might come true, and she went into the house.

A month passed and the snow was gone, two months and everything was green, three months and the buds began to come out on the trees, four months and the flowers were in bloom and trees were dense and tangled and thick and birds sang among them. In five months the blossoms on the trees fell and the air was so sweet that when the woman stood beneath the juniper tree it was as if her heart leaped within her, and so she fell on the ground and gave thanks. After six months the fruit on the trees grew round and heavy—and the woman grew very still; seven months and the fruit grew ripe and the woman ate it—ate it so greedily; eight months and the woman was so sick that she thought she would die—and she begged her husband to bury her beneath the juniper. After nine months she gave birth to a child who was as white as the snow and as red as the blood. She held him in her arms, she looked at him, and she died. Her husband wept bitterly, and buried her beneath the juniper tree.

Time passed and still he wept, and more time and still he wept, and more time, and he ceased crying, and more time and he took for himself a second wife. Now this woman had a child, a daughter—but his son was as white as the snow and as red as blood and every time his wife would look at him [the boy] it would cut her to the heart, for she desired all of the merchant's wealth for her daughter. And so it seemed to her that the boy was always underfoot and it was as if the Evil One spoke in her ear, and she began to pinch him here and push him there and pummel him, so that the boy was always bruised and in a fright and he had no safe place to hide.

One day, when the boy was at school, Ann Marie followed her mother up into her mother's bedroom, and there her mother had a chest filled with apples. And Ann Marie said "Mother, may I have an apple?" And her mother said "Why yes." And she bent over and reached for a red, ripe apple and handed it to her daughter. And as she did so, Ann Marie said, "And my brother—can he have one too?" And that angered the woman, and she said "He can have one when he comes home from school." And then she turned, and she looked out the window and she saw the boy coming.

It was as if the Evil One spoke to her and she snatched the apple out of her daughter's hand and she flung it down into the chest and said, "You can have an apple after your brother's had his!" Ann Marie went downstairs, and when the little boy came up the stepmother said to him in a strange voice, "Would you like an apple?" [Susan draws out each word slowly, using a menacing tone.] And the boy looked at her and he said "Oh mother, you look so wild today, strange and wild." And the Evil One made her speak to him more kindly: "Wouldn't you like an apple?" And she lured him on, and he said, "Yes mother, I would like an apple." She lifted the lid on the great chest: "Take one," she said. And the boy bent in to get an apple—and the mother brought the lid down CRUNCH! on his head. His head flew off and rolled among the apples.

Then the mother said to herself "What have I done! How can I get out of this!" And then she sat the boy's body upon the chair, and she reached in and took out his head and put it upon his neck. She took a silken cloth from her drawer and wrapped it round and round his neck. She set the chair by the door and put the apple in his hand.

Then she went downstairs and was boiling a great pot of water, when Ann Marie came in and said "My brother's sitting in the chair so still and white. He has an apple in his hand but when I asked him for a bite he will not speak to me." And her mother said "Go back up and ask him for the apple. And if he still will not speak to you, box him in his ear."

So Ann Marie went back to her brother and said "Give me a bite of that apple." But he did not speak to her, so she slapped him—and his head fell off his shoulders and rolled across the floor.

"*Mama! Mama mama mama!*" Ann Marie came running into the kitchen—"Mama, I hit him and his head ... *Mama! Mama!*" And her mother turned and looked, and said "*Ann Marie!* What have you done, you foolish girl! Well there's nothing to be done for it now, except to hide it." And she went and picked up the boy's body and laid it upon the table, and gathered up his head and placed it there as well. She took a knife from the drawer in the table and began to hack his body up and throw the pieces in the kettle to boil. Ann Marie stood by the pot and cried and cried and cried, until the water needed no salt.

Late in the afternoon when the father came home from work, he walked in and he said "I'm hungry, I'm ready for dinner." And his wife said "I have a fine stew cooked for you." And Ann Marie cried and cried and cried—and the father said "Where is my son?" And the wife said "His uncle came for him—your first wife's brother—and he's taken him down to his place to live for a while." "But how strange," said the father, "for him to go and not to say goodbye to me." "Oh he'll be back," said the mother. "They'll take good care of him. He'll only be gone six weeks." And Ann Marie cried and cried and cried. The father said "Still, how strange that he would say nothing. Well never mind. I'm hungry. Give me my dinner."

And his wife dished up the dark black stew that was his son, and the man began to eat—and he ate and he ate and he ate. And he said "All of this is for me. None of you may have any of this." And so he ate all of the stew—until it was gone. He chewed on the bones and then flung them beneath the table.

Ann Marie cried and cried, and he said to her "Your brother will be home soon. You'll see—it will be all right." Ann Marie bent beneath the table and she gathered up all the bones of her brother, wrapped them in a silk cloth and took them outside and laid them beneath the juniper tree. And when she laid them in the grass, suddenly the tree began to move. The branches went back and forth like hands that are clapping when they are happy. And a mist rose out of the tree, and from the center of the mist flew a great golden bird, singing. Ann Marie looked down at the base of the tree and she saw the bones of her brother were gone, and suddenly she felt happy—as if he had come back to life. And she went into the house and ate her supper.

The bird flew down into the village and sat upon the roof of a gold-smith's house, and sang out:

[sung slowly] *My mother she butchered me,*
My father he ate me,
My little sister Anne Marie
She gathered up the bones of me
And tied them in a silken cloth
And laid them under the Juniper Tree.
Ohhhhhhhh, What a beautiful bird am I.

The goldsmith came running out of the house so fast that he left one of his slippers behind, and he stood out in the street, one slipper on and barefoot in the other, and a chain—a golden chain—in one hand and his working tools in the other. And he said "Oh bird, that was wonderful. Sing it again." But the bird said "Oh no. A second time I do not sing for free. Give me a gift." And the goldsmith flung the golden chain up to the bird and said "There it is! Sing it again." And the bird caught the chain in his right claw and began to sing his song:

[sung slowly] *My mother she butchered me,*
My father he ate me,
My little sister Anne Marie
She gathered up the bones of me
And tied them in a silken cloth
And laid them under the Juniper Tree.
Ohhhhhhhh, What a beautiful bird am I.

And then he flew away, down to the cobbler's house, and again he sang out:

My mother she butchered me,
My father he ate me,
My little sister Anne Marie
She gathered up the bones of me
And tied them in a silken cloth
And laid them under the Juniper Tree.
Ohhhhhhhh, What a beautiful bird am I.

The cobbler came running out of the house and said "Oh bird, that was wonderful. Sing it again." And the bird said "Oh no, a second time I do not sing for free." And the cobbler called out his wife and his workers and his daughter and said, "See, look—look at that beautiful bird. You should hear the song that he can sing." Then he said to his daughter "Go upstairs and you'll find in the attic a pair of red leather shoes. Bring them out and give them to the bird." And the daughter ran upstairs and she brought down the red leather shoes and she held them up into the air, and the bird flew down and took them in its left claw. And then he sang again:

> My mother she butchered me,
> My father he ate me,
> My little sister Anne Marie
> She gathered up the bones of me
> And tied them in a silken cloth
> And laid them under the Juniper Tree.
> Ohhhhhhhhh, What a beautiful bird am I.

And then the bird flew on until he came to a linden tree beside a mill. And there, there were twenty millers hewing a millstone and the mill went "clickety clack, clickety clack, clickety clack, clickety clack." And the men chopped, chopped, chopped, chopped. And the bird sang out:

> My mother she butchered me,
> (And two of the millers stopped working;)
> My father he ate me,
> (and three more stopped;)
> My little sister Anne Marie,
> (And two more stopped;)
> She gathered up the bones of me,
> (And there were only five millers still working;)
> And tied them in a silken cloth,
> (And now there were only two;)
> And laid them under the Juniper Tree.
> (And now only one—)
> Ohhhhhhhhh, What a beautiful bird am I.

And the last miller lay down his tools and said "Oh bird, what a beautiful song. Sing that again." And the bird said "The second time I do not sing for free. Give me the millstone." And the miller said "It is not just mine to give. It belongs to all of us." And he turned to the other millers and they said "Oh yes, give him the millstone. Give him the millstone, and let him sing again." And so the bird flew down and put his neck beneath the millstone and flew back up into the tree with the millstone around his neck, red shoes in one claw and gold chain in the other—and then he flew away again—flew away towards his own home.

And then he perched on his roof and he sang out:

> *My mother she butchered me,*
> *My father he ate me,*
> *My little sister Anne Marie*
> *She gathered up the bones of me*
> *And tied them in a silken cloth*
> *And laid them under the Juniper Tree.*
> *Ohhhhhhhhh, What a beautiful bird am I.*

And his father said "Ah, suddenly it feels like summer in the air—warm and ... somehow I feel like soon I'll see my son again." And the mother said "No! No! It's cold out, not warm! It feels like a great storm is coming!"

And the bird sang out:

> *My mother she butchered me,*
> *My father he ate me,*
> *My little sister Anne Marie*
> *She gathered up the bones of me*
> *And tied them in a silken cloth*
> *And laid them under the Juniper Tree.*
> *Ohhhhhhhhh, What a beautiful bird am I.*

And the father said "Oh what a wonderful song. Oh look, look at the bird out there, it's singing. I want to go out and see him." His wife said "No! Don't go out there! I'm so afraid! My teeth are chattering and I'm so cold inside—and I'm burning up!" And she ripped open her blouse. And the father said "I'm going out to see what the bird has for me." And he stepped outside and Ann Marie cried and cried, and the mother flung herself down full length on the floor and her cap fell from her head.

The father stepped out and the bird sang:

> *My mother she butchered me,*
> *My father he ate me,*

> *My little sister Anne Marie*
> *She gathered up the bones of me*
> *And tied them in a silken cloth*
> *And laid them under the Juniper Tree.*
> *Ohhhhhhhh, What a beautiful bird am I.*

And he dropped down the gold chain and it fell around the father's neck. And the father came in and said "Look—look what the bird has given me. He's a wonderful bird. And the air outside—it smells like cinnamon." And the mother said "No! No! We're all going to die!" And then she lay still as if she were dead herself. And Ann Marie said "I'm going outside to see what the bird has for me." And Ann Marie went out and the bird sang:

> *My mother she butchered me,*
> *My father he ate me,*
> *My little sister Anne Marie*
> *She gathered up the bones of me*
> *And tied them in a silken cloth*
> *And laid them under the Juniper Tree.*
> *Ohhhhhhhh, What a beautiful bird am I.*

And he dropped down the red shoes, and Ann Marie caught them and put them on her feet and danced and danced and danced all around the yard. And then she came in and she said "Look—look what the bird has given me. I feel so happy."

And the mother said "*No!*" But then she said, "I will go out and see what the bird has for me." And the mother stood up, and walked outside.

Ohhhhhhhh, What a beautiful bird am I, he sang.

The bird dropped the millstone, and it crushed the stepmother. And there was smoke, and a spot of grease, and that was all.

The father and Ann Marie heard the sound and they came outside—and there they found the boy back again. And the boy took his father by one hand, his sister by the other, and they went inside and sat down and ate their supper.

Notes

1 A much briefer version of the first part of this chapter appeared as "And She Lived Happily Ever After?" in *Women and Language* (Radner 1996:14-18). The second part of this chapter was first presented as a paper, "Two Women: Two Stories," at the 9th Congress of the International Society for Folk-Narrative Research, held in Budapest in 1989; it was substantially expanded and revised from a chapter of the same name in *Undisciplined Women* (Greenhill and Tye 1997:250-65).

2 Cristina Bacchilega presents a thorough examination of rewritten fairy tales in *Postmodern Fairy Tales* (Bacchilega 1997).

3 In various European ballads a resentful elder sister drowns the younger into the sea. Her body is found and a harp or fiddle is made of her bones and hair; the instrument sings the song of the murder, but the victim most often remains unresuscitated. One Russian variant ends ambiguously, leaving open the possibility of her return to life (from an unpublished collection of Doukhobor songs).

4 She means either "The Six Swans," "The Seven Ravens," or "The Twelve Brothers." This story (AT 451) was so popular with the Grimms that they included these three separate variants of the same basic story.

5 The text Marvyne sent me, "Snow White: A Reflection," still remains unpublished as of this writing (1997). Her other stories, based on folktales and fables, were published in *The Emperor's Body* (Jenoff 1995).

6 Her master's thesis is a detailed description of her experiences in therapeutic storytelling; she includes the drawings made by many of the clients who took part in her investigation (Gordon 1991).

7 She details this process in her thesis, in which she describes how she draws listeners into the story by having them discuss different possible outcomes in small groups, and also by having them draw parts of the story relevant to their own experiences.

8 "Snow White" was one of the tales that Wilhelm Grimm revised more than most of the others; it changes noticeably from earliest to latest editions. The earliest known text of the story is in an unpublished manuscript sent by the Grimms to Clemens Brentano in 1810. An English translation of this text from the 1812 variant changes the story even further (David and David 1964, 303-315).

9 Marvyne sent me the two texts of "Snow White: A Reflection," first written in 1989 and revised in 1993. I quote from the 1993 text, which is included here. Page references are to this manuscript.

10 The intensive workshop for professional performers was offered at the

Eugene O'Neil Theater Center in August 1982, led by storyteller Laura Simms. Each participant spent the week working on a story of their own choosing, and Susan's choice was "The Handless Maiden." Susan Gordon details her adventures with this story in a separate article (Gordon 1993).

11 Susan sent me both a cassette tape, which I transcribed, and several letters (some undated) discussing her reactions as a storyteller.

12 I was part of the audience at the 1989 American Folklore Society meeting during which Susan used this method of expanding the story. It was an effective means of creating alternate "readings" of the text.

13 For example, I was intrigued by the responses of a group of 13-year-old girls in a Winnipeg working class neighborhood I interviewed in 1974. After rejecting "fairytales" as unrealistic romantic stories, they insisted that the stories were also "real" in their representation of various forms of family violence.

14 I say this as a child who fantasized that my parents were not my true parents at all, and also as a mother with distressing dreams and fears of various disasters befalling my children.

FIVE

BURNING BRIGHTLY: THE DEVELOPMENT OF A STORY[1]

W E have been exploring the experiences of a number of contemporary storytellers, all quite self-aware of the processes
of composing and performing orally. In this chapter I try to
explore this experience from the inside out, examining a story I have
been telling from the 1980s on. My adventures with this single story
have led me on interesting paths.

In one of the lesser-known Grimm tales a girl is warned by her parents not to visit a witch who lives in a strange house in the center of
the forest; she disobeys them, seeks out the crone in the heart of darkness, and is turned into a log for her efforts. This short tale, first read
while I was doing research for my doctoral dissertation, illustrates how
a single text is, in fact, a constantly emerging story. Tellers who com-
pose and recompose orally are aware of the interesting twists and
turns a story takes as they continue to tell it. From our experiences
with written literature we are accustomed to expect a single authoritative text created by one named author. Oral tales, unless they are
scripted or recited by rote memory, are the result of countless variant
texts, not only by different authors (every teller is the author of their
story) but also the same text told and retold by the same teller, since
each performance is unique. Every wondertale that lives an oral life is
multi-textual. (The only exception in this book is Jenoff's "Snow
White: A Reflection," which was composed in writing; even this tale
has two variant texts—and always the possibility of an oral rebirth.) In
the process I describe here a single printed Grimm text becomes oral
and multi-textual.

One of my own pleasantly impossible tasks has been an exploration
of how and why stories come to life. Though I did not see it clearly at
the time, this task was part of my very first academic explorations of
folktale heroines, begun in the early 1970s and developed over the
next two decades (Stone 1975a, 1975b, 1980, 1985, 1988, 1993,

1996, 1998). Initially I was interested in finding out how heroines were portrayed in both traditional and popularized tales and how these characterizations were received by contemporary readers and listeners. While conducting interviews for my dissertation I discovered that, generally speaking, girls and women remembered the fairytales they had read as children, while boys and men generally did not—though some would admit to having read many of the same stories.[2]

My interest in stories continued to grow over the next few years but it began to take unexpected turns. I found it was not satisfying enough to study folktales and to question others about them; I began to tell them as well, first as part of my lectures where a summary of a tale was merely an illustration of a point I made, then as a separate thing, as a "performance" in which tales were told merely for the sake of telling them. As I took part in professional storytelling events and observed other tellers I was able to see firsthand over an extended time how tellers, tales, and listeners interacted in the living process of verbal artistry. Of course my curiosity was expressed in writing, because that is how I learned to tell academic stories (Stone 1984, 1985a, 1985b, 1986, 1993b, 1994, 1996a). I was a "curious girl" indeed.

The words I offer here are my first attempt to express in print what I have learned as a scholar of tales as well as a teller of tales. I describe the evolution of one particular story, "Mistress Trudy" (AT 334, Grimm number 43), from its beginning as the single text I read in 1973 to its most recent telling as of the writing of this chapter.[3] It may sound like a simple task to report how "Mistress Trudy" became "The Curious Girl," but it has been the most difficult writing I have yet done, since I have had to be both the academic and the performer, both the curious girl and the crone. As a folklorist I asked myself how and why the story was learned and told and how it developed in the oral context. As a storyteller I asked myself how the various performances shaped the tale as it was told and retold to listeners, who consciously and unconsciously influenced the evolution of the story.

Coming to terms with Mistress Trudy's adventures was a different challenge from exploring her story in academic writing: her story required me to unravel its patterns of significance from the inside out instead of interpreting it from the outside in. Like the girl in my retelling of the tale, I had to discover the unknown story. I include both texts in full, the Grimm tale as part of this chapter, and my oral variant, developed over several years of performance, at the end of the chapter. My difficult task was to describe how the first text evolved into the second; to discuss my explicit and implicit interpretations and the influences of actual listeners; and finally, to examine the metaphoric relationship of this story to the realities of life.

As I said earlier, I first met Mistress Trudy while reading traditional tales as part of my dissertation research. I spent three years sitting on small chairs in the children's sections of dozens of libraries in Canada and the United States, reading though English translations of the most popular folktale collections (the Grimms, Hans Christian Andersen, and Andrew Lang). When I first met Mistress Trudy in my own copy of the complete Grimm tales she did not offer pleasant company. I was enraged. So much so that I threw my book across the room—something I have not done since I was a child. It split neatly in half. The story inflamed me. I was too sympathetic with that overly curious and disobedient girl who set out so boldly on her path into the woods, and who was eventually overwhelmed and destroyed by the witch she sought out. It was an ugly story, but it was part of what I was studying. I picked the book up and put the two pieces back together, cited the tale, put it into my dissertation statistics, and classified it according to the neat four-part scheme I used for describing folktale heroines into Persecuted, Tamed, Passive, or Heroic categories. After that I occasionally used it as a negative example when I was conducting interviews, but I did not find it useful in any other way. I would never have judged it suitable for oral performances once I began telling stories in the 1970s.

But Mistress Trudy did not wish to be forgotten. Her story returned most unexpectedly, ten years after I had first read it, when I was trying to resolve another story that I had been working on. I carefully reread "Mistress Trudy" to see if I had missed something. To my surprise I discovered one tiny ember that offered possibilities. Here is the text as I found it in 1973 and reread it again ten years later, the whole story told in two brief paragraphs.[4]

Mistress Trudy

Once upon a time there was a girl who was stubborn and inquisitive, and whenever her parents told her to do something, she'd never obey. How could she get along well? One day she said to her parents, "I've heard so much about Mistress Trudy; I'll call on her sometime. People say that her house looks queer and that there are many strange things in it. I've become quite curious." The parents strictly forbade her going there and said, "Mistress Trudy is a wicked woman, given to evil things, and if you go there, we'll disown you."

The girl paid no attention, however, to her parents' orders and went to Mistress Trudy's just the same. When she got there, Mistress Trudy asked her, "Why are you so pale?" "Oh," she answered, shaking all over, "I'm so frightened at what I've seen." "What have you seen?" "I saw a black man on your stairs." "That was a charcoal burner." "Then I saw a green man." "That was a huntsman." "Then I saw a blood-red man." "That was a butcher." "Oh, Mistress Trudy, I shuddered; I looked through the window and I didn't see you but I did see the devil with his fiery head." "Is that so!" she said. "Then you saw the witch in her proper garb. I've been waiting for you for a long time now and have longed for you. Now you shall furnish me with light." Thereupon she transformed the girl into a log and threw it in the fire, and when it was all aglow, she sat down beside it and, warming herself at it, said, "That really does give a bright light."

It is not surprising that this unpromising story did not become part of my repertoire when I began to perform folktales in the mid-1970s. However, a few years later, when I was playing around with a story of my own that refused to resolve itself, "Mistress Trudy" returned unexpectedly to mind. I turned aside this intrusion but the story refused to go away. As stubborn as the curious girl, I resisted until curiosity nudged me into rereading the Grimm text to see if there was something I had missed. I found nothing at first, but I decided to try retelling it as close to the Grimm text as possible to free whatever had caught my unwitting attention. Only after several tellings did I sense something in the girl's transformation by fire that I had not noticed in the first readings: She gave a bright light. More important, the story did not explicitly say that the girl was destroyed. I also heard Mistress Trudy's words with new ears: "I've been waiting for you for a long time now and have longed for you." With these equivocal words the story began to develop new configurations, and after five years of retelling it transformed itself into something quite different from the cautionary tale I first read. Once the story was on its new path it continued to flow, with the theme of transformation, not destruction, as its central motivation. Mistress Trudy lost none of her properly menacing cronishness; she continued to be threatening as she was in the Grimm text, but she was also willing to accept the girl's curiosity and persistence instead of simply annihilating her for improper behavior.

The story as I now told it began in the same way, with the girl's curiosity and disobedience, the parental threat of abandonment. But as she proceeds through the forest I allowed her to become frightened, and to be guided by stubbornness to the strange little house. Here she sees the blazing woman, is questioned by her, and is turned into a log and thrown on the fire, with the exact words of the story as I read it. And here everything changes. As the fire blazes up to warm the crone, a shower of sparks flies out of the flames. The witch recognizes them, catches them, and transforms them into a fiery red bird. She challenges the girl to find one story that has never been heard before; if she fails she remains a bird forever. The girl, as bird, flies into the world and learns stories for a year and a day, returns and tells them all to Mistress Trudy—who of course has heard them all before. In desperation she opens her mouth to protest, but most unexpectedly words come out on their own and she begins to tell her own story. This, of course, is the story that has not been heard before.

On the surface of the text alone, the two stories seemed quite the opposite in their resolution. "Mistress Trudy" was a stark cautionary tale warning of the dangers of disobedience and curiosity for girls, but "The Curious Girl" rewarded these same risks. In the end the two stories, mine and the Grimms', are entirely opposite. Not only does the girl survive, she becomes empowered as well. How could these two stories be related in meaning at all? I was still missing something.

I reread the story as I had first encountered it to check on the wording and to see its relative situation in the Grimm collection. The surrounding stories are similar and might have colored my initial reading. "Mistress Trudy" is placed between "The Godfather" and "Godfather Death." Their similarities were as fascinating; they were almost variations on a theme. In all three tales the protagonists must confront an overwhelming force that threatens their existence and in the end destroys them in two of the stories, almost does so in the other.

In the first story, "The Godfather," a father sets out to find a godfather for his child and meets a stranger who agrees, and who gives him a bottle of magical water that cures death. The man later goes to visit this godfather and on his arrival meets strange objects on the stairway that tell him the way; he sees a shovel and broom having an argument, a heap of severed fingers, a pile of skulls, and fish frying themselves in a pan. When he reaches the top floor he peeks through a keyhole and sees the godfather with horns on his head. The man boldly opens the door and goes inside, and the godfather hides himself. When asked about the strange things he lies: the shovel and broom are kitchen boy and maid, the fingers are roots, the skulls are cabbages. When the man insists that he has seen the godfather through the keyhole the godfather yells, "Now that's just not true." The man leaps up and runs away in fear.

This dissatisfying story seems to be a garbled variant of "Godfather Death," which succeeds "Mistress Trudy." "The Godfather" lacks clear motivation and certain resolution, while "Godfather Death" is strong in each of these: a son is promised as a godchild to Death, who, when the child has become a man, gives him water that cures any illness. The godchild misuses the water twice, is warned but ignores the warnings, and is eventually carried off by Death.

"Mistress Trudy," presents yet another variation on the theme of supernatural relationships. The girl is not promised to anyone by her parents—in fact they warn her against unholy alliances. She sets out in direct disobedience, out of her own curiosity. She does not receive any magical objects either, which is appropriate given her more tenuous relationship: she's an intruder, not a godchild. However, she does see three odd men and questions the witch about their identities, echoing the experiences of the man in "The Godfather." In contrast to him, she knows what she is doing and is definitely more adventurous: "I think I'll go and see her one of these days," she boldly tells her parents. The man in "The Godfather" simply muddles through with no plans. "Mistress Trudy" is also a much more formidable opponent than is the silly godfather, who lies about the objects on the stairs and who yells at the man, but allows him to escape. Mistress Trudy's answers are deceptively more gentle and patient than his—and her quarry does not get away.

In the more forceful "Godfather Death" the deadly godfather, unlike the crone, is initially a mentor who teaches his godchild how to cure illnesses. This motif suggested to me new possibilities for the threatening figure in "Mistress Trudy." As cautionary tales, all three provide negative examples of what happens when one challenges the mentor before being ready to do so. The silly man in the first story gets away because the godfather is even sillier. The other two are not so lucky; they both meet death in the form of fire because of their arrogant disobedience. She is turned into a log and thrown on the fire while he is taken to a dark cave where he watches as the candle flame of his life is extinguished.

In this trio of stories all three of the characters are disobedient, but the first is so incompetent he does not even know where he is going or why, while the last one is calculating and ambitious. By contrast, the girl is self-motivated but not ambitious, and she does not run away. Nor does she have her flame extinguished. Quite the opposite—the fire blazes up.

What caught my unconscious attention was the fiery nature of this girl. Unlike the two men, she single-mindedly seeks out her antagonist against the advice of her cautious parents. She is disobedient, and she is looking for trouble. As the story asks, "How could she get along well?" In other words she deserves what she gets. But other folktale heroines are also disobedient. Snow White cannot resist her witch either, three times disobeying the dwarfs who warn her about strangers. Nor does Sleeping Beauty evade the spindle from which her parents try to protect her. Cinderella sneaks off to the ball three times and returns home, where she lies cleverly to protect herself. It is not difficult to find all sorts of heroines who are disobedient. I came to understand that, in fact, disobedience was a key motivating factor in most of the stories I could call to mind. True, in the case of male protagonists such disobedience was more often than not deliberate and explicit, while for females it was often accidental and implied. Still, disobedience alone did not seem to provide sufficient motive for annihilation. I reasoned that it must be the girl's particular form of defiance that dooms her in the Grimm text, since disobedience is so widespread. She is, after all, stubbornly set on visiting "a wicked woman, given to evil things."

The image of this "wicked woman" began to work on me. I remembered that the "witch" in our neighborhood lived across the street from the house I grew up in in Miami. She wore strange clothing, watered her yard at sunrise every morning in her nightgown and bedroom slippers, and cared more about plants and trees than people—or so I thought as a child. Her yard, a double lot, was a small forest of trees— orange, grapefruit and lemon, papaya and avocado, palm and pine. My sister Janet and I were curious, but also afraid. We did not even like to go to her door on Halloween. Once we sneaked into her "garden" when she was away to see if there were any curious things there but we escaped safely before she returned. I have since discovered that most of my students have had at least one "witch" in their neighborhood, often "odd" people who were misunderstood.[5] This excited my curiosity. Witches were not like anyone else. They might even live in a house "that looks queer and with many strange things in it," as did the woman across the street from me. Mistress Trudy was more than a storybook figure, at least in the imagination. And of course in past times countless women—and some men—died as a result of such imagination.

One reason she exists, then, is to warn us that curiosity is just as dangerous as our parents tried to tell us. If we take her warning as a challenge we might learn something, but we must be prepared to pay the consequences. Innocence is no excuse.

It is easy to be distracted by the negative "noise" about the dangers of curiosity in "Mistress Trudy" and to read it as the cautionary tale it was meant to be. What came through to me between the lines was something else, though. Even when my conscious mind furiously rejected the apparent destruction of the curious girl, something of her determined inquisitiveness remained in my mind for several years. The angry child in me recognized the girl in the story who did not allow her parents to subdue her curiosity even though they threatened her with abandonment. She was more honest, though. I did not usually disobey my parents outright, and was too timid to meet the neighborhood "witch" in her own yard.

She, unlike me, did not sneak into the witch's domain unseen. She arrived at Mistress Trudy's strange house in broad daylight after a harrowing night journey, pale and shaking but still able to open the door, enter, and respond to the crone's questions. Mistress Trudy's ironic words, "I've been waiting for you a long time now and have longed for you," herald the girl's violent transformation by fire. She is told she will burn brightly, and indeed she does. That caught my attention.

In fact, it was the girl's enchantment into a block of wood that sparked my interest when I reread the tale. I was able to see her test by fire as an elemental encounter, and once my mind was open to this more positive possibility, the other elements began to present themselves as I began to reevaluate and reexperience the story. As the story evolved through my oral tellings (all the time I was thinking about it I was also trying to tell it) the curious girl passed through a number of transformations. In early tellings I had her explicitly pass through all four elements—through the fire as a log and then a shower of sparks, through the air as a bird, through earth as a burrowing wild hare, and through water as a fish. These metamorphoses compelled her to sacrifice her self-centeredness, her uncontrolled curiosity, and in the end gave her freedom and, in my mind, full independence. When she spoke the unknown story—her own—she connected herself with all of the other stories she brought back to the demanding crone. The crone remains a deliberately ambivalent figure, able to punish or reward, to transform and to disenchant. One group of women who heard the story suggested that the girl was obviously going to become her apprentice, but that is another story.

In this new light, the Grimm tale seemed to me not so much disagreeable as unfinished, open-ended. Skilled storytellers understand the open-ended nature of traditional tales as well as folklorists do; such flexibility keeps any individual story alive by giving the teller enough room between the lines to convert old into new, and most important, as we have seen with several tellers here, to find themselves in the story.

The conversion of the story did not happen all at once. Mistress Trudy was not an easy woman to live with and I did not want to risk her ire by mistelling her story. I was very cautious when I related it publicly for the first time, opening with the Grimm text word-for-word (it was short enough for me to memorize easily) and then re-forming the story into my version of "Curious Girl." My intention was to emphasize the negative contrast of the two stories, one which I viewed as "bad" and the other as "good." I continued to recount the stories in this way to many different audiences, listening for their responses. Gradually the story began to change.

It was, and still is, a surprise to me how these two seemingly opposite tales started to grow toward each other, until they became two sides of a coin rather than two separate coins. Eventually they united into a single text, so that the beginning of "Curious Girl" echoed "Mistress Trudy." I held to the Grimm words until the shower of sparks flew from the flames and the fiery bird appeared.

Let me go back to my early adventures with this story and begin to bring in the audience responses that helped me to reform it. What continued to push the story into new growth was my own stubborn curiosity. I wanted to know what happened to the girl after she was thrown into the fire. How did she survive, and why? I knew there was something about to happen next but I did not know what it would be. Every time I told "The Curious Girl" I trusted that I would discover at least one thing that I had not noticed before, and each discovery gave its energy to the next telling. In this way the story grew on its own, and it became easier and easier to tell as I became more willing to enter through Mistress Trudy's door.

As I said earlier, when I first began using the story in Winnipeg schools the girl went through various transformations that represented fire, air, water, and earth. This got to be very elaborate. After her fiery rebirth she turned herself into a firebird and took to the air; and as she tried to escape the witch she leapt into water and became a fish, and finally she was a rabbit burrowing into warm earth. She was offered her own shape back if she would emerge and tell a story that Mistress Trudy had never heard. This challenge became the center of the story for me and for many of my listeners, and gradually it gave me a clearer focus that burned away extraneous material. Several audiences in particular have had a direct impact on the continued unfolding of the story, which passed through its most vibrant transformations in the late 1980s.

Here is the first. I spent a week in late September of 1987 in Quebec City visiting Vivian Labrie and her nine-year-old daughter. One night she invited the neighbors and their children over and we had a warm candlelit evening where everyone told a story. Some told stories they had read, some reported stories they had experienced directly, and I told "The Curious Girl." Later as we put the daughter to bed she asked for the story again. When I had finished she looked at me thoughtfully and said, "Why does that girl have to turn into all those animals?" As I pondered her question, it became clear that the transformations into the four elements were indeed becoming increasingly unwieldy and unnecessary. It seemed to me that I was becoming too literal: "Now get all four of those elements in there or this won't work," I thought. It was starting to feel a bit slapstick, as Susan Gordon commented earlier on her own telling of the murder scene in "The Juniper Tree."

So I stopped telling "Curious Girl" for a while and let my mental bird fly to a new place and learn fresh stories. For several weeks I pondered the nine-year-old's question, which I rephrased: "Why do you [adults] make your lives so complicated?" Eventually, I came to understand that the elements of the girl's transformation did not all have to be expressed explicitly. I began to tell the story again and to try out other connections, until only the fiery sparks and the firebird remained explicit. Air, of course, was her element now; the power of water was implied when she stepped over the stream to enter the forest and everything around her suddenly seemed a bit different; earth manifested itself in the trembling that preceded the coming of the three riders. The story had begun to simplify itself, to become more lucid and transparent.

The second experience came in the spring of 1988. I was participating in a week-long workshop in Windsor, Ontario, and was asked to tell a story for an audience of adults at a folk music concert.[6] I stood in front of some fifty strangers in a church basement where they had spent the last hour and a half listening to people sing and play folk music. They were scattered casually about on folding metal chairs that clanked when shifted. I chose to tell them "The Curious Girl" because the story was brief (I did not trust myself to hold their attention for long). Also, it was ready to go again, primed for further transformation. As I aimed the words at that particular group of listeners that night a few new phrases came into the story, but the most memorable change came at the end, when they began to applaud spontaneously before I had spoken Mistress Trudy's final words in which she acknowledges the unknown story and frees the bird. They responded at the point when the curious girl says the first words of her own story, which repeat the opening lines of the text. I was surprised and a bit concerned, wondering if they were anxious to get me off stage. Perhaps this audience was more attuned to poetry, having listened to an hour of folksongs, and found a circular conclusion satisfying—the end is the beginning. I could appreciate the open-ended potential of such a conclusion and its powerful circular movement. I sometimes end the story here if I am telling it to adults, bringing readers/hearers more directly into the act of creation by leaving the full resolution in their hands.[7] The creative ambivalence matches that of the Grimm tale, leaving room for further re-creation. Recreation is play, and playing can be wonderfully serious and seriously imaginative.

In the fall of 1988 the story took another turn when I told it as part of an American Folklore Society panel, "Women and Power." My function on the panel was to provide a direct example of what we had all been talking about, and "The Curious Girl" seemed an ideal choice since both the girl and the crone were powerful women. Five of us sat a the table in the front of the room offering our varied presentations on women in life and in literature to an attentive audience composed largely of women. They were alert and ready. Since I was the last speaker, the discussion that followed our panel began with responses to the story. Many centered their remarks on the girl's belated recognition of the power of her own life history, a topic that was related to the contributions of other panel members as well. Participants also acknowledged that telling one's own tale is only the beginning, that true freedom comes when one's own stories connect with those from others. They also suggested that anyone who fails to go beyond ego-identity would remain in service to the inner crone instead of growing into equality with her. Jung would have called the result of this growth individuation.

The contributions of this audience deepened my own perception of the story instead of effecting more explicit changes. For example, we talked about the story as an academic metaphor; academics have been trained to look into the window and describe what is objectively observed—we say what we see, a woman in flames, and if we are lucky we are corrected to look again and see what is there in essence—"the witch in her proper garb." These listeners suggested that often our academic vision is as limited as that of the curious girl: what is seen through the window is only one aspect of what is there potentially and actually—in this case a woman who is surrounded by flames but not consumed by them. This image strengthened itself in my mind as a result of telling the tale to this particular audience.

Later that year in Winnipeg "The Curious Girl" took another turn, when it was told back to me by a ten-year-old boy at a gathering of Winnipeg storytellers. A dozen of us were sitting around in a casual circle listening and telling tales. A few of the adults occasionally brought older children. This boy had heard "The Curious Girl" told once by me and another time by his mother. At this time in the story's life history the girl was given her own shape back *before* she went off to learn the stories of the world, which (I had not noticed) weakened her motivation to return. When the boy came to that point in the story two things happened: it was the witch and not the girl herself who brought about the transformation into a bird, and he had her retain the bird shape as she learned her stories, transforming her only when she returned and succeeded in telling her final story. These simple changes were much more powerful in motivation, and so spontaneous that both he and his mother were certain I had told it that way. I had not. My initial response was to correct them, but then I saw that this was an effective change.

The Toronto storytelling festival of 1989 offered another venue for the continuing emergence of "The Curious Girl." At this time I was performing with Rubena Sinha, a classically trained professional dancer from India. Because of the archetypal nature of folktales we found it viable and inspiring to work together, with me telling a story and Rubena dancing it, using the classical movements and gestures of her traditional training to the words of European folktales. We had performed "Curious Girl" several times in Winnipeg, but in Toronto, in front of a large audience of adults sophisticated in storytelling, the simple tale expanded almost to mythological proportions in our own experience of the performance. Mistress Trudy was no earthly witch but a dark goddess with the power to transform the world and the girl became an initiate, however unwilling, in a rite of transformation. This intensification of the story did not change our "text," but it changed our heightened sense of it, in the context of its being told and danced in the presence of an unusually receptive audience, many of whom were experienced tellers. Listeners who had heard the story that night might not have noticed anything different about the story but Rubena and I certainly did. It was never a simple folktale again after that experience.

"The Curious Girl" also benefited from the suggestions of those who read this chapter as it developed. The suggestions of Susan Gordon and Jo Radner were particularly helpful in clarifying how the Grimm text and my variant continued to be intimately and necessarily connected. I carefully reread Jo's commentary on decoding women's texts (Radner and Lanser, 1987). As I discovered from this reading, decoding as they defined it did not apply to "Mistress Trudy" because it was a male-translated text of a male-collected tale based on a male-written poem. Still, it was useful to review my own conscious and unconscious retellings in light of decoding feminist messages. Jo also stressed the importance of the girl's telling of her own story:

> Tellers can go all over the world learning other people's stories and they can tell them well; but the story they need to tell (to themselves at least, if not the public) is the only one they have: their own. That is the base from which we really learn to understand the languages/lives of other creatures; the way we save our lives from the strangers who would consume us for their own purposes (letter, 1988).

I was also inspired by Susan Gordon's struggles to tell "The Handless Maiden" as a story of empowerment rather than of victimization and rescue. Susan's challenge was even greater than mine because she retold the Grimm tale as she had read it, making no substantial changes but subtly suggesting other possibility through slight alternations in phrasing and imagery. One small change she made—borrowing from a Russian tale the theme of the mother gaining her own hands back when rescuing her drowning child—motivated me to borrow an incident as well. I found the horsemen from the Russian tale "Vasilisa the Beautiful" more compelling than the three bland figures Mistress Trudy identifies as "My woodsman, my charcoal burner, and my butcher;" for several years Baba Yaga's dramatic riders—Dark Night, Red Sun, and Bright Day—galloped through "The Curious Girl" (the Russian tale appears in Afanasyev 1973:439-447).[8]

The story also evolved in response to my own ripening perspectives as I aged and—at times—matured. As the mother of two curious children I understood that mothers have every reason to fear for their adventurous offspring, and even to threaten them with all sorts of frightening things out of love, however misguided. Parental anxiety has not lessened much even though my children are now mature adults. The world remains a place where unexpected things happen. I have learned, too, that one cannot be a mother without also being a witch at times. The mother's warning and the crone's challenging of the girl contribute to her unexpected transformations. This was latent to me in the Grimm cautionary tale and came into full life in the retold one. The "good" natural mother and "bad" witch-mother become one, both protecting and testing the girl who wants to find out about the world outside the protective walls of her home.

It is easier to accept the dualistic perceptions of wondertales, to sort characters and situations into positive and negative, good and bad, white and black. In this interpretation Mistress Trudy is truly "a wicked woman, given to evil things" and the girl is tragically disobedient, and justly punished. As I said earlier, when I first began to tell the story I split it into "good" and "bad" versions with the intention of contrasting the two. As my own perceptions moved away from dualism, however, I found I no longer needed to split the stories. They became one as I came to accept the girl's treatment in both versions as challenge rather than as punishment, as transformation rather than as defeat. In this way the girl's path to her enlightenment burns brightly before her. Even in the Grimm tale, the potential for transformation is implicit.

"Mistress Trudy" is more than a cautionary tale. This wisdom came to me from telling the tale rather than thinking about it, from listening to what others had to say rather than struggling through intellectual analysis. I am not suggesting that analysis is not useful, but thinking by itself did not solve the mystery of the woman in flames who throws the girl into the fire. I had to experience them both much more directly to feel the fire and understand its alchemical potential. This story more than any other I have told has taught me to risk losing my shape (in this case my shape as an academic) to find out what is beyond the fire.

While writing and rewriting this chapter over the past few years I sensed an unspoken, continuing dialogue between the curious girl and the crone as they related their stories to one another. Because it was a dialogue rather than two monologues, the story of this story felt as if it was growing spontaneously, that it had a life of its own beyond my deliberate revisions. Relevant parts of my personal story entered consciously and unconsciously, presenting themselves in ways that were objectively illuminating, not just subjectively self-indulgent; this was a very fine tightrope to walk while trying to describe the experience of storytelling from the inside out.

Telling the story was one thing, writing about it quite another. I understand the power of telling stories all too well, which has made me uncomfortable with putting them down in print for an unknown audience. I sit here at my modern computer imagining the curious girl typing out all the stories she had learned and preparing to send them off to Mistress Trudy in the morning mail. If she had done that, mailed them off instead of telling them, that girl might still be a bird to this very day. That is a sobering thought.

My attempt to set down this story's story in print compelled me to look at the tale from very different angles and to sketch the different shapes it took as it moved along. In doing so I became more aware of the essences of character and action and motivation: the dynamic union of negative and positive forces that bring about metamorphoses; the dangers and the ecstasies of deep curiosity; the punishments and rewards of freedom-seeking; the absolute necessity of listening to the stories of others as well the necessity of telling our own as part of the ocean of stories.

Most of all this exploration of a single story gave me a highly conscious experience with the multi-textual (and multi-textural) nature of told tales, always shifting in response to the ever unique contexts in which they thrive. But what does this matter in terms of what I have tried to show in this book, whose title was inspired by the transformative fire? It has made me wonder about how oral tales are learned and developed and passed on. I know that others are telling this transformed variant of the cruel Grimm text because I have occasionally been asked for formal permission. It is meant to be retold.

In general terms my experience stands as a model, however limited, for the tellers we have met here and for hundreds of other participants in organized storytelling. While learning the story I imitated my "teacher," in this case a book rather than another teller; as I continued to tell it the story began to take on its own life and moved away from the text as I learned it; it had a rapid period of growth and elaboration midway through its existence and then began a slow process of simplification, during which unnecessary elements dropped away. And all along, the story, and those who responded to it, continued to transform itself.

From the outside in with other tellers, and from the inside out with myself, I have been able to explore and to experience how the oral process continually circles, spirals and spreads, like ripples from a pebble dropped into a quiet pond. The ripples reach the shore and begin to move back to the center again, overlapping, interweaving, like the sound waves of the human voice speaking a story.

THE CURIOUS GIRL

(Kay Stone, 1996)

It was difficult for me to decide how to put my own story down in print. I had a hybrid version of "Curious Girl" that was adapted into print from my oral telling (Yashinsky 1994), but it seemed unfair to simply reprint this "literary" telling. I had taped story texts for the other tellers included here, except for Bob Barton who sent a typed story and Joe Neil MacNeil whose transcribed text was printed in Tales Until Dawn *(MacNeil 1987). To keep my text comparable I chose to transcribe my oral version from a tape made by Earthstory, the performing trio I have worked with for several years.[9] I have included the book version in Appendix II in order to show how oral and written compositions are different in texture; spoken texts do not have the same requirements for description and development as do written stories, and tend to be less elaborate. This transcribed text is noticeably shorter.*

ONCE there was a girl who was curious and stubborn, and always disobedient to her parents. When they told her to do one thing, she'd do another. Now one day, she said to them, "I've heard that there's an old woman named Frau Trude who lives in the dark heart of the forest, and I want to see if that's true." They said to her, "We forbid you to do that. Frau Trude is an evil woman, and if you visit her you'll be our child no longer." But she didn't listen to them. Early one morning, without saying a word, she slipped out and set off for the forest.

When she began to walk in that forest, at first it was bright and the birds were singing, but as she went further in the forest became very silent, and much darker. But she kept on. She kept on until she felt the earth begin to tremble beneath her feet. She turned, and saw behind her a dark horse and a dark rider, and they came galloping towards her, and when they passed darkness fell all around her. She was frightened, but she was stubborn, so she went on. She could feel the path beneath her feet. She went on until she felt the earth begin to tremble again, and this time when she turned she saw a glowing red horse and red rider, and when they galloped past the sky above her turned blood red. But she went on. She went on until the earth began to tremble again, and this time she saw a flashing white horse and a white rider, and when they passed bright day fell all around her, and she saw that she was in a clearing.

She saw a very strange house there. It was Frau Trude's house. It had a fence made of human bones, and at the gate-posts of that fence there were human skulls with glowing red eyes. When she passed through the gate the skulls turned and watched her. In front of Frau Trude's door there was a tree with blood red leaves; no birds sang in that tree. Now she was frightened, but it was too late to turn back, so she went to the window of that house and she looked inside, expecting to see Frau Trude. But instead she saw the form of a woman all in flames—and she heard her own named called. She went to the door as if she were in a trance and she pushed it open very slowly, afraid of what she would see inside. But when she stepped in, she saw a very ordinary old woman. It was Frau Trude.

"Welcome my dear, I've been waiting for you. But tell me, why do you look so frightened?"

"Oh, it's because I've seen such strange things!"

"Have you? And what have you seen?"

"Oh! First I saw a dark horse and a dark rider, and then I saw a red horse and red rider, and then a white horse and a white rider!"

"Did you? Well then, you have seen my Dark Night, and my Red Morning, and my Bright Day. Tell me, what else did you see?"

"Oh, Frau Trude, when I looked in your window I didn't see you at all. I saw the figure of a woman all in flames!"

"Did you now. Ah! Then you have seen the witch in her true form. And now *you* will burn brightly for *me*."

Frau Trude said three strange words, and she turned that girl into a log. She picked that log up and threw it onto her fire. And when the fire blazed up she pulled her chair closer to warm herself, and she said, "Look, indeed she does burn brightly!"

But as she said those words a shower of sparks flew out of that fire. Frau Trude caught them quickly, and she turned those sparks into a fiery red bird, red like the rising sun, with a beak as dark as thunder and eyes flashing like summer lightening.

"Now ... You will be my servant forever ... unless ... you can tell me one story that I've never heard before, a story that has no end."

"But how can I do that!" said the girl who was now a bird. "You know many more stories than I do."

"Ah yes, that's true. So I'll give you a year and a day to learn as many as you like. Surely you'll find one that I haven't heard, one with no end."

Frau Trude carried that bird outside and she let it fly free.

Now, that girl who was a bird flew everywhere, and she learned stories from all living things, and at the end of a year and a day she flew back, back to that tree with the blood red leaves. And she began to sing. Frau Trude came out and she said, "Ah, I've been waiting for you. Tell me a story."

So the girl who was a bird began, and she told every story she had learned from all of creation, from green growing things, from creatures that crawled and flew and swam and leapt, and they were all wonderful. Frau Trude listened carefully, and when the last story was told she said, "Excellent, excellent! But I heard every one of those stories before you were even born. I hope you have another."

But she didn't. She opened her mouth to say "No!" But a story began to come out on its own. It sounded familiar:

"Once there was a girl who was curious, and stubborn, and always disobedience to her parents ... " Indeed that was the story that had never been heard, and, as far as I know, it is still a story with no end.

Notes

1 An earlier version of this chapter appeared as "Burning Brightly: New Light on an Old Tale," in *Feminist Messages* (Radner 1993:289-305), and is used here with the permission of the University of Illinois Press.

2 Most of those I talked to were female, since it was difficult to find males who were willing to discuss "fairy tales" at all. Interview transcripts are in Appendix X of my dissertation (Stone 1975a:261-385).

3 AT 334 is the classification for the tale type called "Household of the Witch" in Antti Aarne and Stith Thompson (1973), while Grimm number 43 identifies this as the 43rd story in the full Grimm collection of 210 tales.

4 I first read "Frau Trude" ("Mistress Trudy," "Dame Trudy," or "Mother Trudy" in other translations) in *The Grimms' German Folk Tales* trans. Francis P. Magoun, Jr., and Alexander H. Krappe (Carbondale: Southern Illinois University Press, 1960), 157; the text is reprinted here by permission of Southern Illinois University Press. I now prefer the more flowing words of two translations that appeared after my dissertation was completed (Manheim 1977:151-52; Zipes 1988:173-74).

5 I have questioned students for several years and found that almost every one had had an eccentric person, usually but not always female, who as children they called a witch—sometimes even playing pranks on these people. One of my students described how she went back to interview children on the block where she had grown up. As she listened to their accounts she realized that their witch was her own mother.

6 This performance was for the Old Sandwich Song Circle in Windsor on May 28, 1988.

7 This inconclusive finale was less effective in writing. It was also problematic for younger children, who needed to have a more clearly marked ending. I now alternate between including and omitting the final words that identify the story as the one that frees her. In the variant I wrote for Jo Radner, for example, I did not include the last lines because Jo thought they were not necessary (Radner 1993). I was still uncomfortable with this open-endedness in print, and put them back into both texts included here.

8 I have retained these horsemen in both texts, one transcribed from my taped telling and the other in a more literary version, included here for comparison in Appendix II; as I continue to tell the story today it has returned to the more simple form, with Mistress Trudy's three strange men.

9 "North From Centre: Tales by Earthstory." Produced by Earthstory (Jane Cahill, Kay Stone and Mary Louise Chown), Winnipeg, Canada, 1996.

CONCLUSION:

THE WEDDING FEAST

ANY tales end with the wedding feast, the celebration of union after disunion, the "happily ever after" conclusion of the wondertale. It is the time when all things come together in a public celebration of the victory of order over chaos. We arrive now at the conclusion of this book; it is a celebration of the tellers and tales that have succeeded in surviving vibrantly and evocatively almost to the end of the twentieth century, despite the difficulties and challenges of contemporary life.

I began by asking who was telling folktales today, what kinds of stories they chose and why, how these stories were learned and passed on, and who was listening. I have admitted to a bias in favor of tellers who prefer traditional tales, and the folklorist in me still prefers traditional oral narrators like Joe Neil MacNeil, not because of purism but because of a deep regard for words that are spoken for the ear instead of written for the eye. This bias has made me even more curious to discover how platform performers have found their own ways of bringing old tales into new light, speaking for the ear.

We have seen how the current revival movement had its earliest roots in the popularization of rewritten French folktales by Perrault in the seventeenth century, and reworked German tales in the Grimm collections in the nineteenth century. We have explored how organized storytelling developed and spread through schools, libraries, and other child-centered institutions in the twentieth century, and how the sudden burst of activity in the 1970s brought storytelling for adults into a festival and performance-stage circuit similar to that of the folksong revivals in earlier years.

The 1970 revitalization arose from four main professional streams: traditional, library/educational, theatrical, and spiritual/therapeutic. There were also strong contributions by writers, broadcasters, musicians, and many other performers as well; but these four streams formed a steady current that carried platform performing along for most of the twentieth century.

I have described how festivals, concerts, and workshops spread across the North American continent as platform performers found venues for carrying on their new profession. Storytelling events like these were sponsored by organized groups of enthusiasts who took part in temporary scenes or more permanent groups and communities. Some of these communities met in formal or informal gatherings throughout the year, others existed largely to maintain an annual festival. Festival-oriented groups tended to put heavier emphasis on promoting the careers of individual performers, usually from outside the community; grassroots groups were often more committed to supporting both amateur and professional tellers, and with stronger encouragement to local tellers, skilled and unskilled alike.

Folktales strongly dominated the repertoires of tellers for much of the twentieth century, reflecting the influence of library and school storytelling which emphasized printed folktale collections. Even when this began to change in the mid-1980s, traditional material was still favored by many tellers; even those who had ceased to relate folktales acknowledged that they had been inspired and motivated by them earlier in their careers. Some tellers could clearly recall childhood memories of hearing folktales which later guided them into storytelling, formally or informally. Their conscious identity as storytellers may have begun in childhood when they told stories to their friends in the neighborhood, or later in life when they came to tell stories as part of a career in teaching or library work, in a theatrical context, through a spiritual or therapeutic path, or in some other form of expression. As the revitalization of storytelling continued into the 1990s and tellers from various streams interacted at concerts and festivals, social identities and performance styles of the tellers grew more complex, as did the varieties of stories told and the motivations for telling them.

These various phenomena were played out in a paradigmatic community, Toronto, as reflected in the patterns of its annual festival and the preferences in stories and performance styles of several active participants. Here the focus shifted to a number of individual performers loosely representing the four major streams of storytelling. Each found personal ways to bring old stories into new life, connecting the fantastic world of wondertales with the mundane world of everyday existence.

At the close of the twentieth century, an era devoted to rationalism, materialism, and technological advances, old stories were still being told by people who, in some cases, regarded themselves as the modern voices of an age-old form of artistic and humanistic expression—one that was often explicitly non-rational, anti-materialistic, and ambivalent about technology. I wondered if these tellers were engaging in mere wish-fulfillment and romantic escapism, if they felt some deeper impetus for telling and hearing old tales in new times. They, through their story texts and commentary, and I, through explorations and interpretations, would choose the latter; the old stories were not an escape from life, but escape from fantasy—a rejection of the never-never-land stereotype of wondertales, a resounding *NO!* to "The Disney Version."

Let us return for a moment to statements I cited in earlier chapters: the first by Cheryl Oxford, the next by Alice Kane, the last by Max Lüthi. Oxford described a particular oral tale in print—and by extension any printed oral tale—as being "preserved in literary amber," with its genetic code dormant but intact:

> In a favorable climate this story's seed could again take root, sprout, and blossom into performance. The breath of a living voice could again resuscitate the story's perennial folk hero (Oxford 1994:68).

This seems to be an obvious statement, but in fact many folktales do remain dormant on the printed page; it is exciting that tellers, some of whom we have seen here, are now seeking out these lesser known tales and returning to them the breath of life. This was certainly true of Marylyn Peringer's "The Horoscope," Bob Barton's "The Honest Penny," and my "Mistress Trudy/Curious Girl." The told story brings the perennial heroes and heroines into the contemporary world, as we have seen here.

Alice Kane suggested that the act of bringing these tales to the living breath was more than a fleeting amusement:

> In a day of highly efficient communication such as the world has never known before, storytelling remains the most effective form of communication. Through storytelling strangers can converse. Even the shyest and most reticent can speak from the heart, and the listener, even the silent listener, responds completely—and no two in exactly the same way (Kane 1990:68).

This, too, is what we have seen with the tellers described in Section II, and many others quoted in Section I; the personal impact of stories told through face-to-face experiences in actual events touches unconscious depths, where inner transformations can take place. Strangers can converse not only as audience members, but in the imagination as well—one can have a silent dialogue with archetypal story characters.

Max Lüthi carried this to another level of understanding by commenting on the nature of the folktale as deeply symbolic, as both related to the everyday world "of events and experiences" and at the same time not constrained by reality in a one-to-one relationship:

> The folktale is free of such fetters. It is bound neither to reality nor to a dogma. Nor does it cling to individual events or experiences, for these are no more than its raw materials .... And yet, in its own way, it does give an answer to the burning questions of human existence, and this answer provides deep satisfaction (Lüthi 1982:84).

Thus, though tellers bring printed tales to life on the living breath by using the "raw materials" of their own lives, the archetypal nature of the stories that allows us to "converse" with them goes beyond time and place and person: in this way the wondertale can be profoundly comforting, all the more so in this era when efficient technological advances in communication can get in the way of meaningful human communication and interaction. Yet people often reject exactly this aspect of wondertales—the seemingly unrealistic fantasy of this kind of story—and can only see them as entertainment for children. It is interesting to note, then, how strange stories turn up in our everyday world, not just on the storytelling stage. I have a small file of newspaper items about odd events from daily life that seem to imitate the world of wondertales directly or indirectly. Some of these incidents echo folktale motifs and others describe unexpected uses of wondertales. For example, the common motif of losing and finding objects turns up in two newspaper accounts: a woman in Norway lost a gold earring in the North Sea and a week later it was found by her husband inside a cod he had caught.[1] In an article with the headline, "Police Use Cinderella Approach," a thief was identified by the police from a shoe he left at the scene of the crime.[2] These occurrences, no matter how unlikely they might seem, are pale echoes of similar incidents in wondertales, where the ring would be a magical ring placed inside a fish by a story character and the shoe, of course, would identify a deserving protagonist and not a thief. Other items I found in newspapers and magazines involve surprising uses of wondertales: people whose sail boat was swept out to sea in a hurricane distracted themselves by relating fairy tales while awaiting rescue; a Norwegian who skied alone to the South Pole took a collection of fairytales with him as his main diversion.[3] What intrigues me is that, whether such accounts are accurately reported or exaggerated, their appearance in print implies that people who read these accounts—and those who write them—want to accept such incidents as true, that there is a yearning to believe there is more to life than the daily struggle to survive. Hurricanes and antarctic cold certainly magnify the daily struggle, of course, but they are still "real" in the limited way we use this term. I sense a hope in the words of the tellers included in this study: the longing to confront the constant crush of reality, internal and external, through stories that, in Max Lüthi's words, offer "a reply to the demons" (Lüthi 1982:93).

For these tellers, wondertales offer a way of deepening reality rather than escaping from it; disbelief is transformed rather than simply suspended. This world allows tellers and listeners to keep one very practical metaphoric foot firmly in the sphere of imagination and internal reality and the other in the waking world as it is lived externally. Is it more fantastic to find a codfish with a ring in a wondertale, or in a newspaper account? Both offer a view of what is real, one emphasizing an internal world and the other an external world.

Lutz Röhrich, in his exploration of the reality of folktales, began his book by asking, "Does anyone still take the folktale seriously?" Röhrich mapped the paths on which fantasy and reality meet, bringing together external and internal experiences. On the most basic level folktales of all sorts rely on some level of belief in order to be convincing. Fully oral tales "live" in their specific communities, filled with local customs and beliefs, food and dress, and all the communal and personal contexts of life. After carefully describing the many ways that folktales and reality do in fact interweave, and deliberately so, Röhrich answers his opening question with a resounding *yes*, emphasizing the innate resiliency of oral narratives: "The relationship between folktales and reality is therefore different in every historical epoch; it takes new shape again and again, and must be interpreted anew as well" (Röhrich 1991:215). This deep reshaping of old stories has been addressed—through the stories they tell and their responses to my interview queries—by each of the artists included here. Though they are not traditional oral narrators like those described by Röhrich, or by Dégh and Glassie and other scholars, they still experience the constant and creative reshaping of folktales and reality. A significant difference between platform performers and traditional narrators in an oral milieu is the emphasis on individual over community . As we have seen, the community at large is far less responsive to and supportive of platform storytelling, and thus provides less of a context for meaningful connections. The touch of reality comes more directly from the personal lives of these tellers. This is illustrated in the folktales told here by Stewart Cameron and Marylyn Peringer, for whom story characters took on the characteristics of known individuals.

For Carol McGirr, the external world entered her story in the form of images and sound—the silver birches from her childhood in central Ontario, the song chanted by the heroine as she calls up images in the golden bowl. The reality of the story landscape keeps a tale rooted in the earth, consciously or unconsciously. Carol also described one listener who was drawn to "The Rosy Apple and the Golden Bowl" by its touch of reality—the girl was "really dead," buried in the earth, not just asleep in a glass coffin or a tower room.

Joe Neil MacNeil found external reality in his stories through his clear memories of the tellers from whom he first heard them. While the tales thus recreated an actual world of the past, they were not told nostalgically. That is, they were living adventures for Joe Neil himself, not dead accounts of someone else's story.[4] He was recalling those he heard the stories from initially, since community was more significant to him that his individual interpretation; Joe Neil was a modest man, but by no means unaware of his narrative responsibilities. But it was not the tellers or the time he was describing with conviction, it was the characters and their situations who were "alive" for him in the present as he relived them in the telling.

Susan Gordon brought story and life together by asking her listeners to engage with the fictional characters as if they were actual people, sometimes too close to reality for comfort. For example, she acknowledged that part of "The Juniper Tree" was too personal for discussion: "I'm not likely to share it with you or much of anybody," she wrote in a letter. This aspect of deeply personal reality can catch a teller off guard, as when Marylyn Peringer found herself in tears at the conclusion of "The Horoscope."

Sometimes an entire story touched on the reality of a teller's life, as we saw with Susan Gordon's story, and with Bob Barton's "The Honest Penny." Bob's serendipitous adventures as a performer matched in spirit the hero's trusting acceptance of his situation as he moved from outcast to drudge to successful merchant, from "luck" rather than through ambition. Similarly, the stubborn heroine in "The Curious Girl", and her less successful counterpart in "Mistress Trudy," reflected aspects of my own struggle to be led by curiosity into an evolving story.

Here we begin to cross over into the murky world of inner experience. I have heard many tellers speak about certain tales that "called" to them, though they were often unable to say why. Favored stories seem to express archetypal affinities with the inner world of these tellers. Narrative scholars who have worked in traditional milieus have noted how narrators skilfully connect external and internal realities in diverse ways. For example Lutz Röhrich suggested that communities provided the actual external context of local geographical and historical background, and also the psychological aspects of tellers' internal worlds: "Narrators bring their personal experiences as well as social environment into the folktale. A folktale can be a very personal reality; unique personal experiences can supply a narrator with a lifelong stock of motifs and give his or her narratives their unique stamp" (Röhrich 1979:202).

Similarly, Linda Dégh explored the endlessly creative ways that traditional narrators brought their tales to life in performance. She used as an example the European tale popularly known as "Beauty and the Beast" (the Hungarian variant here is "The Snakeprince") to show how a narrator makes "the world of fantasy palpable by connecting it with the world of everyday reality":

> The told story also mirrors the narrator's specific conceptualization of the world and its affairs: his or her cultural and personal meanings.... The storyteller is never neutral but emotionally involved when featuring the personality of the cast [of tale actors] (Dégh 1995a:138).

A teller is not just relating the remembered text of a tale, but fully identifying with it, walking through it with the characters, even taking sides in the conflicts between them.

Dégh is one of a number of narrative scholars who have written compellingly on the necessary connections between the lives of narrators and the lives of the stories they tell. Mathias Guenther explored this topic as it arose in his work with a Bushman settlement in South Africa. In a letter to the editors of a book on storytelling he brought together the spiritual and the esthetic qualities of narratives:

> A narrative, then, that addresses the supernatural and the numi-
> nous whole while, at the same time, informing, and being
> informed by, the personal and collective life experience of the
> narrator and his generation does, by virtue of these lineal and lat-
> eral, spiritual and social linkages, conform to some of these
> qualities of the aesthetic (Guenther 1996:177-78).

By placing narrators and life experiences in the social, spatial and tem-
poral reality of their generation and its collective experiences,
Guenther underlined the essential earthbound quality of numinous
(spiritual) narratives. Later he added, "I am struck by how much a storyteller's life is itself a narrative, with its own drama and turmoil, its
text and texture." We have this seen quite explicitly in the stories of
Stewart Cameron and Marylyn Peringer, and implicitly for other tellers
here. Guenther noted that in oral tradition this biographical aspect is,
of course, an on-going process for a narrator whose own life story
becomes interwoven with those featured in the stories. "Storyteller
after storyteller and generation upon generation will put their own
life-stamp on this store of tales, changing details, nuances and
emphases, and, over and over again, substance, form and meaning"
(Guenther 1996:184).

While platform tellers do not have the "generation upon generation" aspect of creativity, they can still participate in what he calls "the
creative spark of stories and storytelling." This is true for platform performers just as much as for oral traditional narrators in their own
communities. The stories they tell will continue to be enriched and
enlivened by their personal connections between wonder and reality
as it is expressed in their own lives, internal and external. Maria Tatar,
in her study of fairytales, stressed that inner realities were central in
the tales despite their apparent emphasis on external material success:

> That fairy tales translate (however roughly) psychic realities into
> concrete images, characters, and events has come to serve as one
> cornerstone of my own understanding of the texts in the
> Grimms' Nursery and Household Tales. In this respect, they resem-
> ble dreams: but rather than giving us personalized wishes and
> fears, they offer collective truths, realities that transcend individ-
> ual experience and that have stood the test of time" (Tatar
> 1987:xvi).

What Tatar called collective truths, and what Jung termed arche-types, contribute to the continuing existence of wondertales. This, of course, gives storytelling a tremendous appeal to those who take a spiritual or therapeutic approach, and explains in part why this stream of storytelling grew so rapidly in the last years of the troubled twenti-eth century. The old stories still express the down-to-earth associations of individual tellers at the same time as they embody archetypal images, motifs, and characters. This is so even when tellers are unaware of the deeper nature of their material, even when an arche-typically rich story is superficially told. Dégh revealed that this essential power was echoed in tales that were parodied or satirized, or used in bits and pieces in modern advertisements and cartoons. She explored such uses of traditional material in her study of folklore in the contemporary mass media (Dégh 1994a).

At their most sophisticated level the wondertales ask questions that we might ask of ourselves: does one person really make a difference? Does it matter what a single person does in the world? Does anyone care? These are exactly the questions that the boy in "The Honest Penny" answers through his actions, challenging his mother's demean-ing chant that "Nobody cares for thee." Storyteller Peninnah Schram asked similar questions to an audience of adults at a synagogue in Winnipeg in 1995, suggesting that traditional stories answered these questions firmly and positively. I was interested but not surprised to see that many of the men in the audience challenged the possibility of such stories having any relevance at all, while the women spoke in favor of the stories. They considered in particular the woman's lot in many traditional tales, and thought that these characters really "spoke" to them in their own lives. They felt that stories responded to the questions Peninnah Schram posed.

The situation of women in folktales offers a particular challenge for tellers to go beyond stereotype and achieve an archetypal understand-ing; a teller can reveal how a story character—and by extension, a listener—can face the adventure of finding themselves in a perilous situation and can overcome it, against all odds. While this is true of wondertales in general, we saw how this came to life in the tales told by Susan Gordon and Carol McGirr, and in the postmodern creation of Marvyne Jenoff. Each was preoccupied with the eventual triumph of positive over negative forces through the inner strength of the tales and of the female protagonists.

What about the more cynical tale characters who, like many of us, choose the rational, materialistic world over the unlikely events in the wondertales? I am thinking of Tania's sisters, Jack's brothers, Snow White's father, the ship captains in the stories of "The Honest Penny" and "The King of Egypt's Daughter." Their commitment to getting ahead, to becoming successful in the materialistic world, brings about their failure. Carl Jung observed that those who "content themselves with inadequate or wrong answers to the questions of life" often do not find satisfaction:

> They seek position, marriage, reputation, outward success or money, and remain unhappy and neurotic even when they have attained what they were seeking. Such people are usually confined within too narrow a spiritual horizon. Their life has not sufficient content, sufficient meaning (Jung 1989:140).

Certainly Cinderella's stepsisters, who thought only of social climbing, offered a negative metaphor for a life story.

By facing the anguish of the external world, and in fact bringing it in to their stories by envisioning familiar people, places, and objects, the tellers we have met here demonstrated that folktales and reality are not as separate as we might wish to believe. They accomplished this seemingly impossible task by accepting and developing stories as serious artistic expressions, by seeing the real potential of metaphor and archetype as potentially transformational.

There is something else, something more than the skill of the tellers and the metaphoric power of the stories, that draws people to oral storytelling. Narrating as an oral, face-to-face event is a powerful and immediate experience; the event itself is as potent as the teller and the tale. A number of contemporary writer/storytellers have commented on this aspect of platform performing, and in particular on the spoken word as a direct stimulus to the imagination. (There are several accounts in Birch/Heckler 1996, especially 106-154.) In some cases the actual experience can put listeners into a state of trance in which they are so caught up in the story that teller and tale disappear as external realities. Oklahoma teller Fran Stallings deserves credit for her work with the trance-producing potential of storytelling (Stallings 1988). She questioned other tellers on this topic, which had been given only vague and cursory treatment by tellers who tried to describe it from their own experiences.

Alice Kane underlined the intimate connections between tale and listener in another way, by insisting that "in storytelling the teller is unimportant; it is the story that counts. The teller's inadequacies fade away as the story unwinds" (Kane 1990:64).

While many tellers would not go that far—since becoming invisible is not a goal for professional performers—I can report that many people have told me that they were indeed unable to clearly recall either the teller or sometimes even the tale, but they could still vividly call to mind the emotional experience of the storytelling event even when it took place many years in the past. Here is one example from an acquaintance who described hearing stories at the Toronto public library as a child decades earlier:

> On Saturday, when the weather was pleasant, we would board the College Street streetcar and get off at a very large, imposing building that stretched over a city block. We would go around to the side of the building, descend a few steps, and enter the Boys and Girls Room of the library. Inside, we discovered a marvellous world, for there would be a storyteller each time we came. I no longer remember which stories were told or who told them, I only recall entering a world of the imagination, of feeling. Through these told stories the printed word became real to me— the characters came alive. Afterwards, on the streetcar, we would talk about those stories all the way home (Anne Dublin, letter and conversation, 1992).

Years later tales and tellers have faded into the past, but the event is still alive in the present, in her living imagination.

Specific storytelling occasions are equally memorable for the tellers; experienced performers can recount many instances where a particular place or a special audience brought new excitement to a story told dozens or even hundreds of times. For example, Carol McGirr said she could tell if a tale and listeners had deeply connected when, at the conclusion of some stories, there was "that moment of silence where the story just hangs in the air, and people don't applaud, they don't even breathe." This semi-trance state goes beyond mere suspension of disbelief. The listeners as well as the teller have been taken into the story, and slowly find their way out again.

I am not claiming that these retold stories are a universal expression, nor a major solution to life's ubiquitous challenges. I only suggest that for some people who tell and some who listen, there are many convincing reasons for the continuing appeal of this genre: the content and form of the stories themselves, the tellers who bring them to life, and the immediate experience of the storytelling event all contribute to this.

Stories and the very act of telling them are deeply playful, not only for children but for all of us. Even a king can still play in the mud—and probably needs to do so, symbolically at least. Serious play is creative, not just diverting.

This seems to be what Max Lüthi has in mind when he suggests that the wondertale responds to "burning questions of human existence" in a deeply fulfilling way (Lüthi 1982:84). When the reality of archetypal metaphor rings true and burns brightly, the wondertales offer a path into the woods of inner vision and creativity; one returns to the external world with new wisdom and new vision, paralleling the journey of the protagonist of a folktale. The wedding feast that concludes so many of the wondertales symbolically marks this union of inner and outer realities.

Notes

1 My husband, Daniel, recalled the story of his stepmother's childhood experience of losing her father's Phi Beta Kappa key in a lake. It was returned some years later by a man who found it in a fish he had caught. He had traced it to its owner by the individual code engraved on the key.

2 "Police used the Cinderella approach to make an arrest in a burglary case. Officers said a thief lost his shoe as he fled from the home of R. M. Police arrested R. T., who was sitting shoeless in a nearby bar. Authorities said that a shoe matching the one found at the R. M. home was found behind the bar" (*The Winnipeg Free Press*, April 14, 1972).

3 "Not So Wild A Dream: Skiing Solo to the South Pole" describes the epic journey of Erling Kagge, in *National Geographic*, September, 1993. I have no references for the other items, which were given to me by friends and by my university students over the years.

4 Carol Birch discusses in depth the importance of this kind of immediate connection with the story for platform tellers, whose challenge is to create the same kind of personal connection and immediacy though their stories come more often from printed than from oral sources (Birch/Heckler 1996:106-128).

APPENDIX I

Four Streams in The Toronto Festival of Storytelling

LET us look at one festival over a period of years to see the general pattern of participation as individuals representing the four main streams came together. The Storytellers School of Toronto has sponsored an annual festival since 1979. I examined programs of the seven festivals I attended (1985, 1986, 1987, 1988, 1990, 1991, and 1995), plus three programs sent to me by Dan Yashinsky (1979, 1981, 1997).

The table below is, at best, an impressionistic view of storytelling patterns. Each annual festival was unique, as would be true for the many annual events across the United States and Canada. But an exploration of individual festivals anywhere would also reveal overall patterns that would reflect the development of storytelling from the four broad streams as they manifested themselves on festival stages.

I placed tellers in loose categories based on their program descriptions, and, when I could, drew on my own knowledge of their backgrounds and on consultations with many of the tellers themselves to clarify their entries. In most festival programs, many of the performers listed could be connected to one of the four streams. I had originally added categories that included those who described themselves as writers and musicians, as well as others with more indefinite descriptions. This was so unwieldy that it obscured the pattern I was trying to reveal, so I have included only the four streams here to show their distribution and development.[1] This method does not by any means provide a model, but it does allow us to see overall patterns.

Year	Traditional	Library-educational	Theatrical	Spiritual-therapeutic
1979	2	10	3	4
1981	1	13	5	4
1985	—	17	6	7
1986	2	21	15	6
1987	3	15	12	3
1988	3	25	10	8
1990	3	24	8	7
1991	1	18	10	10
1995	5	16	15	7
1997	6	18	18	7

As we see from this table, there were never many traditional oral tellers, but they were always given attention and deference out of proportion to their numerical importance. They were often listed separately from "Local Storytellers" in the programs, and frequently given solo stage time. They included, for example, several indigenous narrators from both urban and reserve areas; tellers of African and of Caribbean descent now living in Canada; Irish tellers claiming traditional roots; and Scottish-Gaelic narrators, one from Cape Breton and one from Scotland. There was only one year (1985) that lacked tellers from this stream.

Tellers from the library-educational stream have been dominant throughout the history of the festival, confirming the very strong influence of this stream in the community. The very first festival featured librarian-storytellers Helen Armstrong and Alice Kane, who began their careers in the 1930s and were central in storytelling events for decades. Alice was a founding member of the Storytellers School and was cited by other founding members I interviewed as the steady inspiration for storytelling in the Toronto area. Her conscientious support and participation influenced hundreds of other tellers, and also encouraged (however subtly) the low key style of library-educational performance as a model that was characteristic of the Toronto festival, especially in its first decade.

There had always been children's theatrical entertainment at the festival so theatrical storytelling was always represented, most often in the special children's programs at the festival. After 1985 the number of tellers with training in dramatic arts increased; many of these performers worked with adult audiences. For example, theatrically trained Helen Porter, who appeared in the 1986 festival, described herself as a "storyteller working in schools, prisons, theatres, churches, and galleries." At the 1997 festival there were as many theatrical tellers and library-educational tellers (18), indicating the continuing success of this stream in maintaining a strong presence.[2]

Performers with interests or connections in spiritual-therapeutic storytelling have remained more or less steady over the years. I have already discussed the problems of identifying such tellers, and this is increasingly true each year as experienced performers found new ways of describing their storytelling. For example, Joan Bodger, the Jungian therapist whom I cited in Section I, Chapter 4, clearly identified her therapeutic training in the 1979 program but did not emphasize it in the 1988 program, nor thereafter. In contrast, other tellers' descriptions moved closer to a spiritual or therapeutic approach as they continued to take part in the festivals.

We have already seen that it is misleading to place performers in tight categories; at best such descriptions are impressionistic, since tellers' self-identifications continue to evolve as they gain experience and as they interact with those from other backgrounds. Significant changes in the way they describe themselves in festival programs reflects the results of two decades of interaction and experience of these four major streams of storytelling. Thus the figures above reflect only the surface level of interaction between tellers representing the four streams.

Notes

1 For example, of the 79 entries in the 1997 festival program only 49 could be clearly identified in one of the four main streams. Of the remaining 30, 13 described themselves as musicians and storytellers, another 12 were not clearly identifiable; three were writers and two were youthful relatives of well-known tellers.

2 If we count some of the musical performers in the theatrical stream, this would increase their number considerably, making this stream the strongest one in both the 1995 and 1997 festivals.

APPENDIX II

"The Curious Girl" in Print

This is slightly altered from the text that appears in Next Teller *(Yashinsky 1994:8-14), and is reprinted here with the permission of Ragweed Press. It is longer and more elaborate than the oral text in "Burning Brightly," with more attention to details of description and motivation, largely at the suggestion of the editors who thought a more "literary" tale would read better. I include it here to show the contrast between oral and written composition.*

ONCE there was a girl who was stubborn and curious, and always disobedient to her parents. Whenever they told her to do one thing she'd do another. Now how could a girl like that *not* get into trouble? And she did.

One day she said to her parents, "I think I'll visit Frau Trude one day. They say she lives in an interesting house full of strange things, and I'm ever so curious to see her."

Her parents protested. They said, "Frau Trude is a godless woman who does evil things, and if you go there you will be our child no longer!"

But she did not listen.

Without telling her parents, she set off through the woods one day. Soon she crossed a small stream, and when she stepped onto the other shore the woods around her seemed darker and more dismal. As she walked along she felt a trembling beneath her feet, a sound like rolling thunder coming from behind her. She turned to look—and saw a huge dark rider on a dark horse who came roaring toward her.

She leapt aside as horse and rider galloped by.

When they had passed, deep darkness fell all around her and she could no longer see her way. But she continued on, feeling the path beneath her feet.

After some time the earth again began to tremble and shake beneath her feet; she heard a raging sound behind her and turned to see an enormous rider on a horse that burned red like the rising sun. As they came speeding toward her she leapt aside and they raced on by her. After they had passed, the sky above the dark trees became blood red.

Now she was frightened, but she continued on her way.

After some time she heard a deafening sound behind her and turned again, this time to see a brilliant white rider on a white horse flashing toward her. She threw herself out of their path. When they had passed by, bright day glowed all around her and she found herself in a clearing at the very heart of the dark forest.

And there indeed was a strange house, just as she had heard. It was small and plain, but it had a feeling of oddness about it that made her uneasy. She saw that the house was surrounded by a fence made of human bones. In front of the house was a small tree with leaves the color of blood. The curious girl was terrified, but she was also determined. She crept up to the house, looked in the window, and was astounded to see the figure of a woman, all in flames but not consumed.

She heard her name called. She was commanded to enter. As if in a trance she stepped around to the door, pushed it slowly inward, stepped inside. What she saw there was an ordinary old woman sitting in a chair with the legs of a strange animal. This was Frau Trude indeed, looking at her with piercing eyes.

The old woman spoke politely to the curious girl; "My dear, why are you so pale and shaking?"

"Because I've seen such strange things!" she answered breathlessly.

"Oh? What have you seen?"

"As I was walking I saw a huge dark rider on a dark horse."

"That was only my Dark Night."

"Then I saw an enormous red rider on a red horse."

"Yes, that was my Red Morning."

"But then there was a white rider on a white horse, flashing like lightening."

"Indeed, that was my Bright Day. And what else did you see, my dear?"

"Oh, then I looked in your window, Frau Trude, but I didn't see you at all—I saw a woman all in flames."

"Did you now! Then you have seen the witch in her true form. I have been waiting for you and longing for you for some time now. You will burn brightly for me."

And so saying, Frau Trude turned the girl into a log and threw the log on her fire. As the fire blazed up she sat down next to it to warm herself and said, "Indeed, it *does* burn brightly."

Suddenly a shower of sparks flew out of the fire and into the air. Frau Trude sprang up, changed the sparks into a fiery bird with feathers like the rising sun, a beak as black as night, eyes that flashed like summer lightening. She caught that bird and held it firmly.

"Clever girl! But you'll never get away from me! You will remain a bird forever and my servant for all eternity—unless you can fulfill my bargain: if you can tell me one story that I've never heard before, a story that has no ending, I'll let you go. If you cannot, you will be in my power forever."

"That's not fair," replied the girl who was now a bird. "You know many more stories than I do."

"That is true," said the old woman. "So I'll give you all the time you need to learn more. Go anywhere you like. Return to me when you're ready. I will be waiting for you. And remember, if you fail you'll be mine forever." She carried the bird outside, lifted her hand high, and released it into the air. The bird flew up—a red flash disappearing into the dark woods.

As she flew, the girl thought of all the languages she could speak in her new shape, knowing that the birds understand the speech of all living things, even the stones on the path (for some stones are alive). And so she began her long wandering in the world, flying everywhere, learning stories from all she met.

She went to the east where the sun rises and to the west where it sets; to the white north and to the green south; to the mountains and the seas, the forests and the barren lands. She heard the trees and all other growing things, even the tiniest flowers; she listened to the birds and all others who could fly, and to all creatures who could creep, walk, run, leap, or swim. She wandered through farms and villages, towns and cities, learning stories from everyone who lived there, young and old alike. Nor did she forget the stones on the path.

Much time passed as she wandered in the form of the fiery bird. At times she was so enraptured by the stories that she almost forgot Frau Trude, at other times the stories themselves reminded her that she was not quite herself. And so she listened and she learned. One day, at last, she returned to the strange house in the forest. She saw from above the circle made by the fence of bones, and she saw also the blood-red tree growing near the house.

On that day Frau Trude heard a strange song. She went out to see and found the fiery bird singing from the tree.

"Ah, it's you," she said. "I've been waiting. Have you brought me a story?"

"I have all the stories in the world to tell you."

"Good," Frau Trude answered. "I haven't heard a fine tale for a long time. Begin."

The curious girl began to tell Frau Trude all the stories she'd learned from all of creation. Some were short and some long, some were plain and others fancy, some comic and others tragic, but they all carried truth in them.

When she finished, Frau Trude gazed at her intently and said slowly and carefully, "Ah yes, excellent stories, and well told too ... But I knew every one of them long before you were born!"

The girl who was a bird was speechless. She had no more stories. None at all. But when she opened her mouth to cry out, words came out on their own, first one at a time and then running together like a small river:

"Once there was a girl who was stubborn and curious, and always disobedient to her parents. Whenever they told her to do one thing she'd do another ..."

"Ah yes," said Frau Trude.

That was indeed the story that had not been heard, the story that had no end.

BIBLIOGRAPHY

Aarne, Antti, and Stith Thompson. *The Types of the Folk-Tale: A Classification and Bibliography*, Folklore Fellows Communications No. 184. Helsinki: Academia Scientiarum Fennica, 1973.

Abernethy, Rose L. "A Study of Existing Practices and Principles of Storytelling for Children in the United States." Diss. Northwestern University, 1964.

Adams, Robert. "Social Identity of a Japanese Storyteller." Diss. Indiana University, 1972.

Afandsyev, Aleksandr. *Russian Fairy Tales*. Trans. Norbert Guterman. New York: Pantheon Books, 1945, rep. 1973.

Alvey, Richard. "The Historical Development of Organized Storytelling to Children in the United States." Diss. University of Pennsylvania, 1974.

Arnason, David. *The Dragon and the Dry Goods Princess: Fractured Prairie Tales*. Winnipeg, Man.: Turnstone Press, 1994.

Asbjørnsen, Peter Christen. *Tales from the Fjeld*. Trans. George Dasent. London: Chapman & Hall, 1874.

Ashliman, D.L. *A Guide To Folktales in the English Language: Based on the Aarne-Thompson Classification System*. New York: Greenwood Press, 1987.

Azadovskii, Mark. *A Siberian Tale Teller*. Trans. James R. Dow. Monograph Series No. 2, Center for Intercultural Studies in Folklore and Ethnomusicology. Austin: U of Texas P, 1974.

Bacchilega, Cristina. *Postmodern Fairy Tales: Gender and Narrative Strategies*. Philadelphia: U of Pennsylvania P, 1997.

Baker, Augusta, and Ellin Greene. *Storytelling: Art and Technique*. 2nd Edition. New York: R.R. Bowker Company, 1987.

Barton, Bob. *Tell Me Another: Storytelling and Reading Aloud at Home, at School, and in the Community*. Markham, Ont.: Pembroke Publishers, 1986.

——., and David Booth. *Stories in the Classroom: Storytelling, Reading Aloud, and Roleplaying with Children*. Markham, Ont.: Pembroke Publishers, 1990.

——. *Stories to Tell*. Markham, Ont.: Pembroke Publishers, 1992.

Bauman, Richard. *Verbal Art As Performance*. Prospect Heights, Ill.: Waveland Press, 1977.

——. *Story, Performance, and Event*. Cambridge, England: Cambridge UP, 1986.

Bausinger, Hermann. *Folk Culture in a World of Technology*. Trans. Elke Dettmer. Bloomington: Indiana UP, 1990.

Benjamin, Walter. *Illuminations*. Trans. Harry Zohn. New York: Harcourt, Brace and World, 1968.

Bettelheim, Bruno. *The Uses of Enchantment. The Meaning and Importance of Fairy Tales*. New York: Knopf, 1976.

Birch, Carol, and Melissa Heckler. *Who Says? Essays on Pivotal Issues in Contemporary Storytelling*. Little Rock, Ark.: August House Publishers, 1996.

Bly, Robert. *Iron John: A Book About Men*. Reading, Massachusetts: Addison-Wesley, 1990.

Bolte, Johannes, and Polívka, Georg. *Anmerkungen zu den Kinder-und Häusmarchen der Brüder Grimm*. 5 vols. Leipzig: Dietrich, 1913-32; rpt. Hildesheim: Georg Olms, 1963.

Bottigheimer, Ruth. *Fairy Tales and Society: Illusion, Allusion and Paradigm*. Philadelphia: U of Philadelphia P, 1986.

——. *Grimms' Bad Girls and Bold Boys: The Moral and Social Vision of the Tales*. New Haven: Yale UP, 1987.

Briggs, Charles. "Metadiscursive Practices and Scholarly Authority in Folkloristics." *The Journal of American Folklore*, 106 (1993): 387-434.

Bruner, Jerome. *Actual Minds, Possible Worlds*. Cambridge, Mass.: Harvard UP, 1986.

Cahill, Jane. *Her Kind*. Peterborough, Ont.: Broadview Press, 1996.

Calame-Griaule, Geneviève. *Le Renouveau Du Conte [The Revival of Storytelling]*. Paris: Centre National de la Recherche Scientifique, 1991.

Campbell, Joseph. "Folkloristic Commentary." *The Complete Grimms' Fairy Tales*. New York: Pantheon, 1944, 1972.

——. *The Hero with a Thousand Faces*. Princeton: Princeton UP, 1949, 1972.

——. *The Inner Reaches of Outer Space*. New York: Alfred van der Marck, 1986.

——. *The Power of Myth*. New York: Doubleday, 1988.

Campbell, Marie. *Tales From The Cloud Walking Country*. Bloomington: Indiana UP, 1958; rpt. Greenwood Press, 1976.

Carter, Angela. *The Bloody Chamber and Other Stories*. Harmondsworth: Penguin, 1979.

——. *Old Wives Fairy Tale Book*. New York: David McKay, 1990. (Published in England as: *The Virago Book of Fairy Tales*. London: Virago, 1960.)

——. *The Second Virago Book of Fairy Tales. Strange Things Sometimes Still Happen. Fairy Tales from Around the World*. Boston: Faber and Faber, 1993.

Chase, Richard. *The Jack Tales*. Boston: Houghton Mifflin, 1943.

——. *The Grandfather Tales*. Boston: Houghton Mifflin, 1948.

Coles, Robert *The Call of Stories*. Boston: Houghton, 1989.

Darnton, Robert. "Peasants Tell Tales: The Meaning of Mother Goose." *The Great Cat Massacre and Other Episodes in French Cultural History*. New York: Vintage Books, 1985: 9-72.

David, Alfred, and Mary Elizabeth. *The Frog King and Other Tales of the Brothers Grimm*. New York: Signet Classics, New American Library of World Literature, 1964.

Dégh, Linda. *Folktales and Society: Storytelling in a Hungarian Community*. Bloomington: Indiana UP, 1969, 1989.

——. "Biology of Storytelling." *Folklore Preprint Series*, 1979: 7.

——. "How Storytellers Interpret the Snakeprince Tale." *The Telling of Stories: Approaches to a Traditional Craft*. Eds. N.jgaard, de Mylius, Pio, Holbek. Odense, Denmark: Odense UP, 1990: 47-62. (Rpt. in Dégh 1995: 137-151.)

——. "The Variant and the Folklorization Process in *Märchen* and Legend," *D'un conte ... à l'autre*. Paris: Editions du Centre National de la Recherche Scientifique, 1990: 159-170.

——. *American Folklore in the Mass Media*. Bloomington: Indiana UP, 1994.

——. *Narratives in Society: A Performer-Centered Study of Narration*. Helsinki, Finland: Suomalainen Tiedeakatemia. FFC Publications No. 255, 1995.

——. *Hungarian Folktales: The Art of Zsuzsanna Palkó*. Jackson, Mississippi: U of Mississippi P, 1995.

Dundes, Alan. "Text, Texture, and Context." *Southern Folklore Quarterly*, 28 (1964): 251-65.

——. "Nationalistic Inferiority Complexes and the Fabrication of Fakelore: A Reconsideration of Ossian, *The Kinder und Hausmärchen*, the *Kalevala*, and Paul Bunyan." *Journal of Folklore Research*, 22 (1985): 5-18.

Estés, Clarissa Pinkola. *Women Who Run With the Wolves: Myths and Stories of the Wild Woman Archetype.* New York: Ballantine Books, 1995.

Fasick, Adele M., Margaret Johnston, Ruth Osler. *Lands of Pleasure: Essays on Lillian H. Smith and the Development of Children's Libraries.* Metuchen, N.J.: The Scarecrow Press, 1990.

Finnegan, Ruth. *Literacy and Orality.* Oxford: Blackwell, 1988.

Franz, Marie-Louise von. *Introduction to the Interpretation of Fairy Tales.* New York: Spring, 1970.

——. *Problems of the Feminine in Fairy Tales.* Dallas: Spring, 1972.

——. *Shadow and Evil in Fairy Tales.* Dallas: Spring, 1974.

——. *Individuation in Fairy Tales.* Dallas: Spring, 1977.

Freud, Sigmund. "The Occurrence in Dreams of Material from Fairy Tales." *Collected Works,* vol 12. Trans. James Strachey. London: Hogarth, 1958: 279-88.

Gardner, James Finn. *Politically Correct Bedtime Stories.* New York: Macmillan, 1994.

Georges, Robert. "Toward an Understanding of Storytelling Events." *The Journal of American Folklore,* 82 (1969): 313-328.

Glassie, Henry. *All Silver and No Brass.* Bloomington: Indiana UP, 1975.

——. *Passing the Time in Ballymenone: Culture and History of an Ulster Community.* Philadelphia: U of Pennsylvania P, 1982.

Gordon, Susan. "Invitation and Decision: Storytelling in a Residential Treatment Center for Adolescents." MA thesis, Antioch, 1991.

——. "The Powers of the Handless Maiden." *Feminist Messages: Coding In Women's Folk Culture.* Ed. Joan Radner. Urbana, Ill.: U of Illinois P, 1993: 252-88.

Görög (-Karady), Veronika & Bruno de la Salle. "Qui conte en France? L'apparition de quelques nouveaux types de conteurs." Lecture at the Seventh Congress of the International Society for Folk Narrative Research. Edinburgh, Scotland, 1979.

——. S. Platiel, D. Rey-Hulman, C. Seydon. *Histoires d'enfants terribles.* Paris: Maisonneuve et Larouse, 1980.

——. "Qui Conte en France Aujourd'hui? Les Nouveaux Conteurs." *Cahiers de Littérature Orale* 11 (1982): 95-116.

——. "The New Professional Storyteller in France." Lecture at the Ninth Congress of the International Society for Folk-Narrative Research. Budapest, Hungary, 1989.

Greenhill, Pauline, and Diane Tye. *Undisciplined Women: Tradition and Culture in Canada*. Kingston, Ont. and Montreal, Que.: McGill-Queen's UP, 1997.

Grimm Brothers. *The Complete Fairy Tales*. Trans. Margaret Hunt. New York: Pantheon Books, 1944, 1972.

——. *The Grimms' German Folk Tales*. Trans. Francis P. Magoun Jr. and Alexander H. Krappe. Carbondale, Ill.: Southern Illinois UP, 1960.

——. *Grimm Tales for Young and Old*. Trans. Ralph Manheim. Garden City, NY: Anchor Press/Doubleday, 1977.

——. *The Complete Tales of the Brothers Grimm*. Trans. Jack Zipes. New York: Bantam Books, 1988.

Guenther, Mathias. "Old Stories/Life Stories." *Who Says? Pivotal Issues in Contemporary Storytelling*. Eds. C. Birch and M. Heckler. Little Rock, Ark.: August House Publishers, 1996: 177-97.

Haase, Donald. *The Reception of Grimms' Fairy Tales: Responses, Reactions, Revisions*. Detroit: Wayne State UP, 1993.

Hallett, Martin, and Barbara Karasek. *Folk and Fairy Tales*. Peterborough, Ont.: Broadview Press, 1991.

Harrell, John. *Origins and Early Traditions of Storytelling*. Kensington, Ca: York House, 1983.

Harvey, Margaret Clodagh. "A Contemporary Perspective on Irish Traditional Storytelling in the English Language." Diss. UCLA, 1987.

——. "Contemporary `Traditional' Storytelling: Creating and Mediating Realities." Annual Meeting of the American Folklore Society. Oakland, California, 1990.

Heuscher, Julius E. *A Psychiatric Study of Fairy Tales: Their Origins, Meaning, and Usefulness*. 2nd rev. ed. Springfield, Ill.: Charles C. Thomas, 1974.

Hobsbawm, Eric, and Terence Ranger, eds. *The Invention of Tradition*. Cambridge, England: Cambridge UP, 1983.

Holbek, Bengt. *Interpretation of Fairy Tales: Danish Folklore in a European Perspective*. Helsinki, Academia Scientiarum Fennica, 1987.

Hymes, Dell. *"In Vain I Tried to Tell You:" Essays in Native American Ethnopoetics*. Philadelphia: U of Pennsylvania P, 1981.

Jacobs, A.J. *Fractured Fairy Tales*. New York: Broadway Books, 1997.

Jacobs, Joseph. *English Folk and Fairy Tales*. New York: Putnam, n.d.

Jenoff, Marvyne. *The Emperor's Body: A Book of Thirteen Interrelated Adult Fables*. Victoria, B.C: Ekstasis Editions, 1995.

Jung, Carl G. "The Phenomenology of the Spirit in Fairy Tales." *Collected Works*, vol. 9. Trans. R.F.C. Hull. Princeton, NJ: Princeton UP, 1969. 20 vols. 207-53.

——. *Man and His Symbols*. London: Aldus Books, 1976.

——. *Memories, Dreams, and Reflections*. Ed. Aniela Jaffe. New York: Vintage Books, 1989.

Kamenetsky, Christa. *The Brothers Grimm and Their Critics: Folktales and the Quest for Meaning*. Athens: Ohio UP, 1992.

Kane, Alice. "A Most Ingenious Paradox: The Revival of Storytelling." *Lands of Pleasure*. Eds. Adele M. Fasick, Margaret Johnston, Ruth Osler. Metuchen, NJ: The Scarecrow Press, 1990: 62-70.

Kane, Sean. *Wisdom of the Mythtellers*. Peterborough, Ont.: Broadview Press, 1995.

Lee, Tanith. *Red as Blood or Tales from the Sisters Grimmer*. New York: Daws Books, 1983.

Lindahl, Carl. "Jacks: The Name, the Tale, the American Traditions." *Jack in Two Worlds*. Ed. William McCarthy. Chapel Hill, NC: U of North Carolina P, 1994.

Livo, Norma J., and Sandra A. Rietz. *Storytelling: Process and Practice*. Littleton, Col.: Libraries Unlimited, 1986.

Lord, Albert. *The Singer of Tales*. New York: Atheneum, 1970.

Lüthi, Max. *Once Upon A Time*. Bloomington: Indiana UP, 1976.

——. *The Fairytale As Art Form and Portrait of Man*. Bloomington: Indiana UP, 1985.

——. *The European Folktale: Form and Nature*. Bloomington: Indiana UP, 1986.

MacDonald, Margaret Read. *The Storyteller's Sourcebook: A Subject, Title, and Motif Index to Folklore Collections for Children*. Detroit: Gale Research Company, 1982.

MacNeil, Joe Neil. *Tales Until Dawn: The World of a Cape Breton Gaelic Story-Teller*. Trans. and ed. John Shaw. Kingston, Ont. and Montreal, Que.: McGill-Queen's UP, 1987.

Manheim, 1977 see Grimm (1977).

Marvin, Lee-Ellen, and Doug Lipman "Ethics Among Professional Storytellers." *Storytelling Journal*, 3.3 (1986): 13-15.

McCarthy, William. *Jack in Two Worlds*. Chapel Hill, NC: U of North Carolina P, 1994.

McDermitt, Barbara. "Comparison of a Scottish and an American Storyteller." Diss. School of Scottish Studies. Edinburgh, Scotland, 1986.

———. "Storytelling and a Boy Named Jack." *North Carolina Folklore Quarterly*, 31.1 (1983): 3-22.

McGlathery, James. *The Brothers Grimm and Folktale*. Urbana: U of Illinois P, 1988.

———. *Fairy Tale Romance: The Grimms, Basile, and Perrault*. Urbana: U of Illinois P, 1991.

Mellon, Nancy. *Storytelling and the Art of the Imagination*. Shaftsbury, Dorset: Element, 1992.

Mieder, Wolfgang. *Disenchantments: An Anthology of Modern Fairy Tale Poetry*. Hanover, NH: University Press of New England, 1985.

———. *Tradition and Innovation in Folk Literature*. Hanover, NH: University Press of New England, 1987.

Mullen, Patrick. "A Traditional Storyteller in Changing Contexts." *"And Other Neighborly Names": Social Process and Cultural Image in Texas Folklore*. Eds. Richard Bauman and Roger D. Abrahams. Austin: U of Texas P, 1991: 266-79.

Olrik, Axel. *Principles for Oral Narrative Research*. Trans. Kirsten Wolf and Jody Jensen. Bloomington: Indiana UP, 1992.

Oxford, Cheryl. "'They Call Him Lucky Jack': Three Performance-centered Case Studies of Storytelling in Watauga County, North Carolina." Diss. Northwestern University, 1987.

———. "Jack in the Next Generation: The Intra-Family Transmission of a Jack Tale." Paper presented at the annual meeting of Speech Communication Association in Atlanta, GA, October, 1991.

———. "The Storyteller as Curator: Marshall Ward." *Jack in Two Worlds*. Ed. William McCarthy. Chapel Hill, NC: U of North Carolina P, 1994: 56-92.

Nicoliasen, W.F.H. "English Jack in America." *Midwest Journal of Language and Folklore*, 4 (1978): 26-36.

———. "AT 1535 in Beech Mountains, North Carolina." *Arv: A Journal of Scandinavian Folklore*, 35 (1980): 99-106.

———. "The Teller and the Tale: Storytelling on Beech Mountain." *Jack in Two Worlds*. Ed. William McCarthy. Chapel Hill, NC: U of North Carolina P, 1994: 123-149.

Pellowski, Anne. *The World of Storytelling*. R.R. Bowker, 1994.

Perrault, Charles. *Perrault's Complete Fairy Tales*. Trans. A.E. Johnson and others. New York: Dodd, Mead, 1961.

——. *The Fairy Tales of Charles Perrault*. Trans. Angela Carter. New York: Avon Books (foreword by Carter), 1979.

Radner, Joan N. and, Susan S. Lanser. "The Feminist Voice: Strategies of Coding in Folklore and Literature." *Journal of American Folklore*, 100 (1987): 412-25.

——. *Feminist Messages: Coding In Women's Folk Culture*. Urbana, Ill.: U of Illinois P, 1993.

Riordan, James. *Tales From Central Russia*, vol. 1. Harmondsworth, Middlesex: Kestrel Books, 1976.

Röhrich, Lutz. "Introduction." *Fairy Tales and Society: Illusion, Allusion and Paradigm*. Ed. Ruth Bottigheimer. Philadelphia: U of Philadelphia P, 1986.

——. *Folktales and Reality*. Trans. Peter Tokofsky. Bloomington: Indiana UP, 1991.

Rosenberg, Neil. *Transforming Tradition*. Urbana, Ill.: U of Illinois P, 1993.

Rowe, Karen. "Feminism and Fairy Tales." *Folk and Fairy Tales*. Eds. Martin Hallett and Barbara Karasek. Peterborough, Ont.: Broadview Press, 1991: 346-367.

Sawyer, Ruth. *The Way of the Storyteller*. New York: Viking Press, 1942.

Sexton, Anne. *Transformations*. Boston: Houghton-Mifflin, 1971.

Sobol, Joseph. "Everyman and Jack: The Storytelling of Donald Davis." M.A. thesis, University of North Carolina, 1987.

——. "Alternative Voices: The Storytelling Revival and the Postmodern Condition." Unpublished essay, 1990.

——. "Jonesborough Days: The National Storytelling Festival and the Contemporary Storytelling Revival Movement in America." Diss. Northwestern University, 1994.

——. "Jack in the Raw." *Jack in Two Worlds*. Ed. Wm. McCarthy. Chapel Hill: U of North Carolina P, 1994: 3-25.

——. "Innervision and Innertext: Oral and Interpretive Modes of Storytelling Performance." *Who Says? Essays on Pivotal Issues in Contemporary Storytelling*. Eds. Birch and Heckler, Little Rock, Ark.: August House Publishers, 1996: 198-221.

——. *The Storytellers' Journey: An American Revival*. Urbana, Ill.: U of Illinois P (forthcoming).

Stallings, Fran. "The Web of Silence: Storytelling's Power to Hypnotize." *The National Storytelling Journal* (Spring/Summer) 1988: 6-19.

Stone, Kay. "Romantic Heroines in Anglo-American Folk and Popular Literature." Diss. Indiana University, 1975.

———. "Things Walt Disney Never Told Us." *Women and Folklore*. Claire Farrer, Austin: U of Texas P, 1975: 42-50.

———. "Fairy Tales for Adults: Walt Disney's Americanization of the *Märchen*." *Folklore on Two Continents: Essays in Honor of Linda Dégh*. Eds. Nikolai Burlakoff and Carl Lindahl. Bloomington, Ind.: Trickster Press, 1980: 40-48.

———. "To Ease the Heart: Traditional Storytelling." *The National Storytelling Journal* (Winter) 1984: 1-3.

———. "Macht mit mir, was ihr wollt" [Do with me what you will"]. *Die Frau in Märchen*. Eds. Sigrid Früh and Rainer Wehse. Kassel: Röth, 1985: 164-73.

———. "I Never Told This Story to Anyone Before," *The National Storytelling Journal* (Fall) 1985: 3-7;

———. "Misuses of Enchantment." *Women's Folklore, Women's Culture*. Eds. Jordan and Kalčik. Philadelphia: U of Pennsylvania P, 1985: 125-45.

———. "Oral Narration in Contemporary North America." *Fairy Tales and Society: Illusion, Allusion and Paradigm*. Ed. Ruth Bottigheimer. Philadelphia: U of Pennsylvania P, 1986, 13-31.

———. "Three Transformations of Snow White." *The Brothers Grimm and the Folktale*. Ed. J.M. McGlathery. Urbana, Ill.: U of Illinois P, 1988: 52-65.

___. "Burning Brightly: New Light on an Old Tale." *Feminist Messages: Coding In Women's Folk Culture*. Ed. Joan Radner. Urbana, Ill.: U of Illinois P, 1993: 289-305.

___. "Once Upon A Time Today: Grimm Tales for Contemporary Performers." *The Reception of the Grimms' Fairy Tales: Responses, Reactions, Revisions*. Ed. Donald Haase. Detroit: Wayne State UP, 1993: 250-69.

___. "Jack's Adventures in Toronto." *Jack in Two Worlds*. Ed. William McCarthy. Chapel Hill, NC: U of North Carolina P, 1994: 250-71.

___. "The Curious Girl." *Next Teller: A Book of Canadian Storytelling*. Ed. Dan Yashinksy. Charlottetown, P.E.I: Ragweed Press, 1994: 8-14.

___. "Old Stories/New Listeners." *Who Says? Essays on Pivotal Issues in Contemporary Storytelling*. Eds. Carol Birch and Melissa Heckler. Little Rock, Ark.: August House, 1996: 155-176.

___. "And She Lived Happily Ever After?" *Women and Language*, 19. 1, (1996): 14-18.

___. "Difficult Women in Folktales: Two Women, Two Stories." *Undisciplined Women: Tradition and Culture in Canada*. Eds. Pauline Greenhill and Diane Tye. Kingston, Ont. and Montreal, Que.: McGill-Queen's UP, 1997: 250-65.

Tatar, Maria. *The Hard Facts of the Grimms' Fairy Tales*. Princeton: Princeton UP, 1987.

———. *Off With Their Heads: Fairy Tales and the Culture of Childhood*. Princeton: Princeton UP, 1992.

Tedlock, Dennis. *The Spoken Word and the Work of Interpretation*. Philadelphia: U of Pennsylvania P, 1983.

Thompson, Stith. *Motif Index of Folk-Literature*. Bloomington: Indiana UP, 1955-58.

Wallace, Anthony F.C. "Revitalization Movements." *American Anthropologist* 58 (1956): 264-81.

Warner, Marina. *From the Beast to the Blonde: On Fairy Tales and Their Tellers*. London: Random House, 1994.

Yashinsky, Dan. *Tales For An Unknown City*. Kingston, Ont. and Montreal, Que.: McGill-Queen's UP, 1990.

———. *Next Teller: A Book of Canadian Storytelling*. Charlottetown, PEI: Ragweed Press, 1994.

Zipes, Jack. *Fairy Tales and the Art of Subversion: The Classical Genre for Children and the Process of Civilization*. New York: Wildman, 1983.

———. *Don't Bet on the Prince: Contemporary Feminist Fairy Tales in North America and England*. New York: Methuen, 1986.

———., ed. and trans. *Beauties, Beasts and Enchantment: Classic French Fairy Tales*. New York: New American Library, 1989.

———. *Spells of Enchantment: The Wondrous Fairy Tales of Western Culture*. New York: Viking, 1991.

———. 1988 see Grimm (1988).

ACKNOWLEDGEMENTS

I AM grateful to those who agreed to participate in interviews and to converse and correspond informally, to all storytellers and story enthusiasts, folklorists, editors, and everyone else I can remember who has been part of this very long adventure. They are named here in alphabetical order:

Tigge Anne Anderson, Bob Barton, Carol Birch, Joyce Birch, Ruth Bottigheimer, Lorne Brown, Dianne and Stewart Cameron, Rosalyn Cohen, Donald Davis, Gail de Vos, Elizabeth Ellis, Susan Gordon, Beverly Grace, Donald Haase, John Harrell, Merle Harris, Melissa Heckler, Johanna Hiemstra, Carol Howe, Lynda Howes, Marvyne Jenoff, Christl Kraft, Ruthhilde Kronberg, Vivian Labrie, Celia Lottridge, Margaret Read MacDonald, Joe Neil MacNeil, Carol McGirr, James McGlathery, Elisabeth Nash, Marylyn Peringer, Jo Radner, Barbara Reed, Lynn Rubright, Renate and Robert Schneider, Gerri Serrette, John Shaw, Laura Simms, Rubena Sinha, Joseph Sobol, Ruth Stotter, Diane Tye, Cathryn Wellner, Jane Yolen, Kathryn Young, and the members of Stone Soup Stories of Winnipeg.

I cannot imagine any book coming into being without the comments and suggestions of colleagues and friends, sometimes one and the same, willing to read carefully and objectively—they tell you when they don't agree with you. The conscientious responses of these readers touch almost every page of this book explicitly or implicitly:

Jane Cahill, Harrison Chase, Mary Louise Chown, Pauline Greenhill, Rosan Jordan and Frank de Caro, Marvyne Jenoff, Janet Langois, Mark Mealing, Margaret Mills, Charlotte Milstead, Carol Mitchell, Jo Radner, Elizabeth Stone, Kira Van Deusen, and particularly Dan Yashinsky, for a long and ongoing conversation about stories and storytelling.

I am also indebted to those who provided a place to stay, steady encouragement, and good doses of therapeutic humor:

In Ontario: Elaine and Peter Gold and family, especially Leah and Naomi; Marylyn Peringer; Bob and Doreen Barton.

In Maryland: Norlaine and Morris Schultz; Susan and Ralph Gordon; David, Sally, and Joel Sternbach.

In California: Ruth and Larry Stotter; Allen Mitchell.

In Florida: Joyce and Fred Perlove; Ellen Kempler; my sisters Janet Conner and Jolene Kinney and brother Terry Mitchell; my parents Grace and Glenn Mitchell.

In Tennessee: Jean and Jimmy Neil Smith; Jill Oxendine.
On Block Island, Rhode Island: Bill, Lois and Teresa Bendokas and the students at the Block Island School.

In Quebec: Rosylyn Cohen; Vivian Labrie; Nathaniel Stone.

In British Columbia: Kira Van Duesen; Mark and Jaqueline Mealing and their various wild and domesticated animals.

In New Brunswick: Joan and Robert Meade.

In Whitehorse, Yukon Territory: Jacqueline Parsons, and the hospitable staff and volunteers of the Yukon International Storytelling Festival.

In Georgia: Gail Beck; Donna Andrews; staff and fellow artists and writers at the Hambidge Center in Rabun Gap.

There are also those who scolded me into getting beyond the inevitable periods of self-doubt, procrastination, and paralyzing attempts at perfectionism. Without the efforts of Daniel Stone, Rachel Stone, and fellow adventurer Joseph Sobol, I might still be sitting in the middle of piles of paper looking for just the right way to put this all in order.

PERMISSIONS

INDEX OF AARNE-THOMPSON
TALE TYPES IN SECTION II

INDEX

D

dance in storytelling performance, 230-231

Davis, Donald, 17, 269

de Caro, Frank, 269

de la Salle, Bruno, 70

de Vos, Gail, 269

Dégh, Linda, viii, 6, 7, 12, 16, 32, 243-245
 on audiences, 127-128
 on fact and fiction in stories, 142, 143
 on folklore in mass media, 247
 on gender in traditional stories, 6-7
 on meanings of stories, 193
 on narrators and social context, 11-12
 on personal experience in stories, 245
 on Szekler community (Hungary), 34

"Devil with Three Golden Hairs," 62

"Dick Whittington and His Cat," 110, 272

directories of storytellers. SEE *Canadian Storytelling Directory*; *National Storytelling Directory*

disobedience of women in stories, 223, 224, 225

"Don't Fall in My Beans," 61

drama. SEE theatrical storytelling stream

drama, creative, 101-102

Dublin, Anne, 249

Dundes, Alan, 9

E

Earthstory, 238

Ellis, Elizabeth, 60, 61-62, 63, 67, 76, 77, 269
 on "The Juniper Tree," 70

emergent quality
 of stories, ix, 70-71, 108, 196, 219, 227
 of storytelling, 13, 68-69, 80-81, 91, 243-244

The Emperor's Body (Marvyne Jenoff), 216

ethics of storytelling. SEE performance rights

events, storytelling, ix, 80, 81, 240, 249
 defined, 13
 growing numbers of, 10
 settings for, 27

evil, problem of
 in "The Juniper Tree," 70, 190
 SEE ALSO good vs evil

F

fact and fiction in stories, 141, 142, 143, 217, 243, 244, 248

fairytales, x, xiv-xv, 4, 216
 SEE ALSO wondertales

fathers in stories. SEE UNDER characters in stories

feminist approaches to stories and storytelling, 229-230, 231
 gender stereotypes, 6-7, 58, 177
 SEE ALSO women

festival(s), storytelling, xiv, 10, 17, 28-30, 239, 240
 development of, 38-40, 50, 240
 in library and educational storytelling, 19
 storytelling revival and, 25-26
 SEE ALSO Toronto Storytelling Festival

Fierst, Gerald, 55

Finney, Jake, stories by, 73

fire in stories, 233

Fireside Epic, 77

"The Fisherman and His Wife," 63, 77

Folk Culture in a World of Technology (Herman Bausinger), 11

folk revival, vii, xiv, 7-10, 9, 25-26

folklorists' bias against re-interpreting stories, xvi-xvii, 9

folktales, ix-xi, 4, 58, 148
 origins of, 15, 143-144
 parodies of, 3, 59, 60
 reality in, 248
 SEE ALSO wondertales

H

I

J

Bowl," 34-35, 180, 194-195, 197, 272
    Carol McGirr's text of, 197-200
    fantasy and reality in, 244
    women characters in, 179, 194, 248
Rowe, Karen, 6-7
Rubright, Lynn, 59, 76, 269
"Rumpelstiltskin," 63, 77

S

Saskatoon Storytellers' Guild, 44
"Savitri and Satyavan" (Indian version of "The Horoscope"), 147, 148
Sawyer, Ruth, 10
scene(s), 32, 34, 38, 240
Scheherazade (fictional storyteller), 36, 48
Schneider, Renate, 62, 63, 65, 76, 269
Schneider, Robert, 76, 269
Schram, Peninnah, 247
Schultz, Norlaine and Morris, 270
sermons as storytelling, 23, 24
Serrette, Gerri, 76, 269
"Seven Ravens," 61
Sexton, Anne, 10
Shaw, John, vii, 13, 74, 117-127, 134, 140, 269
    on narrator's techniques, 124-125, 140
    on translating stories, 127
    vocational narrative of, 126
A Siberian Tale Teller (Mark Azadovskii), 12
Siegel, Linda, 25
Simms, Laura, 217, 269
Sinha, Rubena, 230-231, 269
"The Six Swans," xi
    women characters in, 182-183, 184
slapstick in stories, 190, 228
"Sleeping Beauty," 62, 77
    and female stereotypes, 64
Sleeping Beauty (story character), 225
Smith, Jean and Jimmy Neil, 270
"The Snakeprince," 243
"Snow White," 63, 77

and female stereotypes, 64
    Grimm revisions of, 216
    re-interpreted by Marvyne Jenoff, 179, 186
    therapeutic power of, 192
"Snow White: A Reflection," 216, 219
    father in, 248
    Marvyne Jenoff's text of, 201-208
    women characters in, 194
Snow White (Disney film), 4
Snow White (story character), 182, 225
Sobol, Joseph, xiii, xvii-xviii, 24-25, 31, 81-82, 269, 270
    describes Jonesborough festival, 39
    interviews with tellers, 86, 92
    on storytelling communities, 33-34, 36, 41-42
    on storytelling revival, 7, 8, 10
Social Identity of a Japanese Storyteller (Robert Adams), 12, 92
Sondheim, Stephen, 109
The Spoken Word and the Work of Interpretation (Dennis Tedlock), 140
Stallings, Fran, 36, 41, 88, 100, 248
Sternbach, David, Sally, Joel, 270
Stivender, Ed, 23, 59-60
Stone, Daniel, 250, 270
Stone, Elizabeth, 269
Stone, Kay F., xviii, 95, 219-220
    critique of female stereotypes in stories, 177-178
    on gender in traditional stories, 6-7
    personal experience in "The Curious Girl," 245
    reshaping of "Mistress Trudy," 241
    vocational narrative of, 219-220
Stone, Nathaniel, 270
Stone, Rachel, 270
Stone, Ted, 90
"Stone Soup," local variant of, 34-35
Stone Soup Stories (Winnipeg), 34-35, 37-38, 54-55, 269
stories, 70
    authenticity of, xvi-xvii, 80
    bibliographical survey of, 6-8

archetypes in, xv, 6, 192
characteristics of, 5, 6, 66-67, 232
deep meaning of, 58, 193-194
defined, x
emergent quality of, 219
fact and fiction in, 142, 143
happy endings in, 239
literary artistry of, 6
motifs in, 184
parodies of, 60
punishment of evil in, 77
purpose of, 19, 57-58, 250
sociocultural aspects of, 6
timelessness of, 11
truth(s) in, 11, 133, 193, 242-243, 247
women in, 177
The World of Storytelling (Anne Pellowski), 7
Wynne, Elaine, 25

Y

Yashinsky, Dan, 32, 47-48, 49, 54-55, 81, 121, 254, 269
on Joe Neil MacNeil, 124
on John Shaw, 126
on performance rights, 52
on Stewart Cameron performances, 151-152
vocational narrative of, 79-80
Yocom, Margaret, 32
Yolen, Jane, 68, 76, 269
Young, Kathryn, 269
Yukon International Storytelling Festival, 39, 270

Z

Zipes, Jack, 69, 238
critique of female stereotypes in stories, 177
on gender in traditional stories, 7
Zundell, Kathleen, 40-41